Feathered
Serpent
Press

Xibalba: In Search of the Lost Mayan Books

Published by Feathered Serpent Press
1812 Mayfair Dr.
Omaha, NE 68144

ISBN: 978-1-7345949-4-2

English First Edition: May 2020

Printed in the United States of America

Thanks!

"*Xibalba*" would not have been completed without the advice and assistance of many people. Foremost is Valerie, my wife of 40 years. Her intellect, encouragement, and ideas have always sustained me when I doubted myself. She labored tirelessly to ensure that each sentence and idea followed in logical sequence. Fellow Mensan, Jim Bunstock, designed the book covers for the entire *Feathered Serpent Series* and proofed many of my manuscripts. Jim is a wizard – a patient wizard. Harriet Ottenheimer, Professor Emeritus of Anthropology at Kansas State University, proofed the original manuscript. Friend and fellow author Hugh Reilly remains a pillar of support and advice.

Thanks, Thanks!

The Gonzalez - Corso family of Guadalajara, Mexico are special people. Thank you for your friendship and hospitality and for politely suffering my "gringo" ways and wretched Spanish on so many occasions. Your friendship is a treasure.

Thanks Especially

To those readers of mine who enjoy the unusual story set in exotic places and who have read one or more of my four early novels – thank you for your time and interest. Finding people that enjoy the uncommon story in unusual settings is always a blessing.

Special Acknowledgement

None of my books were possible without the enduring friendship of Jose Antonio Gonzalez Corzo of San Cristobal de las Casas, Chiapas. Tony is the rare companion whose interests, personal charisma, humor and life experiences complement your own. From the Yucatec and Lacandon Jungles of Mexico, to the highlands of Chiapas, and from the Valley of Mexico to the mountains of Oaxaca, Tony provided a personal connection and inspiration. He has been my teacher and informant on Mexican culture and history the last 45 years and has guided me through a menagerie of jungle-cloaked Mayan ruins throughout Chiapas and the Yucatan. He also got us out of some tough situations over the years. Thanks, Tony. We're 'Still Crazy After All These Years.'

Praise for the Feathered Serpent Series

"Struble does it again with unexpected new twists on a classic theme. Archaeology and ancient religion are intertwined with corruption and contemporary politics in this compelling page-turner."
— **Dr. Harriet Ottenheimer**, Professor of Anthropology, Kansas State University

"It's here...another Struble mystery! **Gospel of the Feathered Serpent** *is a whirlwind of excitement and an enticing mystery for those who don't like mysteries and religion. When Christianity's long-lost, sacred objects appear unexpectedly in the ruins of a Catholic church in southern Mexico, the great religions of the world contest to own them. Struble's page-turner and prose and plotting will keep you reading late into the night."*

—**Dr. Lew Hunter**, Chair Emeritus, UCLA Screenwriting School

"Full of fascinating historical details, vivid descriptions and enough plot twists to keep everyone satisfied, Stan Struble's new book, **Gospel of the Feathered Serpent** *is a welcome addition to the niche of archaeological thrillers that Struble has carved out for himself."*

—**Hugh Reilly**, Director UNO School of Communication and author of *Bound to Have Blood* and *Drinking with My Father's Ghost*

Very Special Acknowledgement

Without the patience and friendship of Jose Antonio Gonzalez Corzo, Raul Benitez, and Claudia Poel of San Cristobal de las Casas, Mexico, this book would never have been translated into several languages. The significance of their contribution and the depth of my gratitude can't be expressed.

Dedication

This book is dedicated to the indigenous Maya of Chiapas M Mexico and their representatives, the Zapatista National Liberation Army, or EZLN

Author Biography

Stanley Struble is a member of MENSA, the International High IQ Society. He holds an M.S. in Anthropology from Kansas State University, where he taught social anthropology. He is presently an Adjunct Professor of Social Sciences at Metropolitan Community College in Omaha, Nebraska.

Stan has published several mystery-suspense novels, including *Filth Eater, Sins of the Jaguar, Xibalba: In Search of the Lost Mayan Texts, Gospel of the Feathered Serpent, and In the Time of the Feathered Serpent. Xibalba* was translated into several languages.

Stan has worked offshore in the Gulf of Mexico, lived and worked in the Sierra Madres of Jalisco and the lowlands of Sinaloa on the Gulf of Baja. He is married, has three children, and lives in Omaha, Nebraska.

Xibalba
In Search of the
Lost Mayan Books

by

Stanley Struble

Feathered Serpent Press

PROLOGUE

Heart-rending cries and desolate moans–sounds of the hopeless and forsaken–fell on callus, uncaring ears. Muted by the forest, the voices couldn't compete with chattering birds, whistling parrots and a horde of shrieking, rancorous monkeys that rattled the limbs of the jungle canopy.

"He won't talk," said the helmeted, mustachioed Spanish soldier, standing in the shade of the encroaching jungle. Bone-deep fatigue hung on him like wet clothes. Dirt traced the wrinkles on his face and beads of sweat left clear trails down his grimy cheeks.

"Did you try the boiling oil, captain?" asked Bishop Landa, standing in the late afternoon shadow of a faltering Yucatan sun.

"Yes, Eminence. We vexed him greatly. Did you not hear him call out to his wives?"

"Wife?"

"Wives, Eminence. The filthy pagan has three, but one died on the return from the dead jungle city."

Oblivious to the shrieks of those being tortured, the bishop reached for a sandalwood rosary that hung from his belt. A

2

gift from his Franciscan abbot in Grenada, it had been made in the Holy Land in the 12th century and brought to Spain by returning Crusaders. Bishop Landa grasped the cross and stroked it lightly with his thumb while ruminating on the problem of Red Snail.

The bishop remembered Red Snail from ten years ago. They had argued many times, and Red Snail had been one of few who dared speak against Landa, who was then only a young Franciscan priest. The old Mayan had had in his possession folding, accordion-shaped books made from the fiber of the maguey cactus. Landa saw them as the work of Satan and the main impediment to proselytizing the Indians. He already destroyed many of the books ten years earlier before being chastised and returned to Spain in disgrace by the old bishop. But in Spain Fr. Landa's New World activities were greeted with approval. In fact, when his nemesis, the previous bishop died, Fr. Landa was appointed the new Bishop of the Yucatan. Vindicated by his superiors, he returned in triumph, eager to resume his quest. With a fervor born of the Inquisition, he believed that his was God's work, and that any writings inspired by the Dark Angel must be destroyed.

When Red Snail learned that Landa came ashore in Veracruz, the old priest fled Chichén Itzá in the Yucatan with the last remaining books. Red Snail was accompanied by his family and followers, many of them from this town of Mani, into the uncharted Lacandon jungle. But Landa knew that he was God's Hand on Earth and the bishop was not to be thwarted so easily, and so he mustered a small army and sent them in search of the fleeing Indians. The southern highlands and the Lacandon jungle were unmapped and nearly impenetrable. An army of fifty Conquistadors had chased Red Snail and his flock for nearly three months. Pursuing with a

3

righteous vengeance, the soldiers tracked the fugitives south through coastal Tabasco, then southwest, deep into the Lacandon jungle, very near to the ruins of an old Mayan city. When the soldiers arrived, the treacherous priest had already disposed of the books. Where the trove of literature had been hidden, the captain was unable to ascertain. Beatings and torture loosened no tongues. But rather than fail utterly, the captain returned the Indians to the Yucatan and its fanatical bishop.

"Tell me, Captain...what was Jade Snail doing when you caught up to him?"

"Looked like some sort of ceremony, padre." The Conquistador frowned, then sighed, tired of this day's work and anxious to be done. The bishop ignored his indiscretion and listened patiently as the soldier explained again.

"Someone had carved one of those stinkin' stones that no one can read. You know...like those near the pyramid town where Red Snail lived. They were settin' it up in front of a cave."

"What did you do with it?"

"The stone? Had to throw it away, Eminence. We carried it two days, but it was too heavy, and the men complained greatly.

"You transported it two days?"

"Yes, Bishop Landa, much to the disgust of..."

"Is the young wife pretty?" interrupted Landa.

"Pretty?" The captain's face went blank. "She's an Indian, *padre*. All Indians are ugly."

"Kill the old one, then put the pretty one to the fire," said the bishop. "Slowly, mind you, and take care that she doesn't die too soon. Red Snail must be able to see her and hear her cries."

"What if she dies early, Eminence? Some of 'em die for no

4

reason. They just..." the captain hesitated, scowling, "...they just die. They give up."

"Then kill Red Snail," replied the bishop. "He's not going to tell us anything. He hid the books. The record was on the stone and you threw it away. The books will never survive that steaming hell in the south, anyway."

The captain departed and the bishop turned to a trio of coarse-robed Franciscan Friars who witnessed the conversation.

"Well..." Landa shrugged, "there's nothing more here. It's unlikely the old heathen will tell us anything. He'll roast in hell before talking. We might as well return to Merida."

"Yes," agreed a gray-eyed, longhaired friar, rising from his chair. He stood and faced the bishop. The friar's wide smile revealed gaps and yellow, crooked teeth. "It's unfortunate that the methods of Torquemada are now in disrepute, Eminence. We could have made quick work of it. But the Holy Father knows best...be assured of that." The friar bowed and stood aside to allow the bishop to pass."

"Yes...of course," smiled Bishop Landa. "Let's finish here and go quickly to Merida. It will soon be dinner time, and the smell of burning flesh is bad for the appetite."

CHAPTER ONE

Karen Dumas, archaeologist, tossed a manila folder onto her desk, then slumped into the chair of her Smithsonian office. Placing her elbows on the desk and resting her head in her hands, a sigh escaped her lips. Lord, she needed rest; about two weeks' worth, she figured. This project had quickly turned into an obsession, and now her exhausted brain was in full revolt. If she quit moving, even for a few minutes, an overwhelming urge to close her eyes besieged her. But not yet. She must still meet with Dr. Depp, her supervisor, before taking a taxi to American University. Thank God for coffee.

She glanced at the folder. Inside laid her opus, maybe her future; a translation of the Gould Stelae covered with Mayan script. Stelae were tall, flat stones that had been erected throughout the cities of meso-America five hundred to a thousand years ago to commemorate important historical events; wars, ceremonies, marriages, conquest, and alliances. The Gould Stelae, like many others, had been plundered and removed from its original site. Where this was, she didn't know. The previously unknown artifact arrived at the Smithsonian as part of the Roy Gould estate one year earlier. It was chipped, broken, and had critical parts missing. Dr. Depp (Dr. Death to the Assistant Curators) believed the collection to be of no value and had assigned the job of researching and classifying the mismatched odds and ends to her.

After months of study, including weekends and many sleepless nights, Karen, a student of Maya writing, had struck gold. The stelae's previously un-deciphered message made reference to Maya books hidden somewhere in the Lacandon jungle of Chiapas State in southern Mexico. If true and if the books could be found, her discovery was of incalculable importance. Only a handful of the pictographic books had survived the zealous fury and hot fires of the Conquest. The Spanish friars had relentlessly destroyed any reference to native religions. Unfortunately for the Indians, this included all forms of writing, and since the Catholic friars couldn't read the pictographic glyphs, everything had been consigned to the fires. Only a few of the folding, Maguey-fiber books survived.

Her discovery was of such importance that it ranked a presentation at American University today. Quite a coup for a young assistant curator with no credentials. But first, before her moment of glory, she must meet with Depp. His secretary had called and insisted. What did the pompous bastard want now? She sighed, unable to find the energy to go and meet with one of her least favorite people. Her shoulders sagged and she closed her eyes momentarily. Might as well get it over with. She grasped the folder containing the stelae data, photographs, and her translation and exited her office, pausing only to lock the door.

She never left the translation unattended now after an incident one week ago when she believed that her office had been burglarized. Well...maybe not burglarized. Nothing was missing as far as she could tell, but her stelae data had been removed from the folder and lay scattered about when she returned from lunch. She cradled the folder against her chest and unconsciously patted it as she turned to walk down the hall.

"Oh...here you are," said an unfamiliar voice.

Surprised, she turned to see who addressed her.

"I've been looking for you." A tall, fiftyish, deeply tanned man with dark hair smiled at her. "When I saw that you had been dropped from today's agenda, I thought I'd look for you here. Name's David Wolf." He extended a hand. "I'm an archaeologist from the National University in Mexico City."

"What? Who?" Her mouth hung slack. Tired, mind working slowly, she stared at his proffered hand. "Dropped from what agenda? What are you talking about, Mr. Wolf?"

"Call me David...please," he answered. "I see your talk on the Gould Stelae was canceled," he held out a pamphlet. "I wondered why. You see, I knew Roy Gould from the old days. We... er...had some dealings twenty or thirty years ago and I was curious about some things. I remember seeing some of his..."

"What do you mean I'm not on it?" she interrupted. "Let me see that!"

"Uh... sure." He handed her the conference agenda. "Actually, one of the reasons I came all this way was to talk to you about Roy."

"Damn...must be a mistake," she muttered, ignoring him, searching the list for her name. Karen gripped the pamphlet tightly, her mouth a tight, thin line.

"A mistake?" He seemed perplexed by her answer.

"Are you sure this is today's?"

"Got it this morning and decided to come right over. Roy

8

had a couple of things he picked up from some people–grave robbers really–that he wouldn't part with. I think one of them was your stelae. I argued with him...wanted to do a little work on it myself, but he shipped it to the states with a bunch of other stuff. I used to hear of him buying things...you know...but then I guess he died and no one in his family wanted..." The archeologist's voice trailed off when he realized she wasn't listening.

Karen stood mute, her eyes wide, staring at the paper. Another name had replaced hers: Dr. Jonathan Depp, Master Curator, Smithsonian Institute.

"Is everything okay, Miss...er...Dr. Dumas?" David seemed to realize that he had stumbled into an awkward situation. "Like I said...I tried to call first but you weren't..."

"Yes...I mean no..." she hesitated. "I didn't know that I've been removed from the list. Can't imagine why. Must be an oversight. I must call immediately...and...and I have an appointment right now." Her face turned pale and she slumped against her door.

"Miss Dumas!" cried the archaeologist. "Are you ill?"

She shook her head. "Just tired." She looked at the agenda once more to verify her name's absence. This was not an accident, and the reason had been inserted in her time slot–Dr. Jonathan Depp. This is what Dr. Death wanted to talk with her about. The bastard! The sneaky, calculating jerk had done this to embarrass her, she decided.

"Miss Dumas," said the Mexican archeologist, "I'm sorry if this is a bad time. I wrote you two months ago, remember?"

Karen looked at him, puzzled. "Oh...yes...yes. I believe I do remember. I'd forgotten. Please excuse me...I wasn't expecting..."

"If this is a bad time, perhaps later?"

"Yes...please...if you don't mind." She looked at her watch.

"I have an appointment," she repeated. She breathed deeply to gain her composure. "I don't think it will take too long. Say fifteen minutes?"

"Of course. Is there anything I can do? You seem distressed."

"No." Her face turned hard. "No, but thanks anyway. I should have done this a long time ago."

"Is there somewhere I can get a cup of coffee?"

"Downstairs," she pointed, "to the left."

The archaeologist took his leave and Karen turned to walk to Depp's office. Disappointment magnified her fatigue as she contemplated her dilemma. Why? Why would Depp do such a thing without first consulting her? Was it just a mistake? Professional jealousy? Spite? An attempt to put her in her place? Who could ever understand why a man did anything? It just didn't make sense. But what the heck? She would just go and get it over with. There was no excuse for what he did, but she would listen–just for a minute–then she would give him a piece of her mind.

CHAPTER TWO

Gray-haired Mrs. Dinty, Dr. Death's secretary, frowned upon seeing Karen enter the office. A long-time employee of the Smithsonian, the priggish Mrs. Dinty had witnessed numerous directors come and go over the decades. When Karen approached the secretary's desk, the old woman's face colored and her head dipped momentarily, as if embarrassed. She must already know what Depp had done! Without a word, Karen bypassed her and headed for her supervisor's office.

"Please…Miss Dumas," the secretary stood and held up an arm, "I must inform Dr. Depp that you are…"

Sleeplessness and anger overcame Karen's good sense. She ignored the flustered secretary and opened her boss' door without knocking.

"Miss Dumas, please…Miss Dumas…" called Mrs. Dinty.

Karen shut the door on the old woman's protests and turned to confront the enemy. Dr. Jonathan Depp, a small man, sat unmoving in a large over-stuffed leather chair. He stared blandly, his thin face unreadable. In his late fifties, nearly bald except for dark bushy eyebrows and a toilet-seat pattern of hair on his head, he appeared calm but alert. He studied her, as though seeing her for the first time. Suddenly she didn't feel so confident. Until now she had never realized how unattractive and reptilian he seemed. His small, soft hands twirled a pen. Why was he looking at her like that? She glanced away, unnerved, unable to meet his eyes.

"They don't teach social skills where you come from?" he asked.

The sarcasm fanned the embers of her anger. Grasping her file folder with one hand, she waved the conference agenda at him with her other. "Dr. Depp, I just learned that I've been taken off..."

"Just a moment," he interrupted and reached for his phone. He pressed four numbers, then waited. He stared at her again.

Flustered, she tucked a strand of hair behind her ear and began again. "Dr. Depp can you tell me why I've been removed from the agenda at today's meeting?"

Depp held up his hand, then spoke into the phone. "Bill? Yeah, go ahead. Tell me how it goes, okay?"

"Miss Dumas," he said, hanging up the phone and leaning back into his chair. "Have a seat." He pointed with the pen.

"I prefer to stand."

"Suit yourself." He shrugged. "I've been wanting to talk. I left memos in your mailbox. I left phone messages, and Mrs. Dinty put a note on your office door last Friday."

"I've...er, been busy, and I've been working at home a lot lately."

"I see." His pen began to tap the desk. "Tell me...did you notify Mrs. Dinty or anyone else that you were working at home?"

12

"Dr. Depp, I've been working night and day on the Gould Stelae," she protested. "Like I told you last month, I think I might have deciphered..."

"Yes...that's the problem isn't it? The Gould Stelae. Let's talk about the stelae, Miss Dumas." Dr. Depp leaned forward. "Why have you not shared the results of your research with me? Why are you avoiding me? Why, Miss Dumas, are you behaving like a prima donna who doesn't have a supervisor, like someone who doesn't have to come to work like the rest of us?"

She swallowed a lump in her throat. "I didn't know that you were interested."

His tiny fist slammed the desktop. "I'm your boss! Of course I'm interested! It's my responsibility to supervise your research and measure progress. You must share your results with me. You're an employee of the Smithsonian, remember?"

"Yes, but..."

"No but's. Quit interrupting me."

"But I think that someone entered my office and went through my data."

"Preposterous!" Depp waved off her complaint. "Look, Karen, you share with me and the Smithsonian, or you're out on your fanny. Got it?"

"Yes...of course...and I will...I mean..." Karen began to dissemble. Her anger fled and her face felt flush. "But why did you cancel my presentation today? I have valuable data...I've made a remarkable discovery...I..."

"You have nothing, Mrs. Dumas; certainly nothing worth wasting the time of the most premier researchers in the country. I've seen your notes. Your work is worthless."

"What? When did you see..."

"I have my ways. I know what you're doing, and I'm sure it will lead to nothing. Effective immediately, organize your

13

data and notes and deliver them to my office. I'm taking you off the Gould Stelae."

"No," she choked, gripping the folder. The agenda shook in her hand. Good Lord! she thought. The information he intended to steal was in the folder she held at this moment!

"What do you mean '*no*,' Miss Dumas? You're an intelligent woman. Must I remind you that you have no say in the matter? I can assign you any task I wish...and you're done with the Gould project!" His pen punctuated the air for emphasis.

Karen stood speechless. Her eyes felt hot, as if she might burst into tears of exhausted frustration. How had this happened? Why? What had she done to deserve this treatment? She had put all her energy, dedicated her life to the Gould bequest. This project could make her career, and this bald-headed creep was taking it from her. Anger rose within, only this time hard-cold as ice. She wanted to scratch-out his eyes.

"No," she repeated, firmer this time. "I can't...won't, I mean...I..."

"You don't have any choice. Get it done, today." He waved her off, then looked at his wristwatch and smiled. "I have to run over to American University and bail out the Smithsonian's reputation."

"You had no right to cancel my presentation without permission. You have no real reason to take me off the Gould Stelae. I'd be happy to show you my results. I can..."

"Too late, Miss Dumas. And I took you off the agenda because no one," he pointed the pen at himself, "has had a chance to referee your work. Any presentation of data out of this department goes through a peer review process. It's the same at any university, any academic environment, Miss Dumas. You know that." He glanced at his watch again, then

14

frowned. "I must be off. Be sure and have the Gould materials on my desk by late afternoon. You may go." He pointed the pen at the door.

"Please...I wish you would give me another chance, Dr. Depp. The Gould Stelae means a lot to me. I may have made a fantastic..."

"You have made a mess, Miss Dumas. The answer is no, and our conversation is ended." He ignored her and bent to retrieve materials from a bottom desk drawer.

She could barely move. Her jaw clenched. Had she screwed up? Did he have a grievance? No. He'd done a hatchet job on her. Resentment seethed and held her resolve firm. She must force herself to leave. Finally, unable to control herself, she said, "Dr. Depp?"

"Yes, what is it?" He looked up frowning from his desk drawer, annoyed.

"This is for you, creep." She raised her hand and shot him the finger. It felt good, and she finally smiled. Nothing like getting the last word. His mouth gaped wide, and she turned and strode from his office, passing a nervous Mrs. Dinty who sat clenching a handkerchief. Karen wadded the agenda and tossed it onto the secretary's desk.

"Mrs. Dinty," Karen said pleasantly, "please give my copy of the agenda to Dr. Death."

Karen navigated the endless, bland white corridors of the Smithsonian to her office. The hallway's fluorescent lights seemed eerie and surreal, and she felt lightheaded. She realized that she had been hyperventilating, and so she made an effort to control her breathing. What a jerk! What an orifice! How dare he talk to her like that! And take her off the Gould Stelae? Not a chance. She wouldn't do it. She wouldn't comply. She wouldn't, she wouldn't...

"Hello, again."

The professor from Mexico stood outside her door. She glared at him. Not now. She really didn't have time for this.

"Get it all straightened out?" he smiled pleasantly. "Took a while to find the snack shop. Big place, the Smithsonian," he offered.

"Mister...er..."

"Wolf. David Wolf. Please call me David."

"Mr. Wolf...I really can't talk right now. I've just had a...well I guess you could say I've just made a mess for myself." Karen visualized herself standing in Depp's office shooting him the finger. How could she have been so stupid? Now he would probably fire her. "Can we talk later? I need time to sort some things out."

"You look a little flushed. Are you okay?"

"I'm fine...I guess." She pushed recalcitrant locks of hair behind her ear again, then mustered a wan smile.

"I've come a long way, Miss Dumas," he reminded her. "I must return to American University by noon. There are several presentations I want to hear." He smiled again. "You look as if you could use a cup of coffee, too. Want to join me downstairs so that we don't bother your colleague?"

"Huh...what colleague?"

"Oh...I saw a shadow through the window of your door. I assumed that you shared with someone."

Karen whirled to face the office door. She had locked it before going to Depp's office! Who else had a key? She tried the doorknob, and it turned. A large shadow loomed within, then disappeared as she pushed the door wide. "Who's here?" she called out.

"What's going on, Miss Dumas?" asked the professor.

She stepped inside and quickly look around. A window stood open and her desk had been rifled. The outline for her presentation was missing. Some of the data on the Gould stelae was strewn about the desk, chair and floor. Burglarized again! It was planned. She knew it. But who? Depp? He said her research was worthless. Why would he break in if he thought her data meaningless and of no value? Besides, she had just left him in his office. He wouldn't have someone else do it, would he?

"Damn! Damn! Damn!" she stamped her foot, surveying the damage. David joined her inside and together they peered out the window, but saw no one or anything suspicious.

"Gee...archaeology isn't near this exciting in Mexico," he joked. "Shouldn't you call a security guard?"

"Yeah...sure...I guess." She looked at the mess of papers, then placed her folder securely under her arm and began to clean up the mess. Thank God she'd carried her translation with her! What a perfectly horrible day. She ignored the Mexican professor and took stock of her situation. What were her options? She had just terminated her employment with the Smithsonian by shooting Depp the finger. They would never be able to work together again. Now that she thought about it, she didn't really care if she stayed at the museum or not. Problem was, though, that he might try keep her from getting a job elsewhere. Damn! She sagged with disappointment. What next? What now? Someone touched her shoulder, and she turned to face the Mexican.

"How about that coffee, Miss Dumas? You can tell me all about it."

Karen hesitated, looked at the gaping window, and then at the professor. She remembered that he claimed to have known Roy Gould and, though she had forgotten, that she had invited the Mexican archaeologist to talk with her when he attended the conference.

"Sure...why not," she replied. She paused, then said, "I'm probably not going to be an employee of the Smithsonian after

17

today. I...ah...had some words with my boss because he wants to take me off the Gould Stelae."

"No! Really?"

"Yes, and even if he doesn't, I'll probably quit."

The professor hesitated, as if measuring his words. "Roy was a grave robber, you know?" he offered enticingly.

"Do you know where he found the stelae?" His bait had fueled her obsession.

"Maybe the general area. Roy was a bit of a scoundrel in the old days before he made a few legitimate dollars and got respectable."

"See you down stairs," she pointed vaguely toward the door, "I'm buying. I'll join you as soon as I report this to security. I want to hear all about Roy Gould."

CHAPTER THREE

David Wolf sat alone at a table in the middle of the Smithsonian cafeteria. Tourists and staffers on their morning coffee break thronged the facility. White walls and a ceiling of florescent lights provided a familiar setting to anyone having spent time in a museum. Vacationers were easy to identify, as they consisted of noisy families or the occasional individual reading Smithsonian literature. The staff sat in small groups, talking and joking. David idly twirled a coffee stirrer and pretended to ignore the twitters and darting glances of a collection of colleagues and well-wishers that had surrounded Karen. What had she said or done to earn all the attention? He studied her from afar and saw that she was lovely woman; tall, athletic and shapely enough for any man to appreciate. She pushed strands of shoulder length brown hair back from her face and flashed a smile to her well-wishers.

David stared into his coffee and frowned, annoyed that

Karen had not remembered his letter regarding Roy Gould. Very unprofessional. He sighed and shifted his legs beneath the table. The few presentations he had attended at the conference had been lackluster and unappealing, and thus far his meeting with Karen had bordered on bizarre. He took a sip of bland cafeteria coffee and slipped into a daydream, imagining himself sitting on a shaded colonial verandah in San Cristobal de Las Casas, Chiapas, Mexico, talking with his wife, ignoring his unpleasant brother-in-law, while awaiting the arrival of old friends, Luis and Alicia Alvarado. The professor was eager to return to Mexico and resume his vacation.

His first three days in Washington D.C. had reaffirmed why he had deserted this material-rich country for the easy, slower pace of Mexico. Simply stated, the rush-rush, hubbub and racial strife drove him crazy. A fifty-two-year-old American expatriate, he rarely returned to the states except for professional reasons. He held a full professorship in the Department of Anthropology at Mexico City's National University and had spent nearly thirty years in combined research and teaching. Archaeology was his passion, and his wife of two years, Alexandra, joked that she would have him fossilized if he died before her. Theirs was a mixed marriage, so to speak, between a widow of five years and a widower of twenty. His new bride came from a pedigreed, well-connected political family. Whereas some might see him as a lowly academic and a gringo, though he had lived in Mexico many years and thought of himself as Mexican.

David glanced at Karen. He found the whole business unsettling. The woman appeared moody and distracted and quite possibly incompetent–though certainly good looking. Had she been hired for her beautiful face? The situation with her boss and the burglarized office were out of context for a

20

museum. He was tempted to leave and catch the few remaining conference presentations before flying home, but the unresolved issue of Roy Gould and the peculiar events of the last hour tugged at his curiosity. He might as well stay and hear her story. He looked at his watch and decided there was no hurry.

Karen disengaged from the crowd and sat at the table, placing a manila folder in her lap. "Sorry," she muttered. "The rumors around this place are incredible." She nervously moved strands of brown hair behind an ear, then reached and tore open a package of artificial creamer. Her hand shook as she poured. She stirred, then sipped her coffee, holding the cup with both hands. She looked to see if anyone watched, then smiled and leaned toward him like a conspirator.

"So..." she began. "You knew Roy in the old days. Tell me...was he really a grave robber?"

"Perhaps," David returned her smile. "Roy didn't have professional training and never seemed to have a real job. Thirty years ago he hung around the Yucatan a lot. He always hustled for a buck and had a knack for acquiring and marketing unusual pieces. While I don't know of any specific incident of grave robbing, his dealings always seemed shady to me. Pre-Colombian art is worth more when sold with documentation. You must know its provenance. A piece that comes with a written history is worth ten times that of an item without it, but Roy never bothered with paper. It led me to believe he was involved in something illegal."

She chewed her bottom lip and nodded. "Yeah...lack of documentation. I'm almost positive the Gould Stelae comes from farther south in Mexico...Chiapas or Tobasco...maybe even Guatemala." She set the cup down and leaned back into her chair. "Part of the stelae inscription mentions a journey through Palenque."

"When I last saw Roy, he had your stelae."

"Really!" she leaned forward, both hands gripped the table's edge. "When was this?"

"About `65. Ran into him on the Usumacinta River near Yaxchilan ruin. Said he picked up some stuff near Palenque and was on his way to Bonampak."

Her gaze seemed unfocused as she slid deep into thought.

"The stelae, Miss Dumas…what time-period are we talking about here?" he interrupted.

"1500's" she said, refocusing. "Probably about 1570 or so."

"What?" The professor's eyes grew wide. He frowned, disbelieving. "That's hardly a compatible date, Miss Dumas. I...er...surely you're aware that the Mayan culture died out before the Conquest. With the exception of the Yucatan, all the southern Maya cities were abandoned four hundred years before Columbus. I've done considerable work at Palenque and it was abandoned even earlier. No..." David shook his head, "couldn't be. Doesn't make any sense."

"Believe it," she insisted, reaching for a paper napkin. "Here...look." She took a pencil and drew two glyphs, then added a series of bars and dots. "I'm not much of an artist, but does this mean anything to you?"

"Let's see," the professor turned the napkin around and studied the drawings. "It's a date…obviously." He frowned with concentration. "Probably the month and day."

The Maya year was calculated through the Tzolkin calendar, using eighteen times the twenty-day Haab, their equivalent of a month, which comprised three-hundred-sixty days plus five unlucky days at the end of each year. There were twenty name days and thirteen numbers associated with them. Each day was linked to a number. Since there were more days than numbers, the fourteenth day used the number one again. Thus, two-hundred-sixty days passed before the

22

original number came around. In some aspects, their calendar was more similar to astrology than science. The Maya believed that extraneous factors influenced the characteristics of each day; things such as the day number, the Haab character, and a quadrant sign characterized by four gods called Kawils, each one associated with a color and responsible for a quadrant of eight hundred and nineteen days. Years were gathered into katuns, or twenty-year cycles, baktuns were grouped at twenty times twenty for four hundred year cycles. There were much larger units too, such as the calabtun, a one-hundred-and-sixty-thousand year cycle.

"Looks like this one could be Yaxkin and this one Cib," he mumbled, scribbling on the napkin. "That means Tender Sun, then Vulture," he smiled, happy with himself. "Then you have to figure that each Tun was...uh...so that translates to about..." He continued to scribble, then paused and frowned, peering intently at the bars and dots. "1573? But how? Does it say that on the stelae?"

She nodded, smiling. "It does. And it also says that the stelae was erected near Palenque."

"Impossible...couldn't be. Palenque was all but buried in the jungle when discovered."

"Unless it wasn't."

"What wasn't?"

"Wasn't buried at Palenque. Maybe the stelae was erected within Palenque's dominion, but not actually associated with the Jaguar dynasties of Palenque. In other words, erected four hundred years later."

The professor shook his head, confused. "Miss Dumas... there are Mayan sites with inscribed calendar counts that predate the Big Bang!"

She ignored his skepticism. "Are there caves in the area?" she asked.

"Caves? Oh...sure. Probably hundreds. Cenotes, too. You ought to see how big and deep some of those things are. There's also an immense tropical jungle covering the mountains. Lots of rivers and waterfalls in the rainy season, too. No roads, either. Why is that important?"

"Are you familiar with the four remaining Codexes?"

"Never actually seen them, but I know of them. There's several in the national Anthropology Museum at Chapultepec in Mexico City. They're all that remain of Mayan books. Spaniards destroyed the rest. They are named after the places in which they are exhibited in Europe; Dresden, Paris and Madrid. The Grolier Codex was the last discovered...1971 I believe, even though it's the oldest...written in the twelfth century. Everyone knows that. What of it?"

"There's more."

"More Maya books?" He looked doubtful. "Where?"

"I think near Palenque. Probably hidden in a cave."

"Does the stelae say that?"

"I think so."

"You think?"

"I'd bet a year's pay on it."

The professor sat rigid, but his mouth hung slack. Historians and archaeologists believed that Spanish friars had destroyed every written Mayan document except for the four codexes. Friar Diego de Landa, a Franciscan who later became Bishop of the Yucatan, had terrorized the Indians, torturing them for their reluctance to embrace Christianity. Thousands were put to the sword. In the 1560's he had held a full-blown auto-da-fe, burning every written Mayan text he could find. Although many people had searched since, not a single remnant of the Maguey fiber books had been found. This young woman was immersed in fantasy or onto the biggest archaeological story of the last one hundred years. How could

24

it be?

"Does the stone..."

"The stelae was placed somewhere near Palenque in 1573," she interrupted. "The inscription says it was erected by Red Snail, a priest or shaman from the Yucatan."

"A priest?"

"Think about it," she said, stretching her arms wide and yawning.

Karen crossed her legs nervously and reached for her cup. "What were the Spanish doing at the time? Remember?" she prompted.

He shrugged, "Pacifying and proselytizing the Indians."

"Destroying their religion and culture, you mean."

"Yes...yes," he agreed. "It's well documented. There were incredible excesses."

"What if one group of people held out and fled south into the Lacandon jungle?"

"With the books?"

"Exactly."

The professor extended a shaking hand toward his cup. "How do you know? Does the stelae say that? It's a fantastic story." He sipped his tepid coffee and reflected on her words.

Karen leaned forward, checked for conversation voyeurs, then said, "I think the inscription records the flight of Red Snail and his clan from Chichén Itzá–that they carried with them the last of the temple books. If you were a Mayan Indian caught near Palenque and it was already a ruin, where would you hide something precious?"

"A cave," he smiled grimly, nodding agreement. A logical assumption. Caves were holy places to the Maya. Their spiritual ancestors came from Xibalba, the underworld. Even today, throughout the Maya homeland, Indians enacted rituals in caves. Still, this was an incredible story.

25

"You have proof?"

"I have the translation."

"Can I see the stelae?"

Karen shrugged. "Probably not now."

"Why not?"

"I'd be surprised if I'm still an employee here." She frowned, then reached and tucked a strand of hair behind her ear. "Depp and I just had it out. I'm done. He's not going to let me anywhere near it."

"What did you..." the professor started to ask, but shut up. He watched as she looked at her feet.

"I...I do have photographs...and I traced the glyphs with paper and pencil." She removed her materials from the folder.

David wiped his suddenly sweaty palms on his trousers. "So...the stelae isn't intact?" he said, lifting the top photograph by its edges.

She hesitated, then said, "No...but here...look at a couple of these." She handed him three black and white glossy photos.

He shuffled between them quickly, searching for recognition. "It's hard to read...the light..."

"I know, but I have the tracings." She reached and took them from his hand.

"Hey," he protested, "I didn't get a look."

"Not now. Maybe some other time." She gripped them tightly and held them to her chest.

David stared, surprised. Why, that was almost rude, he thought. Did she have something to conceal? Why wouldn't she allow him to inspect the photos?

"Miss Dumas, are you absolutely sure what the stelae says? Have you allowed others to check your work...look at the glyphs themselves and do their own translation?"

"No...there...er...wasn't time. I checked in with Depp sometimes, but he didn't seem to care what I was doing. Not until today, anyway."

"Can I see what you have?" he coaxed. David doubted her fantastic story had any basis in fact, but he had to see for himself. Lord! Discovering Maya books would be an incredible accomplishment.

"No," she said suddenly, pulling her folder away from him and the table. She stood to leave, her mouth set in a thin line. "Thanks, but no thanks. I don't need another male mentor to...to..." She floundered for words, then turned to leave.

To burst your bubble, he thought. Then, with a flash of insight, "You're afraid I'll steal your work."

She spun about, surprised. Her face colored. "I didn't mean...what I meant was that..."

He held up a hand to caution her. "Please...I understand," he sighed and extended a hand toward her chair. "Sit down, Miss Dumas. Are you always so rash?"

"Rash? Me?" her mouth opened, but no words came.

"Miss Dumas, I have no intention of stealing someone else's work. I don't know if your research is of any value. Apparently no one does. And no one will believe you unless and until your translation is verified. Regardless, you're going to need help. I can only assume that you're planning a trip to Mexico?"

Her brows lifted with surprise. "Yes," she answered, avoiding his eyes. "Soon. I'm leaving my office today." She looked over her shoulder. "I need to hurry, before more of my work disappears."

"Ahh..." he said, remembering the incident in her office. "You really think someone wants your data?"

"Positive. You don't know...you haven't been around. This isn't the first time something's happened. What else could it be?"

He stared at her pretty face, but caught himself and looked

27

away. Was this all fluff and fancy, or did the woman really have something? What should he do? All this way for a crazy story from an unknown archaeologist of dubious academic credentials. But if she was right...why would someone break into her office? Discovering Maya books would be the equivalent of finding the Rosetta stone! That rock fragment, found in the Egyptian desert with the same inscription in three different languages, had resulted in the translation of Egyptian hieroglyphics.

"I'm leaving tomorrow for San Cristobal de Las Casas," said David.

"Chiapas?" she looked hopeful.

"There's a war going on, you know," he warned.

"Oh, yes...read about that...the Zapatista rebellion." Her shoulders sagged. She obviously had forgotten this important bit of information.

"It's dangerous, Miss Dumas. Dangerous for anyone...a woman especially."

"I can take care of myself," she retorted, back stiff.

"I'm sure you can," he replied. "But you still need help. You'll never find squat without it."

This got her attention and her eyes locked on his. "Why should I trust you?"

"Why should I trust you?" he countered.

The corners of her mouth fought a smile. She hesitated, then said, "I wouldn't mind a little help." She looked at her feet again. "It's really important to me that I do..."

"Miss Dumas..." he interrupted.

"Karen," she corrected him.

"Karen, you don't have a prayer without help. I have connections in Chiapas."

"What kind of connections?"

"My wife's brother is the diplomatic Consul in Chiapas

28

State."

She laughed. "You're kidding!"

He chuckled, "Yeah...and I know a few others, too. Karen if you want to do this right, I can help. I'll be in San Cristobal for a month. If you make it down, give me a call. This will be my address and phone number while I'm there." He wrote it out and handed it to her. "Karen," he hesitated, choosing his words carefully, "I really must check your data...and frankly, unless I do, I'm probably not interested in working with you." He shrugged. "You have to decide." He stood. "I worked in and around the Palenque area for ten years. If your translation is any good, I'll know. Give it some thought, then give me a call. I don't believe you'll find anyone better to work with." He smiled. "I really must be going. I think I can still catch a couple of the afternoon sessions. Maybe I'll even see your Dr. Depp."

"Yeah. You do that. While you're at it, see if he has my lecture outline, will you?"

"Surely you don't think..."

She waved off his question. "No...yeah...who knows. Someone took it." She looked around the room, then back to the professor. "Look...David, I'll be out of this place in a week. I...I'm coming to Mexico. Maybe I'll look you up when I get there."

"Hope so. By the way, I wouldn't take a small plane if I were you. Fly into Acapulco or somewhere reasonably close, then take a bus."

"Why?" she asked.

"Zapatista guerrillas. Remember? There's a war on."

"Oh...yeah. I forgot."

"Karen?"

"Yes?"

"I can pick you up at the airport in Acapulco if you wish. Think about it, okay?" David extended a hand, and she shook it. He left her standing, deep in thought and chewing on her lip. He walked from the room, navigated several hallways and eventually found his way outside.

I wonder if she'll call? he mused, descending long rows of granite steps that fronted the Natural History Museum. Crazy story, really. Maya books, unknown stelae, burglars, a very good-looking young woman, and jealous academics. What the hell was going on here, anyway? Maybe it would be better if she didn't call. At fifty-two his life was interesting enough without having to traipse all over the Lacandon jungle. Alexandra, his wife, would be unhappy if he decided to work on vacation, especially with a young, pretty woman. And his friend, Luis Alvarado, arrived in San Cristobal within the week. David really didn't have time for this. It sounded like nonsense anyway. Aw, well... He put his hands in his pockets and began walking the path alongside the Tidal Pool. Soon he was whistling a song from his youth. To hell with the conference, he decided. Maybe he would climb the Washington Monument one last time before he was too old.

CHAPTER FOUR

The subway ride home allowed Karen to ruminate and put her situation into perspective. She was juggling a lot of issues and it was time to sort them out. She carried a briefcase that contained her stelae data, photos, translation and a few personal items from her office. The escalator up from the subway quickly brought her to the surface. She began walking the seven blocks to her apartment. The familiar sounds and smells of Washington D.C. greeted her. Stately, broad-limbed trees lined both sides of the street. A few ragged survivors of the devastating Dutch Elm disease of the 50's stood aged and forlorn, casting dappled shade across street and lawns amid the newer, healthier sweet gum and Maple.

Even though she felt fatigued, and certain that she was now jobless, Karen felt uncharacteristically upbeat, more positive about the future than she had in years. Suddenly she had options. She was free! Maybe there was life after the Smithsonian! Her career was no longer constrained by idiots like Depp and, without her job at the Smithsonian, there was little to keep her in Washington; exhilarating–and a little scary. What would the future bring?

Karen knew her translation to be a solid piece of research. But, she realized, it paled in comparison to the possibility of finding the Maya books themselves. That would be an incredible feat! The Mexican professor seemed to be a nice guy, and she didn't blame him for being skeptical. After all, she hadn't allowed him to see her work. No one had seen it. He was right about the dangers of a trip to Mexico, too. An excursion into the Lacandon would require as much luck as hard work–maybe more. Chiapas was the most southern state in Mexico and had long served as a buffer between Guatemala and its larger neighbor to the north. There were few roads, almost no hospitals, and remote areas with well-deserved reputations as lawless enclaves of Mayan sedition. The state's heavily forested mountains and lowland jungle were intimidating to even the most jaded of explorers. And as David Wolf had so succinctly pointed out, she had no political connections in Mexico and a guerilla war was underway in Chiapas. She knew absolutely no one in the country to assist her. What's more, and it galled her to think about it, she was a woman and women were oftentimes treated like crap and not taken seriously in Mexico: a typical patriarchal, male dominated Latin American country. It might be an impossible task without the professor's help. As things now stood, David Wolf was her only potential ally. Fortunately, he might also be the best. In truth, there was really little choice but to avail herself of his services. Her fear of having her research stolen was unrealistic. He didn't seem the type, and so she must include him in the project or forget about the stelae.

Karen turned the corner and continued walking, deep in thought. An unfamiliar man passed by her house on the sidewalk. Across the street a loud Iranian family poured out of their brownstone and piled into a cream colored Volvo station wagon. Her ailing, gray-haired neighbor to the east, Mrs. Slobodnik, wore slippers and robe while kneeling over a well-tended flower garden. As the man on the sidewalk drew near, something about him caught her eye. Tall and skinny, he wore a Panama hat and cream-colored suit. A well-chewed cigar swelled the corner of his mouth, and he stared as she approached, unnerving her and causing her to avert her gaze.

Perhaps a lack of sleep was fueling her imagination, but a woman must be careful in Washington. Areas of the nation's capitol seethed a desperate malevolence, and it was one of the murder/rape capitols of the country. This was the reality of being young and female–you could easily become a victim, and this colored your thinking. A woman must take precautions.

As he drew close, she saw his face. God! A long thin scar trailed from his forehead and a pale, sightless eye, to his cheek. Her flesh crawled and she nearly stepped from the sidewalk as he passed. But she looked straight ahead and feigned indifference. Get a grip! she told herself, and stepped another thirty paces to her apartment before turning towards the door. Glancing back down the street, she saw that he, too, had stopped and turned to watch her. A crooked smile framed by dull, insipid eyes gazed back. He tipped his hat, then turned and strode purposefully away. Weird. What was that about? She shivered, wishing for the safety of her apartment. She unlocked the front entry, climbed one flight of stairs, then changed keys to unlock her apartment door-but the knob turned without the key. *Oh no*, she thought. Not again! Karen pushed the door wide, and–Sweet Mary! Furniture overturned, books spilled onto the floor, papers everywhere. The room stank of cigar smoke. Oh Jesus! Must have been the man on the sidewalk.

"Damn it! Damn, damn!" she cursed. This was too much. She screamed in anger, slammed the door behind her and raced down the stairs and over to Mrs. Slobodnik's to call the police.

****

"You're making a mistake, Karen. Why didn't you ask for help?"

The accusation and disapproval in Aunt Rose's voice lay like a wet towel, smothering Karen's enthusiasm. She visualized the old lady now–frowning into the telephone, faded red hair, wrinkled face, and one hand on her hip. The call to the police had resulted in nothing but a cop ogling her body while taking a report. Nothing would come of it, she was sure, so she made excuses.

"This project could make my career. It could..."

"It could kill you is what it could do, Stinky. A young, single female has no business..."

"Quit calling me Stinky!"

"...has no business wandering through jungles all alone. There might be headhunters or cannibals."

Karen groaned. Where did her aunt read this stuff? National Enquirer?

"There aren't headhunters or cannibals in Mexico, auntie. Besides I won't be alone. I'll be with Dr. Wolf...and...er...others."

"Worse yet. Meeting a strange man in a foreign country. God...what would your father and mother say?"

"They're dead, Auntie. Been dead six years. Besides...there's nothing for me here now. The Gould Stelae..."

"...and Lawrence," the old lady ignored her. "What would Lawrence think if he knew you were going to Mexico?"

"Lawrence? I divorced Lawrence two years

34

ago...remember?" Karen's face flushed warm and she gripped the phone tightly. "He's a jerk, a liar, and a cheat! Who gives a damn what he thinks!"

"Watch your language, young lady," reprimanded the old woman, but her voice showed no displeasure. "Come to Omaha. Please? Let's talk before you decide."

"It's a done deal, Aunt Rose. I sublet my apartment and everything but the furniture is in storage. I meet Dr. Wolf in Acapulco next Wednesday. I'm committed to going. Please...I was hoping...well...you're my only relative and I want your blessing."

Still holding the telephone, Karen plopped onto her living room couch. Why didn't Rose just say okay? Surely she knew Karen wouldn't change her mind! This conversation had gone just like the previous ten–Karen planning and working enthusiastically, Aunt Rose overly cautious and disagreeing. But her aunt was all that remained of Karen's family upon her parents' death six years earlier. The staid and steady Rose was always there for her–initially as guardian and executor of Karen's parents' estate and then as her primary supporter and only living relative. Even though the old lady had disapproved of Karen's playing volleyball and her anthropology major in college, her auntie had helped her through graduate school and been a tower of strength during her divorce.

A silent battle of wills ensued, punctuated by her aunt's occasional sighs. Finally, Rose cleared her throat and said, "Do you have enough money, Stinky?"

Karen smiled. "Yes, Auntie. Money's not an issue now, you know that. I just don't want you thinking badly of me. I have to follow up on this. It's important to my career."

More silence, followed by the inevitable sigh. "Karen, you really must force yourself into a more...more..." the old lady hesitated, seeking an appropriate descriptor, "...into a more natural lifestyle for a young woman, or you'll never find another man to..."

"Aunt Rose!"

"I don't mean to nag, but..."

"Aunt Rose...please!" Karen frowned, then shifted the telephone to her other ear, her patience nearing an end. She dearly loved the meddlesome old woman, but the conversation was veering uncomfortably into recriminations and paths best not traveled.

While her aunt remained silent, Karen plunged ahead. "Auntie, my telephone will be disconnected tomorrow. That's why I called. Just wish me well, okay? I'll call again when I arrive in San Cristobal. Everything's going to be fine. Trust me, okay? I'm a big girl now. This is going to be the best thing I've done. You'll see."

"Oh, Stinky..." Her aunt's voice cracked with emotion.

"Aunt Rose, I hate that name," said Karen with resignation. "Listen, if everything goes well, maybe we can meet in Guadalajara...listen to mariachis and shop at Tlaquepaque. I'll call when I'm close to finishing. We'll have reason to celebrate. You'll be proud, auntie. I promise."

"I suppose I really must trust you again." Sadness and resignation tinged the old woman's voice. "How long will you be?"

"A month–give or take a week. I'll stay in touch."

"Promise?"

"I promise, Aunt Rose. I can do this thing. You'll see."

"If you say so." Aunt Rose sounded doubtful. "Send me a card for my collection. You know how much I like to get cards."

"I love you, auntie. Don't worry."

"Bye, Stinky."

"Goodbye, Rose...and stay out of the bingo parlors."

"I only play at St. Francis Cabrini once a week," said the old woman, defensively.

Karen's line clicked, indicating a call waiting. "Got to go, Rose. Someone's trying to reach me."

"God bless you, child."

Aunt Rose hung up, and Karen switched to the new caller.

"So...you are home. I've been trying to reach you," said the unfriendly voice of Dr. Depp. "I instructed you to leave all your notes and materials at the Smithsonian, Miss Dumas. I'm certain you're withholding valuable documentation from the museum and that you are deliberately..."

"Deliberately protecting my work from being stolen?" she finished the sentence for him. "What you have is all there is, Dr. Depp. Do some work for a change. It's all there if you're smart enough to figure it out."

"How dare you!"

"How dare *YOU!*" she shouted, standing up.

Depp paused, then said with deliberate calmness, "I'll do whatever's necessary to protect the museum's interests, including taking you to court."

"Call someone who cares, Dr. Depp. I'll be in and out of Mexico by the time you can do anything. You lost this time. Might as well get used to it. Go find another female subordinate to harass. I'm hanging up now."

Karen cradled the phone with trembling hand and took a deep breath. There...she did it. She told him to take a hike. She hadn't allowed herself to be intimidated. Of course she withheld some of the documentation. He thought her analysis worthless anyway! Did he think she was senile? The Gould Stelae was her project and she would see it through until the end. Depp could complain to whomever–go scourge himself with a thorn bush and ashes and wear a hair shirt for all she cared. Nothing would stop her. Nothing.

CHAPTER FIVE

Incongruent, Karen decided–the word best describing the handsome, stocky, dark-haired man who had seated himself across the aisle of the Mexicana jet. Dressed in khaki slacks and a guayabera shirt, he gave the impression of being a well-to-do businessman. He fastened his seat belt, looked around to orient himself, and seeing Karen watching, gave her a thin, but disinterested smile before reaching to open a small book he carried aboard. She couldn't read the Spanish title, but the author's name caught her attention. Sun Tzu? Why did that sound familiar? Then she remembered; *The Art of War*, by Sun Tzu. The thought of a classic Chinese strategy book translated into Spanish struck her as peculiar, even a little silly. She smiled and turned her head, but not before seeing the man's shoes. Weathered, scuffed, still harboring bits of red mud–inconsistent with his overall appearance. Maybe he wasn't a businessman. Except for the strong arms and shoulders, he looked a little bookish. Maybe he was some kind of bureaucrat who lifted weights. Whatever. It didn't matter. Karen didn't know why she had even noticed, though she did find him attractive, maybe even a little stirring.

The plane taxied to its designated runway. After a short wait the pilot engaged the engines. The roar and pressure of the takeoff gave way to a sinking feeling in her stomach as the plane lurched, hesitated momentarily, then lifted its nose to the sky. The jet tilted left, then then leveled and headed southwest for Acapulco. The seatbelt light went off and flight attendants began flitting up and down the aisle, pouring free champagne and picking up the passengers' small children to hug and praise. She loved flying Mexicana. It was her third trip, and you could savor the taste of Mexico before ever landing.

Karen had decided to waste no time in Acapulco. Dr. Wolf agreed to meet her plane, though he seemed surprised that she intended to ignore the white sand beaches and towering cliffs of Acapulco Bay. "All work and no play?" he chided. "Not even one day?" His mildly disapproving tone had irritated her, but she let it pass, knowing that she could play later. This was a business trip.

Karen fidgeted and looked around, anxious to be there already. The boy next to her, a skinny studious-looking teenager, was transporting a large plastic statue of the Virgin of Guadeloupe. It stood nearly three feet tall and took up too much space. The Virgin would be lucky to arrive in one piece, especially if she kept bumping into Karen. She made a face at the statue. Only on a Mexican airline would the kid have been able to carry such a thing aboard. Seeing her interest, the latte-skinned teenager grinned, believing that she admired his Madonna. She attempted a smile, trying to be graceful, but grimaced instead. She brushed her brown locks aside, looked across the aisle at the handsome man with the dirty shoes,

40

then bent to retrieve her carry-on briefcase. She would review her notes before landing. Dr. Wolf had asked again to see her data and, better rested, she found his request entirely reasonable. She extracted a clipboard with a wad of loose-leaf paper, noting that she really should have organized better before leaving. The hectic pre-trip preparation had left little time to compile her work into a cohesive, presentable package. He would just have to wait until they arrived in San Cristobal when she could sort it all out in her hotel room. Meanwhile, she would answer his questions the best she could.

She immersed herself in reading, and in practically no time the captain announced in Spanish, then English, that they were about to land in Acapulco. The Virgin bumped her again, and Karen turned to frown at the boy. He apologized, and she lied and said it was okay. She reinserted the clipboard and papers in her briefcase and placed it on the floor between her legs. Upon leaning back into her seat, she noticed the reader of Sun Tzu had put away his book aside and was watching her. She smiled a greeting and attempted a conversation.

"Speak English?"

His head ducked momentarily; embarrassed that he had been caught staring. He answered, slowly choosing his words. "Yes. A little. I...I studied in school many years and I lived in England for six months once." He gave her a quick, embarrassed smile, then turned away.

"Really!" she said, encouraging him. "You speak quite well. Where did you live in England?"

"London...then later I spent a month in Miami."

He pronounced Miami like Mee-ah-mee, and she smiled at his accent. "Are you going to war?"

"Que? I am going to war?"

41

"No," she chuckled at his mistake. "I see you're reading Sun Tzu's *The Art of War*. My ex-boyfriend had a copy and I read it my first year of college."

He warmed to her conversation and leaned toward the aisle with the book in hand to ask a question, but the stewardess stepped between them to admonish the Virgin of Guadeloupe's caretaker to get a grip on the Patron Saint of the Americas and prepare to land. When the flight attendant moved up the aisle, Karen's handsome new acquaintance settled back into his seat and stared stoically ahead. He glanced up, gave her a quick smile, but just as quickly turned to look out the window. The conversation had ended.

Rats. So much for romance. What was it about her that seemed to run guys off? She had been told numerous times that she was pretty, and by the standards represented in women's magazines, she knew that she was. Was it her personality? Aunt Rose, never one to mince words, had told her that she was too intense and intellectual. Was that true? Did it matter? Karen tried to convince herself it didn't. She was here on business, after all.

She turned and looked past the plastic virgin to view the beautiful aqua sheen of the Pacific Ocean. The Maya, Karen recalled, believed the earth was Imix, a water-lily monster like a giant crocodile or a turtle that lay in an immense pool of water with the earth resting on its back. Beneath Imix lay Xibalba, the Mayan underworld, a mythical place of water where the sun became the Jaguar god every night during its nocturnal journey through hell.

The plane's nose tilted as it began to sink and descend into Acapulco Bay. A Pacific wind buffeted the jetliner, and when the wings tipped westward, she caught a glimpse of towering cliffs and hotels surrounding the bay. Suddenly the sun shone strong and brilliant, blinding her and causing her to turn from the window. The Mexicana jet dipped again, leveled, then surged for the runway. The plane whined in protest, the wheels skidded, lifted, and then connected with the ground. Jet engines roared as the pilot engaged thrust reversers to slow the plane. Karen released her breath, unaware that she had been holding it, and looked beyond the Blessed Virgin and out the window. Tall palms stood unmoving and listless, ready to wilt in the Acapulco Sun, their fronds yellow and drooping. Heat shimmered from the runway, distorting the distant buildings, creating a glassy mirage of water on the tarmac. Her Mexican adventure had begun.

CHAPTER SIX

Karen grabbed the carrying strap of her handbag and hoisted it onto a shoulder while scanning the arrival area one last time, searching for Professor Wolf. Seeing no one she recognized, she wandered toward baggage claim. Upbeat tropical music reverberated through the small airport and grew louder as she approached a band of swarthy men in gay, flowered shirts playing a collection of brass and percussion instruments. In contrast to the lively music, the musicians were unsmiling and appeared bored, simply going through the motions of playing. The airport's walls were plastered with colorful posters of Acapulco Bay hotels and restaurants. Sex, sun, beach, and surf they screamed, each promising romance and vacation delights unimaginable. She felt a pang of regret. How long had it been since she'd had a real beach vacation? She frowned, realizing that it had been four years ago—on her honeymoon with Lawrence. Yech.

The mysterious and handsome reader of Sun Tzu appeared

at her elbow and began to accompany her. He offered a tentative smile, and after an awkward moment, gestured at the posters and said, "You'll like Acapulco. Great place to vacation...lots of Americans here."

"I'm not on vacation. I'm an archaeologist and..." she slowed to look around the concourse, "someone was supposed to meet me. We were leaving for San Cristobal today."

"Chiapas?" he asked, sounding surprised.

"Yes. A colleague of mine, Dr. Wolf from Mexico City, will pick me up...or anyway he's supposed to. Hope he doesn't forget." They arrived at the baggage carousel and watched the circular conveyor bring bags into view. She searched again for the missing Dr. Wolf, then turned her attention to her companion. "I hear everything runs late around here. Is that true?" She smiled, trying to encourage him. He hadn't yet told her his name, she realized.

He frowned, then muttered, "Dr. Wolf? His lips pursed and he repeated the name again. "Ah," he said, as if making a connection. "Professor Lobo. I knew a professor Lobo once, but he was not a Mexican. He was from Nuevo Mexico, on the other side." He pointed north.

"Maybe the same person," she suggested, "especially if you were in school."

He grew silent, considering her statement, and his expression turned sober. She saw that the information troubled him. Did he know David Wolf?

"So...where you headed?" she tried again. She found his reticence annoying. If he had a romantic interest in her, it was time to show it. But maybe he was just shy. "Do you live in Acapulco with your wife and children?" If he wouldn't volunteer the information, she would ask, and if he was married, she would drop him like an ugly insect.

"No," he answered, "I'm not married." He looked at his feet, seemingly embarrassed. "I live...er...down south. Not too far from San Cristobal, actually."

"Really! Well, how interesting. What do you do?"

"Do?"

"Work. What kind of work do you do?"

Again he hesitated, and his forehead creased with wrinkles. His mouth opened to speak when, unexpectedly, someone down the concourse called out to her.

"Karen...Miss Dumas!" The professor waved from afar.

Dr. Wolf walked toward her, his white teeth shining through a friendly smile. A sense of relief calmed her. Good. Her ride had arrived. She hated waiting in airports–especially in foreign countries. She waved energetically and walked to meet him. Halfway there, she remembered her handsome friend and turned to invite him along, but saw that he had grabbed a suitcase and strode quickly away. What the heck? He sure wasn't very persistent. Wait a minute–she had walked away first. Guess she wasn't worth pursuing. She stood with hands on hips, watching him disappear through the glass doors. He flagged a cab at the curb, jumped inside, and was gone. He still hadn't told her his name! Strange, she thought, but familiar. Sometimes she just seemed to repel men.

****

"Make a friend?" asked David. "Hope I didn't run him off." He carried her two suitcases and she walked at his side. Fluorescent lights lined the ceiling and cool air wafted down the concourse. A wall of glass protected them from the outside. David tried to follow her eyes, but saw only taxis and buses. The sun blazed high in the sky, a yellow-white corona, baking all within its reach.

"Don't know," she answered, reaching to sweep aside a dangling lock of hair from her face. "Just some guy I met on the plane. He was kind of strange, really. Acted like he wanted to talk, then took off suddenly."

"He looked vaguely familiar," offered David. "Seems like I might have known him at one time. Maybe a relative of his. Something about the eyes."

"Yeah. He said he knew a professor Lobo once."

David stopped and faced her. "He said that? Professor Lobo?"

"Yeah. Why? Who is he? An old student or something?"

The professor frowned, started to speak, then hoisted the suitcases again and walked toward the doors. "I don't know. Probably not...or at least not the student I think. He was killed six or seven years ago by the army somewhere here in Guerrero State, as a matter of fact."

"Killed by the army?"

David nodded. "A brilliant young man. Came from an Indian family somewhere down south, but his politics were radical and he was always in trouble with the police." They struggled with the doors momentarily, then passed through. "I always kind of liked him. He was right about most of it. It's just that things change slowly down here."

"Right about what?"

"Oh, you know...a repressive government, keeping the Indians down, murder...stealing the Lacandon forest from the Maya. The stuff no one wants to talk about."

"He talked about it, though?"

"Did more than talk…died because of it." He glanced to see her reaction and saw shock register on her face. "Miss Dumas, this is Mexico. They've probably had more revolutions here than you've had traffic tickets. This is a great place to vacation, but you have to know your way around if you deviate from the beaten path. That's why I'm here… to help you get started. By the time we reach San Cristobal late tonight, we'll probably have passed through five or six military roadblocks and a

47

couple of federal police checks. There's another revolution starting in the south. Now that I think about it, it's too bad Marcos didn't live to see it happen."

"Marcos?" she asked.

"Yes...that was it. Can't remember his last name. But that couldn't have been him. He's dead, remember?"

"You're sure?"

He chuckled. "The government is. It was in all the papers. Marcos was always one for the bold gesture, but he wasn't stupid. He was a wanted man before he died, and wanted men are very careful in Mexico unless they're ready for the firing squad."

"What was he wanted for?"

"Why all the questions, Karen?"

"I just want to know. You've piqued my curiosity."

"Well," David hesitated. "He was accused of massacring a family in Cuernavaca and stealing their money to finance his guerrilla band."

She stopped short and asked, "Do you believe it?"

"The massacre part?" David rubbed his jaw and considered her question. "No. Not really. Not Marcos. I was always suspicious of the government's report–of any reports they issue for that matter. He was a lot of things, but a murderer wasn't one of them."

They arrived at his car, a cinnamon-brown Chrysler Le Baron, wilting in the heat. She entered while he loaded the trunk. Strange how a face conjured up memories, reflected David. He hadn't thought of Marcos in years. The professor remembered him as a born leader; brainy, talented, well-spoken and quick to smile. But Mexico seemed destined to destroy its best and brightest. Who knows what the young man might have achieved had he not become involved with that group of radical Indians? Joining a band of guerrillas in

48

Mexico, regardless of the cause, always led to a permanent home in a pine box with an unmarked grave.

When he got in, she smiled and thanked him for meeting the plane. She was a beautiful woman, he realized again, and people stared as he wheeled out of the airport parking lot and guided the car through the busy city. Air smelling of salt marsh and cooking food wafted through the windows while brilliant sunshine parboiled block after block of square, whitewashed stuccoes lining the street. High walls or fences, protected the owners from the excesses of a capricious government and crime from the lower classes. They drove east of Acapulco Bay, away from the *malecon* and tourist areas, into the old city where the other 1.5 million inhabitants lived. Suddenly the noise and traffic amplified by a factor of 10. Diesel exhaust, rotting meat, and the rancid odor of sewage was ever-present. They arrived near an outdoor market, and street vendors milled about hawking their wares. Traffic slowed to crawl, allowing sellers of flowers, puppets, quesadillas, and blankets to approach the car. A short, stocky youth burdened with a huge load of serapes and sandals with tire tread soles briefly blocked their path, but David patiently told him no, then finished circling the market and drove east on the blacktop until he found the Pan American Highway. The beautiful bay and its towering cliffs had disappeared. Soon the Chrysler was navigating a range of tall, nearly barren mountains in Guerrero state as they headed south toward Chiapas State, the historic colonial frontier of Mexico and the ancient home of Mayan Indians.

They talked as he drove, the professor pointing out items of interest and Karen peppering him with questions. In a matter of minutes, he felt comfortable with her. But then she became quiet and her questions fewer. They left Guerrero and were now in Oaxaca. The vegetation was different, sparse and

49

mean, and thorny plants grew in abundance. The mountains were rugged and barren and the people dusky and thin. She began to study the activity alongside the road, observing the movements of rural Mexico much as it had been for four hundred years.

Groups of people, mostly Indians carrying baskets of produce or items purchased at el Mercado, stood waiting for aged, brightly painted buses to transport them home to small anonymous villages at the end of tortuous rocky roads deep within grim mountains. The sun hid, partially occluded behind stringy, taffeta clouds, while machete-wielding shirtless men wiped their brows and surveyed manicured banana fields.

"How long before we reach Chiapas?" she asked.

"Nine hours...ten to San Cristobal. Did you reserve a room?"

"No. I looked in a travel book and there seemed to be plenty. Can you recommend a hotel? Two or three days is probably all I'll need."

"I know just the place, *La Flor de Corso*," he grinned.

"What's so funny?"

"My wife's family owns it. But it's nice," he assured her, "very nice."

"Okay with me. I can sort my notes tonight. When do you want to take a look at what I have?"

David rubbed his jaw and considered his options. "As soon as possible. But I've got friends in town. An old federale buddy and his wife are vacationing with us at my brother-in-law's house."

"The Consul?"

"Yes. *Senor* Joaquin Antonio Salinas Moctezuma, Honorary Consul in Chiapas State."

"Has a nice ring to it."

"He's a fool."

She turned to him, eyes shining. Mirth tugged at the corners of her mouth.

"Sorry...shouldn't have said that." He sighed with contrition, frowning at his lapse.

Then she surprised him, remembering his comment at the Smithsonian.

"Are you always so rash, Professor Wolf?"

Irritation swept his face, but he held his tongue. After a moment, he added, "Guess I had that coming."

"No, you didn't. It was a cheap shot, but I couldn't resist. I was just being rash."

He met her eyes and saw that she was joking. She brushed a lock of hair aside with an impish look. This woman had fire in her belly. He kind of liked her, he decided.

"I think we're going to get along fine, Karen."

"Me, too. When should we get together? Sometime tomorrow? I don't mean to invite myself, but I'd like to meet your wife and friends."

"And my brother-in-law the fool," he grinned.

"Of course."

"Tomorrow morning, say ten o'clock? We can do breakfast at the hotel and go over your material. I've thought a lot about our conversation in Washington and I'm eager to see what you have. Afterward, if you wish, we can do some sightseeing in San Cristobal. It's quite famous, you know: churches, museums, outdoor markets and such. Or we can drive out to the consul's ranch."

"Sounds great, David." She turned her attention to the scenery. Following interminable hours of rocky, forbidding countryside, the sierras now appeared very green and lush, covered with plants that were sold in northern floral shops, many of them growing wild at roadside. The air, too, had changed and was now thick with humidity, and smelled of rain. After a moment she said, "Sure are lots of trees and mountains in southern Mexico. How easy is it to get around? Are the roads any good?"

"There are virtually no roads. Those that do exist are dirt or gravel. Some are little more than trails. Where you plan to go has few or none once you get outside the tourist areas. See those clouds?" He pointed to dark thunderheads breaching the peaks of the western mountains. "It's the monsoon season here and sometimes it rains so hard you can't hear. The few roads we have wash out and the jungle becomes beautiful, but deadly."

"How so?"

"Like I said—no roads or hospitals, no places to shop for goods, and no police. You have to find a town to find a telephone, if the town has one. The jungle is full of snakes, biting insects, poisonous plants, and jaguars."

"Jaguars?"

"Yes, jaguars; other cats, too, but not as dangerous as jaguars. But that's the easy part." He hesitated, waiting for her to ask, wanting to see if she was paying attention or if she intended to brave it out and play the fool.

"Okay, I'll bite. What's the hard part?"

"The war, remember?"

"The zapatistas?"

"The truce was broken two days ago. Both armies are on the move. You may not be able to get near Palenque, let alone into the jungle. The forest is a haven for bandits hiding from the law. We still have refugees from Guatemala streaming in because of their government's twenty-year war against Indian guerrillas. Frankly, you couldn't have come at a worse time. You may be denied access to where you want to search."

She reached for a lock of hair and toyed with it, winding it around her index finger. He knew that she was considering the challenges waiting her. The Lacandon jungle could be a forbidding adversary. Would she just return home after looking around and spending a few days in San Cristobal? He certainly wouldn't blame her if she did. Entering into the jungle during the rainy season was daunting enough without the additional hazards of guerrilla armies, robbers, and refugees.

"David...you mentioned in Washington that you might be interested in helping with the investigation. What would it take to convince you?"

He looked her straight in the eye. "Good science...good data. Proof that you used the scientific method."

"That's all?"

"That's plenty. If your data is any good you could be on the track of archaeology's biggest discovery in the last one hundred years. I'd be crazy not to want to be part of that." He glanced at her, then at the road. "Uh oh..." he said, braking hard.

"These weren't here earlier today. They changed location."

"What is it? What do you mean?"

Up ahead a platoon of green-uniformed soldiers were pulling aside cars and searching them. They slowed to a near stop and pulled in behind a short line of cars. "You speak Spanish?"

"Yes...no...a little." Her eyes were wide with alarm.

"Pretend you don't. Let me take care of this, okay?"

"Is everything all right?"

"Probably. But you can never tell. Stay in the car unless they tell you to get out."

"Oh, Jesus," she mumbled, focusing on the car directly in front. Three soldiers that had searched a Ford pickup were leading a passenger away into the woods where a small encampment was erected. Two cars ahead, three men, one waving a half-empty bottle of mescal, tried to offer a grim-looking officer a drink. He refused, resolutely directing the search of the car.

"It's okay," said David. "Be sure and give the officer in charge a pretty smile."

"You're kidding."

"I'm dead serious."

"How's this?" She gave him a broad smile that exposed brilliant white teeth.

"Perfect," he said, "Your orthodontist would be proud."

David exited the Le Baron and pulled his wallet to extract identification. Mexico had no laws against drinking and driving, so the drunks two cars ahead were waved through. The officer and two soldiers turned and, with their guns leading the way, approached the Le Baron. One of the men barked an order at Karen. The professor held up his hand and told her to sit still. He turned to the officer and began a rapid stream of Spanish, protesting their being stopped. The army officer frowned and yelled at the soldiers, who subsequently lowered their rifles, then he turned to examine David's identification. The officer asked a few perfunctory questions, returned the professor's papers, and walked to the passenger side of the automobile.

David followed and motioned for Karen to roll down the window. She bit her lip, but lowered the window, then, as if a light bulb had come on, gave the officer a nervous but gorgeous smile. David smiled also. It was infectious. The officer decided to try his English on her, and she answered, complimenting him on his usage of the language. This encouraged him, and he began to ask questions that she couldn't understand, stuttering and stumbling as he talked. She replied the best she could, trying to be respectful and gracious to the barbarian. Finally he nodded, satisfied, and waved them through.

"Great job," mumbled David, firing the car and guiding it through the roadblock. "He liked you."

"I'm scared to death."

"It's okay, really. We'll probably be stopped a couple of more times."

"What did you tell him?" she asked.

David relaxed into his seat, checked the rearview mirror, and answered. "I told him my brother-in-law was the Consul of Chiapas and that you were a famous archaeologist from the United States coming to visit him."

"You talked longer than that."

"I also happened to mention that it would be truly unfortunate if I had to tell the consul that we were threatened by rifle-toting idiots totally devoid of courtesy."

"Ah. He didn't detain us as long as the others."

They rode in silence, David reviewing the incident in his mind. Hours passed and the sun fled the sky and hid behind the mountains. Long dark shadows stretched across the narrow valley, and the roadside vegetation seemed denser. The air felt thick and smelled of sweet, rotting compost.

Karen seemed fatigued and reluctant to talk, so David offered no conversation and drove the Le Baron steadily south. He was eager to return to San Cristobal to his wife and friends. He would drop Karen at La Flor De Corso. Tomorrow if everything went well at their meeting, maybe he would invite her to visit the ranch.

A half-hour later they successfully negotiated another roadblock, this one manned by swaggering federales waving .45-caliber handguns. But this encounter, too, was uneventful. The federales knew what they were doing, and after a curious stare at Karen, waved them through. They had bigger fish to fry.

"God...is it always like this?" Karen's head lolled back against the headrest.

"In the south, yes, and all up and down the Pan American Highway. Long history of rebellions here. Gun runners and dope smugglers move their product on this blacktop. It's like this all the way to the border."

"Guatemala?"

"Yes, but north too...clear to the United States."

"This is so different from home. The army would never..."

"Karen, you don't know the half of it," he interrupted.

She straightened in her seat, as though offended. Her head whipped around to face him.

"What do you mean?"

David said, "In the United States everyone must pass tests to get into the military. If someone is psychologically unfit or doesn't meet minimum education guidelines, they're rejected. Not so here. Anyone can get in. You don't even have to be able to read or write. And, as you might imagine, the consequences of having an army of illiterates, or worse, sometimes leads to disasters."

Karen offered no reply, reaching instead for a lock of hair. Dusk came and went, and their headlights shone strong on the road. The professor yawned, wishing that he were home, sitting with his nightly glass of brandy on the verandah surrounded by avocado trees, visiting with Alexandra, Luis and Angela. He inhaled through his nose, recalling the scent of his wife's perfume. He glanced again at Karen. Maybe tomorrow's meeting would go well.

He turned to her. "You're pretty sure of yourself, aren't you?"

"You mean my research?"

He nodded.

"I know I'm right. I know it's there."

"Hope so, young lady, I truly hope so," he repeated. David propelled the car into the next curve, then steadied the wheel to keep it between the lines. He looked at Karen. "I'm glad you came," he said simply. "Who knows? This trip might turn out to be something neither of us will forget."

CHAPTER SEVEN

"Two weeks ago she was pretty," chastised David's wife, Alexandra. "Today she's beautiful, you old goat. Are you coming home tonight, or should I send Luis to help with your carousing?"

"Ali, you know I'm a one-woman man. I was merely telling you about this interesting young archaeologist who..."

"Who just happens to be beautiful," she finished for him. "Where are you, anyway?"

"*La Flor de Corso.* She's checking in right now."

"Stay out of her room. I know all about American women. They're over-sexed and act like *putas.* Joaquin had his satellite dish hooked up and we watched MTV tonight."

"What?"

"MTV. Oh, it's really something. Joaquin couldn't get the sound to work, but Luis didn't mind. He likes watching the big-breasted American girls."

"Listen, Ali...I'm coming home. Tell Luis to hold on, we'll

watch together." Two could play this game.

"Not a chance, old man. I've got plans for you. Besides, it quit working when Joaquin left."

"Joaquin left? Where'd he go?"

"His airstrip. An old friend from the Guadalajara Embassy called and requested that he meet a small plane of VIP's from the United States."

"Diplomats?" asked David. "Did he mention names?"

"No. Now that you mention it, he was mumbling about gringo archaeologists and seemed a little irritated. Should be back any time, though."

This stirred the professor's curiosity. Anthropologists were always coming and going through San Cristobal. It was a major thoroughfare and watering hole. In fact, it was because of them that San Cristobal had diplomatic personnel. And since the Zapatista uprising in 1994, the city's population had doubled. But the consul usually only met planes of important people; diplomats and PRI politicos from Mexico City, or army Generals and their entourages. Whatever. It didn't have anything to do with him. He was tired and ready to go home.

"See you in thirty minutes." He looked and saw that Karen had finished registering. Good. His task was accomplished.

"Promise?"

"Promise. I'm tired. Could use a rubdown tonight," he hinted.

"Come home, David. Just come home."

"No back rub?"

"That and more, *senor*."

He heard the smack of a kiss over the phone, and so he whispered a few endearments, his eyes casting about to ensure that no one listened. Life after fifty could be pretty good if you took time to smell the roses.

He walked Karen to the second-floor landing where she

59

had taken a room overlooking the hotel dining room. Lush with tropical plants and traditional Indian art pieces, the dining room had two rancorous parrots that harassed the patrons. She could listen to the birds chatter while watching the other guests come and go. Although her room had no balcony, a large picture window presented a view of the park across the street.

A light sprinkle began to soak the ground, and dark thunderheads, illuminated by flickering luminescent threads of lightning, moved steadily east toward San Cristobal. He hurried toward his car, parked a half block south near the *zocalo*. Remembering that he left his umbrella in the car, he scowled and muttered. The sprinkles and threat of rain began to clear people from the park. Flower and food vendors were packing up, as were two groups of mariachis. Their livelihood at stake, they lingered nearby beneath the protection of the gazebo, hopeful that the shower would pass. But this was the rainy season and no one really expected the storm to spare them.

The sprinkle became a light rain and David walked even faster, berating himself for his forgetfulness. I'm getting old and insensible, he thought, then relented and gave himself an excuse. He had been, truly, distracted. The young archaeologist had proven to be as interesting as she was attractive, and seemed pleased that he was taking her seriously. The professor believed that they could form a working relationship—if she would follow his lead. He worried that she might be over-confident and too full of herself—an affliction common to bright young people.

His attitude of skepticism was changing, he realized, even though he hadn't seen her work. He liked this archaeologist, and she exuded confidence. He hoped that she had indeed stumbled onto the scent of a promising mystery. Tomorrow morning they would review her data; an imprint of the Gould Stelae and her interpretation of the glyphs. Her anecdote of Red Snail, the Mayan holy man, and his flight south from the Yucatan made a good story. The improbable date discussed at the Smithsonian, 1573, and the events she hypothesized invited some pretty fantastic conjecture. He knew that some of it was consistent with written records from the time of the Conquest. But he must see for himself. Interpreting pictographic glyphs was as much an art as science; and symbols of syntax, prepositions and verbs rarely behaved as they did in Roman script.

Unlocking and starting his car, he drove carefully, navigating the aged, bumpy cobblestone streets of San Cristobal. People scurried everywhere, trying to beat the rain and get home to their white stuccoes. As he passed the last Pemex gas station on the fringe of town, he saw a man riding a donkey while his wife walked dutifully behind, balancing a large basket of roots on her head, a common scene in Mexico.

Lightning arced across the sky and rolling thunder reverberated and echoed a response. Large foreboding patches of vegetation crowded the road on a moonless night. David turned on his wipers and leaned forward to focus on the winding, slick pavement. Narrow asphalt roads were dangerous on rainy nights and the professor looked intently for straggling, homeward-bound pedestrians. He slowed at each curve to check for cattle being herded down the highway, another common occurrence in Mexico. A hint of his wife's perfume drifted into memory, and he replayed their telephone conversation in his mind. She had promised a back rub, he remembered. His imagination began to flower as the wipers whisked rain from the windshield. Ten more minutes and he would be home.

CHAPTER EIGHT

Karen tossed and turned all night. The thunderstorm, the excitement of her journey to Mexico, and her conversation with the professor had kept her awake well into early morning. Again and again she preplanned today's meeting with David Wolf. Completely alert, she watched darkness succumb to the first aura of morning's light. She lay wide-eyed in bed, listening to the sounds of food vendors, taxis and the muffled talk of people going to work. She knew when the restaurant help arrived because they uncloaked the parrot cages, which encouraged the birds to screech and squawk and fuss at anyone who walked near.

By 5:30 a.m. she could no longer stay in bed. Though apprehensive of going out alone, the wonders of colonial Mexico lay just beyond her hotel room door. She showered and dressed and checked the time, discovering that she had four hours before her meeting with David. Plenty of time to attend mass at one of the forty beautiful churches she had read about. Afterward she could wander through the market and watch the shops open and the Indians arrive from the surrounding mountain towns who come to sell their handicrafts.

Karen carefully folded two sheets of paper containing a synopsis of her methodology and conclusions regarding the Gould Stelae and put them into her purse. One was a photo of the stelae with her translation, the other data gleaned from her research. She slung the strap over a shoulder, left the room and walked to the handrail overlooking the hotel and restaurant. No one was eating. Indeed, no guests were awake as far as she could tell. A civilized breakfast in Mexico began at 10:00 a. m. Lunch was eaten around 2:00 p.m. and dinner at 8 or 9:00 in the evening. The aroma of tortillas, beans and grilled chorizo wafted upward. Her stomach growled in response, and she inhaled deeply and with longing. She had promised to eat with David. It would take time and effort to adjust her circadian rhythms to the pulse of Latin America.

Karen descended the stairs, walked through the empty restaurant and, hugging her purse, stepped outside into the early morning of a San Cristobal day. The air smelled fresh from last night's thunderstorm and the pure, golden evanescence of the rising sun held her still and reverent. A ripple of enchantment stirred within. She breathed deeply, savoring the magic, then looked about for a church steeple. With so many to choose among, it would be unlikely that she could walk far without encountering one.

Straight ahead, the zocalo beckoned. Broad-leafed diffenbachias and rows of red-orange croton encircled a carousel that sat in the middle of the park. Near a fountain, a trellis erupted a violent red as bougainvillea leaped up and over a lattice frame and poured down the other side. She decided to cut through the *zocalo* on her way to wherever. An

63

urge for serendipity tugged at her, and she allowed herself to be led by whim. She would just walk and see where her feet led. Stepping confidently from the curb onto the cobblestone street, she walked toward the park. Smiling and trusting, she wandered here and there, wherever she wished or where her eyes were attracted.

Had she turned and looked behind her, she would see a man standing in the window of her hotel room. A straw Panama hat sat on his head and a thin scar curved from the bridge of his nose to his chin. He extracted matches from a shirt pocket and fired a thin cigar, puffing until its tip glowed red, illuminating the grim, malevolent set of his eyes. He watched Karen bend to smell the flowers, then walk around the carousel. When she turned south and left the park, he waited until she left his field of vision, then disappeared from the window.

****

David gripped two mugs of steaming black coffee as he stepped through the patio door and out onto the verandah of his brother-in-law's home. A carnival of brightly colored plants sat potted and well-nourished on a red brick floor. Others hung in baskets from sheets of lattice serving as a ceiling. The sun hung bloated and lethargic on the eastern horizon, the Jaguar god struggling to resurrect itself from its nightly battle with darkness.

Luis Alvarado, the professor's federale friend on vacation from the northern state of Chihuahua, sat in an adjacent lawn chair, resting his large feet on a stump of polished mahogany. Luis, a large man with bushy, mobile eyebrows, waited impatiently for David to arrive with the coffee.

"Didn't put any milk in it did you?" asked Luis, reaching to accept one of the mugs.

"No, Luis, just a couple of spoonfuls of sugar."

64

"Tell me you're lying, professor."

"I'm lying, Luis." David plopped into a chair next to his friend. He sipped his coffee and grunted with pleasure. "That hits the spot. Nothing better than coffee to start the morning."

"I would recommend an occasional whiskey," offered Luis, "but I know you're addicted to those damned distilled grapes."

"Brandy is the drink of gentlemen," retorted the professor.

"Then why don't I like it?" asked Luis, his eyebrows arched quizzically.

"You really want me to answer that?" David grinned. Luis had left himself wide open.

"Starting early, are we?" accused Luis, grimacing at his friend.

"You'll get me back." The professor reclined in his chair. "Nice sunrise eh?"

"Beautiful," intoned Luis. "Just like Chihuahua, except here they have trees."

"How's the shoulder?" inquired the academic. Luis had only recently returned to work after recovering from a bear attack a year ago in the Copper Canyon area of the Sierra Madres. A grizzly sow had nearly torn off his arm, but the federale had survived and kept the limb, even though he'd endured terrible hardship for nearly two days before receiving medical attention.

"Ready for a rematch," bragged Luis. He flexed a burly arm for David's benefit.

"Yeah...well...better have a 30-06 next time you decide to wrestle a grizzly."

The house servant, an elderly Mayan woman, appeared with plates of fruit and sweet breads. David retrieved a roll and began tearing away pieces to eat, occasionally tossing crumbs to speckle-chested finches that strutted about the patio.

"Have you noticed all the small airplanes coming and going from Joaquin's airfield?" asked Luis.

"He's an important person, Luis." David shrugged. "Just be grateful we don't have to meet or entertain them."

Luis pursed his lips to offer a retort, but hesitated, saying instead. "So...you're gone again today?"

"Probably be back about noon. I need to meet with Miss Dumas and look at some data she's prepared. If no one objects, maybe I'll drag her along later to meet everyone. I may be involved in a research project with her."

"What kind of project?' Luis's eyebrow arched again.

"Mayan books. Could be a cadre of them in the Lacandon jungle."

"That figures."

"Huh?" David turned to see what Luis was hatching. "What does that mean?"

"The zapatistas control the jungle, David. You know that. This sounds like another one of your lame ideas that'll get you killed."

"You don't know anything about it, Luis. These books could..."

"Not the books, David. If you say the books are there, I believe you. Problem is, you'll have to sneak past everyone to get inside that jungle."

"I'm not going today, Luis." David scoffed at the federale's concern. "The army's winning the war. It can't last forever."

"It's lasted almost two years, my friend. It isn't well publicized, but the army, in case you haven't noticed, hasn't exactly routed the guerrillas from the forest. Hell...they can't even find them." Luis snagged a slice of mango from the plate and bit into it. Beads of juice hung from his mustache. "You won't get permission to do any archaeology around here. Too much at stake. They don't want any hostage situations,

66

especially with Americans."

"I think Joaquin can help if I need him," said David.

"Joaquin?" Luis sounded doubtful. "Have you said anything to Ali about this?"

"Well...I really haven't had time to think it through. You know...I...er...haven't had the chance."

"Yeah...I thought so." Luis reached for a slice of avocado. "Let's take a look at this here plan of yours, David." Luis took a deep breath and sighed with pleasure, relishing the opportunity to score on his friend for the "gentleman" remark earlier. He paused for effect, then said, "Joaquin is Ali's brother, and they're obviously very close. What if Alexandra doesn't want you to go on this here treasure hunt?"

"Books, not treasure, Luis." David knew what was coming. Worst of all, he suspected that his friend might be right.

"I stand corrected, but if Ali doesn't approve of you running off with a pretty archaeologist into the jungle," continued Luis, "just how likely is it that Joaquin will pull strings for you?"

The professor didn't respond. The answer was obvious— zero to none, that's how likely. He frowned. Why had he deluded himself? Why hadn't he thought of this very obvious encumbrance? He'd said much the same to Karen himself. It might take months, even years to settle with the zapatistas. He turned and saw Luis' face fixed with a sly smile. The federale knew he had scored.

"You got me back, Luis."

"Thanks for noticing, professor. When do we get to meet your American friend?"

"Beautiful...beautiful," boomed Joaquin, his arms spread wide, embracing the sunrise as he strode through the door to the verandah's edge. He turned and beamed at his guests. Every hair on his head lay perfectly manicured; mustache and hair trimmed precisely. He wore an Armani suit, necktie and wing tips polished to a mirror shine. His smile revealed pearly white teeth.

The perfect host, thought David. God, I despise him. Too bad one can't choose his family.

"I trust you gentlemen slept well. Sorry I arrived so late...business you know," he winked. Joaquin lifted a roll from the plate and bit into it, pausing overly long to assess its flavor. "Some of your people, David." The consul gestured with the breakfast roll. "A Director of that...a...famous museum in Washington...a..." he frowned, unable to recall its name. Then he had it. "Smithson, that's it." He snapped his fingers.

"Smithsonian," said David. The Smithsonian? How unusual. Perhaps Karen knew them. He would have to ask when they met later this morning. If so, it was a strange coincidence. Had she known and not told him they were coming?

"Yes...yes...the Smithsonian. A rock hound like you, David," said the consul.

The professor bristled. What a pompous, self-serving ass. Joaquin looked down on any profession not associated with business or government. He believed that his sister, wealthy in her own right, had married beneath her station. David found his brother-in-law's affectations and voice inflections to be maddening; always insinuating, never forthright, behaving like the rich, snotty patrician that he was. He possessed little in terms of character or ability. To David he was just an empty suit–a man totally void of charm and personal integrity. But the professor bit his tongue and remained civil.

"Why did they fly here, Joaquin? Are they friends of yours?"

"Of course not." Joaquin waved off the idea as nonsense.

"The governor called from Tuxtla Gutierrez and asked me to greet them." Joaquin's chest swelled with self-importance. "He received a call from Guadalajara. Someone called them from Washington, D.C. You know how it works."

David knew how it worked, and he didn't like it. Smug insiders showing each other special favors with taxpayer money; another reason he didn't like Joaquin and his self-serving brethren. But the diplomat was family, and they must all accommodate the other's character flaws.

"Did you take them to La Flor de Corso?"

"Of course," replied Joaquin, smiling broadly. "Bill and Dr. Depp were very pleased. *La Flor de Corso* is a first-class hotel, you know. The governor would expect no less of me than to ensure that they received the best treat..."

"Bill and who?" David jerked upright, spilling coffee into his lap.

Joaquin motioned for the servant to bring a towel. "Bill something or other," he said, "never caught his last name, and a Dr. Depp. He's the one from the museum. Do you know them?"

David dabbed at his lap. "Well...yeah...one of them anyway. Depp, maybe...if he's the same one. Never met him...actually just heard of him."

David finished with the towel and excused himself. An occasional coincidence was nothing to be concerned about– depending on the situation. This, however, could not be coincidence; not with what he knew regarding Karen's departure from the Smithsonian. Had she brought trouble with her in the form of an angry boss and the Smithsonian Institute? Had the U.S. Government sent someone to locate her? Maybe she didn't have the legal right to be pursuing this investigation! Was she involved in a deception? Whatever the situation, he intended to find out. Immediately–or, at least, after he changed his pants.

CHAPTER NINE

Karen exited the old Franciscan church through wide oak doors embellished with beautifully carved representations of biblical scenes. She paused briefly to admire the craftsmanship, then descended broad limestone steps worn uneven by five hundred years of prayerful churchgoers. Her own religious fervor had quieted many years ago following the death of her parents and years of anthropological study. Religion, in its myriad forms, interested her greatly, though she now found herself in the passive role of ethnographer, academic, and observer. But the ancient church with its gilded interior, flickering candles and cloying incense evoked pleasant memories from her childhood when she had attended St. Margaret Mary's with her parents in Omaha, Nebraska.

The air stirred with the fragrance of frying foods, and the sun lolled behind pine forested hills surrounding the town. Rays of light leaked through long shadows cast by the trees, encouraging a benign lethargy. A quick glance at her watch revealed it was time to head back to the hotel to meet with Professor Wolf. A twinge of anxiety gripped her and she pressed her handbag to her side. Assured of her data's safety, she strolled toward the market that lay between her and *La Flor de Corso*.

The scent and sounds of el Mercado hinted its proximity. The aroma of cooking food–chorizo, tortillas, and black beans–drifted on a light breeze, accented with undertones of leather and rotting fruit. She breathed deeply, absorbing the odor of the market. Shallow puddles of rainwater reflected light from the street, and the sidewalks were busy with people visiting or going to work. An occasional pre-teen girl in braids and brightly embroidered blouse swept the sidewalk clean in front of her door. On the other side of the street, a cheerless donkey saddled with large milk cans stood on the sidewalk over a pile of manure while its owner chatted with the proprietor of a small corner *abaceria*. The windowless store had no signs advertising its food and wares, but customers lingered within while the owner talked outside with the milkman. She paused on the market's periphery to recall the way that she had passed earlier and saw that it now hummed with activity.

Upon turning the corner, she found herself following a family of Indians toting twine baskets bursting with traditional handicrafts to spread out on a blanket and sell at the market. Most of the proprietors had already arrived and were busy preparing for business. Karen picked her way through the maze of stalls and aisles. Surrounded by every imaginable enterprise, she nearly ran into a curtain of plucked chickens. Hanging by their claws, strapped onto a yellow polyester line, blood pooled on the floor beneath them. The butcher talked while his knife flashed, paring fat and gristle from a rack of ribs. The head of a steer, its black eyes staring

72

balefully, had been placed on a spike so all could see from where today's beef had come. Large black flies licked blood from the severed neck. She could easily imagine them laying their eggs in the decaying flesh, and quickly turned away. A shoe and sandal merchant, nodding his head at the butcher's discourse across the aisle, used wire hooks made from clothes hangers to suspend his wares from horizontal poles that hung in concert from the ceiling.

Karen moved on, alert, threading her way past blankets, onyx chess sets, jewelry, toys and puppets, and an occasional food vendor. Finally she saw daylight and what appeared to be her street. She navigated the remaining clutter and exited the market, pausing briefly to turn and look over her shoulder. A sense of regret tugged at her. An old-world market place with its color and odors tempted her to linger. She wanted to spend more time looking and shopping–but mustn't. She touched her handbag again, recalling her purpose in coming to Mexico: the Gould Stelae. Playing tourist would have to wait.

Karen glanced at her watch and saw that it was now 9:34 a.m. She walked briskly, and two blocks later the *zocalo* and cathedral across from *La Flor de Corso* came into view. She held her shoulder bag firmly, eyes on the ground, her mind attuned to the Gould Stelae, she reviewed what she knew, recalling the glyphs and the secret therein. How would David react? she wondered. Would he help, or would she have to go it alone? Now that she had arrived in Chiapas, Karen realized that she had undertaken a daunting, maybe unachievable task. This investigation would require more than a positive attitude and determination. She needed help; someone who knew influential people, a person who could fix things with a telephone call. Most of all she needed an experienced, knowledgeable archaeologist who knew Chiapas and the

Lacandon jungle. So much hinged on this meeting. "Oh Lord," she whispered, "I hope he agrees with my translation."

She bit her lip and gripped the bag tighter as she crossed the wide apron that fronted the cathedral. *La Flor de Corso* beckoned, and she exited the park and crossed the cobblestones. The professor was nowhere in sight, so she paused momentarily at the doors and looked both ways. Then she moved through the entry and walked into the hotel. The desk clerk seemed startled to see her, and his gaze followed as she passed. What was that all about? she wondered. Was he ogling her, or had she received a message? She thought to ask, then decided against it. It was poor form to stop and talk with men who stared at you, and she had long ago learned to ignore staring males.

Karen entered the restaurant commons and looked around for David. Several couples, mostly tourists, enjoyed their breakfast. Her stomach growled again. The morning walk had added to her hunger. She glanced above at the balcony and walkway leading to the hotel rooms. Still no David. Perhaps he hadn't arrived. Removing the room key from her purse, she turned toward the stairs to begin her ascent, when a movement from above caught her eye. A bedroom door had just closed. She looked and saw that it was her room! The number 21 was clearly visible. What the heck? Then she relaxed; it was probably just the maid cleaning her room. She took another step, then heard a familiar voice. But it wasn't David. She listened again, her eyes wide with alarm. A stab of fear pierced her gut, and she grasped the stairway banister for support. She tried not to panic as her heart thundered, and she strained to listen. The voice talking to the desk clerk sounded like Dr. Depp. But that wasn't possible. *Please, God*, she prayed. It can't be him!

Karen looked for a hiding place, questions flooding her

74

mind. Why had he followed her to Mexico? It could only be the Gould stelae! The crazy, domineering jerk had pursued her. He must be desperate to go to such extremes. But why, and what did he intend to do? Did his appearance in Mexico lend support to the value of her data? She had not imagined the string of events culminating in the office burglary after all. Perhaps Depp had been responsible all along! She gripped her handbag. What should she do? If he'd steal from her in the U.S., he'd certainly steal from her here! This was Mexico–a foreign, sometimes lawless country. Washington D.C., Omaha, and Aunt Rose seemed very far away.

She placed herself behind a broad-leafed dieffenbachia near the stairs, listening to the desk clerk answer Depp's broken Spanish. They argued, and Depp's voice grew louder. The ruckus disturbed the parrots and they squawked and fussed in protest. Their cage, suspended from a bamboo tripod, began to sway back and forth as they flapped their wings. Those damn birds! They were drawing everyone's attention, and she couldn't think! She must hide the translation somewhere. If Depp accosted her or brought the police to help him, she would lose it–lose everything. The parrots continued to screech. She grimaced, wanting to smack the cage and tell them to shut up. Then she saw it–the perfect hiding place until she could get this mess sorted out. The birdcage!

She stepped from behind the plant and set her purse and keys on the table. She extracted the papers from her satchel. A pan at the bottom of the cage slid in and out to catch their droppings. She grasped the tray handle, slid it out. The birds went into a frenzy. A stranger was messing with their cage! She tried to shush them, but saw that everyone in the restaurant watched her. She smiled sweetly and nodded a greeting, acting as though she did this often, and then returned to the task.

75

There was no time for niceties, so she laid the two neatly typed pages on top of the existing bird mess and tried to shove it back, but the pan jammed. She wiggled and manipulated it, grinding her teeth and holding her breath, her hands trembled and felt numb and leaden. By this time everyone had stopped eating to watch. She gave them a nervous laugh, then wiggled the tray up and down, trying to slide it in the groove. Finally the tray moved, and she was working it forward when she realized that the voices in the entry had died down. She glanced toward the hall leading to the front desk and saw Depp handing money to the clerk, who in turn looked about to see if anyone watched. The clerk's demeanor changed and the acrimony disappeared. After he pocketed the money, the two behaved as friends. The desk clerk bent to whisper like a conspirator. Damn!

Karen gave the tray one last push, grabbed her purse, and nearly ran for the stairs. While all the diners watched, she took them two at a time, then hurriedly walked toward her room, her eyes on the restaurant and hallway below. She reached into her purse for the room key, only to remember that she had left it downstairs on the table.

"Mother of God, I'm losing it!" she whispered. Angry, she gripped the door handle and wrenched it hard, but the knob turned easily, unlocked. She stiffened, surprised, then remembered that the maid was inside cleaning. Karen pushed the door and burst inside. Her heart thumped dully and she gasped for air. She closed the door and leaned against it for support. She tried to calm herself and regain her composure. Should she call David? But no, he was due to arrive any moment. She would just stay in the room until he called for her. If Depp knocked on the door she wouldn't answer. She turned to face the door and fumbled with the latch, then a pair of strong hands closed around her neck and squeezed tightly,

76

preventing her from crying out. She clawed at the hands and tried to scream, but managed only a gurgle. She was whirled about to face a knife directly in front of her eyes.

"Make a sound and you're dead, bitch." A tall, thin man with a milky eye and long scar streaking his face smiled grimly. He flashed the knife close to her face, then scraped it across her cheek so that she felt the blade's keen edge.

She struggled, but he held firm, just tight enough to keep her from screaming. The knife flashed and pain seared her upper arm. She stiffened and moaned, terrified. His one good eye pierced her with a black, dead look of cruelty and indifference. She felt herself swoon, go weak in the knees, then everything went dark.

****

David parked the Le Baron at curbside near La Flor de Corso and hurried toward its double oak doors. He stepped inside and looked around. As he walked past the desk clerk, a man he knew, David smiled a greeting. The clerk, however, turned away. What was that all about? he wondered. Realizing that he was late, David ignored the snub and strode into the dining room. A quick survey of the tables revealed tourists eyeing plates of suspicious-looking black refried beans and red-orange sausage. Karen was nowhere to be seen. He glanced at his watch–10:15. Tardiness, of course, was no crime in Mexico. Everyone arrived late–it was a cultural trait. Karen, however, was not Mexican, and therefore likely obsessed with punctuality. She should be here, irritated at having had to wait for him. Should he knock on her door or wait a few more minutes? Perhaps she was putting on makeup or doing whatever women did before appearing in public. He decided to give her a few more minutes, and sat down at one of the tables. His morning coffee had been interrupted at Joaquin's and he craved a cup of the local

77

variety. He summoned a waiter and ordered.

It arrived black and steaming, just as he liked. He sipped cautiously, then centered the cup on the saucer and turned to watch the parrots. They were especially noisy and active today; jumping about in their cages and squawking threats. Something had agitated them, he decided, amused at their antics. He liked birds, but had never had one for a pet. They were colorful, but dumb as mud—messy, too. He took another sip, savoring the dark rich brew, and noticed that someone sitting next to the cage had left their room key on the table—not the brightest thing to do in Mexico. He stared at the key, wondering to whom it might belong, but then he recognized the room number—21—Karen's room. Why would she leave it lying on the table? He took a drink from his cup and eyed the key, tempted to pick it up. He checked out the restaurant more thoroughly, but still didn't see her. Apparently she had already been down, but returned to her room when he didn't show. Just like an American to be on time, he groused.

Five minutes later, his cup nearly empty, his patience expired. The key begged to be picked up. It could easily be stolen and her room burglarized. No one left hotel room keys lying about unless they had forgotten them. Maybe he should go up and knock on her door. Better yet, he would ask the desk clerk if he'd seen Karen and check if number twenty-one was, in fact, her room. Maybe she had taken breakfast alone? He retrieved the key and walked to the front desk.

The clerk seemed nervous and would not meet David's eye. He rubbed his hands and said that, "yes," he'd seen her several times. Some while ago she'd left with two other Americans to do whatever it is that tourists do.

"She left with other Americans?" David repeated, unbelieving. But she had an appointment with him at 10 o'clock? "You're sure?" he asked again.

"Yes...yes...of course," mumbled the clerk, "thirty minutes ago. She...er...looked a little ill too."

David's brow furrowed and he shook his head, disgusted, unsure what to think. Why was the clerk behaving so strangely? Did he know more? Enough. He would call at her room. He paused at his table to down his coffee, then climbed the stairs and walked to her door and rapped loudly. No one answered. He knocked again, but still no answer. Looking left, then right, he tried the knob. It opened easily and he pushed the door wide. The room had been tossed and everything lay in disarray. A hollow feeling grew in his stomach and his heart began to pound. He called out, expecting no answer. He got none. He walked cautiously into the room, then slipped on something gooey. The professor lifted his shoe to see what he had stepped in, and jerked upright, startled, realizing that it was someone's blood! Whose? Karen's? An involuntary shiver wracked him. He must call the *policía* immediately! He would call Joaquin, also. The consul owned the hotel and knew people—including the *policía*. This was serious, maybe terrible. The clerk had said she left willingly with other Americans, but had appeared sick. What did he mean by sick? What the hell was going on? Whose blood was this?

Her purse and its contents lay scattered on the bed. He shoved the key into his pocket, then tossed everything into the purse and carried it with him as he retreated from the room, carefully retracing his steps. He shut the door and nearly ran down the stairs. He breathlessly told the clerk to call the *policía* and hotel manager. The clerk sniffed disapproval and started to argue, but David insisted, reminding the clerk that Joaquin was his brother-in-law. Irritated, but apprehensive, the clerk picked up the phone and complied.

The calls completed, David looked around, checked his watch, and shifted his weight from one leg to the other. What should he do? Had she hurt herself accidentally and the American friends taken her for medical attention? He asked the clerk, who looked out the window and stated that he didn't know. He hadn't really noticed.

David returned to the dining room, his dread growing with each moment. He looked about the room and spotted the table on which the room key had lain. This had probably been her last stop before going up stairs. Had he missed something? The tabletop was empty and nothing lay below it. What was he looking for? He heard a voice and turned to see the desk clerk huddled with a man dressed in a suit. David presumed him to be the manager. He turned to join them, but noticed that the birdcage seemed somehow awry. The mess pan on the bottom stuck out noticeably. He almost ignored it, but something caught his eye. Not only was the tray extended, the paper inside was white. Everyone used cheap newspaper for bird droppings. He reached for the pan and pulled. It gave on the first try, and he gently pulled the papers from the pan. The paper was an English publication. In Mexico? Very unusual! Looking closer, he recognized the words, and saw that Mayan glyphs were strung across the page. His hand began to shake. Karen had placed them in the cage! He knew it. Something would have to have been terribly wrong for her to hide it here! The professor reached for a napkin and cleaned the bird mess from the papers. He folded and tucked them away in his back pocket, then turned to meet the approaching manager and desk clerk.

****

Karen cradled her throbbing arm and cowered in the back seat of a rusty white Ford Fairlane as it lurched and bucked on a muddy, rutted road leading to a small airfield somewhere near the forest. Fight or run, her instincts told her. She longed to open the car door and jump, but knew that escape was

80

unlikely. Where would she go? If she were still in town it might work and certainly draw attention to her plight, but Depp had explained that escape wasn't a good idea. Bill held a knife to Karen's ribs to ensure her cooperation and, if she gave them what they wanted, her aunt wouldn't have to meet Bill.

"Sweet Mother of God," Karen whispered under her breath. How could this be happening? How had Depp known about Aunt Rose? Why was he doing this, and who would have suspected that he'd go to such extremes? Was he desperate, or just crazy? Maybe she should have paid more attention to the stories and gossip about him when she was at the Smithsonian. For now, though, her only alternative was to go along until an escape opportunity presented itself.

She felt the gentle stroke of a finger on her arm. Bill smiled lewdly, then wiggled his tongue at her. She jerked her arm away and scooted even closer to the door.

"There it is." Depp pointed into the distance at a small single-engine plane parked near a shiny Quonset hut. The road worsened, and the car slowed to accommodate large ruts.

"Damn Mexicans," complained Depp. "They built pyramids, but never learned to make a road." The car slid sideways, wallowed in the mud, and then hit a large chuckhole. Everyone bounced upward and banged their heads on the ceiling.

Bill smirked and looked at Karen. "*A los zarcos y los mujeres, hay que entrar in media.*"

"What'd he say?"

She saw Depp's smile in the rearview mirror. "It's an old Mexican saying. The women and chuck holes must be entered in the middle."

"You're a creep and he's a pervert," she retorted. "Where'd you find him, under a rock?"

81

"Listen, you snotty bitch. I'm in charge here. If I want something from you, I'll step on you. Keep your mouth shut and do as I say, or I'll give you and your Aunt Rose to him."

"You won't get away with this."

"I already have, idiot."

"How did you find me?"

"It was easy. I still have connections down here, especially in Guatemala. I work in D.C., remember? I spent nearly twenty years doing archaeology in Latin America, and I just called in a few chits from the old days. I knew I'd get the chance to score again."

"Score again? Sounds like drug lingo. What kind of archaeology did you do?"

"Nothing you'd appreciate, bitch." He cast a malevolent glare by way of the rearview mirror. The car lurched again, accelerated and then stopped. "Okay, time's up. Where are we going?" Depp turned to face her. "No more games, Karen. Where are we heading? Veracruz? Tobasco? Guatemala, I hope," he added.

She glanced toward the plane. "My guess is Quintana Roo," she lied.

"The Yucatan peninsula?" He seemed perplexed. "Limones?"

Karen shrugged. "Wish I knew for sure." She moved strands of hair from her face and stole a look at Bill. "Never been there. May even be Belize," she lied again. "Probably somewhere in the jungle. It's just a guess, that's all."

"Then what're you doing in San Cristobal? Quintana Roo is four hundred air miles east." Depp glowered, as if daring her to dispute him.

"I have friends here. Someone was going to help me..."

"Oh, yes...Dr. Wolf. I heard he was in Washington."

"He's a fine scholar and a..."

"You wouldn't know a scholar from an illiterate. You have a graduate student mentality."

Karen returned Depp's scowl, but then checked to see that Bill kept his distance. The knife in his right hand hovered near, and his one good eye held her steady. She found the milky eye repellent and couldn't hold his gaze.

"Where's the translation?" Depp demanded, holding out his hand.

"I left it in the hotel."

"Bullshit. We checked your room." Depp's eyes darted to Bill, and the knife drew close to her head. She cowered against the door, trying to disappear into her corner. "It's the truth," she squeaked. "It was in my purse. I left it in the side pocket."

"Your purse?" Depp glanced at Bill, who shrugged. Neither of them had spotted a side pocket in the purse. They couldn't check her story without going back, and that wasn't going to happen.

"I've got it memorized...all of it...even the glyphs." She was betting they wouldn't kill her if she had the information in her head. Karen eyed Bill's knife, and an involuntary shudder shook her.

"Let's go," ordered Depp. "Everyone in the plane. Got to move before someone follows." Depp exited the old Ford and slammed his door. "Shit," he groused. "Came all this way and now I've got to fly over a fucking jungle. *Chingada!*" he cursed in Spanish, whirling to face Karen. His finger pointed accusingly. "I've waited twenty years for this chance. I've risked everything. If you're lying or gaming, you won't survive this, Karen." The hand dropped, but his mouth was a thin line of fury. He took a step toward the plane, then stopped and turned again. "And neither will your Aunt Rose. Understand?"

Bill grabbed a cheek of her butt and she yelped in protest.

"Hands off asshole, unless you want to lose them," she threatened the scar-faced antagonist, but he leered and blew her a kiss. He raised the knife again to remind her.

To Depp she said, "Are you going to let this creep keep pawing me?"

"Get in," Depp motioned to the airplane door, "and quit bitching unless you want to learn to skydive without a parachute."

Karen took her first close look at the airplane, and her stomach waffled. The paint was faded. It was old and small, and pocked with dents. Were those bullet holes? People crashed in these things all the time, didn't they? From the corner of her eye she saw Bill's free hand moving toward her bottom and she jumped away, hissing as she did so. This time he jabbed the knife toward her and she said, "Okay...okay," and stepped backward toward the plane.

Depp entered first, then Karen, expecting Bill to goose her at any moment. Depp sat in the pilot's seat and directed her to the seat behind him. Bill motioned for her to fasten the seatbelt, then took the adjacent seat, a sadistic leer pasted on his face. He folded the blade and pocketed the knife. Depp hurriedly flipped switches and pre-flighted the plane. Finished, he lifted an aviation map from beneath the seat and studied it while chewing his lip.

"That way east?" he asked Bill, but got no answer. Depp glanced at the sky to get a bearing, mulled over the map a moment, then sighed and closed the book.

He flipped the ignition switch and the engine turned slowly–too slow to start, she hoped. It caught, sputtered and then fired, belching black smoke. A deafening roar and vibration enveloped the cabin. Soon they were bouncing and lurching on the unkempt airfield, every bump jarring her wounded arm. Depp kept up a steady stream of chatter as they approached the runway's end, but Karen couldn't hear a word over the engine's bellow. Bill paid him no attention, ogling Karen's breasts while stroking the outline of the knife in his pants pocket. She shuddered and looked away. Cold dread enveloped her and nausea caused her stomach to lurch.

The engine roared again and the plane sped along the grassy runway. In no time they were airborne. Depp banked hard right, and she looked out a small window. San Cristobal lay to the west. She could see its numerous church steeples and red, dusky hills. Ant-sized people moved to and fro, all of them unaware of her personal drama. They gained altitude, and the dark green vegetation of the forest approached. Mountains shrouded in dark clouds stood huge and protective to the south and west. Two, narrow, serpentine rivers heavy with silt wound their way south and east into El Rio Usumacinta, Mexico's southern border with Guatemala. Within five minutes they were over the Lacandon jungle heading east toward the Yucatan peninsula. Depp continued to talk, but no one could hear above the engine roar. She glanced at Bill and saw his one good eye staring at her breasts, but now the knife had reappeared. "Oh, God," she mouthed silently. "Oh, dear God!"

****

The professor tightly gripped the steering wheel. "Damn!" he exploded, slapping the wheel in frustration. What the hell was going on? Karen had left with two men, apparently of her own volition—one whom she must have known, John Depp, her former supervisor at the Smithsonian. But Karen and Depp were at war, according to her. Why would she miss a meeting with David to go with a man she despised? She claimed to have been fired by Depp, but now he appeared Mexico. Why had he followed? That was the question.

85

Apparently she had not made a clean break with her job or with Depp. Trouble had followed.

The professor wasn't surprised. Although he didn't know Jonathan Depp personally, the professor had heard stories, most of them twenty years old–the kind of unsubstantiated talk that swirled around coups and revolutions. The American government had supported a CIA inspired Guatemalan coup in 1954 and assassinated a democratically elected head of state to do so. But the Indians living in the highland jungles had resisted. Depp, then a young social anthropologist, had been studying the various Mayan tribes of Guatemala and Mexico in the late 50's and early 60's. Rumor had it that he'd become a government asset. Whose, David didn't know, but he suspected the CIA. Depp, who had acquired intimate knowledge of the Indians with whom he worked, had ultimately served as the catalyst to destroy the people he had studied. Depp, so went the scuttlebutt, had passed on names of anyone opposing the new military junta. These individuals, in turn, were hunted and slain by the army. But three decades later Depp had somehow become a respectable museum curator in one of the finest museums in the world. That in itself was a mystery. Depp had virtually no publications or research projects to his credit. This, of course, implied that he was well connected in Washington D.C. If you ever had trouble making sense of something crazy in D.C., one only had to factor in politics, then everything made sense.

And what of Joaquin, David's brother-in-law? The consul had been more impediment than help. Of course he didn't want problems in his hotel, but a woman's life might be at stake! Joaquin had downplayed the incident to the *policia*. They had listened respectfully to his analysis and nodded their acquiescence. He was, after all, the Honorary Consul in Chiapas and a well-known, moneyed patrician from an old family. There probably wasn't anything to investigate, they had decided.

The maid had noticed nothing. She wasn't about to dispute her boss. Five dollars a day in pay wasn't much, but it put tortillas and beans on the table. Karen had left with two men, apparently under no duress, according to the desk clerk. But the room had been tossed and her purse emptied, complained the professor. Her room key was found downstairs on a restaurant table. Blood was found on the carpet. What more did they need? The *policía* shrugged. Who knows, they replied, she was a woman. Maybe she had a nosebleed or had cut herself accidentally. Besides, she was a single female traveling alone in Mexico, they sniggered–a moral crime for sure. Things happened to women like this. She was probably sexually involved with the two. This scenario had credibility, the *policía* agreed.

Joaquin had tried to soothe David, and the policía had dismissed his protestations as so much donkey manure. No crime, no case, they had decided. If anything resembling evidence appeared, call them. Meanwhile, the woman would probably appear within a few hours, they predicted. She was an American. Americans were unreliable and promiscuous. Apparently everyone but David knew this. Joaquin thanked them, shaking hands all around, making personal inquiries about their families while David stood aside seething with resentment.

The desk clerk was a liar, David decided, and the consul a duplicitous snake. But the professor had known this many years. It was Joaquin's chosen profession.

"Damn!" exploded David once more. His own hands weren't clean in this matter. He hadn't mentioned the purse or the documents he'd discovered in the birdcage for fear of having them snatched as evidence.

"Damn! Damn! Damn!" He slumped back into the car seat. What to do? What could he do? After ruminating on the dilemma, David decided that the *policía* were probably right about one thing. If Karen was okay she would appear soon, none the worse for whatever had befallen her, if anything. The professor would return to the ranch and talk it out with Luis. The federale, despite his macho affectations and country bumpkin demeanor, had a sharp mind that cut to the quick and fleshed out truth. Luis' many years as a Mexico City street cop would be invaluable.

David now had what appeared to be a translation of some sort, probably of the Gould Stelae. And if what he suspected was true, the stelae and Karen's translation were what this matter was about. Whatever it said, she must have struck gold. Depp would not have followed her to Mexico and risked so much unless he believed this to be an enormous opportunity for personal gain. David started the Le Baron, looked in the rearview mirror and pulled away from the curb. Deep in thought, he navigated the familiar cobblestone streets with ease, analyzing the morning's events and trying to make sense of it all. Soon he navigated the blacktop leading to the ranch. He guided the car through one curve after another, his mind focusing on the problem at hand. He saw a small silver plane to the east, a mere reflection in the sky, but dismissed it. The plane gained altitude and disappeared behind the forested mountains.

As the Le Baron approached the ranch, the professor's mind shifted modes. He began ruminating on the folded papers in his pocket he retrieved from the birdcage. He believed they likely held the translation and location of Karen's Mayan books. A growing sense of anticipation held him firmly as he drove resolutely toward the hacienda. Thank God he had brought his resource books from the National University in

Mexico City. Without them, any appraisal of her translation would be guesswork and become a comedy of frustration and errors. He would be lacking Karen's input, but would somehow make sense of it all. Even though he had been in archaeology thirty years, Maya writing had only been deciphered in the last decade. It had been right in front of their face all the time. Bishop Landa, the infamous book-burning priest from the Conquest, had left a translation of symbols to sounds that had finally been understood. Now, after ten years of study, David had become one of the leading authorities in the world.

His mind slipped into academic recall and his driving automatic as he shut out all distraction and began to speculate on what and how the glyphs would present themselves when he examined Karen's work.

CHAPTER TEN

Karen's eyes were riveted to the knife. It was the center of her Universe. Her chest tightened and she breathed with difficulty. Sweat stung her armpits and trickled down her sides. As she watched, the creamy-eyed cretin stared at her while pulling the blade across his hairy forearm, leaving a cleanly shaved path where the knife's edge had touched. An incipient scream tugged at her fear and threatened to loose itself.

"Bill!" Depp twisted in his seat and glared at his miscreant assistant. "Put it away and get up here!" Depp motioned to the seat next to his. "I need some help with this." He waved the aviation map. "Come on, move it." He glanced quickly at the gauges, then again at his miscreant friend. "We're going to head east over Guatemala before turning back north. I want to see what Yaxchilan and Tikal look like from the air."

The knife disappeared, but Bill's one good eye stared unwavering and lifeless. He sat motionless. Seized with dismay and trapped against the plane's wall, Karen held her breath. Why didn't he follow orders? Bill glanced at Depp, then back at Karen. He mumbled something and a faint smile tugged at his mouth. He wiggled his tongue at her, and she turned away toward the window, too sickened to watch. Finally, he crouched and moved to the vacant front seat. Depp tossed the map into Bill's lap. Karen exhaled and her shoulders sagged. She eyed the back of Depp's head–her captor/savior. He had kidnapped her, but was now the only person who could save her from the pervert–for the moment, anyway.

"Kind of scary, isn't he?" Depp yelled over the engine whine. "Should've seen him twenty years ago in *El Encanto*, Guatemala. Didn't make any friends there, did you Bill?" Depp smiled at his accomplice.

Bill ignored the comment and retrieved the map. He looked, quickly rotated it ninety degrees to get his bearings, and then bent to study it.

"I'm going to take her down a little and look around. Been a while since I've flown over this area." The nose tilted and the plane dropped precipitously until they were a few hundred feet above the ground, skimming the treetops. Karen wiped sweat from her upper lip and tried to regain her composure. Meanwhile her captors conversed and jabbed fingers at the map, occasionally pointing outside to a mountain or river to confirm their location. Bill, surprisingly, seemed interested in the map and began a lively discussion with Depp. Mr. Nightmare had become all business. She shivered, slumped forward and hugged her knees.

How had she gotten herself into this mess? She should have just given Depp the damn translation! Holding out had been stupid. Shouldn't have been so pig-headed. This Bill creep meant business–so did Depp–and now she was on a death

91

flight over the Lacandon jungle, and no one knew where she was. All illusions were shattered. It would be a miracle if she survived. How could they release her to tell the world what had happened? They'd have to kill her. But, at least then they'd leave Aunt Rose alone, rather than call more attention to what they were doing.

She peered out the oval window and studied the dusky mountains and sparsely forested hillsides. The terrain had changed. The red, rocky hills had been replaced by verdant stands of old forest. They were over the Lacandon jungle. Tall, ancient trees stretched to the sky, creating a shady canopy over the jungle. A riot of tropical vegetation wound like a sensual ribbon of green through the lowland foothills up into the distant mountains.

"Aw...shit," cried Depp.

Karen's head shot up.

"Aw Jeez...damn it anyway."

She watched Depp's hands grip the steering wheel, and he backed off the speed. The engine whine subsided and the plane slowed. She could hear better.

"What's up, Death Man?" The cretin's head shot up from the map.

"Don't call me that, Bill!"

"Something wrong?" Bill looked at the plane's numerous gauges. "Looks okay to me. Why do you..." He stopped in mid-sentence. "That oil?" He pointed to the plane's small windshield.

"It isn't bird shit."

Bill's back became ramrod straight. He looked at the oil-stained windshield, then out the window and all around the forested mountainsides. "How far back?" he asked, swallowing visibly.

"Who knows...fifteen or twenty minutes?" Flecks of oil

continued to spot the window, then streak and smear from the force of the wind. Dr. Death craned his neck in a hopeless effort to find the leak. "Can't see it. Gotta' land before the engine burns up...damn it!"

"What's that?" asked Karen. "Is something wrong?"

"Shut up, cunt," growled Bill. He flung a malevolent glare with his good eye.

She gave him a face, but then thought better of it and turned away, not wanting to provoke him. She wished Depp would answer her.

"Let's go back," said Bill.

"Can't. Might be someone waiting for us." Depp motioned to Bill. "Find us a place to land on that map."

"Won't work. None of these villages have an airstrip."

"Look anyway. It's been twenty years. Things change." Worry lined Depp's forehead. "I'll look below, you check the map. We got to find something."

"You said this engine only had fifty hours on it," accused Bill.

"Shut up and look."

"You shut up, ass eyes! This was your idea." Bill's white eye began to dart and his face to twitch. "You and your fuckin' junk airplane. You CIA fucks never got shit right." Bill turned and glared at Karen and his lip curled, seeking an outlet for his hostility. "We should've cut the bitch 'til she told us. You've gotten soft. In the old days..."

"Shut up, damn it!" said Depp. He glanced at Karen to see if she followed the conversation, then back to Bill. "Just find us somewhere to land." Leaking oil fanned out across the windshield. Depp stretched to see around the dark, spreading goo. "I'm going to take her back up so that we can see farther. Gotta' be something around here. Can't all be jungle anymore? Hell, it's been twenty years."

"There's a small village over there," offered Karen, pointing out the side window.

"That's a mountain, idiot. Where would we land, in the zocalo?"

The plane struggled south toward Guatemala, ever deeper into the jungle. They passed over small villages, all with narrow winding trails leading to and from them. The mountains had become islands of floating emeralds in a sea of green forest, the vegetation so dense that the jungle floor lay hidden and unknown. The glint of an occasional creek reflected from below as it wound through the underbrush and flowed toward El Rio Usumacinta and Guatemala.

"Maybe we ought to go back, Death Man," repeated Bill. "We can make it if we turn now."

"I said no. There's only trouble back there."

"Look..." said Bill. "We can land somewhere different. There are roads back there."

"Are we going to crash?" interrupted Karen, alarmed at their conversation. She tried to stand and look out the window.

"Sit down, bitch!" Bill's face twisted in rage.

"The federales will be waiting. We have to keep going," said Depp.

"I thought you had connections?" fumed Bill. "The Station Chief in Guadalajara owed you a favor?"

"Had is correct," replied Depp. "I don't have shit now. I cashed in all the chits to get us here."

"The fuckin' heat gauge is goin' up!" Bill's voice took on a shrill, nearly hysterical quality. "I hate fuckin' airplanes."

"We got three minutes at most if we lose the oil." Depp's voice sounded hollow, as if struggling to maintain control. His jaw clenched. "Look at the goddamn map!" he commanded, speaking through his teeth.

"Maybe we should radio someone?" suggested Karen, rising to a crouch.

"Yuppie whore!" Depp's rage exploded and his doubled fist swung backhand, striking Karen flush in the face.

Her head snapped and her sinuses flooded with pain. Her knees buckled and she collapsed into the rear of the plane, wrenching her back as she hit the floor. "Ahhg...you bastard," she cried. "You filthy..."

Depp and Bill ignored her, their eyes glued to the spreading oil stain on the window. Karen tested her back, groaned and slowly made it to her knees. She gingerly touched her face. Blood ran from her nose and her cheekbone swelled. Her shoulder ached, and the cut on her arm started to ooze again.

Three minutes, Depp had said. Three minutes after the oil was gone the engine would burn up. Tears sprang to her eyes. This couldn't be happening, she told herself. It's too unreal. Her eyes overflowed and she sobbed silently, a bitter sadness overwhelmed her. Twenty-nine years old, divorced, no children, no career to speak of and quite probably she would die in this plane. She toppled back into her seat to await the inevitable. Her life lay in the hands of murderous criminals flying a broken airplane. So much for hope.

And still the plane flew on. Depp and Bill squabbled and hurled invectives at each other. Depp jabbered to himself and Bill tottered on the verge of emotional chaos, unable to sit still, cursing anything and everything. He began to shoot hateful, malicious looks at Karen.

"At least let me do her before we crash!" His right hand hovered above the outline of the knife in his pocket.

"God damn it...no! Back off!" Depp swore vehemently, and began striking the plane gauges with pent-up frustration.

Kaboom! An explosion shook the plane and the nose tilted

slowly downward. Smoke roiled from the engine in steady streams while Bill screamed obscenities. Depp's knuckles shone white, gripping the plane's steering wheel. He glanced quickly back at her and she saw that his eyes were wide and his face pale. Beads of sweat dotted his upper lip and forehead. He frantically tried to see around the smoke and oil-grimed window down into the jungle. The plane lurched and yawed as Depp fought to keep the nose up and forestall a headlong dive to the jungle floor. Bill was now silent, staring like a catatonic out the passenger window at the deadly jungle below.

Karen witnessed the drama as if observing a play. Then plane stalled and the nose sank one final time. The tree tops loomed suddenly closer, and an icy heat surged up her spine. She tugged to tighten her seat belt, then leaned back into her seat and gripped the chair's arm supports. Her heart beat madly and fear pierced her like a blazing laser. She began to silently intone the hoary prayer she had heard that morning. *"Our Father, Who art in Heaven. Hallowed be Thy name..."*

CHAPTER ELEVEN

David frowned, staring east into rolling foothills that rose like stairs into pine-forested mountains. The afternoon sun shone blissful and content on the languid scene–winding trails and terraced, manicured fields of corn. An occasional assemblage of mud-brick homes with thatched roofs clustered on the mountainside. Behind him, dark cumulus clouds gathered strength on the western horizon. He normally loved the bucolic lifestyle it portrayed, but today it brought no enjoyment. He had just argued with his wife over Joaquin's unconscionable indifference to Karen's ransacked hotel room. His self-serving brother-in-law remained a festering thorn in his mind. The professor wasn't too happy with his wife, either, as she had sided with her brother. David had brought *'that woman'* to Mexico. The beautiful foreigner wouldn't be in San Cristobal if not for him. Thus, there would be no problem if not for David. Good grief, he thought, helplessly. What had Joaquin told her? She had sounded almost uncaring, even jealous, her accusations dripping with innuendo.

David knew that Joaquin would do nothing unless forced to, which, of course, was totally unacceptable. After two hours of worry, the professor had called the hotel to verify Karen's continued absence. In an effort to cover up the whole event, Joaquin and the *policía* had, no doubt, packed Karen's belongings and cleaned the room by now. It was even likely that the room had a new occupant. They would waste no time. Corruption was endemic and appearances easily substituted for reality in Mexico. One hour ago the ranch foreman had appeared to inform them that the "gringo plane" had left sometime that morning. When or where to, the foreman didn't know. No one had seen it leave, and David had thought this an ominous development. He feared that Karen was on board, likely under duress, and surely in danger. Now he sat mired in recrimination, his wife's argument resonating in his mind. Though he had disagreed at the time, some of her words rang true. He had invited Karen down, playing the role of the omniscient professor, baiting a lesser to bring their prize into his lair. *What if she was already dead?* he worried.

David buried his head in his hands. "Do you think she's still alive?"

"Probably," answered Luis, his bushy eyebrows arched in concentration as he tried to read Karen's notes. "We've got the translation. Depp's only got what's in her head. She'll be okay until she gives it up."

David raised his head to stare into the foothills, his mood mirroring the dark clouds gathering over the western Sierra Madres.

"Quit blaming yourself, professor," consoled Luis. He strode to the patio table and tossed Karen's translation to David. "Thing is...nothing's going to get done on this unless someone in Mexico City orders it."

"Then it won't happen," said David, flatly.

"Then we need to figure out what's happened, where they went. Can you read that stuff?"

"The English?" asked David.

"All of it. The pictures and everything."

"The glyphs?"

"Yeah, the glyphs. Does it make sense?"

David retrieved the papers and patiently began to examine them. One page appeared to be a Photostat of the stelae itself, the other her translation. While Luis walked to the verandah's edge, David laid the pages side by side, opened two resources books and placed them on the table. Ignoring Luis, he gave the papers his first serious examination, shifting his gaze between the photocopy, the books, and back to the translation. His brow wrinkled as he tried to remember what he knew of Mayan glyphs. He chewed his lower lip, studied the pictographs for nearly thirty minutes, then quit. He leaned back into his chair, his hands clasped behind his head. An incipient euphoria rose within. Nothing was certain, but her work appeared good. If the stelae was genuine and the books could be found, the discovery could turn Latin American archaeology on its head.

"Well? Luis inquired.

David spread his hands. "It may be brilliant...if it's true," he leaned forward. "It seems to make sense. Most of it, anyway. She's done her homework." He picked up the translation and held it up into the light, searching for minute detail in the pictographs. "She's identified a place west and south of Palenque near the highlands as the probable location of the cave." He lay the paper on the table again and sighed. "I wish I could see the stelae myself. Some of the shading on this thing..." he frowned, then gathered the two pages together. "It could be someone's name, someone's mother's name, or someone reenacting the role of a myth. It could be..."

"Yeah, yeah..." interrupted Luis, not in the mood for scholarly discourse. "But could she be right?"

The professor leaned back into his chair and swiveled to face Luis. He smiled broadly. "Yes...easily. Might even be probable."

"It doesn't give the location of the cave?"

"No. Doesn't even mention Palenque. Loosely translated, it identifies the area as the land of the Jaguar Kings."

"That's Palenque?"

"That's Palenque," affirmed the professor, "or the area south and west into the Lacandon."

The federale, tall and broad-shouldered, stretched and yawned. He rubbed his nose, then frowned. "Well...looks like we need a plan." Luis returned to the patio table and David. "Look...Angela and I probably need to go..."

David wanted to protest, but Luis held up his hands, smiling benignly. "It's okay, gringo. Things are going sour for you here. You and Ali are fussing and we don't want to be around to watch you punch-out Joaquin. Angela and I were leaving in a couple of days, anyway. This way I can stop by Mexico City on the way back to Chihuahua and talk to some friends about this thing...maybe pull a few strings for you and get somebody interested."

David felt a flash of hope. "That would help. Otherwise I'll have to call some people I know in Washington and tell them what I know."

"That isn't going to win you any friends, David. Could even cause problems...some of them personal."

"Yes, but it's the right thing to do." The professor stood to go, but stopped and faced Luis. "Could you do something for me in Mexico City?"

"Anything but murder, gringo."

David pursed his lips, the said, "Do you know anyone at the *zocalo*?"

"*Federal Policía*?"

"No, someone who does intelligence stuff."

Luis drew a blank, scratched his head, then asked, "Interpol?"

"Exactly!" David smacked the tabletop. "Can you check into this Jonathan Depp character, or this Bill he brought along? I think Depp has a history with us."

"Who's us?"

"Mexico…Guatemala…and probably the other side," David pointed north.

"The United States?"

"I'd bet money on it."

Luis hesitated, "Well…lessee…don't know who I could…" he shook his head, unable to make a connection with whom he might tap for information.

"How about Jose, your ex-boss?" suggested David.

Luis looked as if he'd just smelled rotting flesh. "Jose is a sneaky, back-stabbing, secretive, conniving asshole," growled Luis, remembering his old Mexico City precinct captain. "I don't trust him."

"He got promoted after the Vicario murder investigation. He owes you."

"Yeah…maybe." Luis sounded reluctant. "Haven't seen the jerk in years. He's a spook now I hear. Hard to believe. Yeah…maybe I'll try Jose. Can't do any harm." Luis glanced toward the dark clouds hovering over the western mountains, then kicked at an imaginary clod at the verandah edge. He turned to David. "What'll you do? Hang around until I call? I'll know one way or another in a couple of days."

"Actually, I'm going to check on the departure of any small planes, especially any carrying three gringos, one of them a

woman," replied David. "Then I might take a short sabbatical."
He glanced into the house to see if anyone overheard their
conversation. He gave Luis a rueful smile. "Ali and Joaquin
would probably appreciate it if I took a little vacation. I'm
thinking of visiting an old friend near the Palenque
ruins...guy by the name of Balaam Reyes. He used to work for
me on a dig near Socorro. He's actually a curandero/shaman
type guy that likes to hang out around Palenque now."

"Indian?" asked Luis.

"Quiche," confirmed David, "and a damn fine worker.
Knows a thing or two about archaeology, too."

"You gonna check on the cave thing?"

"Who knows," David shrugged, trying to hide his
excitement. Of course he intended to confirm Karen's
translation and follow up if he could. "It's a place to start.
Balaam knows things that I could only guess at. He's lived his
whole life in the jungle."

Luis frowned again. "What are you thinking, David? I can
see the wheels turning in your head." Luis sat at the table and
plunked a booted foot onto the tabletop.

"I told you..."

"Wait a minute..." Luis snapped his fingers. "You mean the
Bone Man, don't you? You're going to see the Bone Man."

David stiffened. "His name is Balaam..."

"I heard you. It's that drunken, mushroom-sucking
reprobate that left us in the lurch at Agua Azule five years
ago."

"He's a holy man, Luis, a shaman."

The federale sneered. "I've never considered mescal as holy
water, David."

"You're a cynic," David waved off his friend's protestations,
but failed to meet his eye. In fact, the Bone Man, who,
coincidentally, happened to live in a bone-frame hut on the

edge of the Lacandon jungle, was a little peculiar, maybe even bizarre by Luis' standards. But the professor liked him, even though the shaman's dependability and sanity were at times questionable. Balaam ate psilocybin mushrooms and chased spirits in the ether world so often that you could only have spent considerable time with him in order to know him. The Bone Man drank only when he had money, which was rare, and survived by trapping animals and trading his services as a spiritual advisor and performing rituals and healings for the Indians. But David had discovered that, without warning, the Bone Man would sometimes vanish into the countryside to pick magic mushrooms from piles of cow manure and spend the next several days and nights in or near a cave communing with spirits.

"He stole the mescal and food when I came to visit," reminded Luis. "He stank, too."

"Balaam wanted to offer food to the spirits. It was a holy day of sorts for the Indians."

"I thought they were Catholic?"

"They are...sort of." David sighed, tiring of Luis' criticism.

"Sort of?" Luis scoffed, sarcastically. "Lookee here...it's a great image; an Indian holy man who uses dried mushrooms and mescal for Holy Communion." He smiled at his own joke. "What could he possibly know about this here book thing?"

"He knows the Lacandon like you know your town."

"He's probably dead by now."

"Balaam? Dead?" David considered the idea, but then shook his head. Not likely. The grizzled Indian had been spry as a goat five years ago when traversing the forested mountains around Agua Azul. David would bet money that the Bone Man was alive. The trouble would be locating him. As a young man the shaman was known to have disappeared into the jungle for months, or even a year at a time, living a spare,

103

aboriginal existence off the plants and animals. It was a chance David would have to take. The only way to know for sure was to go look for him.

"It's going to rain, professor."

"Huh? It's the rainy season, Luis. It rains almost every day."

"Julio's coming."

David cocked his head toward Luis and waited for the punch line. "Julio?"

"Hurricane Julio, gringo. There's a toad floater due any day."

"There's a hurricane coming?" David looked west. This was news. He'd been immersed in Karen's coming to Mexico, the stelae, and today's mess. San Cristobal lay one hundred fifty kilometers and a range of mountains away from the Pacific coast. If anything, the storm would be an inconvenience. A quick look showed the clouds to be layered gray and black and be growing thicker. Hurricanes were usually preceded by a series of smaller thunderstorms. Today's rain would soon blow in like it usually did this time of year.

"Where's it supposed to land?"

Luis shrugged. "Maybe north near Acapulco, maybe south of here. Doesn't matter. We'll get rain, lots of it, regardless of where it hits. You better not be traipsing off into a jungle."

"When will it hit?"

"Tomorrow evening, the next day…who knows?"

"We're too far inland…"

"David, it's going to rain like hell for a long time and you know it. I worry that you're gonna to do something stupid again."

"You know me better than that. Besides, I need to be here to get your call. Two days, right?"

Luis vacillated. "No…I'm going with you. If it's just for a couple of days, the women can stay here and commiserate

104

with Joaquin and agree on what asses we are. Angela and I can stop in Mexico City on the way back and call you."

"I can be back tomorrow night, Luis. Really, I will. Trust me."

Luis leaned his chair back on two legs. "I trust you, gringo. It's just that there's been some crazy stuff happening here and you don't seem to have a clue what's going on."

David's back stiffened. "Well...I'm not going to figure it out staying in this place, am I? Joaquin isn't going to help and Ali is...well...she'll get over it."

"You get over it, David. We're friends and I'm going. Understand?"

The professor wanted to argue, thought of kicking Luis' chair from beneath him, but held his tongue. What the heck, he thought. Better Luis for company than Joaquin, or Ali either, for that matter.

"You're going to miss the MTV girls on the satellite dish."

"Yeah," Luis grinned. But I can get over something, too."

CHAPTER TWELVE

Karen awoke to the sound of crackling thunder and gunfire. Acrid cordite stung her nose and made her want to sneeze. Her head ached and throbbed and a viscous fog of cobwebs impeded her thinking. The ground shuddered, mortar fire contesting with a thunderstorm as she fought to regain consciousness. A stiff westerly wind blew sheets of rain against the plane's broken fuselage, and a bolt of lightning stabbed the nearby earth, startling her and igniting violent pain in her head. Shouts of surprise came from outside. But from whom? She forced her eyes to focus on the wrecked, jumbled interior of the plane. The pop-pop-pop of gunfire continued, joined by curses and frantic, unintelligible shouting. Had they crashed in a war zone? Where had they gone down? Guatemala? Mexico?

Now she remembered. Skimming the dark green canopy of the Lacandon jungle, smoke billowing from the engine, the nose of the plane had flown flush into the leafy upper branches of a tree. The collision had bashed her face into the back of Depp's chair, but her seat belt had held–no doubt saving her life. The wings of the plane had snapped off and the fuselage flipped over, slipping and sliding downward through broad branches to the jungle floor where it now lay on its side.

Miraculously, she lived, strapped into her seat inside the wreckage. A look out her broken window revealed pieces of wreckage: a broken wing and metal scraps. Gusts of rain blew steadily through the mostly missing windshield. Water splattered her face and ran in a steady drizzle from above.

She groaned at the effort of moving a hand to touch the mass of bruises on her face. What didn't hurt? Her body was a fluid tapestry of pain; every joint throbbing, a piercing ache in her forehead. The cut on her shoulder from Bill's knife play blazed. Breathing hurt and she felt dizzy. She must have cracked or bruised her ribs.

But with pain came awareness. The gunfire and shouting continued, drawing her attention to the firefight outside. What was happening? With effort, she unfastened her seat belt. Bill's seat was vacant, but Depp sagged lifeless and limp, his head cocked at an unnatural angle. Blood had run from what used to be his face, down his shoulder and arm to pool on the floor. Dead, she assumed, but she felt nothing for him; no stirring of emotion, no sympathy, only relief. His death had a certain symmetry. Whatever his aspirations as a young man, he had ended his life little more than an educated criminal and terrorist–and based on what she had heard in his conversation with Bill–Depp had returned to lose his life in the area where he had committed most of his crimes.

Where was Bill? Her neck protested as she turned to look around. Definitely not in the plane. Had he been thrown clear and survived the crash? If so, where had he gone? She recalled his milky eye and scarred face, and shuddered, repressing a growing urge to vomit. She hoped he had been hurt badly, maybe even paralyzed, but knew this was unlikely since he wasn't in the plane.

The shouting increased and the gunfire diminished. Someone barked orders, and she heard men approaching the plane through the trees. A rifle-toting, green-uniformed soldier appeared at the broken cockpit window. He stooped to stare inside, and was joined by others. They jabbered among themselves and pointed, and then one called out to another still in the forest. She understood little of their conversation, but a sense of relief flooded her. Thank God! It was over. How or why the army had appeared so soon after the crash she didn't know—or care. She was alive, and though battered and hurt, knew that her injuries were not life threatening. She was saved, and without thinking she called out to her saviors, startling one of the soldiers who fired his automatic rifle into the fuselage. She screamed! And then someone cursed and struck the soldier from behind.

"*Cabron*! *Chingada*!"

Through the windshield she saw an officer waving an automatic pistol standing over the offending soldier, berating, then kicking him for good measure. The officer cursed again and shouted orders to the growing circle of men. The soldiers slipped away into the forest, pursuing the enemy. She called for help and tried to stand, but the fuselage was tilted and jagged sheets of metal inhibited movement. The army officer issued another order and two soldiers unceremoniously dragged Depp from his seat and dumped him onto the ground. The officer leaned inside the plane, a flashlight in one hand, pistol in the other.

"Please…help me," pleaded Karen. "Thank God you're here." She extended an arm, but he ignored it, instead shining the light throughout the plane and then directly into her eyes, causing her to flinch. He frowned.

"*Parece que no hay contrabanda,*" he mumbled, seemingly disappointed, moving the light beam around the interior, then back to Karen.

She saw his eyes grow wide with amazement. What had he expected? Contraband? Then she understood. Drugs. He thought the small plane had been shot down transporting drugs to the United States. Was this the reason for the gun battle, a fight over the spoils of a wrecked plane? This was not what she had expected!

"Please," she repeated again, reaching toward the officer. "Help me."

****

Captain Chavez, wet and disgusted, looked back out into the forest at his men scrambling about outside, then shone the light one more time on the woman. It was a gringa, a foreigner, and what she was doing in the Lacandon jungle would make an interesting story. He saw that she was hurt; her face was swollen and blood soaked her shirt from the left shoulder down her arm.

Chingada, he cursed silently. He didn't need a damaged woman to hamstring his operation. Mobility was paramount. It was hard enough to control the roads. The guerrillas moved at will through the jungle, attacking unexpectedly and disappearing just as quickly. If not for the temptation of discovering a mother lode of cocaine in the plane, he would not have ventured from the village into the zapatista's forested domain.

The woman extended a hand to him and spoke English. He knew a little English, but remained silent. Best to play dumb and let the woman talk. Maybe she spoke Spanish? He stepped away from the fuselage and issued an order. Two

109

soldiers leaned their rifles against the fuselage and began helping her from the plane.

Rain fell steadily and thunder rolled through the heavens, hesitating, tantalizing, before ending with a violent crack. Two soldiers, Castro and Alvarez, sauntered toward the captain from the forest to report that the guerrillas had again slipped the noose and fled into the jungle. *Chingada*! Again! No cocaine, no guerrillas, two dead soldiers, and all for nothing! It would've been better if the woman had died in the crash.

A *gringa* complicated matters. Captain Chavez and his men had captured the small community of Piedra Blanca one week earlier, driving its inhabitants into the surrounding forests. The locals of Piedra Blanca were either zapatistas or sympathizers and Captain Chavez had shown them no mercy. He was now the supreme ruler of the area. The Mexican army would borrow Piedra Blanca and its women for a few days until he had completed his mission—to receive an illegal cargo of drugs for his boss, Colonel Herrera. Two cocaine mules were due to cross the Usumacinta from Guatemala with a shipment in three days. Captain Chavez would then move to transport the goods to the Colonel in Tenosique. Where the drugs went from there, Chavez didn't know, or care. It was stupid to know too much if it didn't pay good money. People moving cocaine were excitable and prone to over-reaction when it came to drug deliveries and money. He must be prompt and ruthless. He would listen to the woman's story before making a decision. If he could assist without endangering his mission—fine. If not, he would get rid of her somehow, regardless of what that might entail.

While he considered this and more, he heard the woman's moans and protestations as she struggled from the crumpled fuselage. His eyes fell momentarily on the pilot's bloody face. Another *extranjero*. Probably an American like the *gringa* in the plane. Chavez snarled an order to a stocky young soldier who moved with alacrity and began emptying the gringo's trouser pockets. The soldier brought Chavez a passport and billfold, then returned to strip clothes from the dead man's body, searching for a hidden money belt or other valuables. Captain Chavez gave the passport a cursory look and stuffed it in his vest pocket. The soldier had Depp's pants and underwear to his knees when the captain barked an order. The soldier backed away and Chavez lifted the bloody shirt. A money belt, just as the captain had suspected. He quickly unstrapped it from the gringo's waist and rolled it around his own fist. Tucking it inside his vest, he turned to watch his soldiers pull the protesting *gringa* from the plane.

Stooped with pain, she whimpered and slowly, carefully straightened herself, rising to her full height which, he realized, was several centimeters above his. Amazed, he stared at the shapely woman with the bloody, swollen face. Though hurt, she stood proud and returned his stare, a wary look in her eye. She had long hair and shapely legs, and her breasts strained against a blue cotton blouse. Her eyes closed and she coughed, groaning as she did so, holding her ribs, her face contorted in pain. She noticed that her male companion lay stripped and naked, his pants to his ankles. She turned to the captain, said something he didn't understand, then her eyes glazed over and she collapsed onto the ground.

Time to go, the captain decided. He squeezed the money belt inside his vest. He would rather have cash any day. Drugs were easy to come by. This venture had been worthwhile after all. He ordered the woman placed on a stretcher and carried through the forest to be loaded in one of the trucks.

His men would be upset about their dead comrades, and some of them had seen the money belt. They would talk and grumble, so Chavez would give them several cases of posh, a

111

fermented sugar-cane beverage he confiscated from the last town they captured. The men could drink the cane liquor and celebrate something–even if it was just getting drunk. Soldiers didn't need an excuse to drink. And maybe, just maybe, he would give them a few of the women they had captured from the village. The women were all zapatista scum, of this he was sure, and deserved nothing better. After the mules delivered the cocaine, Chavez would give the Indians back their town– slightly used–like the women, but that was the life of the powerless in Mexico. It would send the treacherous bastards a double message: traitors are punished, and you don't fuck with Captain Chavez.

CHAPTER THIRTEEN

"David, that raisin-faced dwarf is wasting our time," complained Luis. He reluctantly followed the professor, who trod a shady jungle path behind the Bone Man. "Have your talk and let's get out of this friggin' jungle."

He huffed a few meters further, then said, "Jeez it's hot…and these damn mosquitoes…they punch holes in you like a drunk dentist." He brushed one from his sleeve, then slapped the back of his neck. "Damn it…" he fretted again.

"Quit bellyaching…you wanted to come," David replied between gasps. The humidity and hills were taking their toll.

"Damn it…" continued Luis. "Didn't even bring any water…damn Indian…friggin' jungle."

"Shut up, Luis," said the professor, benignly, trying to maintain his composure. But he, too, was tired of running after the Bone Man. After a fruitless two-day search around the Palenque ruins, David had received a tip from another ruins guide to check with Colonel Herrera, who had a platoon stationed just outside the town of Palenque. As it turned out, the Colonel knew exactly where to find Balaam Reyes, and during the discussion let it be known that he didn't hold the old Indian in very high esteem. In fact, he had spoken disparagingly and frowned as he did so.

"How much farther, Balaam?" called David.

No answer was forthcoming. Seemingly indifferent to his panting pursuers, ignoring their conversation and protests, the old shaman threaded the jungle path with practiced silence. They followed the winding trail and struggled through thick, sinuous vines and tall cane grass before coming upon a creek swollen with yesterday's rain. A tree trunk bridged the stream, solidly connecting the two banks. The Bone Man never slowed his pace. He tossed a cloth satchel across the stream, then moving like a cat, leapt atop the log and put even more distance between himself and the two ladinos seeking his company.

Still swatting mosquitoes, cursing his bad luck, Luis went next, followed by a worried David. The professor cautiously placed one foot in front of the other, his arms out-stretched for balance. He appeared to be walking a tightrope, and tried not to look at the rushing white water as he carefully and firmly planted one foot at a time before moving forward. Halfway across he found that he had been holding his breath, and so he paused to calm himself.

Luis, frowning, waited impatiently on the eastern bank. When David arrived, Luis extended a hand and helped his friend down from the trunk.

The Bone Man was nowhere in sight, so they scrambled up a shady, grassy bank and over a steep incline to a clearing in the forest where, to their surprise, they found a sprawl of mud-brick huts. The treeless area lay exposed to the sun, except when an occasional gray thunderhead from yesterday's storm floated lightly overhead on unseen wind currents. The huts had round palm leaf roofs and varied in size. The more prosperous homes boasted makeshift fences constructed of tree limbs. A few had vegetable gardens. South of the village, rows of tobacco leaf sprouted beneath hilly orchards of coffee.

Five men in ragged, soiled white pants, homemade sandals, and dirty gray pull-overs, loitered and smoked homemade cigars in the shade outside one of the houses. Nearby, a group of women in pleated black skirts and brightly colored smocked blouses gathered around the door of another bungalow. A woman knelt over a metate, grinding corn kernels with a hand stone while two neighbors stood watching and gossiped.

Unsure what do now, David and Luis loitered and caught their breath. The smell of wood smoke and rotten garbage mingled with the rank odor of human feces and urine. Luis bitched and cursed in a whisper, and both swatted mosquitoes. David spotted Balaam, the curandero, talking to the women. The shaman smiled broadly, greeted old friends and accepted their thanks for coming. He chatted briefly, but then broke away and went inside the shanty. He quickly reappeared and held a door wide so that a mother could carry her small child outside. Hearing that the Bone Man had arrived, other villagers came to greet him. Soon a large group had gathered to watch the curandero do his stuff.

David wiped his brow with a sleeve and took a good look at San Angelo de Montanez, an Indian village of no more than ten or twelve mud-brick homes twenty kilometers south of Palenque. There were no roads to San Angelo, only well-worn paths trod by the Indians when traveling to surrounding villages or to the town of Palenque to sell homemade goods. San Angelo was not to be found on any map, and lay well hidden in a forest of mahogany and ceiba trees. Over 200 feet

115

tall with massive trunks, the ceiba were sacred to the ancient Maya and had once covered hundreds of square miles of southern Mexico and Guatemala. Unfortunately most had been logged, and only a few stands remained in the Lacandon jungle.

The strident cadence of jungle insects disturbed an otherwise quiet day, and thin tendrils of gray camp smoke rose unmolested to the sky. Luis groused and shifted his weight from one foot to the other. David's shirt, soaked with sweat and clinging to his back, reminded him that the highlands of San Cristobal were far away.

All eyes were on Balaam Reyes, the Bone Man, as he prepared to treat a feverish, red-cheeked child lying prone on a woven mat of palm leaves. Done with his prayer and his medicinal preparations complete, the curandero took a small sheet of paper and tightly wound it into a funnel shape. He then inserted the point into the girl's ear canal. The child, about six in age, whimpered with fear. Tears ran in a steady stream down her cheek. The girl's mother brushed aside her daughter's thick black hair to protect it from the flame, then held her daughter firmly while Balaam extracted a glowing coal from the fire and lit the cone's outer edge.

Mesmerized, David and Luis watched the smoke cling to the funnel's inside surface and swirl downward, as though the ear was inhaling the smoke. The child squirmed, but the mother tightened her grip and spoke soothingly in a tongue neither David nor Luis understood.

Fire rimmed the cone's edge, turning it to ash as the flame raced toward the child's ear. With a practiced hand, waiting until the last moment, the Bone Man snatched the paper fragment away and tenderly brushed ashes from the side of her face. He instructed the mother to turn the child on her side, ear downward, and wait. The task completed, he began

116

to chant and throw tobacco leaves on the fire. Seconds later, the child cried out and the mother tensed, then blood-streaked pus oozed from the girl's ear.

"I'll be damned," muttered Luis, shaking his head. "I'd heard of this, but never seen it done." He spoke grudgingly, unable to express approval of the gnarled, but spry shaman. "He's lucky he didn't catch her hair on fire or burn her face," he added.

"He's done this a thousand times, Luis. Balaam knows more curing techniques than you can imagine."

Luis frowned and looked at his watch, impatient to be off. "David, when are we going to..."

But the professor held up a hand to quiet his friend. The Bone Man approached David and was speaking.

"Her companion soul is opossum," explained Balaam. "This good because opossums hard to kill. The animal is probably lying sick somewhere. Maybe a child hit in the head with stick. But it be get well now, also." The Bone Man turned to the mother and gave more instructions. He patted the child and offered encouragement, then repacked his sack of medicinal herbs and supplies.

Luis snorted and grinned ear to ear, tempted to make a sarcastic comment on the opossum soul statement, but David gave him a warning glare.

"Look...Balaam...I know you're busy and everything, but I need some help. It's taken us a long time to find you, and I've got to be back in San Cristobal in two or three days. Can you help out...you know...work for me a day or so? I can pay you."

His face brown and wrinkled, his hair straight and black, the Bone Man stood to his full height of 4'8". He wore gray, coarse cotton trousers and an off-white pullover. Soiled, tire tread sandals were strapped to his filthy feet and looked as if

117

they had never been removed. His age was unknown, but David suspected the Bone Man to be nearly eighty years old. Balaam Reyes was affluent by Indian standards, though he rarely had available cash. The old curandero had acquired three wives that David knew of, and had eleven children at last count. The wives stayed in different villages and his children lived throughout Chiapas and Mexico, some of them laborers for rich ladino coffee and corn growers.

Balaam traveled the lowland jungle, going where he wished or was needed, guided by spiritual and family needs and by his own internal compass–a truly free-spirited man. He had lived most of his life as an itinerant holy man, wandering the Petén and Lacandon jungles of Guatemala and Mexico, performing religious rituals and cures. He was well known throughout hundreds of square miles; respected as a curandero and by many and feared as a witch by others. To David, who knew him as well as any ladino could, the Bone Man was an enigma and an anachronism–a fascinating, but mysterious man living in the wrong century. Balaam's religion was a blend of Catholicism and thousand-year-old Mayan beliefs. There were few, if any, of his kind left wandering the jungles. He was the last of a pre-revolution generation of curanderos and shamans still practicing their healing arts the old way. His medicine was a combination of herb lore and practical knowledge developed before and after the Conquest. His spirituality embraced the ancient concept of two Mayan souls: the inner soul and accompanying animal soul.

Although the western highlands had quickly succumbed to the ravages of Catholicism, the Lacandon jungle was near impenetrable and its Indian inhabitants never fully proselytized or converted to Christianity. Lancandon religious beliefs were more similar to those of their thousand-year-old ancestors than to that of their highland Mayan neighbors. In

118

fact, the lowland Lacandon were joked about and look down upon as savages by their highland counterparts in Guatemala and Mexico. To this day the Chamula and Totzil Maya threaten to send misbehaving children to live among the Lacandons.

But civilization, if you can call it that, arrived in the jungle in the 1970's in the form of Ladinos; Indians and mixed bloods who had taken on the ways of city Mexicans. These Ladinos logged the mahogany forests and stripped the lowlands of vegetation to plant corn, destroying the fragile jungle soil and pushing the already bereft Lacandon Indians deeper into the remaining forest, landless and poverty stricken.

"What want, *ahua*?" asked the Bone Man, using the respectful address of leader for David. The shaman spoke poor Spanish and frequently uttered something amusing or unintelligible. Holding the tote sack by its drawstring, Balaam tossed it over his shoulder, ready to be off.

"Two things," said David quickly. "First...I need information. Have you heard of a small plane landing near here two days ago?"

"Where? Palenque? San Martin?" asked the Bone Man.

"Yes. Two men and a tall woman. We believe the woman was kidnapped and forced to go along. I think she was looking for an archaeological site somewhere south of here."

"*Gringos*?"

"Yes."

"No," said the shaman, and turned and walked toward the forest.

"Wait just a minute you..." protested Luis.

But David again raised a hand to stifle Luis' protest. Motioning for the federale to stay put, the professor hurried to join the Bone Man.

"Look, Balaam...give me a second here, will you? What's

119

the hurry? I'm offering to hire you for a couple of days. Can't you use the money? I'm looking for some caves south of here. Something you might be interested in...Mayan books. I got a lead on something from the woman in the..."

"Books?" the old shaman slowed his walk. "What book?"

"Your ancestors, Balaam. You know...the folding books with the pictographic writing."

"No book," said the Bone Man, decisively. "Black robes burn all book. Ladino priest kill Maya with religion."

"Maybe not," said David. "I just need someone who knows the jungle to keep me from getting lost. Do you know of any caves south of here?"

The Bone Man stopped at the forest's edge and peered into its shady, beckoning interior, then gazed back toward the mud brick village and the frowning Luis.

"You friend no me like," said Balaam.

"Balaam, you don't care whether ladinos like you or not. Come on...what's the deal?"

"I have job."

"Aw jeez..." disappointment registered on David's face. "With who? Look...maybe I can pay more," offered David.

"Me pay me nothing, but I no can refuse."

"What the..." David's brow wrinkled with confusion.

"Big Colonel...pig's ass Herrera threaten burn San Martin if I no guide on Ceiba Trail to Tenosique. I have daughter San Martin."

"Why doesn't he just take the road?"

"He want trail can chase guerrillas. Army move soldiers Lacandon. Take villages. He think guerrillas move walk Ceiba Trail."

"Wishful thinking."

"Yes," agreed the Bone Man. "Pig's Ass no find wart on penis, but he burn San Martin if Balaam no help." The

120

curandero shrugged. "No matter. I go now important thing. My son important hombre. Take cargo (religious obligation) for Festival San Francisco. I promise help can come. Festival come two week. He need have more money pay cargo. He bring much shame on him family if cargo no be good okay."

"For fifty dollars could I tag along?"

"Eh...why, *ahua*? Why is important?"

"The caves, remember?"

"Are hundred cave, *ahua*...yes know you. It be find spot fish in a river fish. One cave is same all cave." The Bone Man shrugged. "Lacandon and Petén are many cave. Look...*ahua* say have two days, remember you?"

"How about if I tag along with a map...you know...as we walk the trail you can point out the general direction to places where you know there are caves and I'll mark them on the map for later."

"What Herrera?"

"My friend will talk to Herrera," said David. "Luis can be very persuasive sometimes."

"*Ahua*..." the Bone Man frowned, looked at the ground, then at David. "Fifty dollars buy much posh for festival...but zapatista ready. Maybe fight shit army try burn corn. Dangerous be Balaam. Dangerous be *ahua* if come. Ladino *ahua* best stay Palenque."

"I trust you, Balaam. Just give me two or three days and Luis and I will be out of your hair."

"That one tall no smile?" The shaman turned to appraise Luis. "That one die in jungle, *ahua*. He hands soft and clean fingernails."

David laughed. "Don't worry, Balaam! Come on...what do you say?"

The Bone Man squinted into the sun, looked back toward the frowning federale, then to David. "Is federal *policía*?"

"Yes."

The shaman nodded, understanding how they intended to pressure Herrera to come along. "Okay, *ahua*. I no forget you bring ladino doctor when wife Dolores maybe snakebite die. I help you. Maybe no work. Fix thing Pig's Ass first. I no talk talk him unless must."

"Thanks, Balaam," smiled David. "Here...here's the money." David extracted several bills and handed them to the shaman.

"Is more much, *ahua*. No have change."

"Keep it, Balaam. Give it to one of your wives or buy some extra posh for your son's cargo."

The Bone Man stared at the money, as if trying to remember when he had held so much at one time. He stuffed the paper into his pants pocket, then slipped over the edge into the forest. David motioned for Luis to follow, then hurried to catch up with the Bone Man.

"Tell me...Balaam. Are there caves along the Ceiba Trail?"

"More no count you, *ahua*." The shaman strode purposefully on the winding path.

Deep in thought, the professor followed dutifully, sometimes coming abreast when the path widened, then falling behind again as it narrowed, imagining unexplored caves and great discoveries. Luis, disgruntled and complaining, brought up the rear.

Balaam stopped abruptly and turned to face David, gazing up into his eyes. "Tell Balaam, *ahua*, you know hear La Cueva de Vidrio?"

David pursed his lips, frowned and shook his head no. "Where is it?"

"Fifty kilometers south and east. No far Ceiba Trail, by rock canyon. Maya call Council Valley."

"Is it special?"

"Yes!" exclaimed the shaman, "Is good place. I hear gods

122

sing when I me child."

"Really!" exclaimed the professor. "What's so special about it?"

"Is river glass deep in the belly cave. Gods walk talk on river."

"Oh yeah?" said David, trying to remember if he'd ever heard this particular legend. "I don't recall ever hearing that one before."

"No ladino hear gods sing, ahua...you deaf stupid all ladino. But soon come loggers will find in Lacandon jungle. Is best I show ahua before ladino logger find."

They walked together another hundred feet, David considering what the Bone Man had revealed. Had he understood him correctly? His Spanish seemed to be worse this time. Was the legend of Council Valley the truth, or was Balaam just telling him what he wanted to hear? Was it just another Indian myth?

"*Ahua*..." said the Bone Man, "you not find nothing no book. Old black robes, old priests Catholic kill burn all. My wife is thank *ahua* that soul of the snake no overpower her. I think I point you on map where find *La Cueva de Vidrio*."

CHAPTER FOURTEEN

"Well that's just great!" Angry, Luis threw his hat to the ground. "Another one of your damn fool adventures...traipsing off after a witch doctor looking for holes in the ground. Why couldn't you be a bird watcher or somethin' instead of a damn rock hound?" Luis glared at his friend.

"Now you sound like Joaquin." David winced, careful not to say too much. He knew that Luis would cool off as quickly as he had become angry. The federale was too good-natured to stay mad long. David bent to retrieve Luis' hat and handed it to him. Luis jerked it from his hand.

"That ferret-faced Indian isn't to be trusted, David. Besides...how are we supposed to get back?"

"We can grab a bus on the paved road to Tenosique and return to Palenque. We'll hire someone to watch the car. This is too good a chance to pass up. Balaam knows..."

"He knows how to take your money and make you like it.

When are you ever gonna learn? What's Alexandra going to say?"

"We're not going to tell her."

"Who's we? You got a turd in your pocket? I ought to call and spill my guts. David, there's a war going on...or haven't you noticed? I thought we were here to check on your female archaeology friend. She's joy ridin' in an airplane with some bad guys, remember?"

"Balaam said he hasn't heard anything."

"Of course he hasn't heard anything. He doesn't know anything. He's unreliable and doesn't know shit." Luis shook his head mournfully, positive that his friend had taken leave of his senses. "And tell me this...what are we going to do when the zapatistas jump us in the jungle? Can the Bone Man talk us out of that one?"

"The army's going to protect us, Luis. That's the beauty of it. Balaam will point out the location of caves on the map while we walk the Ceiba Trail. The army will accompany us for protection. It's a no-brainer."

Luis squinted and stared suspiciously at his friend. "No-brainer huh? And why is the army going to protect us while we're trying to get lost in the jungle?"

"Well...I was going to talk to you about that before you became so irrational."

"You're lookin' in a mirror, gringo. Irrational describes you...not me." Luis glared a challenge.

"Luis...I told Balaam that you could fix it with Colonel Herrera. Now listen to me before you go off again..."

Luis' hat hit the ground again and his eyes grew large. "You didn't? Tell me you didn't, David," he pleaded.

"You know his brother, Raul. Go talk to him about one of your cases in Mexico City. If that doesn't work...offer him a *mordida* of a hundred dollars. Bribes always work."

125

"You're kidding?"

"Luis...this is really important. Balaam could show me where..."

"Screw Balaam...and screw you, too, David." Luis' fists were clenched and he appeared ready to swing at any moment. But he hesitated. Finally, he shook his head and said. "God...David. What's come over you, man? You want to walk into the middle of a war? Are you loco, or what?"

David sighed. "Look...do you want me to grovel? Here...I'll get down on my knees for you if you'll..."

"Aw knock it off, professor." Luis turned so that David wouldn't see him smile. "Okay, loco. I'll talk to him. Gettin' someone killed for a hundred dollars is probably the best offer he's had all day."

****

It was late afternoon in the colonial town of Palenque. Heat waves waffled from the cobblestone and a stifling humidity soaked the air, making it difficult to breathe. The town's small *zocalo* was nearly empty. Rows of red-yellow croton lined the sidewalks and elephant ear alocasia and broad-leafed banana trees circled the gazebo. Coconut palms that lent little shade stood tall and serene, their leafy fronds rustling in the breeze. A typical day in the tropics, thought David.

The professor had chosen a park bench in the shade of a gazebo to sit and study the topographic map in his lap. Balaam had shown them the approximate location of Council Valley, the purported location of *La Cueva de Vidrio*. Luis had no patience for maps and had quickly grown bored. After mumbling an excuse, he headed for the police station. Weary from his trek into the jungle, the professor waited for Luis to return from his errands. A slight breeze began to blow and David looked west into the forested highlands. Towering thunderheads were being swept along by gusting winds. Dark and heavy with rain, the clouds swallowed the sun, and it suddenly smelled of rain and the air felt almost refreshingly. Fluorescent flickers hidden deep inside the clouds promised a violent deluge. There was much to do and he couldn't sit idle much longer. He glanced at his watch–6:06 p.m. Luis had been gone an hour. Why was he so late? Had the calls to Mexico City and San Cristobal taken so long?

Despite his brother-in-law's denial, David and Luis were certain that Karen had been abducted. And, as incredible as it seemed, probably planned and executed by someone who knew her. Jonathan Depp. Why had he and his accomplice staged the kidnapping? Depp must feel certain that acquiring the Gould Stelae promised more than he would ever gain through honest research. The rumors of his CIA involvement in Guatemala and Chiapas twenty years ago now seemed very credible. Actions speak louder than words. Depp had risked everything–his job, what little was left of his reputation, and who knew what else? He was behaving like a grave robber and criminal, not an archaeologist. Riches and fame awaited the person who found the only remaining Maya books; strong motivation, indeed, to break the law. But would the prize be worth it?

David and Luis agreed that the federale should call his superiors in Mexico City and insist that they report Karen's disappearance to the American Embassy. Since Joaquin was covering up the incident, the consulate in Tuxtla Gutierrez, the Chiapan capitol, would otherwise never know of the incident. It was anyone's guess whether the Americans would actually be told–politics being what they were these days–but it was the responsible thing to do.

Luis would also call Angela at el rancho in San Cristobal to test the waters and see if Ali and Joaquin were still angry with

David. If things had calmed down, he planned to phone later this evening before bedtime. Even though he didn't want to argue with his wife and brother-in-law, David remained upset at their reaction. Although Joaquin's behavior was predictable, Alexandra's lack of concern had stunned and confused him. It was a side of her personality he'd never seen and didn't know what to say when he did call her.

Colonel Herrera had readily agreed to allow them to accompany his troops–especially after Luis' "gift" to the colonel for his "trouble." Everything would be fine, Herrera had assured them. The zapatistas were unskilled rabble, hardly a match for the exquisitely trained and well-armed troops of the United States of Mexico. Their journey along the Ceiba Trail would likely be uneventful. He would be amazed if they saw any guerillas. The rebels were cowardly women to hide in the jungle.

Luis had introduced David to Colonel Herrera and let drop that David's brother-in-law was the Honorary Consul of Chiapas. Herrera, much impressed, had quickly found someone to watch David's car. The colonel then secured a room for them at El Hotel Palenque across from the *zocalo* and insisted that they join him later for dinner. There was no entertainment in Palenque, the colonel explained, not even a good whore; thus brandy and conversation among educated men was better than a lonely hotel room–yes?

But now the professor wished that he hadn't agreed. An evening with a boasting, drunken, marionette–which is what Herrera appeared to be–was poor use of what would otherwise be a pleasant evening in a small colonial town. If it didn't rain too long, a mariachi band would probably play in the *zocalo* after dark and the young people would gather under the watchful eyes of the town. Besides, he really needed to go over Karen's data and translation once more.

David frowned and looked at his watch again, but at that moment Luis strode from the *farmacia*. Very tall and broad-shouldered for a Mexican, Luis' size commanded respect in Mexico. He waved and turned to join the professor at the gazebo. Luis ambled when he walked, and a look of resignation, almost a frown, had settled on his face. Uh-oh, thought, David. Bad news? The professor shifted in his seat. Luis worried too much. He'd enjoy this much more if he wasn't so suspicious...but that's probably what made him such a good detective.

"So...will I be sleeping in the servant's quarters when we return to San Cristobal?" asked David.

"Worse," replied Luis. "She gave your clothes to the mission and your rock hammer to Sebastiano, the gardener."

David lurched forward, alarmed. "Really?"

"Nope. No one home. Joaquin took the ladies shopping to Tuxtla Gutierrez while he attends some meetings. We're supposed to call the consulate if we want to leave a message."

"Did you?"

"No...why?"

"I don't know...maybe just cause more problems, I guess. Let them cool off." David moved aside so that Luis could sit. "Did you call the *policia*?"

"Sure did. They wanted to know why I was reporting it instead of the San Cristobal Policia. I told the smart-ass that they were too busy shaking down tourists and stealing license plates to file a report."

"You certainly have a winning personality, Luis."

"So says Angela."

"I thought you said she liked your hands?"

"That and other parts of my body," Luis grinned.

David stood, stretched, and then pointed west. "It's going to rain, big guy. Let's get a Tecate and figure out what we're going to say to Pig's Ass tonight."

"It's what you wanted, David. Be careful what you wish for."

"Yeah...yeah. Let's just make it short. I've got lots to do before we take off in the morning...and I can't seem to find Balaam anywhere. You see him?"

"Don't get me started, gringo. For all we know he may be out tellin' the rebels what Herrera's plan is. I don't trust that little turd of a witch doctor for nothin'."

CHAPTER FIFTEEN

The darkness brought no respite, and the need for sleep gripped Marcos like a constricting snake. Exhausted from nearly thirty-six hours of travel, he tried again to give his attention to Rafael's story of the federal army's attack on the village of Piedra Blanca. But his mind wandered to the events of last week and his circuitous fund-raising trip. The Zapatista Rebellion, though well organized, had always operated on a shoestring budget. His army remained poorly equipped–some had only homemade .22 rifles–and was composed of peasants who divided their attention between farming and revolution– and sometimes farming took precedence over revolution. By airplane and train Marcos had traveled from Chiapas in southern Mexico to New York and Toronto, finally arriving in Amsterdam. His plea for money had fallen on deaf ears. It had all been a waste. The zapatistas had never been ideologically rigorous. While they definitely planned to redistribute land to the Indians and embrace some form of benign democratic socialism–it was a position that pleased no one, or promised the world's power brokers any future toehold in mineral rich Chiapas.

In retrospect he knew that he had been naïve, and the humiliation of failure was now a constant companion after returning. He felt like a child that must be disciplined for his behavior. The men in Amsterdam had listened patiently to his impassioned plea for assistance, smiling benignly at his immature and callow arguments. Then they patiently explained the facts of life to him. No one gave a damn about a good cause. "Where is the money to be made?" they inquired. "What's in it for us?" they wanted to know. What government did he represent? Was he in position to make commitments to them regarding their access to the natural resources in Chiapas once the zapatistas controlled the state and ceded from Mexico? Promises, they said, make poor collateral. It was, after all an investment, and they were businessmen. If he wanted a loan that could be easily written off, perhaps he should approach the World Bank or the International Monetary Fund. "Sorry…but no thank you, Mr. Reyes. Revolution is rarely good for business." As a group they opened their wallets and tossed several thousand dollars onto the table to assuage for their lack of conscience. It was a hateful recollection, and his jaw clenched in resentment.

Rafael was waving his arms and building to a climax in his story, and Marcos turned to his friend and listened.

"They came at night, Marcos. We weren't expecting them to arrive so early. They have mortars and fired their automatic rifles to drive everyone from the village. Several of the women and teenage girls were captured." Rafael's head hung momentarily. "Guess you know what's happening to them."

Marcos knew, all right. They were probably servicing their captors at this very moment. But most of the men, all of them zapatista sympathizers, had escaped into the forest. The most pressing concern was that the army would burn the town and corn and cane crops that grew in the fields. Though comparatively small, the crop was the life-blood of the villagers. Without corn, they would starve. The fields were ripening when Marcos had left for Europe–obviously a bad decision. Now it was time to focus and put Amsterdam behind him. That embarrassing debacle was a world away. Here there was revolution–and he was charged with protecting the villages and crops from the counter-insurgency of the Mexican army.

Marcos had expected the army to come, but not so soon. Two years had passed since the San Andreas Accords, but the government had done nothing but stonewall and prevaricate since. Now they reverted to old tricks–harassment, intimidation, and murder. The Zapatistas now refused to enter into any further talks until the Mexican government met conditions already laid down in the previous accord.

Marcos' attention returned to his adjutant.

"We decided to cross the Usumacinta into Guatemala because we knew they wouldn't follow. Except for a brief skirmish over the airplane, we've done nothing but wait for your return. But we must counter-attack soon or they will surely burn the…"

"What airplane?" interrupted Marcos. "What are you talking about?"

"The drug plane, Marcos…an old single-engine Cessna crashed in the forest. We saw smoke from the engine and followed, but the army arrived moments later and drove us off. They have mortars you know," he repeated, his voice trailing off, as if making an excuse.

"So…what did they find?"

"What makes you think I know?"

"I know you, amigo," smiled Marcos. "Either you or someone else observed what happened. Come on...out with it, Rafael...drugs, contraband, politicos...whom or what my friend."

"A *gringa*," grinned Rafael, "a tall one with big chi-chi's!" He held his cupped hands in front of his chest to show the size of her breasts.

"A *gringa*?"

"Si, Marcos...an American, I think."

"She survived the crash? Anyone else? There were no drugs or contraband?"

"The pilot died...another gringo. He was carrying a money belt. Julio watched from his perch in a tree and saw Chavez take it from him. The *gringa* was hurt, but probably okay, he thinks. She stood for a moment outside the plane, but then collapsed. Chavez had her carried on a stretcher to Piedra Blanca. Maybe he will fuck her...eh Marcos. You ever fuck a *gringa*?"

Marcos waved off the question, looking around instead, surveying the makeshift encampment of rebels sprawled without pattern beneath sheltering, broad-limbed trees. He turned in his chair and looked through a clearing in the trees, a path leading to the muddy Usumacinta, and stared across the river at the campfires of the Mexican army strung along the river bank. Moonlight peeked from behind whispy clouds and glazed the river in iridescent, flickering streams of light. The air, heavy and moist, carried the sweet rot of the river and decaying jungle vegetation on its breath. Hundreds of fireflies blinked enticingly.

"Marcos...we must move before they burn the village and crops. We have waited too..."

"Yes...yes, Rafael. Tomorrow...amigo." Marcos smiled grimly. "We will surprise them tomorrow night at this time.

134

Have reinforcements arrived from Dolores and Agua Negra?"

"Yes...and listen to this...we stumbled onto a band of twenty guerrillas. They are leaderless and hungry and cannot return to their villages."

"Guatemalans?"

"*Si, Commandante*...and they have agreed to join us."

"Feed them. Give them posh to drink. They are welcome and will lead us into Piedra Blanca tomorrow night." Marcos rose from his chair, stretched and walked down to the banks of the wide, dark river. Rafael followed dutifully.

Marcos turned to his second in command and said, "So, amigo...why have you not spoken of Consuelo? Why was she not here to greet me? Is she ill?"

"*Si*, Marcos. Sick or dead." Rafael stared across the river. "Or wishes that she was. Your sister is with the Mexican army across the river."

CHAPTER SIXTEEN

The acrid odor of campfires, refrying beans and baking tortillas wafted on the morning breeze, causing Karen's stomach to rumble in recognition. She had eaten only *posole,* a corn soup, and a few leathery tortillas since yesterday. But her appetite had returned with a vengeance, and the smell of cooking food was just one more thing to create discontent.

She lightly touched the swollen bumps and scratches on her face, then stretched her arms high and slowly swayed from side to side. With her arms tied together at the wrists it was difficult. She felt stiffer and sorer than she could ever remember–but she was whole. Her arm ached and throbbed from Bill's knife-play, but an army medic had taped the sides of the wound together and given her a shot of penicillin. The cut and a minor concussion were her worst injuries. A golf ball size bump hid beneath her hair. For the hundredth time today, she touched it gingerly and winced. Lucky it wasn't a fracture, or she wouldn't be up walking around for a long time.

The day after the crash was the worst. When she rose too quickly, dizziness and nausea would bring her to her knees. But yesterday was better, and today she moved about carefully. She had much on her mind, and a restless energy simmered within, causing her to ruminate on her situation and the events that brought her here. She had survived the nightmarish plane ride and plunge to the forest floor. Upon regaining consciousness, and against all hope, she awakened virtually unscathed, believing that she escaped from the brink of hell. Her survival appeared to be a grace from God, a spiritual epiphany. For a few brief moments she believed in miracles. Nothing like a brush with the Grim Reaper to put you in touch with your spiritual core. But not now. After three days in this small hamlet, she knew it was a lie. Hell had followed and come to stay, leaving the foulness of humanity with her and the other four women in this adobe hut. Now she was learning firsthand what she had only read about previously; knowledge acquired on the visceral level, through the shocking reality of "being there."

Why the Mexican army held her captive with her hands bound, incommunicado in a house with women forced to service the sexual needs of invading soldiers was a mystery. Why hadn't they questioned her about the airplane and the circumstances surrounding the wreck? Why was she a prisoner? Surely they intended to transport her to the nearest embassy. But what took so long, and what happened to that army officer she remembered seeing after the crash? Her memory remained stubbornly hazy. Gunfire, pouring rain, being helped from the plane by stinking, wet soldiers and Depp stripped naked on the ground were vague, disjointed recollections.

Sighing, she lay her head down on a table of rough pine

planks. Patience was not one of her virtues and the lack of it had landed her in trouble more than once. Somehow she would bear up, she knew. She was determined to survive this ordeal. If only the guard outside the door would untie the ropes binding her wrists and take a message to that army officer she remembered seeing.

Her Spanish had quickly returned, and she learned new words daily. After an initial reluctance and embarrassment in speaking so badly, she had just decided to blaze away. Hardly a time to be concerned about appearances. Her teachers, the captive women being used as sex slaves, were at first surprised to see a giant, white-faced *gringa* thrown in with them. Though wary at first, they had warmed to her and managed to communicate the helplessness of their situation. Stunned, then sickened at what was being perpetrated, Karen protested each time the soldiers came and went. Consuelo, the boldest of the Indian women, argued with them also, but always received a beating for her efforts. When Karen objected again this morning, a soldier slammed a gun barrel into her stomach, then dragged Consuelo crying and protesting from the hut. Bastards. From the rear of the hut, behind the table, a small girl sobbed helplessly in the darkness. Two women in their early twenties, their hands bound also, tried to comfort her. The women were worried about who would be taken next to service the soldiers.

Held captive four days now, all but Karen had been raped repeatedly. The women endured stoically, all but the twelve-year-old girl who had been a virgin. The bestiality of the soldiers and the intractable horror of their actions had shattered her fragile psyche. She babbled incomprehensibly, cried much for her mother, and clung to the women who could not console her.

And now Karen could hear Consuelo arguing and men

laughing. Other soldiers yelled obscenities and whistled lewdly as she approached the hut. They must be done and were returning her to the house. Karen heard her curse the soldiers, but this only resulted in more laughter. One of them slapped her, and both soldiers roared with laughter. Angry, Karen stood with difficulty and walked stiffly toward the door.

This time Karen would make them listen, she decided. They had to. She would demand it. She had practiced what she wanted to say over and over in her mind. They must take her to see the officer in charge. The outrage must end. She was a U.S. citizen and had rights, and so did the poor souls in the hut with her. This was the twentieth century, for Christ's sake. Barbarism and crimes against women had been outlawed in numerous treaties. She swore that heads would roll when she was released.

The soldier guarding the hut swung the door wide and Consuelo was shoved inside, landing in a sprawl on the dirt floor. She groaned, but reached her knees and turned and spat at the soldiers, her eyes steely with hatred. They jeered, and one grabbed his crotch and told her what he would do to her next time. Consuelo, even though her hands were tied, scooped dirt from the floor and threw it toward the hecklers. The dirt hurt no one, but the guard took two steps forward and firmly planted his boot toe into her stomach, leaving her gasping in a fetal curl.

Karen snapped, forgetting her rehearsed speech and sore body. Their senseless brutality lit a flame in her soul and she leaped upon the soldier's back and began clubbing him with her tied hands. She was nearly a foot taller, and he collapsed beneath her weight. She continued to strike him, venting her anger and frustration. Cheered by her response, Consuelo staggered to her feet and the women raced from the back of

139

the hut to help, but two soldiers stepped inside with their rifles in hand. A shot rang out and Consuelo fell to her knees, grasping a bloody stomach. Rifle butts to the head dropped the other two females unconscious onto the floor. The twelve-year-old in the back grunted and quit wailing, her eyes wide in horror.

Karen was lifted bodily from the soldier's back and dragged kicking and fighting from the mud hut. While one man held her from behind, the other slapped her twice, then grabbed her shirt and ripped it, exposing her brassiere clad breasts. The one holding her arms laughed and licked her neck. Still she struggled, but he held her firm. The one who tore her shirt pulled a knife and cut each bra strap above the cup, then the snap in the middle. Her breasts sprung free and the men gathered to cheer.

Enraged, she planted one leg and kicked upward with the other as hard as she could, solidly connecting with the knife-wielding soldier's crotch. Surprise turned to twisted agony as pain gripped and held his face. He groaned mightily and sunk to his knees. Karen launched a kick at his head, but it went wide when her captor flung her to the ground.

"*Basta!*" (Enough!), shouted Captain Chavez, striding toward the melee. He rubbed his nose and sniffed loudly. "*Que paso*, Rangel?" he demanded, continuing to rub his nose.

But Rangel knelt on the ground, his face twisted with pain, his hands holding bruised genitals. The other soldier began a rapid, scorching accusation of Karen, pointing at her, and then to the hut as he explained the shooting and Karen's beating.

The captain frowned, asked another question of the soldier, which resulted in a shake of the head and more denials. Chavez rubbed his nose and watched contemptuously as Rangel tried to gain his feet. Captain Chavez turned to Karen and sniffed, and it seemed that his eyes were large, like obsidian plates. He had a feral, wild look this time–much different than her recollection in the jungle after the crash. He eyed her breasts greedily.

"You...American woman," he pointed to her. "You no bother with our business, eh? Or you help them," he pointed toward the hut of women. "You will help with the fuck-fuck and the men," he threatened, his arm sweeping wide to indicate the soldiers. He watched to see her expression.

"I find a man today," he continued, "a man who knows you, senora. He has a long scar on his face. His name is Bill. You are criminal, he say. He say you steal the Indian treasures from Mexico and you have map worth much money." The captain reached to lift Karen's chin, but she jerked her head aside and glowered, unafraid.

"Stand up, *puta*!" he barked.

She stood, reluctantly, trying to cover herself, and faced her tormentor.

"What say you, senora?" He persisted. "This Bill...he has a long knife and a strange story for a man alone in the jungle. Should I believe him, gringa? Do you have a treasure map? Me...I don't believe such nonsense. But maybe I take you to him. Maybe it loosen your tongue...eh? He seems very sure and is anxious to talk with you again."

Karen, with all the dignity she could muster, her arms folded over her breasts, held the captain's eye. "I, too, have a good story to tell...a true story. Bill is the criminal. He and the pilot kidnapped me in San Cristobal. Bill gave me this." She pointed to the cut on her arm. "Untie me and take me to the nearest embassy. I'll see that you are rewarded. You have no right to keep me or these women prisoners. Please...help me...help us and I'll...I'll do whatever I can to get you some money."

"Money, *senora*? Yes...everyone likes the money. But what

141

of the map, *gringa*? This Bill does not appear to be the kind of man a lady would go with. Are you a lady, *senora*, or are you a *puta* that goes with men on trips for their pleasure?" His large black eyes stared brazenly at her chest, then he extended a hand to touch her face. Again she jerked away.

"Bastard!"

"This is not time for the conversation...eh, *gringa*? Tonight we fiesta. The men...they will drink posh and fuck-fuck with the women. But I am a gentleman. After dark you come and entertain me...eh?" he leered, appraising her body. "We have much fun, I am sure." He winked at her. "I never have complaints from the *senoras*, you know?" He struck his chest with his fist. "I am very strong. You will see." He rubbed his nose again and sniffed. "I have something special...something better than posh to offer you, *gringa*."

"I wouldn't go with you if you were the last man on earth." She spat at his feet. "Take me to an embassy...I demand it!"

Captain Chavez shot her a malignant look. "*Senora*...tonight you entertain me," his hand reached to cup his genitals. Then he pointed to the soldiers. "Your interference has cost them the use of a good whore. So I send for you later and show you what a real man is like. You please me, or I give you to them, or maybe I give you to this Bill. But..." smiled the captain, "I no think he want to fuck you." He gripped her cheek with a hand and pulled her face to his. "You have pretty face, *gringa*. But with cuts on it you would just look like another whore. Remember...you are in the jungle...and you are alone."

CHAPTER SEVENTEEN

His mind simmering with anger, and saddled with guilt for what he had not done, Marcos thought of the village across the yellow-brown Usumacinta River. Doubt gnawed at him like a jaguar worrying a bone. During his ill-fated fund-raising trip to Europe, the village had fallen and some of its women captured. His younger sister Consuelo and other village women were now captives of the Mexican army, but no one would ever know. He gazed south of Piedra Blanca into the distant green of well-manicured, terraced cornfields. They, along with the town, would burn if he didn't act soon.

Not wanting to tempt fate and present a target to a drunken federal soldier, Marcos knelt behind a cover of broad-leafed staghorn ferns to view the village. Scraggly trees, tall grass and exuberant tropical plants lined the coarse, sandy riverbank. The fluid snake moved like a mighty boa constrictor, flowing strong and sinuous; a timeless, vibrant artery in the heart of Meso-America–the ancient highway of

Maya civilization. Its clear waters began in the highlands of Guatemala and carried the detritus of composted jungle soil through a series of spectacular cataracts into the hot, lush lowlands of Tobasco state before spilling into the Gulf of Mexico. The dead cities of Bonampak and Yaxchilan, subsumed by the jungle, lay near the river's edge. Palenque, the home of the Jaguar Kings, lay only 40 miles to the west, and Tikal, in Guatemala, to the east.

Marcos had drunk cane liquor and talked with the new Indian rebels late into the morning hours. His mind, dulled with alcohol, felt like the river—murky and slow. He slept not at all, and the fervor of the night's conversation left him disturbed. The Guatemalans were good soldiers, as they had known nothing but war since childhood. Because of a CIA sponsored coup, the Guatemalan Indians had battled their government for twenty years. Marcos had known many of the war's major players.

Both sides had committed uncounted atrocities. Whole families—women, children and the elderly—had been murdered and entire villages exterminated. But these guerrillas had no families waiting their return, no villages to welcome them home, no fields to call their own. Even though peace had finally come to Guatemala, the rebels knew only two things—war and retribution. Despite the peace accords and a generous offer of amnesty, many had chosen not to turn in their guns and return to mainstream Guatemalan society. They wanted revenge against the government. Children who grow up without mothers, fighting wars and hating at an early age, have festering sores on their souls and lack essential traits basic to wholeness of character.

Marcos recalled a two-year-old conversation with Guatemalan Nobel-prize-winning peace activist, Rigoberta Menchu. Her entire family had been killed in the internecine war. Against all expectations, she had become an ardent peace advocate and beacon of hope for the anguished armies of Guatemala. She argued that the war had lasted so long because the rebels and government soldiers had become entrenched in a cyclical abyss of anger and retribution, and that the original issues had become secondary. Reprisal and vengeance were now primary–replacing the goals of justice, land reform and self-determination among Guatemala's Maya. Spanish descendants who ruled Guatemala had lost touch with the soul of their country and succumbed to the rule of an oppressive military brought to power by the United States by way of a CIA backed coup. Sentiment and passion, not injustice, had fueled the war.

Marcos had vehemently disagreed with her, but now the truth of her words gripped and chilled his heart. The reptile part of the lower brain flooded the mind with hormones, causing man to act violently and without compassion. The constant pressures of war created a besieged mentality. The urgency of survival and the subsequent rancor and drive to settle old scores dominated. Rationality and compassion succumb to emotion and hatred

His sister was across the river, probably being used like a Zona Rosa whore–or worse, being gang raped. War was so terrible for women. What sort of life remained for a young girl so terribly abused? How did one recover from something so horrible? Would she find a good husband to help her? Would she have children and a family to nurture her? His leaden heart beat dully and his face felt flush. His fists clenched. He wanted to kill the bastards–slowly and with much pain.

It was tempting to cross the river right now, in broad daylight, but this would be foolish. Surprise and speed were the only hope against superior fire power. Better yet, his spies reported that the army had somehow procured several

145

carboys of posh and that the soldiers were drinking and reveling. Marcos believed that a big fiesta was likely planned for tonight. He also knew that an American *gringa* who spoke passable Spanish was held in the same hut as his sister. He knew these things because the zapatistas had captured two cocaine mules and interrogated them before and after their meeting with Captain Chavez. The mules, poor *campesinos*, were father and son, wanting only money, not trouble. They had been eager to cooperate with the rebels. The father claimed to have fought many battles against the soldiers of Guatemala. After talking with the Guatemalan guerrillas that had joined his platoon, Marcos had relented and cut a deal with the mules. They were allowed to deliver the cocaine in exchange for their lives and information. Both men were now on their way to highland homes in Guatemala. No one would ever know of their deception.

The zapatistas planned to retake Piedra Blanca this very night. They would drive-out the Mexican army, save the women and cornfields, and steal the cocaine. The drugs would be sold for cash or traded to buy arms–which is what Marcos should have brought on his trip to Amsterdam, not ideas and principles. Arms dealers don't give a shit about causes, injustice, and the little people–only money.

He heard someone treading the river path and turned to see Rafael searching the trail for him. His old adjutant walked bow-legged, his broad face etched with worry, deep in thought. Marcos rose and gestured for his friend to join him.

"Commandante…" began Rafael, "a messenger just arrived from Santiago's company. He's pleading for us to come and help. The Federal army and Colonel Herrera are in Palenque and plan to move along the Ceiba Trail. He believes they will burn many villages and fields. What should I tell him? We have our own problems, you know." Rafael pointed across the

146

river, and then extracted a handkerchief from his back pocket to wipe his forehead.

"The Ceiba Trail?" repeated Marcos.

"Yes...says that Balaam Reyes has been forced to act as a guide."

"Balaam, eh?" Marcos considered the news. Surprising, but not unlikely. Balaam Reyes was his father, and Marcos knew he would never willingly help the federal army. He was coerced. But Balaam would also know that the Zapatistas were aware of the army's planned foray into the jungle. Thus he would probably find a way to sabotage the army's efforts, or lead them into a trap.

"Tell him..." Marcos hesitated, "tell Santiago he's on his own for three or four days. Tell him to attack in the evening when the Mexican army is tired. Their soldiers are weak and have no heart. After two or three days of heat and mosquitoes, the jungle will soften them up."

"But what of Balaam?" inquired Rafael.

"Don't worry about, father. His medicine's too strong to get hurt. If the army's forcing him to help, they're dumber than I thought. They'll be sorry he was forced to help."

Each stared across the river, imagining what the night would bring, what friend or family member might not see the morning sunrise. It had become a too familiar contemplation: resolute, dedicated peasants who had learned war much as they had religion, by succumbing to the realities of a small universe and adjusting their beliefs to accommodate the urgency of their material misery.

"Rafael?"

"Si, Commandante," responded Rafael without looking.

"We will execute Chavez with a firing squad."

"What about Consuelo and the other women? What about the *gringa*?" asked Rafael.

Marcos knelt by water's edge and plucked a blade of grass. He slowly wound it around his finger, considering his reply, then allowed it to unravel and fall into the river.

"I'll go in first with the Guatemalans. The women are being held in Jose Chiapa's house."

"You can't be risked, Marcos," objected Rafael. "You plan like a hothead, not a General."

"I'm a man…nothing more."

"Quit being stupid. You are El Commandante. Without you we are helpless farmers."

"I promised to lead."

"A leader does not lead by getting killed. Your mind is clouded with posh and thoughts of revenge. Send the Guatemalans to Chavez's hut. We must take him first, then seize their weapons."

A long silence ensued.

"Yes…" said Marcos, finally. "I suppose you're right." This is why he trusted Rafael; the old man gave sound advice and never hesitated to contradict him–in private–never in front of the men. Balaam Reyes had assigned Rafael to Marcos' command. The unlikely pair had quickly bonded; each immediately recognizing valuable qualities in the other. The old man was right. Marcos must deny his anger regarding his sister. Despite what might happen to her, the Zapatistas must fight another day, and he must be there to provide leadership. Otherwise the Indians would never overcome the tyranny Mexico imposed on them.

Rafael, however, was still planning the method of the Mexican captain's death.

"Then we can cut off Chavez's cojones and send them to his wife," added Rafael. "Or maybe chop off his hands and shoot his knee caps like they did Ortega's wife at La Palma.

Marcos extracted a small bag of tobacco and rolling papers.

148

He expertly spread the leaf, then rolled, licked and sealed the paper, placing it between his lips. "I'm afraid not, old friend. We must be careful to not become like them. We must fight the good war." He lit the cigarette and tossed the match into the river.

"Eh...that sounds like more of your philosophical bullshit, Marcos."

"It's true, though, Rafael. In order to keep public opinion on our side, we can't commit atrocities. Even when we lose on the field we must win in the newspapers. The war of words is just as important as bullets."

Rafael sighed. "So you say...but tell me that we can shoot him, Marcos. The man has no heart. Surely we can fill his chest with good zapatista lead."

"We will shoot him dead, amigo," smiled Marcos grimly. "But we will give him the chance to give the order himself to show that he is a man, so that we do not anger them in Mexico City. But...who knows," Marcos struck a match and lit his cigarette, "maybe he will befoul himself and the story of his shit-filled pants will spread to the federal army."

"When given the chance to prove himself a man, he shows himself to be a coward?" asked Rafael.

"Si, old friend."

"I like it. I know of an emetic he can drink to ensure it."

Gunshots erupted and faint whoops of laughter echoed across the water.

"Starting early, aren't they?" Rafael shaded his eyes and peered to the other side.

"Yes...and so will we," said Marcos. "Post guards and tell everyone to get some sleep if they can. No more drinking."

"Even the Guatemalans?"

"Especially those crazies. We must be rested and at our best tonight."

"What happens if they start burning the fields today?"

"They won't. Spaniards and ladinos play before working. With posh and cocaine available, they may party for days."

Rafael smiled grimly, nodded acquiescence and turned to go.

"Rafael?"

"Si, Marcos?"

"Clean your rifle, old friend."

"I keep it clean, Marcos. But you, Commandante…you need sleep. The men depend on you," chastised Rafael.

"I'll be up in a minute," said Marcos. "First I must plan Chavez's execution."

CHAPTER EIGHTEEN

A stew of soaking humidity and heat paralyzed the jungle, discouraging enterprise, causing one's head to hang as if a heavy burden lay on the shoulders. Captain Chavez could hear the strident cries of river insects beginning their nightly mating chants, staking out territory and calling out their location to others. He had set up quarters in a small wooden slat and mud building south of town. The home had dirt floors like the others, but was cleaner and better furnished, and the shitter outback was a two-holer. Talk about prosperity-the hut even had a kerosene lantern that glowed brightly on the table. He liked to be on the periphery, away from the men. It was good to distance himself from the lower classes, and it was none of their business what he did. With all the bad habits he had acquired, it would be foolish to flaunt them in front of others. Envy and resentment were well-developed sentiments in Mexico and remained the favored response of the ignorant to the affluence of the upper classes.

A guard stood impatiently outside the hut. Chavez could hear an occasional cough, or the sound of a boot nervously kicking the dirt. The soldier was anxious to partake of the *ponche* and women. The captain had dismissed his two non-commissioned officers, Sergeants Gomez and Cuero, so they could join the fiesta and keep an eye on the enlisted men. Except for a few designated guards, everyone had put aside their guns. Chavez wanted them to party-but keep the lid on. Cane liquor and young, illiterate soldiers were a volatile mix. He hoped that they contented themselves with drinking, fucking the women, and bragging about it. Tonight, even the lowly privates would get their dicks wet if they wanted a shot at the zapatista whores.

Chavez's head hummed like it was in orbit and his knees were too weak for him to stand up. Posh hit hard and stayed too long. Damn fine stuff on occasion. While the captain watched, the gringo chopped cocaine rock into powder and divided it into lines with his sharp, lock-blade knife, all the while spouting a steady string of chatter. Who would believe a man could talk so much? Guatemala, Honduras, El Salvador...where had he not been? Hell...for all Chavez knew the gringo was a Yankee spy. But American spies didn't chase pretty women with treasure maps in old planes, did they? He didn't quite know what to think of this Bill, but was quickly growing tired of talking to the scar-face. By rights, Chavez ought to shoot him and be done with it. But for some reason the captain just watched and listened. He really should lay off the rock, but opportunities like this occurred so rarely. It was one of the perks of the job. It was time to drink, talk, and have sex. Tomorrow they would move out. Chavez must meet the Colonel in Tenosique, Chiapas in four days to deliver the cocaine, but first he must burn the corn and tobacco, and maybe even the town if he decided to.

Bill was talking about the *gringa* again. Maps, treasure, maya books–these were not the fare of professional soldiers. Besides, it sounded political. Anything to do with archaeology was political these days. If you wanted to get your tit in a wringer, just mess with one of the stuffed suits in Mexico City. Captain Chavez didn't give a shit about archaeology, only money–and talk of treasure was so much bullshit. The only treasure in Latin America these days was drugs, especially cocaine. The gringo was an idiot. Chavez had plans for the *gringa*, and they didn't include turning her over to Bill. Anyone who had traveled and done as much as the one-eye claimed to have done should know better.

Captain Chavez stomped his boot to get Bill's attention. Enough, it signaled. Bill's knife paused its chopping, and his head shot up expectantly.

"Listen, *senor*...I have plans for the *gringa*." The captain cupped his genitals and grinned knowingly. "You need to leave...quickly. You have enjoyed the courtesy of the Mexican Army long enough. Your story is bullshit and you have no business playing at intrigue in a war zone. I should shoot you as a spy. But since I like a man like you, I'll have someone take you to the road in one of the Humvee's. My advice is to get out of Chiapas...get out of Mexico if you can. You don't look like a person who has many friends."

Chavez felt the urge to empty his bladder, and so he told the gringo to chop a couple more lines. He carefully pushed himself erect and staggered outside to relieve himself. He barked an order for the guard to fetch Bill's belongings, then ambled unsteadily into the darkness. After the *gringa* arrived the captain would put Bill in a jeep with the guard and have him dropped off somewhere.

The forest to the west loomed black and impenetrable–an ominous encroaching wall. Velvet shadows of gray-black stretched long and eerie as nebulous thunderheads with impassioned lightning moved stoically over the jungle, threatening a summer deluge. The captain could see the glare and flying sparks of distant bonfires as his men milled about, feeding the hungry fires. Laughter, shouts and the singing of drunken soldiers echoed through the village. He heard a woman scream and curse loudly, and he smiled. The captain unzipped his fly and extracted his penis. He stroked it a few times and sighed. He hadn't used it for much lately but peeing and the cries of the woman reminded him of the *gringa*. He visualized her struggling and fighting outside the hut, her pendulous breasts jiggling with each exertion. Her kick had put Rangel to his knees, probably destroying his only asset. Chavez chuckled. Jesus…what a woman, what chi chi's! And tall! The *gringa* had legs all the way to her ass. What would it feel like to have those wrapped around you…eh? He shivered. Time to get rid of the scar-face and send for the woman. But first a drink and a few more lines of rock. Let her worry. It could only make things better.

****

Tico Rodriguez, small in stature but very horny, was the youngest soldier in the company. He sat sipping the last of his posh–a difficult feat for an inexperienced drinker. He knew he was making progress–knew that he could drink like a man now because it no longer made him gag and retch. Sweet and syrupy, the cane liquor burned like fire and smelled like paint thinner. It seared a path, trickling into his stomach, and brought tears to his eyes. He wiped them and looked around for Andre. His fellow guard had brought Tico a cup of liquor nearly an hour ago, which he had nursed, trying to make it last in hopes that his buddy would soon bring a refill–but such had not been the case. With deep appreciation, but partly out of necessity, he took a deep breath, exhaled fumes and

154

looked longingly into the empty cup.

Sweaty, dirty, drunk and pissed at being assigned to guard the *gringa*, Tico squashed a biting mosquito, crunching it flat against his forehead. He hated bugs, hated the jungle, hated Captain Chavez, and now he hated Andre for not bringing more posh. Where was he? Probably fucking one of the women at this very moment while Tico covered for him by standing guard. Tico knew that if he vacated his post to drink or fuck, he would probably be shot for desertion. It just wasn't fair. From where he stood on the southern edge of town, Tico could see groups of soldiers milling about campfires, and knew that the smoke protected them from biting insects. He watched them tip their cups to toast one another's lies and stories, all the while bragging about their sexual prowess with the women. *Chingada*, he thought. He wished the captain would send for the woman so that he could join the others.

Tico looked toward the palm mat door that stood between him and his captive. It was dark inside, he knew, but Tico's imagination worked non-stop. He could still visualize the *gringa's* swaying breasts when she struggled with the guards earlier. *Caramba*! What a woman, that one. She had put Corporal Rangel to his knees with that kick. Were all American women so big and sexy? He massaged his crotch, imagining what it would be like to have sex with a *gringa*. Andre said that American women like oral sex. Tico believed it, too. It made sense. He knew many stories about promiscuous foreigners and had once verified them himself. When Tico had turned thirteen, his uncle had brought him along to Acapulco to deliver a load of mangos. After unloading the truck his uncle had smiled slyly and asked if Tico wanted to go pick up some *putas*. Fearful, yet curious, he had said yes. They prowled the Costera along Acapulco Bay in their truck. They didn't picked up any whores, but the experience was as unbelievable as it was unforgettable; scantily dressed women, their *nalgas* (buttocks) and chi chi's bulging from every imaginable fold, wearing bathing suits that exposed nearly everything and left little to the imagination. Incredible! The women might as well have been from another planet. They either ignored you like an insect, or stared brazenly into your eyes–even the fat ones and the old, wrinkled, sun-dried ones.

Tico's penis grew erect as he recalled the boardwalk of nearly naked *gringas*. Then his thoughts turned to the captive women scattered about the camp. He was missing it. Damn! He rubbed himself again, barely stifling a moan. He thought again of the *gringa*, and he visualized her on her back, legs spread, smiling and welcoming. He wanted to penetrate her...now...with one violent thrust! His imagination run amok, he stood stiffly and adjusted his painful erection. If only he didn't have guard duty. Where was that damn Andre? He turned and walked toward the hut, wondering if American women really did like oral sex.

****

Karen sat despondent inside her mud-brick prison. The heat was enervating, the mosquitoes voracious, and the house nearly dark. Very little light leaked between the slatted walls. With her hands still tied and almost numb from lack of circulation, she leaned forward and rested her weight onto the heavy plank table. The water pitcher was empty and she craved a drink. Her blouse, ripped and shredded, hung from her shoulders like a sodden rag. She was alone. The other women, including the twelve-year-old, were out being used as punchboards by the soldiers.

If her situation hadn't been clear before, she no longer harbored any illusions. Chavez's threat of a scarred face and his insinuation, "You are in the jungle and you are alone," resonated with her. She would be raped like the others. Karen could still visualize his dead black eyes, shining like obsidian plates, his face bloated with lust.

The plane had crashed into a bacchanalian hell of violence and hedonism, and she had discovered that war was worse than hell if you were a woman. Men were such beasts. A quick death now had a singular appeal when considering the scenario that Chavez had outlined for her. It was highly unlikely that he would turn her over to the American Embassy after what she had seen. And though it made her tremble to think about it, she knew that Chavez would probably share her with his soldiers when he finished with her. Worse, he might give her to Bill.

The ex-CIA monster had somehow been resurrected to threaten her again. She recalled his absence after the crash. Had he escaped unharmed? Incredible–but then, she was alive too. Why not Bill? Chavez's threat to turn her over to Bill was not to been taken lightly. The pervert seemed obsessed with her discovery and believed that she had access to treasure. God! What had Depp told him? She just didn't see any acceptable options. Chavez would likely rape and kill her. With Bill, however, she might live long enough to deceive him into believing that she knew where the Maya books were hidden. But once he discovered her deception, she would die slowly and horribly at his hands. These weren't options, they were just different death sentences.

She shuddered. Her throat constricted and she couldn't swallow. Panic and fear pushed her inexorably toward the precipice of mental collapse. She felt more alive than she ever remembered, wired for 220, her glands pumping hormones, insisting that she fight or run. She could barely sit still. But she must. She had to think of something quickly, but what? How could she escape? What did women do when faced with this

157

situation? Fight and resist? Manipulate? Commit suicide? Go and be raped and hope for the best?

Complete darkness threatened to overwhelm the remnants of dusk, and light was barely visible beneath the door. The muffled sounds of drunken laughter and an occasional chorus of song filtered into the dark hut. The merrymaking was moving toward crescendo. She shivered in the stifling heat.

Why hadn't Chavez sent for her? Had he changed his mind? Where was the cretin, Bill? Was something important occurring of which she knew nothing?

"Damn it!" she cried through clenched teeth. "Damn, damn, damn!" She stood and kicked the chair on which sat and, though her hands were tied, doubled her fists and slammed them to the table, venting her rage and frustration.

"*Que paso*, senora?" called a guard from outside. "*Estas bien*?" he inquired.

Karen gave no answer. How many guards were there now? she wondered. There were two earlier.

"*Oye*...senora..." the soldier called. "*Contestame!*" (Answer me!) he commanded.

Was he alone? If so...then maybe this was her chance! She desperately searched the room for a weapon, but saw nothing. Only a thin length of sisal rope tied to a thick stick, probably a child's toy, caught her eye. Or, maybe she could hit him with the empty pitcher on the table. Her eyes returned to the stick, and an idea began to crystallize.

The door, a curtain of woven palm leaves, rustled slightly and the guard peeked around the edge. Receiving no answer, he pushed it wide.

"*Hola, senora...estas bien*?" (Are you okay?)

This might be her only chance, she decided. It was now or lay down and die. She walked slowly toward the door so as not to alarm him.

158

"Que quiere?" (What do you want?) she asked. *"Vayase."* (Go away.)

Dim light shone through the doorway and the guard stepped inside. He was alone, she decided.

Though her shirt hung in shreds, she made no effort to cover up. She watched his eyes move to her chest and stare, then to her face and back again to her chest.

"Tengo sed," (I'm thirsty) she said. *"Puede llevarme agua?"* (Can you bring water?)

The soldier, young and small, glanced over his shoulder to see if anyone was watching, and then again at Karen. His eyes focused on her breasts. "Si, senora," he smiled. His shoulders relaxed perceptively. He said, *"Soy muy solo."* (I'm lonely). *"Voy para el agua, pero tu me debera un favor."* (I'll go for water, but you will owe me a favor.) He smiled shyly, almost pathetically, took another look at her chest and said, *"Quedate. Estoy en regresar pronto."* (Stay put, I'll be right back.)

When he exited the hut, Karen moved quickly to retrieve the stick and rope toy. Her heart thudding dully, she looked around for something to use as a hammer, saw the ceramic pitcher on the table and grasped it. Judging the distance to be about right, she sat on the ground and placed the stick upright between her feet, then pounded it into the ground like a stake. She looked around for something to which she could attach the other end, but saw nothing.

"Shit!" she cursed, slamming the pitcher on the floor. The she saw it…the leg of the table. In the darkness, she scrambled to her feet and over to the table. Dragging it near the door, she tied the rope to the leg and moved the table until the rope held taught, creating a trip line a few inches above the ground.

Flush with exertion, her heart racing, she moved the tatters of her blouse aside to fully expose her breasts. She grasped the pitcher by its handle and waited two meters on the other side

159

of the trip line. Looking through the door opening, she saw flickering shadows and a red-orange corona dancing above a large bonfire attended by eight or ten men near the center of town. Their laughter and boisterous bravado stung her sensibilities. Bastards! All of them. She hoped they burned in hell.

Here came the guard–and still alone. Her heart pounded dully and she felt as though she sweat steel splinters. Feeling light-headed, almost weightless, the pain and stiffness of her injuries dissipating into a swell of endorphin-induced euphoria.

He hummed a tune as he approached, stopped outside the door and lowered his head to peek inside. "*Senora*," he called, not seeing her clearly. "*Tengo su agua.*" He offered the cup.

"Gracias," she mumbled, but made no effort to take it.

He leaned his rifle against the wall and again presented the cup. "*No te olvido mi favor,*" (don't forget my favor) he reminded her. He took another step forward, then froze. His mouth hung slack when he saw her breasts fully revealed. He stared, mesmerized.

Karen thought she heard a moan. He glanced at her face and she gave him her best "come hither" look.

He returned her smile, said "Oh *gringa...eres tan bella,*" and moved quickly into the dark room, the cup extended. He tripped on his third step, and Karen saw a look of puzzlement on his face as he tried to keep his balance. He fell forward and as his head ducked toward the floor, she kicked his jaw as hard as she could with her heavy hiking shoe, connecting solidly but nearly falling herself. He landed on his hands and knees, but she jumped on his back and pounded his head with the pitcher. It broke on the third blow, but still she hit him with the handle, grunting with each two-handed blow to the head. He didn't fight back, groaned once and lay still. She struck him until her hands were bruised and bloody. Her energy spent, she rolled to the side, her chest heaving. She quickly rose and removed the knife sheathed in his belt. Although it felt awkward, she grasped it between her hands so that the blade cut the light sisal in two. There...it was done! Elated, she ran to the doorway and peeked outside. No one paid them any attention. The rifle lay near the door, and she took it. She hadn't fired a rifle since her freshman class in marksmanship at New Mexico State. It felt awkward and unfamiliar, so she examined it. It appeared to be a simple bolt action with a clip of shells. She found the safety and moved it back and forth a few times, then left it off. She hefted it and put it to her shoulder. It would suffice. No one was raping her tonight. She would take a bullet first.

The guard groaned and her heart skipped a beat. His arm pushed against the ground as he sought support. She moved quickly to slam the rifle butt against his head—once, twice, then silence. He never uttered another sound.

She panted from the exertion. Now what? she wondered. Run? Go out firing like crazy? Try to sneak away now that it was dark? She didn't have a plan; this was all serendipity–so far a miracle of luck. But she must act quickly. Chavez might send for her at any moment.

Karen stopped to catch her breath and regain her composure. None of the choices seemed right. She had no clue where she was other than deep in the jungle. Or did she? That river outside–was it the Usumacinta? She bet it was. They had flown far enough south–almost to Guatemala before crashing– and the great river served as a border between the countries. She didn't feel good about her chances of making it in the jungle. She was a single female, and David had been very explicit about what awaited her–snakes, jaguars, insects, heat and guerrillas. The river, on the other hand, might be the best

161

way. All rivers had small towns along them. And the towns, in turn, were at the end of roads. Roads went to other towns; sometimes highways if you were lucky. She recalled hearing outboard motors on the river. Maybe someone would find and transport her back to civilization? She knew how to swim, but were there snakes in the river? She would need a boat, or at least something like a raft. Maybe she would just disappear into the jungle and circle back downstream, following the river until she found a boat or something on which to float. But how would she escape unnoticed?

Karen peered outside into the darkness. The soldiers still milled about the fires where the smoke warded off mosquitoes. She must go now before it was too late. To hesitate was to fail. She ready to leave the hut when her eyes fell on the battered soldier. She needed a disguise, no matter how poor. The darkness would be her friend. She quickly stripped away his fatigues and ammunition belt, only to find that the pants were too short. The shirt almost fit, but Lord it stunk! She put it on anyway, then retrieved his helmet and tucked her hair beneath it.

Taking a deep breath, she stepped outside. The river lay to the right. Two fires blazed on the shore and a larger bonfire lay straight ahead, in the middle of town. She moved left and headed for the jungle, walking naturally to not draw attention. She barely breathed, her nerves raw and strung tight like piano wire. Her stomach clenched into a knot and her mouth felt as if it was lined with cotton balls.

Twenty meters from forest edge she bolted, breaking into a full run with the gun in hand. Then she was in the jungle, but still she ran, stumbling and slipping, unable to see anything clearly. Sudden shadows unnerved her and vines and bushes grasped at her legs and arms. Flying insects struck her face, and her heart pounded to near bursting, and so she stopped

162

and turned to see if anyone followed. She heard nothing but her heart and the chirping of insects. Dark, odd-shaped shadows formed intangible three-dimensional barriers around her. The village had receded into darkness, now back-lit in the orange glow of fires. Calmer now, she turned and slowly threaded her way into the jungle, moving downstream, away from the village. She could do it, she told herself. The worst was behind her.

She tried to make no sound, carrying the rifle at her waist like she had seen on TV. Progress was steady, and then she found herself on a path and picked up her pace, anxious to put as much space as possible between herself and the army. The trail was serpentine and laced with roots, but moved steadily east toward the river. A faint flicker of alarm, like startled birds in flight, caused her to slow her walk. Why the feeling of dark foreboding? She didn't know. As she passed between two trees, she noticed, too late, a movement on her left. In an instant the gun was torn from her hands and she was lifted by the neck and thrown to the ground, the wind knocked from her and her helmet rolling aside. The sour, stinking breath of the man that held her in a death grip stung her nostrils, making her want to retch.

"*Adios cabron*," he grunted and his hands squeezed her neck like a vise.

****

Captain Chavez finished urinating, massaged his penis a few times with anticipation, then tucked it back inside and turned towards the mud shack. Light from the kerosene lantern glowed dimly through cracks in the wall. He could hear the tap, tap, tap of Bill chopping cocaine on a small mirror. Chavez rubbed his nose and sniffed. A couple more toots and he would be ready to taste the *gringa*. He walked toward the hut, visualizing the tall woman's breasts and long

163

legs. He hoped that she wouldn't be a bitch about it. It would be more fun if she just went along with everything. He would make sure that she enjoyed herself. But then what? Should he give her to the men? Keep her around a couple more days, then feed her to the crocodiles? Maybe he would sell her to a whorehouse in Guatemala?

The tapping had stopped, so Chavez pulled the door aside and, stooping to enter, stepped inside. When he straightened, a bolt of pain rocketed through his head. He stumbled, then another blow landed, felling him. He attempted to rise, but collapsed onto the dirt floor instead.

****

Karen struggled mightily; kicking and scratching, trying to throw off her attacker. Her adrenaline surged and she began to buck.

"*Parate!*" shouted the strangler's companion. "It's a woman! Look at her hair."

The rock-like hands loosened their grip and the soldier clumsily grasped a breast to confirm this ridiculous statement. She yelped in protest.

"*Caramba,*" muttered her attacker, but he made no move to let her rise. "Go get Rafael or Marcos," he whispered urgently. "This is not one of our village women. Maybe she is with the federal army."

Karen gasped for air, and her lungs slowly filled. She protested again and he placed a hand over her mouth, shushing her. She fought half-heartedly, but then lay still. Her attacker didn't look like a Mexican soldier. He wore a bandanna to hide his face and dressed in peasant clothing.

A robber? she wondered. No, she decided. There were more men. This one had sent the other for someone in charge. Then it struck her. Zapatistas! The rebels were near the village. But why? Were they about to attack? Incredible. She must

164

leave quickly. When bullets began to fly, she wanted to be way down river.

Within moments several men appeared, all toting rifles and machetes. They looked like silhouettes in the darkness. Someone growled an order and she was lifted and carried deeper into the forest, jolted and bounced painfully as they did so. How could they move so fast in the darkness without running into something?

"Be careful, damn it," she complained, trying to adjust herself. They gripped her tightly and were hurting her arm near Bill's knife wound.

Minutes later they stepped into a moonlit clearing in which fifty or sixty men milled quietly about. She could see better now. A sense of urgency pervaded the air, and Karen smell their pungent, male body odor. Her captors released her arms, but stood close by. She ached all over, and her lower back felt as if it were sprung. While she regained composure and began to assess this new situation, groups of men, four at a time, slipped silently into the jungle, all of them carrying rifles and wearing bandannas. Zapatistas for sure, she decided, and they meant business–no one talked or joked.

Not-so-distant thunder rolled through the heavens, and she looked upward in time to see white lattice fractures of lightning back lit in towering thunderheads. Great–now it was going to rain. What else could go wrong? Then the mosquitoes found her, and she cursed and slapped them helplessly.

Within minutes only a few guerillas remained in the clearing. The rest were dispatched to await a signal, she supposed. But what of her? What would they do with her when they attacked? The soldiers who carried her whispered among themselves, and she understood enough to confirm that her guess was right. The rebels, worried about their crops, were counter-attacking.

165

Karen spotted a man who appeared to be in charge. Of medium height, but with very broad shoulders, his walk and manner of carrying himself seemed oddly familiar. She watched carefully as he moved from group to group, reassuring and dynamic, occasionally raising a fist for emphasis when he spoke.

When all were dispatched, the leader approached her group and gave orders. Her guards disappeared into the forest also. Unlike the other soldiers, he wore a ski mask.

"Do you speak English?" she asked. "What do you want with me? Let me go. I'm an American."

He spoke haltingly, and his voice seemed vaguely familiar.

"You are the *gringa* in the village with the other women?"

"Yes," she answered, surprised. What else did he know?

"Did you see a woman named Consuelo?"

Even in the faltering light she saw that his eyes shone with fire. Passion exuded from his pores, and his presence unsettled her. She felt attracted, yet repelled, and turned from his eyes. She lowered her head, feeling sad and ashamed, remembering the women in the hut with whom she had bonded in such a short time.

"Dead," she said, finally. She looked up at him. "The army shot her when we tried to escape."

He blinked, and his eyes closed momentarily. Dead," he repeated. "You're sure?"

Karen nodded. "She was very brave. She fought every time they…they…er…took her to…"

He held up a hand to quiet her, showing that he knew what they had endured.

"And you *senora*…how are you? You seem to have survived the plane crash and now you have escaped the woman killer, Chavez. How were you able to do this? Tell me, what is happening in the camp?"

166

Karen repeated what she knew, which was very little, she realized. But he listened carefully, asked questions, then turned and gave orders to an old man called Rafael at his right.

"*Si*, Marcos," agreed Rafael, who hurried to the other side of the clearing to where a man carried a radio on his back. The radio pack was removed and placed beside a tree. Rafael called other radio operators and spoke urgently, relaying their orders.

Marcos? she wondered, realizing the name held significance for her. But why? She looked at him carefully, aware that she was missing something. Why was he familiar?

"So...you do not recognize me yet?" he asked.

"Should I? Why would I know you?"

He peeled the ski mask from his head and she squinted to see. Yes, she knew him. He was...she struggled to remember, then she had it. The reader of Sun Tzu! She had talked with him on the flight from Dallas and in the Acapulco airport. Then she remembered her conversation with Professor Wolf.

"But...but...you're dead...I mean...David said that you were killed in...ah..."

"Guerrero," he finished for her. "Yes. Burned beyond recognition, but it wasn't me. It was a federal officer who killed two children in the town of Tlecopliota. Bastard had it coming."

"David said that..."

"Professor Lobo?" he interrupted.

"Er...yes. David Wolf said you were accused of a massacre."

Marcos' mouth became a tight line. "And does he believe this?"

"No," she replied. "He said you were a lot of things, but a murderer wasn't one of them."

"And you? What do you believe?" He caught and held her

167

eye.

"I don't know what to think," she answered, honestly, "but I trust Dr. Wolf."

He nodded agreement. "Yes, Lobo was a good man, but he had no…" Marcos struggled for the word… "commitment," he said finally. "Many good ideas, but not willing to…to act."

The sky above flickered and a warm breeze drifted through the jungle. They both looked up at the same time.

"Marcos…it's time to go. We must start before the rain comes," chastised Rafael. Three soldiers, rifles in hand, stood behind the old man.

"What do you want to do?" he asked her. "I can't stay here. It isn't safe."

"What are my choices?"

"I can have a man show you the trail the army brought their Humvees over, or you can try to follow the river until a jaguar or crocodile kills you."

"Anything else?"

"You can come with us and pay a visit to the woman killer."

"Captain Chavez?"

"Yes."

"Then what?"

"I'll arrange for you to get back to San Cristobal or wherever you wish."

She considered the options, but none were palatable. "What does Sun Tzu say your chances are of winning tonight?"

"Excellent. Decide. I must go."

"Do I get my gun back?"

Marcos hesitated, but then said, "*Si*, why not?" He barked an order to one of the soldiers who came forward and returned her rifle.

She hefted it and checked the bolt action. "Aunt Rose will never believe this," she muttered.

"Que? What did you say?"

"I said let's go. Captain Chavez thinks he has a date with me tonight and I don't want him to think I stood him up."

****

The shadow was moving toward Chavez again. He must get up, must escape, or it would hurt him again. A searing headache grew worse with each beat of his heart. A dull pain constricted his chest when he breathed. Was he having a heart attack? A moan escaped his lips.

"Get up, asshole!" ordered Bill.

The boot struck again. This time the pain curled him into a fetal position.

"Up, I said." Bill's leg was cocked, ready to kick again.

"*Basta!*" (enough), croaked the captain. He held up an arm to fend off another kick. The gringo had knocked him senseless with a rifle butt, and now demanded that he rise from the floor. "*Basta...*" mumbled Chavez again, pleading, trying to regain his faculties, certain that an ax had cleaved his skull. Blood dripped from a gash in the back of his head and soaked the earthen floor. Impatient, Bill stuck the tip of his rifle barrel into the captain's nose and lifted upward.

"Ahhg!" screamed Chavez, struggling to rise. "*Cabron!*" he pleaded as pain rocketed through his sinuses. But Bill steadily applied pressure until the captain gained his feet.

"Don't touch it," warned Bill when Chavez reached for the gun barrel.

The Captain withdrew his hand and moaned pitifully. "*Chingada! Cabron!*" he cursed.

"Out." Bill motioned with the gun. "Move it, asshole."

"Where...what do you want?" Befuddled, Chavez attempted to stall. He had to cut a deal, had to find a way out. Where was the crazy American taking him? Did he want the gringa that bad? Or was it the cocaine?

"*Oye,*" (listen) said the captain. "What is it you want? Some cocaine? The *gringa*? We can cut a deal. You don't have a chance without...ummph!" The gun barrel jammed into his solar plexus.

"Move, or I'll put you in the ground," threatened Bill. "Go..." he motioned again, "out the door and to the left, asshole."

"Where...?"

"The river, Senor Big Shit...and don't try to escape." Bill flashed a knife, "Or I'll cut out your eyes...understand?"

The river? thought Captain Chavez. *Cabron* is going to kill me and throw me in the river! He nearly charged the gringo, but resisted the impulse. If the rifle didn't get him, the knife would. The *gringo* looked very handy with a blade. How far to the river, he wondered? Thirty-forty meters? A field of cane stood to the north, then a thick band of trees. Bush and bramble lay between the river and village. He would make his move there, he decided. A storm was nearly upon them, and the moonlight would soon fade. Besides, he had in his boot a surprise for the pinche *gringo*. Captain Chavez threw Bill a fearless, hateful look and stepped for the door.

"Wait," said Bill, appraising the captain.

"Que? What is it? First I go, then I wait. *Chinga tu madre, gringo.*"

"Get em' off," pointed Bill.

"What? My clothes? Surely you don't intend to..."

"Off...all of them. I need the uniform without bullet holes."

"*Cabron!*"

"Keep the boots, though. They look too big." Bill gave him a sly smile. "Do it...now."

A choleric anger raged within, but the captain assumed a stone face. He was allowed to keep his boots! Gracias a Dios! Chavez wore dress high-tops with thick heels instead of the standard issue lace boot. He gingerly removed and set them to the side of his chair away from Bill's eyes, then reluctantly unbuttoned his trousers and stepped from them. He would kill this gringo pervert–slowly and with much pain.

"You can keep the underwear, too," smiled Bill.

The captain put on his boots. "You'll never get away with this, *cabron*."

"I already have." Bill slung the pants and shirt over his arm, then motioned toward the door. "Move...slow and easy."

Moments later, stripped to his underwear and a gun at his back, the captain trod gingerly through the brush at river's edge. A sprinkle of rain fell and a sallow moon hid behind the clouds, dropping a sullen blanket of darkness over the forest. Only an occasional lightning flicker illuminated the area. A monotonous, perpetual drone of insects filled the forested solitude. Mosquitoes, drawn by the odor of sweaty, near-naked bodies, swarmed to the feast. Chavez kept up a steady string of talk, all the while cursing and slapping mosquitoes, trying to buy time, waiting for his chance. He was tempted to run. It might work, he reasoned, but must be done with surprise and in the densest brush near the river where the one-eyed gringo would have trouble seeing. There could be no fuck-ups, no errors when he drew the derringer from inside his boot holster.

"Slow down," commanded Bill. "Can't see shit. This isn't a path. Where the hell you going?"

The gun barrel jabbed his back and Chavez stumbled forward, then stopped. "It's the *pinche* mosquitoes, *cabron*. They've..."

"Here...turn right," pointed Bill. "This looks like a trail. Can you feel this?"

Chavez winced with pain. The knifepoint had drawn blood. Dios, he wanted to choke the one-eyed white man! Hatred

171

simmered within, allowing him to forget the insects and focus on the need to escape. He must endure, and so he plodded onward, waiting for the right moment. He knew the Usumacinta lay nearby when the trail began to narrow. How far? Ten meters? Five? Unexpectedly, he had his answer–the splash of bullfrogs leaping into the river. He decided. Chavez bent the palm leaf of a cycade and let it fly into Bill's face, then dove to the side over a stand of alocasia. He rolled toward the river, gained his feet and ran, stooping forward, hiding behind a grove of leafy cycade trees.

"You fuck! You greaser!" screamed Bill, rubbing his one good eye.

Captain Chavez, already hurting, had now added more scrapes and bruises. Though his heart beat painfully, he tried to control his breathing and make no sound. He pulled the two-shot .25 derringer from his boot and waited. When he looked again, the gringo had disappeared. To where? He strained to listen, but heard only the grunts of breeding crocodiles slapping their tails on the water as they wallowed near river's edge.

Lightning continued to flicker, bolder and closer, accompanied by the distant rumble of thunder. The sprinkle threatened to become rain, and the jungle floor slowly dissolve into viscous mud. The cloying odor of decaying vegetation and rotting fish assaulted his nose.

What was that? He wheeled around, and the mud clutched at his boots. Shouts? He listened closely, then heard the unmistakable sound of gunfire coming from town. A twig snapped, and more frogs leaped into the river. He wheeled and fired. The *gringo* yelped, only three meters away, knife in hand, his mouth hanging slack. Bill tottered on the bank, then slipped and fell backward into the swift Usumacinta.

Crocodile bait! thought Chavez, grinning gleefully. Got the

cabron! He crouched and walked to where the American scum had fallen. Good riddance, he thought. But now gunfire broke out everywhere, and the shouts of men in drunken pandemonium echoed in the night. Dios! What was happening? Hadn't he ordered all the guns placed in the gazebo before the drinking, and....zapatistas! The thought rocketed through his mind. His army was under attack. But how? His army had scattered them into the jungle. They were cowards–women pretending to be warriors. They were... At that moment he stumbled over his clothes and rifle where Bill had laid them. In the darkness, not knowing that the captain had a gun, the *gringo* had tracked him with his weapon of choice, the knife.

Gracias, Dios! thought Chavez. He quickly donned his clothing. But now an inchoate fear gnawed at his gut. Why had Bill done this? The *gringa*? The cocaine? "*Chingada*!" he cursed. Captain Chavez would never know. The loss of his army would be a disgrace, but the loss of Colonel Herrera's cocaine ensured that Chavez, too, would take an unwanted swim with the crocodiles. He grabbed the rifle and sprinted through the brush toward the village. *Dios...oh Dios*! he thought.

CHAPTER NINETEEN

A resident of Piedra Blanca had led the way through misting rain and dense tropical growth. Karen followed Rafael, Marcos and two soldiers, one of whom had a radio strapped to his back. They moved silently, single file on a muddy path known to the guerrillas. Karen, anxious and sometimes slipping in the mud, felt her heart thudding as she followed the radioman. Twice they stopped and knelt in the brush while Marcos and Rafael whispered and motioned with their hands, arguing about "Guatemalans." Marcos seemed disgusted, but Rafael, surprisingly, behaved as a stern father with a willful child. Lots to learn about that relationship, she decided.

They arrived on the periphery of a dense field of sugar cane, some of it nearly five meters tall. Nothing looked familiar to her. The huts set farther apart here, and all were dark inside except for one. It sat very near the cane field. Flickering yellow light leaked through walls of wood slats and mud. Karen moved to the front and kneeled abreast the men so that she, too, could see into the village. Three bonfires, one in the middle of town and two others near river's edge were surrounded with soldiers. The sounds of a fiesta in full swing—drunken laughter and loud voices—were clearly audible. While Rafael whispered urgently into the radio microphone, a woman's scream pierced the night, followed by the hoots and cheers of the soldiers. Beside Karen, Marcos gripped his rifle and swore. The drama had begun, and her stomach waffled in protest.

Rafael returned, and Marcos peppered him with questions.

"How many?"

"Thirty or forty."

"That's all?" Marcos seemed surprised.

"That's plenty."

"Guns?"

"Mateo says they've all been placed against the inside rail of the gazebo."

"The mortars?"

Rafael shrugged, "Who knows? Could be with the Humvees, or even in there." He pointed to the lighted shack.

"No," Marcos scowled, shaking his head, "that would be stupid."

"Exactly," argued Rafael, "like everything else they've done."

Rather than argue, Marcos asked, "They know to capture the guns first?"

"Si, Marcos." Rafael seemed impatient. "It's time, hombre. They are waiting."

"Okay," said Marcos. "Send three groups to the gazebo while the Guatemalans attack the hut. Tell Delpino's group to hide in the corn, and…"

"Shhh…" urged one of the soldiers. "Mira." He pointed to

the hut.

They ducked low and peered through the brush. A man clad only in his underwear and boots exited the door, followed by a tall, thin man who held a rifle to the nearly naked man's back. They stopped and argued at the door, then the man with the gun pointed the barrel toward the river. The prisoner, however, was reluctant and looked instead toward the trees where they hid. His captor's gaze followed, as if searching out their hiding spot. The one with the rifle scanned the area for soldiers, then with a parting glance toward town, shut the hut door and ordered his prey into the forest. While Karen and the small group watched, baffled, the men disappeared into the shadows.

Karen exhaled loudly, unaware that she had been holding her breath. Was that Bill? She started to say something, but Marcos held a finger to his lips to shush her. She chewed her lip and gripped her gun, suddenly recalling the terror of her flight over the jungle. She shivered, remembering the cretin's knife and dead white eye. Her throat felt parched and her stomach waffled. It was him. His shape and body movements were forever imprinted in her mind. She took a deep breath to dispel a creeping fear, but still his image lingered. She visualized her tormentor playing with his knife, a sly smile on his face, his dead white eye staring, but unseeing.

"Bastard!" she hissed through her teeth.

"You know him?" whispered Marcos.

"Yes. Too well...it's...it's Bill. He's a..."

"Marcos," interrupted Rafael, "it's time!"

Marcos ignored his adjutant and shot her a questioning look, but she gave no answer. His gaze returned to the shadowy blackness where the two figures had disappeared, then back to Karen. "We'll talk later," he promised. To Rafael, he said, "Do it...but send the Guatemalans to Chavez's house

176

first. Drive the soldiers into the river or south of town. Tell Delpino…"

"I know what to tell them." Rafael motioned to the radioman, who removed his load. The radio was placed on the ground by a tree, while everyone else checked their guns. Marcos pulled Karen aside and examined her rifle to make sure it was loaded. He took the safety off, told her to be sure of what she shot, then they knelt together in the bush to watch. Rafael counted in a whisper, staring at his wristwatch. "*Ahora,*" (now) he muttered anxiously, glancing toward town. At that instant six masked soldiers carrying AK-47's and bandoleers rushed from the forest's edge toward the hut.

Karen tried to breathe evenly, but fidgeted, barely able to hold still. Beside her, Marcos and Rafael whispered urgently. Just as the Guatemalans approached Chavez's door, shouts and gunfire erupted from the center of town when the zapatistas charged pell mell toward the gazebo to capture the federal army's armament. Straight ahead, a Guatemalan kicked the flimsy shack door open and rushed inside, firing wildly, followed by his companions.

"Stay here," ordered Marcos. Rifle in hand, crouching low, he trotted toward the shack.

"Marcos!" barked Rafael. "*Cuidado, hombre!*" But the commandante ignored his protest.

"*Chingada!*" muttered the old man between clenched teeth. He, too, stood and rushed after his commander.

"Sweet Jesus," muttered Karen, galvanized by their charge into battle. But panic held her firmly. She swept her hair aside, lingered a moment longer, then cast caution aside and followed with rifle in hand. She could hear the pop, pop of gunfire. Rifle shots erupted nearby as she entered the open area between the forest and shacks. Shadows were in motion. Near chaos ensued. The confused, drunk federal army quickly fell into disarray. Soldiers in full flight deserted the campfires and ran for cover. Many hoofed it south toward the jungle, some dove into the river while others took cover behind huts where they were eventually captured. Halfway to the house she stopped to watch three uniformed men, running and stumbling toward the cane field. A zapatista appeared in their path but was knocked to the ground and his rifle stolen. They fled in unison toward the field, but must pass her and Chavez's hut in doing so.

"Marcos!" she cried, "Marcos!"

Hearing her voice, the soldiers stopped abruptly, and one of them pointed her out. The other placed the rifle to his shoulder and aimed. Trembling, Karen dropped to one knee and hefted her own rifle. It felt heavy and cumbersome, but she sighted and fired, hearing other shots simultaneously.

****

Upon hearing Karen's call for help, Marcos stepped quickly from inside Chavez's hut to fire at the oncoming soldiers. But Karen fired and shot the gunman. Marcos took aim at the second one, but Rafael fired first and felled him. The third soldier turned and stumbled toward the jungle, where he was met by gunfire from the radioman and two waiting zapatistas.

"*Que buena mujer!*" exclaimed Rafael. "Did you see her shoot, hombre? She has *cojones* (balls) like a man!

"Inside...hurry." Marcos motioned for her to join them in the hut. She rose unsteadily and walked wild-eyed to the house. Rifle fire resounded through the town, and she jerked and looked behind with each volley.

She arrived at the door. "My legs are going to give out," she said in a hoarse voice.

"All good soldiers are afraid...unless they're stupid," soothed Rafael.

"Well done, Karen." Marcos extended an arm and pulled

178

her close. She lay her head on his shoulder. He felt her tension slacken and breath exhale. Killing your first man was a memorable, life-changing event. Violent death, especially in war, caused permanent damage to the personality. Many soldiers became inured and callused to the horror of death–indifferent to the butchery and slaughter of war. Others succumbed to guilt and fear, obsessing on the smallest details of the event, unable to quell the waking nightmares that stalked their memories. He would watch her in the coming days to see how the killing affected her. But based on what he had seen thus far, he felt confident that she would respond well. This woman had proven herself a survivor, and perhaps a warrior.

The radioman and zapatistas in the bush approached the hut now. Rafael met them and talked on the radio with his men to see how events had transpired. Marcos led Karen inside and sat her at the table.

"What's this?" she asked, puzzled. "Looks like drugs or something." She touched the powder on the mirror with her finger. "Is this what I think it is?"

"That, Karen, is the new currency of Mexico–the most sought-after commodity and the worst sickness to afflict the country since the flu, the smallpox, or the measles. It's the latest white man's disease inflicted on the Indians."

"You knew this was here?"

"We captured the couriers crossing the river yesterday. They gave us their story and we let them go."

"Why...why didn't you...er...do something else? Or...I guess I mean..." she foundered for the right words. "I guess I don't know what's going on."

"It's typical. It's part of what this war is all about to the government?"

"Drugs?"

179

"Drugs and land. Our land was stolen hundreds of years ago and is still being taken by politicians and ladinos. The Indians of Chiapas are the poorest people in Mexico. We want our land back. PRI has been losing elections all over the country and wants to protect its interests, which are the landowners. The military wants to control the area so that they can run drugs. This war is about money, Karen." He rubbed his thumb and fingers together. "Big money. Easy money. The army, PRI bureaucrats, the Mexican Mafia, many drug cartels, and evangelical Protestants-just about every greedy fool in Mexico wants in on it. Only the Catholic Church supports our cause."

"That's insane."

"It's the truth."

"Then taking this village...this whole war is..."

"Just another opportunity to make money," he finished for her. "Chavez was probably sent by a superior officer to pick up this cocaine and transport it back safely. Who's going to check on the Army or stop them? No one. The Indians are blamed for the war, and the government responds by burning villages and crops. It's how the PRI political party deflects attention from Mexico's biggest problem–government corruption."

"God...that's so sick." She swept hair from her eyes and slumped in her chair. Kerosene fumes wafted steadily towards the ceiling, causing her nose to wrinkle with disgust. She eyed the weak flame in the lantern and sighed, realizing how very tired she was.

Marcos found it hard not to stare. She had long legs and auburn hair, and breasts that swelled beneath the federal army shirt she had taken from a soldier. In the dim light of the lantern he could see that she was beautiful–even with one side of her face swollen and scratched. Dark, puffy bags lay below

180

each eye, revealing the dread and horror of the last few days. Still he found her enticing, exotic. War and violence stoked the libido. He felt his loins stir and imagined himself pulling her into his arms. He wanted to touch the injured face and reassure her, caress her ample breasts and stroke her thighs. He wanted to make love to her.

Karen must have felt him watching because she caught his eye, then blushed and looked away. She sat up in the chair and avoided his eyes by looking toward the door. The air sizzled and seemed to explode as exclamations of surprise rose outside when a bolt of lightning struck a nearby tree. The heavens opened with pouring rain and the wind gusted, driving water through the poorly caulked slats of the hut. The thunder and fury of the hurricane finally reached the center of the Lacandon jungle, cleansing the air and forest just as the zapatistas purged the federal army from their village. Gunshots were sporadic now, but the glad shouts and hoots of villagers rang loud through the storm.

"What now?" she asked. Her head lolled back onto the chair. "Where do we go from here?"

"We secure the town, then gather all the weapons and supplies left behind. Rafael will send word to the others across the river to cross tomorrow. Most of the villagers are camped along the Usumacinta. After they arrive, we'll bury the dead and…" his voice faltered, remembering his sister, Consuelo. "…and we must make ready in case the army tries a counter attack."

"I thought you got all their weapons?"

"We did…we think. Other armies are on the prowl, though, and many of Chavez's soldiers fled into the bush. They're still around and could make trouble. We'll have to be careful. I'll radio in a report tonight and see what I can find out. Tomorrow I'll know more."

"Where's Chavez?" She swept a matted tangle of hair from her face.

Now that's a good question, he thought. Where was the woman killer? Why was this cocaine lying on the table for anyone to see, and who were those two men, one of whom appeared to have captured the other and marched him nearly naked toward the river. Was one of them Chavez? He doubted it. The Captain would have someone else do his dirty work. Yet the incident remained unclear, an unnerving prelude to their attack, and would surely make a good story. He must investigate it further.

"Good question," he replied. "Wait here." He walked to the doorway and whistled to the radioman and Zapatistas waiting in the rain. "Get more guards here," he ordered the radio operator, "and find Rafael. Tell him to have a patrol search the bush along the river where the two men disappeared. Ask if he's found Chavez yet."

"Si, *Commandante,*" said the radioman, and quickly attempted to locate Rafael.

"You two," he pointed, "stand guard–one on each side of the house. Shoot anything that looks federal, okay?"

"Si, Commandante!"

Marcos returned to the hut and approached Karen at the table. "I've got a million things to do. Stay inside here until morning. Try to get some sleep."

"Are they going to stand outside in the rain all night?" A fleeting look of fear stole across her face.

"If I tell them to."

"Am I a prisoner?"

"You can leave any time. They're here to protect you."

She paused and studied her feet, choosing her words carefully. "Will you return?"

"I'll check on you later if you wish."

She nodded. "Please...I...I'm afraid that...I don't think I can sleep."

"I understand." He placed a hand on her shoulder. "You're a very brave woman. No harm will come to you."

"Promise?"

"*Te promiso,*" (I promise), he said, and bent to kiss the top of her head. He turned to go, but she grasped his hand. He looked into her eyes and imagined that he saw sadness and, yes, a little longing. For what, he wondered? He gave her a reassuring smile, then reluctantly lifted her hand from his. "Adios, *gringa,*" he said.

"Adios, Commandante." She gave him a coy smile. "If you get yourself killed tonight, I'll be mad."

"Yes," he chuckled. "I'll be mad at me, too." He turned to go, but she called out again.

"Marcos?"

"Si, Karen?"

"Oh...nothing. I was just wondering...are you going to bring a bunch of people with you later?"

"I come alone when I visit beautiful women."

She blushed and turned her head in a futile effort to hide a smile.

"Good," she said, finally, and turned to seek his eyes. "We can talk more about your beautiful women later."

****

Karen watched her savior move with fluid grace toward the door. Attractive, with broad shoulders and muscled arms, he carried himself with confidence, secure in his manhood. She felt safe with him, and a twinge of regret at his leaving. So much had happened, and she was still trying to make sense of it all. Was she truly okay now? Marcos stopped short of the door, gave her a promising smile and disappeared into the tropical fury unleased by the remnants of hurricane Julio.

183

A steady downpour accompanied by vigorous wind and lightning battered the jungle. Although the hut roof was made of palm leaf, she could hear raindrops hitting the side of the mud-plank house and feel drafts of air wafting through the cracks. The lantern flickered, projecting grotesque shapes onto the walls and ceiling. She glanced around the small, messy room. A dusty, smoked-stained image of the Virgin of Guadeloupe hung askew on the wall. A small altar with an unlit candle and bowl of uneaten food sat on the floor below the picture. Two rough-hewn chairs beneath a cedar plank table were the only real furniture. Mud bricks supported rows of shelving, most of it made from scrap metal or wood. Pans, plastic bowls, baskets and unidentified tools were strewn throughout. Two hoes and a shovel lay against the wall near the door. A tree stump piled with blankets sat on the opposite side of the room. Two hammocks hung from the walls and a pallet of corn leaves covered with blankets lay in the corner. She eyed it with longing, exhausted and in need of sleep, but her mind raced.

Shouts and sporadic gunshots heard over the storm revealed that the Mexican Army was routed, but not quite pacified. Was it possible to sleep with a fire-fight going on outside? She glanced at the bed and hammocks again, then at the door, remembering Marcos' smile and the touch of his hands when he had reached and gently drawn her close to him. Would he return later tonight? If so, then what? She had brazenly invited him back, but now questioned her motivation. Was she enamored with him because he had saved her and now saw him as her champion? Maybe she was being too pushy? Worse, was she making more trouble for herself?

Her sigh was more of a groan. She shoved hair from her eyes again, and stared into the lamp. She ached all over and couldn't think straight. Adrenaline made her jittery and nervous, and the army fatigues taken from the soldier smelled of musty body odor. Her nose wrinkled. She had to get out of these things and get a bath soon. Maybe if she just laid down for a short time she could calm herself and sort out her feelings. She must make a plan for returning to San Cristobal de Las Casas. Aunt Rose was probably worried sick by now. Karen looked at the lamp and decided to leave it on. She had spent enough time in a dirt-floored hut without light and had no desire to be insect food again tonight. She rose stiffly, unbuttoned and removed the soldier's stinking shirt. Her bra lay in tatters somewhere on the other side of town, and she made a mental note to search for it tomorrow. Perhaps it could be repaired. She unlaced and removed her hiking boots, then slid her soaked, clinging jeans over her hips. She had never slept in a hammock before, and eyed it with misgivings. They looked comfortable, but how did you turn on your side in one? Just do it, she told herself and chose a thin blanket from atop the tree stump. She laid the blanket over the twine netting and hoisted herself up. The fit was amazingly comfortable, and she relaxed immediately, succumbing to the soothing sway of its rocking motion. She stared at the ceiling and imagined that she saw familiar shapes in the shadows cast by the flickering lantern. A groan of exhaustion escaped her lips and she closed her eyes. An image of Marcos in the clearing before the attack came to mind. She recalled the pain on his face when told of his sister, Consuelo, then visualized him leaping the bush and charging into the darkness with rifle in hand. She remembered the feel of his broad chest and the smell of his hair when he hugged her. And then she remembered nothing, and her breathing became slow and regular. She began to dream.

****

185

Marcos stared at the lovely *gringa* and drank her beauty. He hoped her dreams were not too bad. She lay dead to the world, oblivious to the drama being enacted outside. Sweat streaks lined her forehead and beads of perspiration dotted her upper chest, sometimes trickling into the valley of her cleavage. Her shoulders lay bare and one very substantial breast lay exposed. It made him catch his breath, and an overpowering sexual desire seized him. He yearned to caress it, to bury his face and take it into his mouth, but knew that she would awaken.

Though he ached with longing, now was a poor time for romance. He was responsible for too many. The guerrillas, the villagers, the Indians of the Lacandon all depended on him. The expectations of so many were an onerous burden to bear alone, and long-repressed resentment tugged at him. He learned many years ago that command was lonely, most nights spent only with one's fears and recriminations. To be responsible for decisions that resulted in death or injury, success or failure, remained his biggest challenge. Guilt, always unwelcome, was an ever-present companion. He turned his eyes from the feast in the hammock and sat at the table.

Much was underway, even in the storm. The captured munitions and Humvees were being transported to where the need was greatest. He intended to release the eight captured federal soldiers about twenty-five kilometers from Palenque so that they could straggle home with the news of their defeat. The Zapatistas, a mobile army, had nowhere to intern them, and it was important not to give PRI an issue with which they might rally the country's support. Prisoners of war were bad business and, unlike the government, the Zapatistas were not murderers. Not yet, at least, not if he could help it.

The villagers across the river prepared to return, and as the early morning sun rose, the river would be dotted with log rafts plying the currents. Everyone was eager to recover their property and inspect crops. These, at least, were intact for the most part. A disaster had been prevented from which the Indians would not have recovered. But then, of course, a few wouldn't. People had died, and others wished that they had. He glanced at his wristwatch and saw that it was nearly four o'clock in the morning. This victory would not be celebrated. Today they would mourn. Two of the four captured women, including his sister, were dead and were thrown into the river to feed the crocodiles. The others would likely never recover from the brutality they had suffered. Those who equated war with conquest and acquisition should experience the misery and heartbreak of innocent people victimized by the greed and rapacious appetites of the powerful.

A painful swelling grew in his throat and his eyes leaked tears. His vision blurred and a sob escaped. His head lolled forward onto the table. Their father would be grief-stricken at the loss of Consuelo. Balaam reluctantly allowed her to join Marcos three months earlier, prior to the federal army's crop-and-village-burning offensive. Her husband was killed in a massacre while tending his tobacco field. A cabal of PRI officials and protestant Indians from a nearby village had conspired with their mayor to murder the entire town of Acteal, a small village in the highlands near San Cristobal. Forty-five people, mostly women and children, were gunned down with AK-47's while the *Federal Policia* stood by, fully aware of what occurred.

Consuelo was the second sibling in the family to die for the cause. Mahogany loggers had assassinated Antonio, Marcos' older brother, fifteen years ago for organizing resistance to their encroachment. He remembered his older brother as a charismatic speaker and brave man. Antonio died for the cause; and others, like Marcos, stepped forward at the urgings of their father.

Marcos was a good student at the mission school. Three years prior to Antonio's death, their father, who wished to groom Marcos for a role in the movement, insisted that he enroll at UNAM, the National University in Mexico City. Marcos never asked why. It was an opportunity to get an education. Optimism was a drug in those days, and he saw the world through rose-colored lenses. He knew that Balaam was far seeing and that he planned many things that his children did not understand. But upon arriving in the big city, a country boy tossed into a metropolitan nightmare, his father demonstrated that there were expectations for Marcos. He was required to study political science and languages in order to understand the ideologies and tongues of those who held power. He traveled to Europe and the United States to study. In retrospect, it was now obvious that his father had groomed him. Like his male siblings before him, he was expected to enter into his father's service–a job requiring that he become a guerrilla fighter and leader.

Father was old, but no one knew his exact age. Marcos' mother related that Balaam Reyes was born in Guatemala and that he was active in the revolution before leaving that country one step ahead of the death squads before fleeing to Mexico. She also said that he had other wives and that he took care of them all, and that Marcos had brothers and sisters that he had never met. She spoke proudly and with genuine affection for her husband and displayed no sign of jealousy when he departed to visit his extended family while weaving his net to cast over the ladino colonizers and hacienda owners.

As the storm raged, Marcos sobbed and his will ebbed. It all seemed so futile. He had grown close to the sister he had barely known, and the guilt he felt from her misery at the

188

hands of the federal troops threatened to paralyze him. Like many Indian women supporting the revolution, she had taken up arms like a man, traversing the jungle and sharing the hardships of a meagerly equipped and poorly trained, but zealous army. If only Balaam hadn't sent him to Europe to beg for money. The patriarch didn't understand that the world had changed. The Cold War was ended and the West had won. The Soviet Union no longer had currency to finance revolution in the Third World. The Americans didn't have to buy influence now that their communist competitor was broke. The rich industrialists with whom he met in Amsterdam to solicit money were no better allies than the corrupt politicians of Mexico. Borrowed money came with strings attached. Investors wanted something in return: booty in the form of trade, land or natural resources–the same problems that had caused the Zapatista rebellion. Doing business with them would merely exchange one group of oppressors for another.

His conversation with Balaam Reyes days earlier had left a sour taste in his mouth. He knew the old fox well enough to sense that much was happening and that Marcos and his men would be drawn further into the conflict. Armies were on the move and Balaam would use them as chess pieces to capture an unknown prize. Marcos felt as if he had put his whole life on hold for the zapatista cause, and now, even with tonight's victory, he found himself at a low point in his life. He had hoped for a reprieve, a little time off, and would like to accompany the *gringa* back to San Cristobal. He would ask permission, but felt certain that his father had other plans. After all, there was a war on, and wars required leaders.

Karen shifted in the hammock, and he turned to see if she was awake. Her eyes blinked with awareness and she pulled the blanket to cover herself.

"What time is it?" she asked.

"Early...a little after 4 o'clock." He stood and wiped his eyes, then gave her a wan smile.

"Is everything okay? Is the army gone?"

He approached and gave the hammock a light shove, causing it to glide to and fro. She enjoyed the movement and her eyes closed.

"Everything's fine. You're safe," he said.

She caught his eye and stared. "Did you find your sister?"

"No...she was thrown into the river, but...ah...I...heard from the others about it."

"She was very brave. She was...kind of our leader. She talked to us and comforted the other women after the soldiers raped them. She never gave up and always said that we would be rescued."

"I was too late."

"Too late? I just saw you three days ago on the plane. How did you get here so fast?"

"By car, by foot, and by air boat on the river. I arrived a day and a half ago."

She nodded her understanding, then looked around the hut. She tugged nervously at the blanket. "Well," she said, "do I have to get up? It's still dark out, and I could use a little more sleep."

Feeling that the moment was right, Marcos bent to kiss her. She didn't resist, but didn't loosen her grip on the blanket. He drew back to gauge her response. The flickering light of the lantern was mirrored in her eyes. She held his eye boldly, and he thought he saw a quiver of yearning, a spark of desire. He kissed her again and held it longer, this time wrapping her in his arms and holding her close. He felt her relax and release the blanket, and she returned his embrace.

He nuzzled her and tasted her lips again, feeling his loins

190

stir. The blanket edged downward and he felt her tremble.

"You have me at a disadvantage, commandante," she teased, then lightly pushed him away and shifted awkwardly in the hammock. "I'm not dressed and..." she tried to sit up, causing the blanket to slide and reveal her breasts. She reached to cover herself, but he caught her hand and stared boldly, first at her chest, then into her eyes. Even in the dim light he saw her face color with embarrassment and look away.

"I want to make love to you, Karen."

She gave no struggle, but said, "I don't know...I don't see how. Not in this thing. I mean...no...I don't think..."

He shushed her and bent to kiss her. Their lips met again and he felt her passion, knew that she wanted him too. When he caressed a breast, a moan escaped and she pulled him closer.

But then she struggled and broke from his embrace. Her face was pink and her eyes mirrored his ardor.

"What is it? What's wrong?"

"Well...it's just that..." She looked around. "This isn't a good place, is it? How could we anyway?"

"There's the bed," he pointed. "Here...I'll help you."

"No," she protested. Her nose curled with distaste. "It might have bugs or...I don't know. Isn't it dirty?"

"No insects, Karen. The perimeter of the houses is treated with bark resin to keep crawling insects out."

"Really?"

"Look...I'll show you." He circled the hammock and walked to the pallet. He drew back the cover to reveal a multi-colored cotton blanket with a picture of an Aztec warrior in full regalia. He inspected it for insects, then turned and took two blankets from the stump in the corner. As he spread them and straightened the bed, he thought he heard her leave the hammock. "There," he said. "That ought to do it."

He turned to see her clad only in panties, her arms crossed at her chest, trying unsuccessfully to cover her breasts. His heart leaped and he mumbled, "*Eres tan bella* Karen," and sighed with repressed passion. He moved to embrace her, but she quickly leaned over the table and extinguished the lantern. They found each other in the darkness and began a long kiss, then another, and then his hands roamed and explored the curvature of her body. She was smooth and firm, and he felt his own body responding. She reached to grasp him, but he was still clothed. With her help, he, too, was soon naked. He led her to the bed and they entwined as one. They fondled and petted, and he suckled her breasts and stroked the carpeted cloven spot between her legs. Then he was above her, and she took him in hand and guided him home. A barely audible moan escaped her lips as he entered and lay securely within her embrace. He paused to taste her lips, then began to move slowly, coaxing her body to move with his in the ancient rhythm of lovers.

A distant roll of thunder drew near before a lightning bolt crashed into the nearby forest, causing her to jerk. Yet another curtain of rain slammed through the jungle. The outside voices disappeared and sought shelter from the storm. Gone was the sound of gunfire and combat. Only the storm prevailed; a torrential rainfall accompanied by the crackle of lightning. Wisps of ozone-laden air blew through cracks into the hut, but the lovers took no notice. The war and its terrors were temporarily out of mind. Tonight, in the midst of misery and revelry, they would steal their pleasure, for they knew not what tomorrow would bring.

CHAPTER TWENTY

David sipped the last of his black coffee, then rattled the cup against the saucer, trying to center it. The hotel restaurant in which he sat was plain but clean and furnished with cheap bamboo furniture. Ficus trees, broad-leafed dieffenbachia and colorful red-orange croton sat evenly spaced throughout the dining area and lobby. Framed posters and photographs of the Palenque ruins hung from the walls. On verdant hills surrounding the ball court sat the *Observatorio, El Templo de Inscripciones* and numerous other pyramids. The towering Lacandon jungle loomed large in the background, lending a surreal mystical aura to the classic Maya city. It was six o'clock a.m. His breakfast eaten, he sat alone near the west windows, enjoying a spacious view of the town's *zocalo*. Although the hotel was air-conditioned, the humidity already transgressed, promising a miserable day. His shirt clung to his back and the air felt thick to breathe.

A thunderstorm had pummeled the area much of the night.

Marbled gray-black clouds, the remains of Hurricane Julio, floated heavy and thick in the sky, slowly pushing eastward from its Pacific landing. Puddles of water blotted the uneven cobblestone. Even the bright red flowers surrounding the gazebo appeared ragged and drooping from the gusting wind and rain.

The professor yawned uncontrollably. The rolling thunder and sudden, startling cracks of lightning had made it difficult to rest. What little sleep he found was fleeting and unsatisfying. He had lain in bed ruminating on today's planned trip into the Lacandon jungle—and then Luis had arrived from his night out and added snoring to the list of distractions. Feeling very tired, yet unable to sleep, David finally gave it up and rose around five a.m. and waited downstairs to greet the restaurant help as they arrived.

Luis, who decided it was not politic to turn down the colonel's invitation, drank brandy until the *madrugada*, the early morning hours, when the storm's fury lessened enough to allow him to stagger home. Before falling asleep the federale had thrown a wet towel on David's enthusiasm by reporting that the Colonel remained undecided as to whether or not they would leave today. *Chingada!* David cursed silently, annoyed at Herrera's lack of professionalism. It would appear that Pig's Ass was not really as keen on finding Zapatistas as he claimed. This, coupled with the disappointment of not being able to locate Balaam Reyes, and especially Karen's disappearance, had the professor champing at the bit. He was ready to move, to do something, anything. He shifted in his chair, on the verge of standing and pacing, but instead yawned and stretched again.

Finally he ordered another coffee and looked through the window, out toward the *zocalo*, his gaze drifting upward to the Catholic Church with its wide, ornate oak doors. Nearly

194

three hundred years old, it was built on a hill sacred to the Indians. Broad limestone steps rose from the *zocalo* to the church doors and, as he watched, morning mass ended and the portals opened, emptying a stream of worshippers into the town's center. He lifted his cup to drink, then jerked with surprise, nearly spilling it upon seeing the Bone Man exit the church. The shaman was accompanied by six men, all of whom appeared wary and uncomfortable. Standing at the top of the steps, they slowly appraised the town. The Bone Man seemed impatient, as if wanting his companions to leave.

Who were they? What was Balaam doing in church? David had never known him to be particularly devout–just the opposite, actually.

The professor stood to go. His mind overflowed with questions and he must talk to the shaman before he slipped away again. Did the curandero know if they were leaving today? Could an alternative plan be made? How long to the caves that he had promised to show David? At that instant, three Humvees full of soldiers pulled into the *zocalo*. Almost immediately the shaman and his associates (accomplices?) turned 180 degrees and re-entered the church. What's that all about? David wondered. Were they avoiding the soldiers?

He tossed money onto the table and headed for the lobby. As he exited the hotel, he saw that the soldiers placed themselves at regular intervals about the courtyard. One yawned, and all looked bored. Just another day, nothing unusual. David crossed the street, strode to the other side of the park and climbed the thirty steps to the church. He reached for the door handle, but then stopped when he heard voices, one of which sounded like the Bone Man's. The professor looked around, confused, and heard voices again. He walked to his right and peeked around the corner of the church. To his surprise, an elderly priest held a door open and was shooing Balaam and his friends outside. Anxious for them to be gone, the priest waved off their thanks and hurried back inside. While David watched, the Bone Man embraced two of the men, then turned to admonish a callow, pouting Indian youth of about sixteen. The shaman shook his finger and lectured the boy, then paused to watch its effect. The boy grimaced, then gave a wan smile. Balaam embraced him also.

Afraid that Balaam would disappear again, David hurried toward the group. He waved and called out. "Hey...Balaam...sorry to bother you, but I've been wanting to go over this map with you before we get started this morning."

The Bone Man's associates reacted with wary surprise, turning quickly to go, wanting to avoid the professor. The Bone Man turned to David and scowled disapproval. He quickly issued instructions to his companions in an unfamiliar dialect. They traded traditional goodbyes, then split into two groups, one disappearing around the corner of the building, the other shuffling down the hill in back of the church.

More intrigue? David remembered Balaam's quick meeting yesterday with a similar group in San Angelo. Today's circumstances were similar, and thus suspicious. Why did the shaman meet with groups of men who didn't want to be noticed? The professor was tempted to ask, but knew that the shaman would give him grief instead of an answer. Always laconic, and sometimes terse when speaking, the Bone Man revealed little of what went on in his head or his life. David hoped that the shaman wouldn't get distracted from pointing out caves on the trek to Tenosique.

When Balaam turned and walked toward him, David stopped, smiled and reached into his pants pocket to extract the map. The shaman, however, continued past, ignoring him as he would an insect.

"Hey…hey! Balaam!" He hustled to catch up, peeved at the shaman's snub. "What's going on? Did I interrupt something?"

"Busy, *ahua*…must meet *Senora* Cardona after mass." Although he used the respectful form of address, his manner bordered on rudeness. Balaam disappeared around the corner of the church and called out to someone.

Disgusted but determined, David doggedly followed the curandero around the corner, but then stood aside upon finding him smiling and chatting with the senora. How did he switch moods so quickly? Was the shaman bi-polar? Both ignored David. The woman, a middle-aged matron, wore a black skirt and colorful smocked blouse with tassels hanging from the sleeves. Even though the morning was warm, she had a multi-colored *rebozo* (shawl) on her shoulders. A chicken squirmed under her arm and her other hand held a brown plastic bowl. They spoke in one of the Mayan dialects and David, though he understood not a word, believed that she was describing a litany of woes. The Bone Man nodded sagely, showing sympathy for her situation, then gestured toward the church doors. He held them wide, then followed her inside.

"David! Wait up!" called a voice from the *zocalo*. The professor turned to see Luis cross the cobblestones and climb sprightly up the church steps.

Moves pretty good for someone who's been up all night drinking, thought David.

"What's happening, gringo?" Luis' mustache and bushy eyebrows accentuated a broad smile.

"Everything and nothing," snapped David, gesturing toward the doors. "Balaam's being unreasonable this morning."

"Unreasonable!" snorted Luis. "He's a jerk, David. Let's give up this stupid cave 'n map thing and go home? Let the Feds handle it."

"Not me, Luis. Not when I'm this close."

"Close to dying?"

David ignored the jab, tired of Luis' Chicken Little routine. "Stay here. I've got a few things to say to Balaam, then you can tell me about Herrera."

He opened the church door and stepped inside, but Luis shadowed him anyway. They stood at the back of the middle aisle and let their eyes adjust to the dimness. Votive candles cast frolicking shadows on the walls and ceiling. The sweet aroma of copal incense wafted through the church and a large crucified Jesus, his face wrenched in agony, hung above the altar. Saints with unmistakably Mayan features lined the side aisles, each within their own small alcove. Because it was cloudy outside, the stained glass windows seemed dull and lackluster, almost sad.

"There's the shyster," pointed Luis.

David followed Luis' finger to the altar. Nearby, but to the side, Balaam and the *senora* stood in the midst of the saints. While Senora Cardona knelt and prayed before the Virgin of Guadaloupe, the Bone Man lit copal incense.

The professor gestured for Luis to follow, and led the way down the center aisle. Having already endured the shaman's coarse greeting, David motioned for Luis to sit and watch until Balaam appeared more approachable.

Alert and curious, the chicken under the senora's arm had remained amazingly quiet, but now it began to struggle and cluck loudly, suspecting foul play. She gripped the bird tighter with one hand and removed an egg from a pocket at her waistband with the other.

"Oh no…" groaned Luis. "Not again."

"Shhh…" cautioned the professor, watching closely.

While the chicken squawked and wriggled, the Bone Man

held the egg between his thumb and index finger and moved it up and down, all along the outline of the woman's body, chanting as he did so. This task completed, the woman extended a small bowl and the shaman cracked the egg, depositing the yolk in the bowl. Now the chicken screeched louder, its legs pumping and running in place.

"What the hell's he doing?" whispered Luis. "This guy one of the Dark Angel's buddies?"

David responded with an elbow to the ribs and a warning glare.

The matron and the Bone Man discussed the egg yolk's features, Balaam pointing out characteristics that were especially meaningful. Surprised at his prognostication, her jaw dropped and her mouth took an O-shape. She sighed and her shoulders sagged. So be it. The divination had verified her suspicions. *Senora* Cardona handed the squirming chicken to the curandero who promptly grasped the head and wrung its neck.

"Whoa..." said Luis, jerking in his pew. He stared raptly at the shaman. "Can you believe this shit?"

The professor offered no reply, but enjoyed the spectacle immensely. He had once witnessed the Bone Man using the liver of a goat to divine spiritual sickness and, on another occasion, watched him throw stones into a circle scratched in the dirt. When questioned, Balaam had given a nebulous, barely comprehensible answer on relationships; points on lines, shape, texture, color, and direction. If there was a system, it wasn't easily discernible.

The professor glanced at Luis, who stared wide-eyed at the shaman. Following Luis' gaze, David saw that the curandero had produced a knife and was slicing the chicken's throat. Blood trickled into the bowl.

Luis' eyes sought David's and the professor shifted

uncomfortably in his pew. He looked above to the crucifix, acutely aware that he sat in church, then attempted a casual glance about the room to see if anyone watched.

"Uh-oh," said Luis.

A short stocky priest with a Mayan nose, his face flushed with indignation, stepped from the vestibule and strode angrily toward Balaam and the *senora*.

"I'm out of here," said Luis, grabbing his hat and heading for the center aisle. The echo of his boots slapping the tile floor reverberated through the cavernous church as he retreated from the priest's wrath.

David hesitated, intrigued at the divination and reluctant to leave without finishing his conversation with the shaman. The padre spoke the local dialect and began to harangue the offenders. The priest gestured emphatically toward the doors, telling Balaam and the *senora* to take it outside. The *senora*, incensed at the priest's words, replied in kind. An argument ensued, angry, threatening and loud. Balaam stood passively, seemingly surprised at the fuss.

The time for vacillation had passed. Leaving was a moot point. The professor caught the shaman's eyes and gestured with his head toward the church doors. The Bone Man nodded agreement, then turned his attention to the fracas he had instigated. David exited and followed Luis' steps to the front doors.

The professor found him sitting on the church steps, watching bored soldiers make little effort to patrol the area. They stopped no one, talked among themselves and, in general, looked as if they wished to be somewhere else—bed perhaps.

The *zocalo* was a remnant of the Conquest, a period when the Iberian Peninsula's culture was forced upon and assimilated by the Indians in the New World. Every town in

Mexico has a *zocalo*, a central park that serves as a meeting area and focus of social intercourse. In this *zocalo* small groups of citizens conversed and gossiped in the shade, much as they do everywhere in the tropics. While a food vendor served up a breakfast of quesadillas and refried beans from a push cart, three men stood and held plates while eating, talking of last night's storm. A sandal-footed, pre-teen in white cotton pants and dirty T-shirt pushed a cart toward the shade of the gazebo where he would shave ice from a frozen block and make snow cones.

"I'm leaving, David," said Luis. "Herrera got bad news last night and everything's off for today."

"What? Why? What happened? That guy is so..."

"I think they got their ass kicked."

"Who?"

"The army...who else? Herrera went into a rage about two o'clock last night. Someone handed him a note and he started yelling about some guy named Chavez. I think the Zapatistas jumped his men somewhere southeast of here."

David groaned. Now what? Seemed as if everything was against his going into the jungle with Balaam.

"...and I'm out of here," repeated Luis, "with or without you. Tell you something else, too. Herrera has good reason not to like your buddy Satan in there." Luis' thumb jerked toward the church to indicate Balaam. "The reason he wanted him as a guide is that he didn't think the Zapatistas would attack with him along."

"That's crazy." David frowned. "The guy's harmless. He runs around..."

"Look...save it for someone who cares. I don't like him. Herrera doesn't like him. His wives don't like him or they'd have him around more. No...don't protest, professor," warned Luis. "If there's ten men in a room and they all say you're an

201

asshole, you're probably an asshole."

"Ahh…the scientific method. Have lots of success with it?"

"Works for me." Luis ignored the sarcasm. He sighed instead, and a look of resignation settled on his face. Crowsfeet radiated from the edge of his eyes and his broad shoulders slumped, his elbows resting on his knees.

"I'm going anyway," David replied, flatly. "With or without you."

"Somehow that doesn't surprise me." Luis lumbered to his feet and placed his hat on his head. "What about Alexandra?"

"Ali…is…er…tell her I'll call. I need some time to get this thing straightened out. Maybe someone will hear from Karen or something about the plane."

"Give it up, David. Let those who know do their jobs."

"Sure, Luis. Who do you mean? Guys like Joaquin and Herrera? Thanks, but no. I'll throw in with Balaam and the Indians."

"Criminals and traitors," stated Luis.

"Don't, Luis. Don't start, okay?" David's jaw clenched and his pulse quickened. "Look…" he reached into his pocket.

At that moment the church doors flung wide and the priest's tirade shattered the quiet, languid morning. The *senora* breezed by without saying a word. Balaam, appearing amused, ignored the vitriol of the priest and surveyed Palenque's rooftops from where he stood at the top of the steps. While David and Luis observed, the shaman pursed his lips and stroked his chin, as if deciding what to do next. The priest's fury disappeared with the closing of the church doors. The quiet returned, but the tense moment that David and Luis shared seemed more acute in the silence, their acrimony bordering on hostility.

"Balaam," asked David. "How long to the caves?"

"To hear gods sing? Two days…no more."

David extracted car keys from his pants pocket and tossed them to Luis. "Here...no hard feelings. I'll be here in two days."

"What if I don't come?" offered Luis, upping the ante.

David stiffened. "Then send Alexandra."

"What if she doesn't come?"

He looked Luis in the eye. "Then I'll ride the bus."

"This isn't right, professor."

"Tell Karen Dumas that."

"This isn't about her. It's about those books...those caves. You won't admit it, but..."

"Luis," he interrupted. "Are we still friends?"

"Hey, David. You know better than that."

"Then be a friend and go. Tell Ali I'm sorry."

"About what?"

He shrugged. "Don't know. Just tell her, okay?"

Frustrated, the federale hesitated, as if to argue. But then he noticed the Bone Man watching, and Luis transferred his anger to Balaam. But the shaman had an innate knack for averting bad humor and simply ignored Luis. Unable to get a fight out of either man, Luis grasped the car keys and descended the stairs without a word. He crossed the *zocalo* and entered El Hotel Palenque.

"I hear Herrera plans to stay awhile," offered Balaam. "He got a surprise last night, I think." The hint of a smile tugged at his mouth.

"How'd you hear that?" asked David.

"There are no secrets in Mexico, *ahua*...only rumors."

David peered closely at the shaman's face, looking for the truth. "Balaam...are you a zapatista?" he asked bluntly.

"All Indian zapatista or like zapatista, ahua–except damn Protestant. Some have gun. Some no." The curandero hitched his baggy pants and threw the ever present satchel over his

203

shoulder. "I leave sun high. We back cave four-five day you want come anyhow."

"I thought you said it was a two-day trip?"

The Bone Man looked disgusted. "Si, *ahua*. Two there…two back. We go southwest to mountain, then south on Ceiba Trail. Then go east Tenosique." The shaman glanced over the rooftops and into the jungle that framed the vista. "Decide, *ahua*. I have things, must do we leave."

"That's almost to Guatemala. Will you guide me back again?"

"No…I go Tenosique help son cargo important. Festival begin one week."

David simmered with indecision. Fish or cut bait, he thought. Four days was twice as long as two, but what the hell? He'd already messed up everything with his in-laws, his wife and friends and this chance wouldn't present itself again. Balaam was old, as was David, and the contrary shaman might balk when asked next time–if David could even find him again.

"Ah…*ahua*. I hear fly plane crash jungle."

"What?" David stood riveted. "What do you mean?"

"*Gringa* plane you ask Balaam. Crash Lacandon many day…" the shaman held up four fingers. "Four day," he said.

"Four days ago? Why didn't you say something? I could have told…"

"No, *ahua*." The Bone Man frowned. "No tell *policia* friend. He tell Herrera. Who know what pass?"

"What do you mean, Balaam? Why would Herrera's knowing mess up anything?"

"Herrera secret *sicario*, *ahua*. Drug man. Zapatista rob army…take drug…cocaine drug."

This was certainly news, but rather than show his ignorance, David said, "So…" and shrugged. The Mexican

204

army had long been accused of running drugs. Corruption in the military and PRI were the new normal in a successful career in the Mexico of the 80's and 90's.

"*Gringa* survive but take by soldiers. Not good...no, not be good. Chavez bad man. zapatista beat Woman Killer Piedra Blanca."

"Cut to the chase, Balaam. What's that got to do with Karen?"

"Captain Chavez no is found. Is gone and no find forty kilo drug."

"Oh Jeezuz!" David smacked his forehead with his palm.

"She dead woman if Pig's Ass find. She see army beat. Maybe know cocaine...maybe know Chavez be have cocaine him too. He worry...be careful now. Depend who pay for drug."

David's eyes narrowed and he stared hard at the Bone Man. The grizzled Mayan wasn't telling him everything. How did he know so much, anyway? What were his sources? The professor looked at Balaam with new respect. "You really are a zapatista, aren't you, Balaam?"

"Maybe you zapatista, *ahua*. I hear you talk Indian. You know? No worry. You come Balaam, you no must have gun." Balaam Reyes gave the professor his first smile, then turned and descended the stairs, leaving David to brood on their conversation. The shaman turned one last time.

"*Ahua* David know jungle trail behind Jaguar Temple and Temple of Inscriptions?"

"Of course."

"*Ahua* David walk two kilometers *Senor* Medina. Bull pasture at forest. Balaam gather medicine. I meet when the sun top great pyramid." The shaman hesitated, then said, "*Ahua*...I want you know—I give message watch big *gringa*. Maybe she us meet us at caves." The Bone Man took two more

205

steps, then added. "No say goodbye Pig's Ass, ahua. He know we leave soon now."

****

David sat on the only chair in his room. It was uncomfortable and unsteady and felt as though the glue in its joints would give at any moment. Drab, putty colored walls and a low-wattage bulb dangling from the ceiling cast a spell of gloom. His topographic and contour maps lay spread out–one on the unmade bed, the other on a small circular table. The professor knew the importance of orienting oneself before traipsing off into the jungle. Your life depended on it. He studied the maps a dozen times the last several days, but experienced trouble maintaining focus. His mind refused to wrap around the task at hand, centering instead on the many unresolved issues of the last week–Karen, the Gould Stelae, his dispute with Joaquin and, in particular, Alexandra. Now Luis had walked. All this within the context of the zapatista rebellion was very distracting, and now worry and guilt gnawed at him like a rat chewing a baseboard. He knew that he couldn't justify going along with Balaam without clearly defined goals.

Karen was the issue, he reminded himself. Luis' accusation stung and resonated with David. Regardless of his own professional aspirations, he mustn't lose sight of the Karen dilemma. From what Luis gleaned from Colonel Herrera and what Balaam shared with David, a jaunt into the jungle with the Bone Man was ill-advised at best. Karen was traveling with zapatistas who had bested Herrera's troops and stolen his cocaine. Drugs were a terrible danger and a treacherous business, especially when powerful people were involved. Herrera would be forced to act quickly, but as to how, the professor had no clue. Did the colonel know the location of the guerillas and his cocaine?

206

To complicate matters, the shaman intimated that the colonel had spies watching David and Balaam, a scary thought when you considered the stakes–war, zapatistas, cocaine and Karen. Could he pursue his own agenda, yet stay out of harm's way? He suspected that the Bone Man's offer to show him the Cave Where the Gods Sing was not a gesture of goodwill. It was possible that he was bait, or at least a pawn in a game–either Herrera's or the shaman's.

The last few days with the Bone Man had been an eye opener. The shaman was up to his neck in intrigue–zapatista intrigue–something that David would never suspect from prior dealings with him. Would accompanying Balaam be viewed as collusion or conspiracy by Herrera? The shaman had warned David not to reveal their plans because the colonel already suspected them. Of what? Although David desperately wanted to find Karen and the caves, he didn't want to make an enemy of Herrera, as it seemed inevitable that their paths would intersect again.

A quick look at his watch told him that he must decide: accompany Balaam or return home. He must meet the shaman at two o'clock south of the Palenque ruins on a trail near the Medina Rancho. He sighed, looked again at his maps, then out the window into the *zocalo*. The safe, rational choice was to suck it up and follow Luis to San Cristobal, but David didn't think he could live with that decision. Joaquin, Alexandra and Luis would be waiting–all of them smugly self-righteous, all insisting that he admit his error–an unpleasant scenario. And why? For offering assistance to a kidnapped woman whom he enticed to Mexico to share her work with him? He was morally obligated. How could he pretend, like everyone else, that nothing had happened? It was unlikely that Luis' call to the federal police would result in an investigation and would likely come too late if it did. Joaquin or Herrera would kill an inquiry before it started. What's more, the Bone Man said that Karen had survived the crash and would be traveling with the guerillas. Everyone would meet near or at the Cave Where the Gods Sing. Problem solved? A nagging doubt told him that it sounded too easy, too good to be true, but the thought of returning to San Cristobal to lick his wounds and be contrite in front of his gloating brother-in-law was even more unpalatable.

I'm going, he decided. Balaam made it clear that he was traveling to Tenosique to help a son with a ritual obligation. He would not guide David back to Palenque. Karen would be on her own, stranded in the jungle in who knew what circumstances? It was David's responsibility to see that she returned safely. He rerolled the maps and placed them in his overnight satchel, realizing that he was not really prepared for a trip into the Lacandon jungle. He didn't have the basics–tools, clothing or equipment to survive on his own. He would be totally dependent on the curandero for his survival. The shaman was a master at surviving in the forest, but the professor feared that the Bone Man's ability to sustain himself was far beyond his own. His level of commitment to this enterprise would require much more effort. But what the hell, he thought–I'd rather eat roots and berries around a campfire with Balaam than dine in the finest restaurant with Joaquin. This insight clarified the matter immensely. He called a cab and arranged to be picked up in back of the hotel in fifteen minutes.

CHAPTER TWENTY ONE

Two men conversed outside the hut. Karen opened her eyes, but lay still listening. Even though the voices filtered clearly through the walls, she didn't understand their meaning. She concentrated, trying to eavesdrop and learn news of last night's battle, but then realized that they were speaking in one of the Indian dialects.

She yawned and stretched like a cat. Time to rise and dress. Today would be eventful and she was eager to depart for San Cristobal. Marcos had promised to leave as soon as possible— maybe today after the dead were buried, the remaining federal soldiers escorted toward Tenosique and after the villagers had re-crossed the Usumacinta to retake their homes. All this, in addition to supervising a small army, sounded time-consuming and Karen hoped that they didn't delay too long.

The depression where Marcos had lain last night retained whiffs of his manly odor and she recalled his body against hers when they made love. A year had passed since laying with a man–too long, she realized, but then she hadn't really found anyone that attracted her. After breaking up with Lawrence, she immersed herself in work to assuage the pain of divorce and the loneliness of returning to an empty home each night. She frowned at his memory–a philandering, lying asshole. No–a rich, philandering, lying asshole. A reptile cloaked in the skin of a charming, caring patrician. Good riddance, she told herself, then bent to breathe deeply of the impression next to her.

The hut had no windows, but it was clearly daylight outside. In the gray twilight she could see the outline of the table, the hammock and other household items. The rifle Marcos gave her leaned against the wall near the door. She must remember to take it with her when she left for San Cristobal. She hoped never to use it, but had no intention of losing control of her life again.

Karen sat up to consider her next move, and the sour smell of her own body assaulted her. She would give anything for a hot shower–but this was a hut in the jungle, not a hotel room. Already she sensed the rising humidity. She was in the middle of the jungle and last night's thunderstorm would only make things worse. The blankets, the whole house smelled of earthen mildew, smoke, and kerosene. With dismay she remembered that her only clothing was the stinking uniform she had taken from the soldier. She grimaced. Surely she could secure something cleaner and better fitting, perhaps even wash herself at the river. She let the covers fall away and stood, feeling each ache and pain in her body as she did so. Her hands rose lightly touched her scabbed, puffy face. Dark purple bruises, some with scratches and abrasions, blotched her arms and rib cage. For once she was glad to not have a mirror. Too bad she didn't have access to antibiotics to ensure

210

that the scratches didn't become infected. Scarring was a definite possibility. Better to let the swelling subside and the scratches heal before assessing the damage. She stretched again, this time touching her toes, then swiveled her upper body left and right to coax the muscles and joints to cooperate. Though stiff, much of the pain had subsided in the last several days. She felt better than yesterday and a hundred times improved over four days previous. Very few people survived plane wrecks. She was lucky to be alive, scratched face or not.

The dirt floor felt strange on the soles of her bare feet. She took each step carefully, still wary of scorpions and insects. Unable to see clearly, she decided to turn up the lantern. Light filled the room and exposed the home's meager contents. The two backpacks of drugs were missing, as were the lines of cocaine and mirror from the table. She assumed that Marcos had removed them. A rack of shelves lined the north wall. Two lumps suggested piles of cloth or garments. Hopeful that her clothing problem might be resolved, she walked over to inspect them. There, folded neatly and lying beside a pair of sandals, lay clothing. She lifted and inspected them closer. One stack appeared to be a man's cotton pants—the type she had seen on the Indians in San Cristobal. The other contained a black skirt and two beautifully smocked blouses embroidered with colorful Indian motifs. Normally she would have asked permission or offered to buy them, but circumstances were anything but normal. She must have something to wear besides a filthy army uniform.

Both blouses were tight across the chest and reached to just above her navel, but the black cotton skirt fit—or at least it did so around the waist. The hem barely reached below her knees instead of the ankles as it did on the local women. Certainly not Saks Fifth Avenue, or even Walmart, but it beat the stinking, soiled discards she had worn until last night. Karen retrieved her socks and hiking boots and laced them tight. They had served her well and she didn't want to leave them lying around for hungry eyes. She stood and looked down at herself, again glad she didn't have a mirror. She suspected that she looked like a giant caricature to the Indians. The incongruency of her boots and height only added to her feeling of ridiculousness. So what, she shrugged–they would have to do. She must locate Marcos and ask when they were leaving. Maybe she could bathe? She tugged at the bottom hem of the blouse again, took a deep breath, opened the hut door, and stepped outside.

Tall grass, bent from the fury of driving rain and wind, extended to the edge of town. The air felt thick and humid, and gray-black thunderheads floated above, the remnants of last night's torment. The sun had not yet risen above the jungle canopy. Two Indians with black bandanas, the identifying mark of the Zapatistas, jumped to their feet and stared when she stepped from the house.

"*Buenos Dias,*" she greeted them. "*Está* Marcos?" she asked.

They stared with gaping mouths, and then glanced nervously at each other. One of them said something and motioned with his head. The other ran toward town–she hoped to find Marcos. The remaining soldier smiled a greeting, but didn't speak. She tried again, but got no answer. Embarrassed at her attire and feeling awkward at the soldier's silence, she turned and walked toward the village. If nothing else, she would find the house which held her and recover that damn bra to see if it could be mended. The soldier fell in behind and followed. When she stopped and turned, he stopped also, still smiling. She decided that Marcos had assigned her an escort, and that was just fine. She had encountered enough trouble in the last week to last a lifetime. Having an escort with a gun left her position much improved.

Many of Piedra Blanca's residents had already crossed the river from Guatemala and were busy cleaning and taking inventory of broken or missing items. Rifle-toting Zapatistas lounged near the gazebo. They, too, stared. She watched while two rubbed their eyes in disbelief. To them she must have appeared as an alien from the sky, or a goddess striding through their town. *Good Lord*, she thought, I'm only 5' 11". But gape they did, as if they had never seen anything like her in their lives. Some, she knew, had never left the jungle or seen a white woman in person. This was a remote Indian village and many of the inhabitants had never traveled to Palenque, let alone a large colonial town like San Cristobal or Tenosique. Many of them wouldn't speak Spanish—only their native Mayan dialect. This, she realized, was probably why her escort only smiled when she spoke to him.

She passed a charcoaled pit where the federal soldiers had enjoyed a bonfire last night. This served as a reference point and she looked south toward the rim of the village and river's edge where she believed she and the other women were imprisoned. There, she thought. It must be the one with soldiers and Indians milling about. Her curiosity piqued, she turned and walked toward them. But a cold, sinking feeling caused her to hesitate. The palms of her hands were wet and her heart quickened. This was where she was held captive and the place in which she had killed a man; something of which she had thought little since last night. The rapidity and intensity of events had allowed her to shunt it aside, but now the enormity of the deed came home to roost. Not that she regretted it. She was alive and intact, and had not been raped and beaten like the others. Still a tug of remorse accompanied a feeling of guilt, and now she fretted. Was she in trouble? What would happen if the authorities discovered the killing before she left the country? And she had shot a man last night during the battle for the village. Was he dead or alive? Get a grip, she told herself. She took a deep breath and exhaled. Her palms were damp and she rubbed them on her skirt. Maybe she should return to the hut and wait for Marcos like he instructed? When she looked toward the hut, she saw the entire group had turned to look at her. She glanced at her skirt and boots, feeling inelegant and oafish. She considered turning and running, but that would appear fatuous, so she steeled herself, tugged at the hem of the blouse and walked toward them.

What would she say? She couldn't begin with, "Have you seen my bra?" Or, "Hi! I just spent the last four days in here with some women that…you know…were being raped by the soldiers." Finally she settled for a hello, but then Marcos and Rafael stepped from inside the hut.

"*Senora!*" A smile creased his face, but quickly disappeared, and he turned sober and business-like. He stood ramrod straight and officious and turned to introduce her to the others. Her lover was replaced by the *commandante*, and the moment turned clumsy. She greeted everyone, a collection of soldiers, two shoeless children and what she assumed were their parents. The children stared open-mouthed and others mumbled welcomes–all except the soldiers–who blatantly stared. This hut was the couple's home, she discovered, and they began to pepper her with questions. She didn't understand much of what they asked as the spoke in both dialect and Spanish, and she found herself losing ground. She cast a beseeching look to Marcos. She didn't want to recall the last four days and had no idea where the couple's belongings were. She just wanted her bra and information from the *commandante*. She gave Marcos a tight-lipped, wide-eyed look that she hoped demanded his intervention. He finally created a diversion by sending Rafael and the soldiers to check for rafts crossing the river. He promised the Indian couple that they would speak again later, then took her arm and guided her toward the gazebo.

She wanted to speak, but felt tongue-tied. Finally she blurted, "I was looking for my bra," but then realized how stupid it sounded. What an asinine thing to say! Now she felt foolish, and she had just made love to him four hours earlier. She face felt flush and warm. "Er...I mean...I thought I'd try to find some of the clothing I lost...and...maybe get some river water to wash..."

"Yes...yes...of course." He glanced at his men near the gazebo and motioned them aside with a nod of his head. "Here...let's talk. I was planning to see you later, but we can talk now."

He seemed nervous, and Karen thought this curious. Was it because of last night? Was it the soldier she had killed?

"Listen..." she avoided his eyes and looked toward the swirling, rapid Usumacinta river. "When can we leave? I'm anxious to go." When he didn't readily respond, she turned and saw that his hands were in his pockets and that he frowned. He looked away, as if embarrassed.

Oh sweet Mary! she thought. "Something's wrong, isn't it? What is it, Marcos? Why are you acting like this?"

"Karen...I...we have to go somewhere first. You see..."

"Then have someone else take me," she interrupted. She placed her hands on her hips and challenged him. "You promised me, Marcos."

"Look...I got a call and we've been ordered somewhere else temporarily."

"A call?" she repeated, disbelieving. "There aren't any telephones in this place." It was happening again. A damn man taking advantage of her, jerking her around. He had used her!

215

"No, Karen...the radio..."

Her slap sounded like a rifle shot. "Bastard!" A collective gasp followed by titters and guffaws were clearly audible.

Stunned. His eyes registered disbelief and his fists clenched. His face turned dark and sullen and frost tinged his voice.

"*Senora*," he began, clearly enunciating his words, "we have been ordered to reconnoiter near ruins some forty kilometers northwest of here to join with other troops. You will accompany us for your own safety. The federal army is looking for you."

"Yeah, right." She doubled her fists. "I'm leaving." She glared a challenge. "Just try and stop me!"

"Professor Lobo will be there," he added as she huffed away.

Already down the stairs, she stopped and whirled around. "Professor Wolf? Why? What ruins? Why will he be there?"

"Aren't you worried about the army?"

"Marcos!" she hissed. "Quit playing with me."

He held up his hands as if to fend her off. "Caves...something about caves, *senora*. We'll meet in two or three days, then you and Lobo can do as you wish. I have a war to fight." He took his leave, ignoring her as he strode past, then stopped after a few paces and turned and growled, "We leave this afternoon after a...a short funeral service. Be ready and don't get in the way, senora. I'll have one of my men fetch you a bucket of water from the river."

Her anger dissipated as quickly as it flared, and she watched the *commandante's* broad back as he strode away. *Ah...Mary*, she thought. I've done it again. Everything I do turns to poop—and there's always a man around when it happens. But Professor Lobo? Caves? Could it be the cave she sought? The one mentioned in the Gould Stelae? How? Why?

Where? She had a million questions, but had just angered the only person who could answer them. She had struck the commander's face in front of his troops. *Aw Jeez...Damn! Damn! Damn!* she cursed silently. How stupid. She glanced about for a hiding spot, but saw no available abyss in which to cast herself. Maybe she should just go throw herself in the river. She felt that everyone was watching, studying her like an insect. Finally, she circled the gazebo and strolled slowly back toward the hut she had shared with Marcos last night. She wondered if the real owners were back yet. Her mind whirled with questions and her stomach ached, hollow with hunger. She would give anything to be playing bingo with Aunt Rose in Omaha.

****

David watched the cream-colored, rusty '62 Buick that had deposited him at the entrance to the ruins struggle and slip in mud on its way back to the asphalt road. Too many times, riding in a Mexican taxi became an adventure, and this occasion had been no different. It was necessary to place his feet on the back seat floor hump to ensure that his legs didn't fall through the rusted, mostly missing floorboards. The car's seats were wallowed out and stank of dogs, and the driver was gregarious to the point of distraction. Exhaust fumes leaked into the car, forcing David to stick his head outside, a difficult task with both feet on the hump. As the taxi crept away, he noticed a ceramic Chihuahua in the rear windshield. Its head bobbed continually and its red beady eyes lit up each time the driver applied the brakes. But the professor arrived intact, no worse for wear, and now received a momentary reprieve from the heat as a quilted layer of clouds floated overhead and cast dark shadows across the Palenque ruins. His shirt stuck to his back and he wiped sweat from his brow. Even though he would soon be in the shady forest, there was

217

no escaping the humidity–or the mosquitos.

He stood at the entrance to Palenque, a city built and inhabited during the Classic Period of Maya civilization, but abandoned five hundred years before the Conquest. David knew the area well, as he had performed excavations in and around the ruins many times. He quickly looked about and counted at least eight carbine-toting soldiers patrolling the site. Several guides milled about aimlessly, patiently awaiting employment. They sat in the shade, drinking warm cokes, appearing relaxed. Tourists were surprisingly few–a result, no doubt, of the conflict with the guerillas. He must be as unobtrusive as possible, then slip away on the trail behind the Jaguar Temple in order to join up with the Bone Man.

He sauntered forward into the old city, then stopped and made a big deal of looking at the huge, well-preserved Temple of Inscriptions. Pakal, one of the great Jaguar Kings, lay buried beneath the pyramid in a subterranean sarcophagus. After judging that he had lingered long enough, he turned left and lost himself in the ruins of the palatial Observatory that fronted the southern edge of the ball court. It was a massive, but decrepit ruin where astronomic and religious studies had taken place for fifteen hundred years. Splotches of faded red and blue paint still clung to the friezes. Mortared limestone lay broken and strewn about the ground. He moved the portico of the Observatory hall and noticed a famous frieze that an American author had asserted in a book to be proof of extraterrestrial visitors on earth. Must be the hats, thought David, smiling. Mayans had the largest, most intricate and outrageous hats of all pre-Colombian civilizations. In fact, one of David's students had jokingly called the Maya 'The People of The Hats.'

The professor didn't believe he had attracted any attention, and when he judged the time right, he would walk south behind the Jaguar Temple and into the jungle and take the trail west to Medina's bull pasture. With luck no one, especially the soldiers, would notice his departure.

Hoping to appear a curious tourist, he casually inspected the ruined observatory. Moments later he located a secluded place to rest in the shade. Then, judging that no one watched, he took his bag in hand and slipped into the forest behind the temple and briskly walked the two kilometers to the bull pasture.

Tall, old-growth ceiba and mahogany trees reached for the heavens. The sun peeked through only occasionally. Trees and lush tropical foliage contested for every space. Again he wondered at the miracle of so many hues of green and leaf shapes. He heard, rather than saw animals scurrying in the bush. And of course, the relentless mosquitos were ever present. Initially wide and well-worn, the trail narrowed and the sun disappeared. The vegetation grew dense and lush during the rainy season and in some places, encroached and obstructed the path. A tingle of apprehension stirred in his gut. Although the ruins were close by, they lay somewhat remote from civilization. He was alone on the periphery of the jungle, pursuing what he hoped was a clandestine mission of mercy. If he wanted to turn back, now was the time.

The trail grew wider and the bushy greenery more sparse as the path wound north. Ranchers had cleared this area of forest nearly a hundred years ago and as he trod toward the pasture, sunlight leaked through the jungle canopy. The trail connected the forest to the bucolic vista of Medina's spacious ranch. Famed for its fine studs and breeding stock, it was known throughout Mexico and South America for its production of bulls for El Corridor. Medina's bulls were found in the fighting rings of Mexico City, Monterrey, Veracruz or any place that could afford their substantial price tag.

David hoped that he wouldn't have to go looking for Balaam in the pasture, but as yet he couldn't see him. Fighting bulls were high strung and dangerous. He had seen enough bullfights to hold their abilities in respect. Bulls were immensely strong, fast and fearless, and he had no wish to be caught in a pasture with the safety of a fence far away.

Unfortunately the Bone Man was nowhere in sight. The pasture was large, encompassing rolling hills and a stream-eroded arroyo that cut through the northwest corner. A fine, thick carpet of grass extended in every direction, leaving little in the way of plants and herbs. What kind of medicine would the Bone Man find here? Irritated, the professor decided to walk the fence line in hopes of finding the diminutive Indian shaman, perhaps in the shade of that tree grove centered in the pasture some hundred meters distant. He didn't want to trespass–not that Medina would mind–David had known Eduardo Medina twenty years. It was the bulls he didn't wish to incite. It had been many years since he had tried to sprint, and running from a bull would definitely require an all-out effort.

Walking the fence line revealed nothing but livestock, an occasional rodent or birds flying to and from the trees. Unseen dogs barked in the distance. He arrived at the southwest corner post and turned north, when someone called out from behind.

"*Ahua*...good see you me."

The professor whirled around to see the Bone Man tracing his steps along the fence. From where had he come?

"Balaam, where were you hiding? I didn't know you were behind me."

"Me you follow from Palenque." The short, gnarled Indian dropped his satchel at David's feet, then stooped to loosen its drawstring.

"Eh? Been following me? Why?"

"We make sure no stop follow soldiers."

"Who's 'we', Balaam...and why would soldiers stop me?"

"No see soldier, *ahua*? Four, five watch *ahua* David."

David's mouth opened, but he said nothing. He didn't know whether to feel embarrassed or angry. He was observed after all. Why had Balaam given him instructions to come this way rather than warn him off?

"And you too, I suppose," said David. "Did they see you trailing me? What is this, a game?"

The Bone Man ignored the retort and extracted a small canvas pouch from his bag. It looked similar to the kind in which David had kept marbles as a child.

"Be not much time." The shaman looked toward the sky, then into the pasture. "Sun high. Much rain in night. This good. Bulls strong and leave medicine." The old shaman placed his hand on a post and easily vaulted the fence. Whoa! David was surprised at his agility, but then thought, *What the hell is he talking about?*

"Balaam, I don't know if this is a good idea." David saw that two bulls had wandered from the trees and stopped to check them out. "You're kind of old to be running from bulls, aren't you? Why don't you tell me what you want and I'll get it for you?"

"No, *ahua*. Stay no go. Bulls see you worry. When worry, bull worry, but no long. They mad. Wait," he repeated, and ambled off, looking at the ground, paying no attention to the bulls.

Not wanting the shaman to think he was a coward, David, too, jumped the fence—or nearly so. His right boot heel caught and he tripped and landed on his backside, one hand still holding the barbed wire.

"Damn it!" he groused, embarrassed, then slowly picked

221

himself up and brushed the moist black earth from his pants. His back hurt, and so he checked himself for damage, stretched a little and turned to locate Balaam. His guide wandered ahead some thirty meters, paused, and then bent to collect something. Curiosity overcame David's wounded pride, and with one eye on the bulls, he walked to join the Bone Man.

"What are you looking for, Balaam?"

"No talk or bull hear."

This, of course, David viewed as the very same thing that the Bone Man had stopped to inspect–a pile of bullshit. "Yeah...sure...I'll keep it down," he promised.

"What's with the cow patties? What are you looking for?"

"Strong medicine," said the shaman.

Cow manure? Strong medicine? As an anthropologist he'd heard many unconventional stories, some of which he'd later discovered to be accurate. But bullshit? He groaned inwardly. The Bone Man's eccentric behavior and unorthodox beliefs made it difficult to sort fact from fiction.

The old man continued to seek out fresh manure piles, and then David heard him grunt approval and reach to retrieve something.

"What is it?" David asked, looking over the shaman's shoulder.

"Medicine...release soul. Go spirit world."

He saw that Balaa had lifted a mushroom from a manure pile.

"Here...hold *hongo*. I look find more." Balaam handed him the mushroom and sack.

"When stem is purple, put bag." He motioned with his hands.

The professor was too surprised to protest. He realized that the Bone Man was collecting mushrooms that contained psilocybin, a hallucinogenic drug that had long been used by curanderos and shamans for religious and curing rites. He knew psilocybin mushrooms were plentiful in southern Mexico, but he'd never known exactly which one was the "magic mushroom." While Balaam went searching for more, David inspected the fungus closely. It appeared very ordinary. In fact, he saw many that looked much like what he held in his hand. He also knew that there were look-a-likes that were poisonous. How did Balaam discern one from the other?

He had just finished asking himself this when his eye fell upon a mushroom. *Aha!* he thought. "Here's one Balaam," he called and reached to extract it from the ground.

The shaman returned with three more, and handed them to David, who in turn gave the shaman the one he had found.

"Uh uh...*ahua*," the Bone Man shook his head. "Is make spirit sick. Cramp and shit the burning water."

"It's just like yours," protested David. "Look!"

Balaam tossed it aside and walked east toward a fresh pile of manure.

David retrieved the mushroom and compared it to those the shaman had given him. Identical, he decided–no doubt about it. Why wouldn't the shaman admit that David, too, had found a good specimen? He decided to press the issue.

"Here, Balaam...this one's just like yours. What's the difference?" he challenged.

The Bone Man, a mushroom in hand, reached to extract another from a manure pile. He inspected them closely. Satisfied, he handed them to David.

"Come on Reyes," demanded the professor. "Why isn't this a good mushroom?"

"No has wings fly spirit world, *ahua*."

"Eh...?"

"No wings," repeated the shaman. He flapped his arms.

"This," he pointed at the stem, "is must have wings. Here...Balaam show." He motioned for David to follow.

Wings? thought the professor. On the stem? He looked at the one in his hand, then at those Balaam had picked. Their stems were now dark purple, almost black, but otherwise appeared no different.

"Ah...here!" He motioned for David to come. "Look, here two; one of bull, other is of dirt."

Side by side one stood taller than the other. He didn't see...or did he? What was that thing on the stem? The professor stooped for a closer look. There...just below the umbrella head, a very thin black ring, fragile-looking and barely visible, circled the stem. Though it ringed the stalk, it didn't seem to touch anywhere. Amazing! he thought, just like one of the rings of Saturn. He reached and plucked it from the manure and drew it close for inspection. He still couldn't see how it was attached–perfectly round and so thin. He assumed that the ring was connected by tiny, nearly invisible tendrils or fibers. He handed it to the shaman and pulled the other from the ground. Sure enough, it was missing the tiny Saturn-like circle.

"Yeah," he nodded to the Bone Man. "I see the difference."

"Strong medicine." Balaam showed the small harvest in his palm. "Bad mushroom is hurt soul make sick."

And the bloody shits, thought the professor. No, he didn't doubt it, nor did he intend to test the shaman's statement. He knew the Bone Man frequently ingested hallucinogens when divining spirit sickness and doing healings. In fact David remembered at least two occasions when the shaman had baffled and mesmerized the camp laborers with his prognostication skills.

Balaam sacked his mushrooms and started walking toward the fence. He glanced over his shoulder, then said, "Hurry, *ahua*. Come the bulls," and began a quick jog toward safety.

The professor's head jerked upward. "Huh? What did you say, Balaam?"

He saw the old man running for the fence. "Aww shit!" cried David. He, too, leaped and ran for the barbed wire, never bothering to look behind. A cold terror rippled down his spine. Fear propelled his fifty-two-year-old legs to pump as hard as they could, but they felt leaden and wobbly. Though his mind raced, his muscles responded poorly. He imagined that the two bulls gained with each step and that he could hear hooves pounding the earth as two-thousand-pound horned beasts pursued him. With twenty meters to go he passed his guide, but felt that his heart might burst. Finally he arrived, and with his last remaining strength, vaulted the barbed wire and collapsed onto the ground.

Meanwhile, the Bone Man, seeing that the bulls had lost interest, pulled up short, and traipsed unconcernedly toward the fence, recovering his own breath.

"Okay, *ahua* David? When breathe okay, we go. Birds wait. Bird is need help. No be late Balaam and *ahua* David."

The professor lay on the ground gasping for air. Cardiac arrest would commence at any moment. What birds? What the hell was the curandero talking about? He watched incredulously as the shaman approached. No bulls had chased them! Was this Balaam's idea of a joke? If so, David vowed he would kill his guide. He would hang him on the barbed wire for the vultures to peck out his eyes. He would push him down the steps at the Temple of Inscriptions. He would…he would…if he could only breathe.

CHAPTER TWENTY TWO

To add insult to misery, it rained during the funeral ceremony. When the downpour stopped, dark thunderheads remained above that mirrored Karen's mood. Driven by a moist breeze, they cruised steadily east toward Guatemala and the Yucatan peninsula. When the sun did appear for short periods, the humidity became enervating and oppressive.

The ceremony piqued her interest–she was, after all, an anthropologist. Too bad that she hadn't understood much of it. The villagers spoke a Maya dialect. They burned incense and presented food and alcohol as gifts at an altar near the edge of town. The altar appeared to be ancient. Made of limestone, a foot thick, and standing about three feet high, it was broken with large chunks missing. Well-worn hieroglyphics were still visible on its front. Clearly Mayan in design, she estimated its age at a thousand or more years. Its presence intrigued her greatly and suggested that more ruins were likely in the area. It would be wonderful to explore the forest, but time constraints and the war made it impossible.

Marcos had not come around to visit, leaving her in the hut to mope and fret about her situation. After a basin of river water had arrived and she had sponged off the worst of the dirt and stink, there was nothing to do but study the two guards standing outside. She had left the hut door open in hopes of getting a breeze, but to little benefit. It was just plain hot and sticky, and the mosquitos soon found her inside the hut. When Mother Nature called, she sought out the bush near river's edge to relieve herself, always followed by the guards. They showed no interest in her bowel movement, only her safety, but she felt mortified as they stood nearby, occasionally glancing to assess her progress. She couldn't wait to ask Marcos to relieve them of their duty.

Karen had heard much talk while waiting for the funeral to begin. The missing were assumed dead and to have been thrown into the river by the federal soldiers. Only one body was recovered near the river. A zapatista had turned up dead–his throat cut from ear to ear. A federal soldier had killed him for his rifle was the speculation. Even though the army had fled into the jungle without their guns, the unarmed villagers were worried that the soldiers were lurking nearby and might attack when the zapatistas left.

Finally, the service was over and smiles mixed with tears. Neighbors hugged and reassured each other. Karen watched the diminutive Indians as they turned to reclaim their lives. Their crops and village stood intact for now, but much work awaited them. Life, always hard, was sometimes short as well in the Lacandon. But these tough, leathery people had survived when others had not. In the short time she had known them, her respect had grown exponentially.

Aw...well, she thought and glanced at the sky. She estimated that it was around 3 O'clock in the afternoon, probably too late to depart, but leaving this tropical hell-hole remained her number-one priority.

Marcos broke away from a group of guerillas and approached. Her gut clenched with trepidation, remembering his anger. Would he tell her when they were leaving? His face conveyed nothing but perhaps a little sadness. She knew that he was thinking of his sister during the ceremony and wished that she could say something to ease his grief. Unfortunately her one attempt at communication this morning was aborted by her temper tantrum. She would let him lead the dance this time.

"*Senora*..." he began.

"Please call me by my name," she interrupted, forgetting to shut up. "You slept with me last night...or have you forgotten?"

His eyes focused beyond her, then flicked back to meet hers. "No. I haven't forgotten...I..."

"Look...uh... I was a real bitch this morning. It's been tough, you know? I shouldn't have hit you. I...I'm just..."

"Karen...do you always interrupt?"

Her shoulders sagged. "Well...sometimes...I guess...mostly when I'm nervous." She found a stone on the ground to divert her attention.

"Do I make you nervous?" he sounded amused.

"Yeah," she said. "You're so...so..." words failed her. Finally, she blurted "male...I guess."

"Male?" His eyes grew wide and a smile tugged at his mouth.

"No," she corrected herself. "I mean...well, you're a little intimidating."

"Did I intimidate you last night?"

A sudden warmness cloaked her face and she sought out the stone again. "No...I really...er...enjoyed last night. I thought that we hit it off pretty good."

He seemed puzzled. "Hit it off?" His hand formed a fist.

This time she smiled. "Yes," she said. "That's what a couple does when they…er…make love."

"Ahh!" Understanding lit his face. He reached for her arm and coaxed her to accompany him back to the hut near the sugar cane field. They walked slowly, enduring an awkward silence, but neither willing to break the peace. Finally, he asked. "You are ready to go?"

"Oh yes!" she exclaimed, then stopped and bit her lip. "Go where, Marcos? What's going on with Professor Wolf and these caves you're taking me to? How did you know about the cave?"

His shoulders shrugged. "I know nothing of a cave, only what my father told me. He insists that you come along and meet him and Lobo west of here, near the highlands. Lobo is supposed to take it from there." A question formed on his lips.

"So…Karen…maybe you should tell me about this cave. Why is it so important? Why do we have to meet Lobo when there's a war going on?"

Where should she begin? How much should she tell him? The Gould Stelae had disappeared from her mind the last four days. Survival and escape was her total focus, to the extent that the cave and books no longer seemed important–but that was then. Now the matter had been dropped in her lap again. Fate? she wondered, or someone else's design?

"What are you doing in Chiapas, Karen?" He stood with hands on hips, as if challenging her, his head cocked with interest, his eyes boring into hers.

She glanced away. "Got a couple of days?"

"Just the important stuff."

She hesitated, then began. "I used to work at this museum and I discovered this stelae that…"

"Stelae?"

"A big flat rock with writing on it," she explained.

"Ahhh..." he murmured understanding. "And what did the rock tell you?"

What was it about his voice tone? Was he mocking her? She frowned, but continued. "The rock said that I might discover something important in a cave southwest of Palenque. Professor Wolf was going to assist me."

"Professor Lobo has seen this rock?"

"Er...actually...no he hasn't. You see...I was kidnapped by my boss and this creep and..."

"Your boss? At the museum?" A look of disbelief spread across his face.

"Yes!" she cried indignantly. "And forced onto a plane that crashed here."

"Incredible," he said. "And now Lobo has found this cave for you?"

"No...I mean...I don't see how. I never shared my data with him." She considered how unlikely it would be, then asked. "Are you sure this isn't a setup?"

"Setup?"

"A trap. You're not leading us into a trap, are you?"

He pursed his lips and considered the question. "Karen...if father says there's a cave and that Lobo will be there, then it's true. How or why, I don't know." He sucked the side of his cheek. "Is it a trap? Maybe," he added, "but not for us."

"Did I hear you say, 'father.'

"Yes. Balaam Reyes is my father."

"What's he have to do with all this?"

Marcos looked surprised. "Why...everything. Father is in charge."

"In charge? What do you mean?"

He looked aside, faltered momentarily, as if reluctant to

speak. "Can I trust you?"

"Better shoot me now if you don't think so."

He gave her a sour look, then his arm swept wide as if to illustrate a point. "Balaam Reyes organized all this. He's the main link in the rebellion."

"The main link?"

"The jefe, the General."

"He ordered us to meet him? Why? Why not let me find it on my own?"

Marcos shrugged, then sighed. "That will be a mystery for a few more days. Sometimes he doesn't tell me why."

He sounded sincere, even a little annoyed. "What if I say no?" she argued.

They arrived at the hut and he pointed toward the doorway. "After you," he said.

She stopped, gave him a hard look, and then ducked to enter. Once inside, she felt him touch her arm. When she turned, his face was very close, and she found herself eye to eye with him.

She made no effort to resist, and so he kissed her. The first was short, a prelude that promised more. Then he held her close and kissed her with passion. She acquiesced and returned his embrace.

Then he broke away, drew back and looked at her with longing. "We leave in thirty minutes, *querida*. Be ready to go." Then he was gone.

****

A good soldier, thought Marcos as he watched Rafael stride purposely through the mud, dogs, chickens and grass huts toward the river to find the village cacique, the village boss. The old Indian had seen and done much in his life, and now served as the linchpin in this small army. He was respected by the young soldiers and, like them, Rafael was a Tzotzil Indian

231

from the highlands. He had experienced the same degradation, near slavery and poverty of the Indian working for the rich ranch owner. He was landless and could find no work that paid a living wage. Like the others, he had joined the Zapatista Rebellion because the future promised nothing but what the past had wrought. The two had quickly bonded. Marcos, the educated charismatic leader, Rafael, wise in the way of the jungle, a folk sage with good instincts for survival.

The guerillas had gathered their supplies and were grouping at the gazebo. The Humvees remained hidden in the jungle for later, when they would be needed. Most of the weapons and equipment, including the mortars, were loaded onto the backs of the guerillas. The zapatistas had exchanged their own pitiful guns for the newer, more powerful firearms of the federal army. They talked and compared weapons, strutted like roosters, bragged and behaved macho. They placed the rifles to their shoulders and sighted them, eager for the opportunity to shoot a green uniform.

Marcos knew that roads were non-existent where they were going. They must trek through the eastern hills before descending into the lowland jungle, where they would cross several rivers in the middle of the Lacandon jungle. From there they would hike tortuous trails into the foothills of the highlands to meet with Balaam Reyes and Professor Lobo. *And for what*? Marcos asked himself. What was the old fox planning? Not a joyous reunion between old friends and colleagues, of this he felt sure. Although his father had given no reason, he had instructed Marcos to bring the cocaine along instead of destroying it. This in itself was peculiar, as Balaam hated drug merchants. Was it bait? If so, for whom? Or did he intend to sell it and raise money to buy arms? What role did Lobo and Karen play in such a scheme? When would the plan be revealed to Marcos? He shook his head. It didn't make sense. He wished that father would confide and show more trust in him. Marcos believed that he had proven himself a leader and that he belonged in the inner circle. He wanted a voice in the war planning. Father and his secret clan of advisers needed to let the young warriors inside. They grew impatient.

He hefted his rifle and walked toward the gazebo, scattering a pack of dogs fighting over the remains of a child's diaper. Halfway there he spotted Karen approaching from the south, the rifle he gave her hanging by a strap over her shoulder. Tall and leggy, her hair stringy and her blouse straining to confine her bosom, she looked like a cartoon character. The skirt was okay, if too short, but her boots seemed incongruous where most women wore sandals. Maybe she would find something more appropriate along the way, but he didn't know where. She waved, and he waited for her to catch up. As she approached, his eyes sought the curves of her body and he recalled her smell and the feel of her body last night. The memory caused him to ache with desire. Maybe they could steal a few moments tonight? Or perhaps tomorrow in the Valley of Rivers? In two, maybe three days they would meet with Balaam. Marcos was determined to enjoy this remarkable woman's attentions one last time.

"I'm ready," she said. "I don't have anything but this." She tapped the gun. "What are we going to eat on this trip?"

"You are hungry?"

"I'm always hungry lately, but I can wait. I'm anxious to be off."

"It won't be easy, Karen. You can't fall behind," he warned.

"I can hold my own...you'll see," she replied confidently.

"We'll travel about twenty kilometers before making camp–maybe forty tomorrow."

"Sounds like a lot." She looked toward the forest.

233

"It is...and it's dangerous." He knew that she had no knowledge of what awaited her. The jungle was the perfect predator; a graveyard where your remains were recycled by scavengers, insects, and microbes. It would be difficult enough to move his army through it, let alone a woman—and a *gringa* at that.

"So," she insisted. "When do we leave?"

"Right now," he replied, seeing Rafael breast the riverbank. The old guerilla had donned a filthy baseball cap and wore a black kerchief around his arm, the symbol of the zapatista. He approached muttering to himself and, like the other guerillas, carried a machete in addition to a rifle.

"What is it, old friend?"

"They're going to shit themselves after we leave," he growled, disgusted. "They're afraid the federal army will return if we leave."

"I don't think so."

"That's what I told them. We got their guns. Can't stay forever, anyway. I told them this village is just one of hundreds. They got theirs back. The corn and sugar are okay." He spread his arms towards the fields. "Go to work I told them." He shook his head. "Bunch of old women," he groused, then sauntered past to join the dozen or so remaining troops.

Fifteen minutes later they followed a well-worn path west into the jungle. Two machete-wielding soldiers were sent ahead to scout and clear the trail of vines and cane grass. Rafael, Marcos, Karen, and the remaining soldiers walked single file, two of them with the stolen packs of cocaine. The forest was shady and the pace brisk, but the stifling humidity sapped one's strength. Marching west from the river, they entered the hill country. Here the trail became more grueling; every mound, every depression choked with brush. At times visibility was limited to less than ten or twenty meters. Vines, some thicker than ropes, looped through the boughs of trees. Broad-leafed plants, ferns, and palms found purchase in rocky soil. Sunshine intermittently leaked through the leafy canopy, and the steady whoosh and whack of slashing machetes accompanied the grunts of men struggling to widen the path. Nearly all carried extra rifles and packs stuffed with supplies stolen from the federal army. The nice hike was over. The remainder of the day would test everyone's endurance– especially Karen's. The zapatistas, though, had entered their own domain and they moved with confidence and precision. A half-hour later Marcos glanced over his shoulder to see how she fared. She was breathing deeply, but not yet panting, occasionally moving her hair aside, concentrating on the trail. Good, he thought, feeling proud of her. Maybe she wouldn't be a burden after all. He turned and picked up his pace, drawing abreast of Rafael. They were making good time, and Marcos wanted to talk about his father and hear what Rafael thought of their strange mission.

****

Captain Chavez scratched his mosquito bites and grumbled. *Cabrones*, he thought. *Pinche* traitors. He would kill them all. No, he would torture them first–then kill them– especially the *gringa*. He would slice her from stem to stern. It was because of her that Bill arrived in the airplane. It was because of the *gringa* that Chavez drank too much and snorted cocaine while listening to the one-eyed pervert tell of his former life in the tropics. After escaping Bill, Chavez hid in the sugarcane field and watched the rebels depart the village with their new guns and cocaine–both his property. It would have been difficult enough to recover the drug satchels, but now the guerillas were equipped with new fire power–AK-47, hand grenades and mortars. *Chingada!* he had thought, watching them file by until they disappeared from sight down

235

the trail. They had even taken the rope, lanterns and field rations. He'd done more to arm the rebels than all the liberal swine in North America. *Que mal suerte!*

From where the zapatistas had come, he didn't know. It wasn't important–only the cocaine mattered now–and he watched with elation upon spotting two of the sandle-footed soldiers toting the familiar bags. It would be his again–he swore it. If not, he would die trying. Colonel Herrera might excuse the loss of his army and equipment, but not the cocaine. The government's pockets were deep–not so the colonel's. He would take Chavez's failure personally. No one would believe the story about Bill, and the captain couldn't return empty-handed. He didn't know whether to try and capture the *gringa* and somehow blame her for his debacle, or attempt to recover the cocaine himself–both daunting tasks. For now he would think and consider and follow. His belly was full of tortillas and he had recovered a nearly full bottle of cane liquor someone had dropped during the night. His derringer was gone, tossed into the river after he had fired its only two shells. He had his rifle and had recovered a .45 automatic from the body of a young zapatista near the river with a slit throat.

After ten years in the Mexican Army, Chavez's brutality and callused indifference to death when carrying out orders resulted in his selection to attend the best war college in the United States, courtesy of the U.S. government. There he learned much about guerilla warfare and survival. Now he must put his training to use and stalk the Indian vermin one at a time. He would follow the path they hacked from the jungle and give them a taste of their own cowardly tactics. He would be patient, plan carefully, then execute them without mercy. He would hit and run. Never fight a battle he might lose and never confront them directly. He would use surprise and fear.

236

Now he was unencumbered and they were the ones heavily laden with equipment. "What goes around comes around, *cabrones*," he whispered. And as the last soldier filed from view he raised his middle finger in salute. "*Chinga tu madres.*"

CHAPTER TWENTY THREE

The Bone Man set a blistering pace. Seemingly tireless in the enervating heat, he strode steadily forward, his machete a blur of motion, hacking and paring vegetation that impeded their path. David, however, did not fare as well. He walked on trembling legs and his thigh muscles burned. His appeals to slow down fell on deaf ears and he had long since quit asking. The aged Indian ignored him. Instead the shaman walked briskly onward through the lush fern and brambles, up a hill and down, deeper into the jungle, the machete blade whooshing through the air with practiced ease. The air was soaked with humidity and the cloying odor of rotting vegetation wafted from the jungle floor. The ancient forest canopy extended nearly two hundred feet into the sky. The trail wound through dense growths of alocasia, yautia, and mimusops, from which a milky latex sap was taken. Red epiphytes with their bare, exposed spongy roots, an adaptation to gathering moisture and nutrients from the air, found purchase in the boughs of trees. Thick vines wound around tree limbs and hung in loops, blocking progress every few steps. Flowers of every color were in bloom, especially orchids, but after two hours of hills, humidity and biting mosquitoes, David toyed with the idea of turning back. They had traveled only fifteen or twenty kilometers and their destination was probably fifty kilometers further. When and where would they stop for the night? When would the Bone Man take a break?

David berated himself for not being better prepared, then scolded himself for what now, in retrospect, appeared to be a run of bad decisions. Marching stoically behind his guide, he revisited the dispute with his wife and brother-in-law, his arguments with Luis and the disaster that had befallen Karen. With Balaam ignoring him, guilt and recrimination were his only companions. As David struggled to keep up, he engaged in silent but righteous argument. This trip, he rationalized, was his only chance to make things right. He would show them-all the doubters and detractors—and find Karen and bring her back. Her surviving the plane crash was a miracle and a good omen. Just how he would pull this off, he wasn't sure, but as his fatigue and annoyance with the jungle grew, so did his determination.

A troop of Howler monkeys, perhaps eight or ten, had followed—but stayed just out of sight. The professor caught fleeting glimpses and could see limbs and leaves sway and hear foliage rustle. The monkeys screamed raucously and tossed leaves and sticks at the intruders. Their noise distracted him and he thought to hurl something back at them when, suddenly, he heard voices. He stopped abruptly and looked around, finally locating the Bone Man up ahead on top of a hill, barely visible through the brush. The shaman shaded his eyes and peered east, searching the jungle in the direction from which they'd come. He turned and spoke to someone who, it appeared, had arrived from nowhere. Balaam glanced again at the professor, then turned and disappeared down the other side. Who was he talking to? Had they arrived already? Balaam hadn't mentioned meeting anyone. David struggled upward, wading through knee-high grass and bind weed until reaching the same spot on the hill. Looking down, he spotted Balaam sitting alone on a rock outcrop extending into a creek. Woody Passion Flower vines with violent red-orange blooms shaded the bank, and gurgling clear water broke against the rocks before slipping downstream. It appeared positively refreshing. The professor slid and shuffled downhill until he reached the muddy bank, then knelt and gulped water from his cupped hand. The clear liquid carried sediment and topsoil from the rain, but was rejuvenating. He took a deep breath and drank again.

"You okay ladino, *ahua*," praised Balaam. "No think keep up."

"What is this, a race?" grumped David. He slumped backward onto his elbows. "What's the hurry, anyway?"

"Birds must be prepared. Feed birds. Touch them....they must..."

"Who was he, Balaam? The guy you were talking to," demanded David, peeved that he was never consulted. He gave the shaman his best 'I mean business,' look. "You didn't say that we were meeting anyone. Is this more of your zapatista intrigue?" He mashed a mosquito feasting on his ear.

"We rest 1-2 minute, *ahua*. No go ahead fast."

"Eh? Ahead of who? What's going on, Balaam?" David sat up, alarmed.

"You me see black *gallo*, *ahua*." The Bone Man resumed his earlier conversation. "Beautiful bird...strong. Like fight kill."

The professor crushed a mosquito feasting on his hand.

240

"Your what? Your rooster? What the..." David wiped sweat and grime from his forehead. Had he heard correctly? Maybe it was the heat. Why was Balaam concerned about getting too far ahead of a rooster?

The shaman hefted his bag and extracted two shiny pieces of metal. "New spurs sharp. Spurs cut bone." He displayed them proudly.

Rooster? Spurs? What the hell was he talking about? "Balaam...who was the person you..." then the professor got it. The shaman was talking about his fighting cock! "Balaam... we're not going to a cockfight, are we?" David glowered at his guide.

"Two hours, *ahua*. No more." The old man rose and pointed. "Follow creek west is *cascada*, then south. Two kilometers Dolores. Good town, good Indian have fiesta. I have wife. She is cook good. You hungry?"

"Balaam, why do you answer my questions with a question? What are you hiding? What's going on? What's this nonsense about your rooster?"

"Oh...we're going to Council Valley, ahua. Don't worry. You see *The Place Where the Gods Sing*, but tonight we stay Dolores. I me meet people...business, eh?" he winked. "Soldiers come is not good. No want in jungle when come soldier." The shaman rose, brushed his pants, and motioned for the professor to follow.

"Balaam!" David called. "What soldiers? Why would they come after us? Balaam!" But the Bone Man struck a mighty blow and sliced a four-centimeter vine blocking his path. Then he was off, wading through knee-high grass that rimmed the stream's edge before disappearing from view.

"Damn it!" cursed David. "Damn, damn, damn!" he tore a handful of sod and tossed it into the stream. "Wait up, Balaam!" he cried. David stood, groaned with stiffness as he

241

gained his full height, and lurched painfully after his guide. He slipped near the bank, but righted himself and ducked beneath the branches so that he pursued the shaman again. He flexed and gripped his hands, visualizing the old man's neck in his grasp. David would choke him until he got a straight answer. He would drown the little bastard in the stream. He would...he would, if he could only find him.

****

Karen's personal bodyguard, Chonala, a youthful but wary Tzotzil Indian from the Chiapan highlands, knelt beside her and took a swig from his flask. He wore dirty cotton pants, sandals, a T-shirt and carried a rifle nearly as long as he was tall. When he offered a drink, she declined. Having drained her own at the last stop, she was now considering a quick dash into the bush to relieve herself. Unfortunately, he was certain to follow and she didn't feel like playing charades to make herself understood. She wanted to be up front with Marcos instead of dragging up the rear with this zapatista boy who didn't speak Spanish. Occasionally he would say something, then realize that she didn't understand. After exchanging a few sheepish grins, she realized that he, too, was uncomfortable with the arrangement. For now, awkward smiles would have to serve as their only form of communication.

They had followed a well-worn road the first two hours. Karen could still see remnants of tire tracks made by the Humvees and personnel carrier that had arrived to capture the village four days earlier. She had found the jungle dense with foliage and hilly and rocky beyond belief. Eroded limestone ravines with shale outcroppings were becoming more common. Though vegetation abounded, the jungle soil was thin and did not appear suitable for farming. For some reason she had visualized the Lacandon as flat, but nothing

242

could be further from the truth.

The sun shone intermittently through thick thunderheads drifting east toward the Gulf of Campeche and the Yucatan peninsula. After an hour they happened upon a poorly tended, gravel road running perpendicular to the jungle trail. They laid low in the shade and rested nearly twenty minutes while the guerillas scouted to see if anyone watched their progress. Believing it safe, they had crossed and hiked double-time into the thickest maze of trees and brambles she'd ever experienced. Huge spider webs, appearing as silken mosaics on a jade background, blocked the trail–some with large furry spiders waiting to trap a meal. Vines, some as thick as her leg, draped from the broad boughs of thick-trunked trees, and Howler monkeys swung limb to limb, screeching threats at the intruders invading their domain. Piercing parrot cries echoed from above through the sunshade. Her imagination ran amok and she believed that she could hear slithering creatures and see their movement in the tall grass. A cloud of mosquitos hung above their heads, following their every step. The jungle was alert to their trespassing and issued warnings to the animals ahead.

Once they stopped abruptly and stood still upon encountering a foraging jaguar and her three kittens. The cat's head dropped low and menacing. She curled her lip and issued a throaty growl, displaying pearly teeth before turning and vanishing into the shadows of the tall grass, a black-spotted wraith disappearing into a jungle netherworld. The kittens trailed unconcernedly behind.

By the time the troop stopped for another break, Karen had begun to lag behind. She thunked her rifle butt onto the ground, wiped her brow and drank from Chonala's canteen. She estimated that she had already seen nearly ten caves, and on two occasions they had encountered what were obviously ruins; completely unknown, she suspected. One such site was entirely covered with trees and brush and invisible from above or below; perhaps a thousand years old, she estimated. Another opportunity missed, she thought, sighing with melancholy. Maybe someday after the war she could return and retrace her steps, but not now. Then the guerillas were on their feet again, ready to move out. No time for lollygagging.

"Time to go," called out Marcos, coming down from the front of the line. He exhorted everyone to hoist their loads and fall in.

"You okay? Going to make it?" he sidled up to her, a look of concern on his face.

"I'll make it. Just make sure I don't end up as cat food."

"Cat food?"

"A jaguar's meal. You know."

"Ahh…yes…no need to worry." He smiled at what he assumed was a joke, stood awkwardly for a moment–then, unable to think of a reply, returned to the front where Rafael awaited.

Chonala stood at her side, smiling expectantly. She groaned and stood, retrieved her rifle–it seemed to weigh a ton–and fell in behind the others. Minutes into the march she felt as tired as before they had stopped to rest. At this stage, she suspected that she must battle intense fatigue until they arrived. Each step required a conscious effort. Forested rocky mounds lay in every direction, and as they skirted one hill after another, she lost all sense of direction. When the troop stopped again, she collapsed in the shade of a bamboo stand and sat with her head bent in exhaustion. Though strong and athletic, the combined misery of the heat, mosquitos and rough terrain quickly sapped her reserves. Sweat ran in rivulets down her spine, soaking the waist of her borrowed skirt. Mosquitos had feast for hours, and she scratched welts on her legs and arms where they drew blood. She hadn't felt this tired since volleyball practice days.

"Not much farther," encouraged Marcos, sitting heavily beside her. He wiped sweat from his brow and offered a canteen.

She accepted and drank deeply.

"Take all you want. There's more just ahead."

She gulped more, exhaled. "Thanks." She swatted two blood suckers on her leg. "God it's humid...and these damn mosquitos..." she waved her arm at the relentless pests. "I feel like a pin cushion."

"We'll have mosquito netting tonight. I know it's hard, but you've got to keep up. We'll be coming to the lowland swamp soon."

"Swamps? Tell me you're kidding?" a groan escaped her lips. "It'll be worse than here."

"We'll skirt around them and camp in the foothills to the west. It's about three hours more." His hand caressed her shoulder and he hunched forward to place his mouth close to her ear. "I know a place...it has a..." he paused to think..a *cascada*...a..."

"A waterfall?"

"*Si!* A stream that has a small waterfall." His hand softly traced the outline of her spine and back. "We'll camp downstream. If you want to bathe..."

"If I want to bathe? At a waterfall?" She stood, excited at the idea, eager to leave. "I'm ready."

But a voice from behind cried an alarm. Marcos grabbed his gun and sprang to his feet. Two young guerillas sped by and he rushed after them.

"What is it? What's happening?" She stood to follow, but the strong hand of a guerilla shoved her back into the bamboo. She stumbled, then whirled around to complain, but someone

245

grabbed her from behind and placed a hand over her mouth. She struggled until the soldier that pushed her raised a finger to his mouth to silence her. As she watched, he knelt low with his rifle and crept out onto the trail, looked about, then called out instructions to the others.

Karen waited, barely breathing, seeing quick darting shadows in the rustling cane grass. Muffled voices carried back down the trail, and then Marcos called out an order. Moments later Rafael and a group of four guerillas jogged by, toting the body of a soldier. They placed him beside a tree and she exited the cane to look. His neck was twisted at an impossible angle. She stared, mesmerized, sickened at the sight, then gasped, realizing that it was Chonala, the soldier assigned to protect her. He had wandered off when Marcos had appeared and sat next to her. No one had noticed his absence. She stole another look, felt her gorge rising, and turned and vomited. The light touch of Marcos' hand stroked her back.

"You okay?"

"Yeah…sure," she lied. "I see stuff like this all the time back home."

"You do?"

"No, Marcos…aw…sweet Mary." She bent and retched again. "He was so young," she gasped.

"We must go," he insisted. Rafael stood at his elbow watching her with jaundiced eyes

"I'm sick!"

"Karen…"

"Just give me a minute, okay?"

Marcos growled an order and two soldiers retrieved Chonala's gear. A makeshift travois was constructed and the dead boy placed upon it. Two guerillas were each assigned a pole. They would drag the body until a safe place was found to bury him. Marcos and Rafael sent several men into the forest to locate his killer, but they returned empty-handed fifteen minutes later. The Zapatistas, many of them boys themselves, huddled in groups and spoke in subdued voices. Meanwhile, Marcos and Rafael had stepped aside and were arguing. She could see their faces and urgent gestures. Finally, an agreement reached, Rafael tramped toward the waiting soldiers and issued orders.

Marcos joined Karen. "We're being followed."

"By who?"

He shrugged, but looked worried. "Maybe the feds gave us a tail back by the road."

"But you don't think so?" She chewed her lower lip.

A twisted smile gave her his answer. He gripped his rifle and looked toward his men, then at the dead soldier strapped to the travois. "Federal soldiers rarely come into the jungle," he offered. "Even then they don't stray far from the roads. But this is…different." He pursed his lips, as if thinking. "Could be several people. Maybe just one…but I doubt it. He would have to be incredibly brave…or stupid. We'll know soon." He glanced again at the travois, then at the path, "I want you up front this time."

She followed his gaze to the soldier. "I'll keep up…I promise."

"If you see or hear anything unusual…anything at all–say something." He rose to join Rafael.

"Marcos?"

"Si, Karen?"

"I'm scared," she admitted.

"Good…it'll keep you alive."

CHAPTER TWENTY FOUR

Well-named town, thought the professor. *Dolores*, meaning pain, described his own physical condition as well as his impression of the jungle hamlet-a big pain. The town was a Lacandon Indian village of grass huts framed with tree limbs, topped with palm-leaf-thatched roofs–each with a narrow roof-like overhang that extended from the entry, supported by two poles. Every house appeared similar in structure, though some were larger than others. Unlike most towns in Mexico, Dolores had no zocalo. The huts were placed haphazardly along two streets, both of which were muddy and stinking with refuse. The village boasted the usual population of chickens, scrawny dogs, and the occasional wandering, rooting, snorting pig. Electricity and plumbing were unknown, but a clear-running mountain stream lay forty meters downhill. Carved from the jungle, small garden plots and terraced corn fields rimmed the foothills above the village.

Considered primitive and ignorant by the other Maya of Guatemala and Mexico, the Lacandon lived in the remotest areas of the jungle. They eschewed civilization in general and few, if any, spoke Spanish. But they were friendly and their excitement evident when the Bone Man and David arrived. Visitors were not a commonplace occurrence.

Gowned in what appeared to be white, one-piece cotton sacks with head and arm holes, the lacandon had yet to adopt western dress. Most wore homemade sandals, and a few were barefoot. Their personal ornamentation consisted of river clam fetish necklaces, bits of hair, rock, or animal bone. Their black, thick hair hung long and stringy in the old manner and their short stature and impressive bent noses identified them as unmistakably Mayan.

Balaam Reyes was greeted by all, including a dignified middle-aged woman who stood close by while he engaged in conversations. Was this the wife of whom he had spoken? After an exhausting trek through the jungle, David found the cheers and laughter of the children heartening. They crowded around, wide-eyed and deferential, while Balaam told a story. When the old man opened his bag and gave them hard candy, the tumult began anew. The smiling elders watched their antics with benign amusement. Some eyed the candy with envy.

The professor gratefully accepted a gourd of water and promptly downed it. The sun had long since faded into a burnt orange haze behind the western hills, and the entire area lay cloaked in the shade of a thousand trees. The earlier, threatening storm clouds had drifted eastward looking for a more suitable target. The oppressive humidity remained, as did the mosquitos, but the heat had relented somewhat. Their journey from Palenque, he realized, had been a gradual but steady incline into the foothills. Hopefully the higher altitude and the night would bring relief from the heat.

Not all the villagers were lacandon. The mystery of Balaam's secret day visitors was solved. Four gun-toting zapatistas had awaited their arrival. That they were expecting Balaam and the professor was now obvious. By now David surmised that the Bone Man was connected to a cadre of couriers who constantly came and went with information. The old man continued to amaze him. Never would David suspect his old camp laborer of having the charisma and political savvy to aid and abet a revolution. That he had done so was a measure of how desperate the economic plight of the Indians was. The wily shaman traveled widely his whole life and was as well-known as any Indian could be. Curanderos and shamans were more respected than local caciques and majordomos, the village political bosses. His divination and curing abilities had reached legendary status and the Bone Man was highly sought after to deal with cases of soul sickness, which were believed to be the primary cause of illness among the Maya.

The hike into the wilds had given David time to ruminate on his own situation. He alternated between cursing and reviling the shaman and minimizing his own involvement by making excuses for coming. His motives were strictly altruistic, he assured himself. He wanted only to assist in the kidnapped archeologist's return to safety. La Cueva de Vidrio (The Glass Cave) and the promise of an archaeological discovery were secondary—or so he told himself. But he had not lived so long or prospered at the National University by deluding himself. After a punishing six-hour trek through jungle, most in silent denial, he arrived at what he thought was an accurate assessment of the situation—he was up to his neck in shit, no doubt about it.

Balaam had admitted that he was a zapatista, that the

250

federal government suspected him, and that they monitored his movements. Worse, the shaman also admitted to robbing their drug couriers. For three days David had watched a steady string of skulking, suspicious-looking men come and go after surreptitious meetings with the Bone Man. These informants appeared every two or three hours with news and carried instructions when they left, and now the shaman had let slip that the army followed them. Why? What Balaam was orchestrating, David didn't know, but his anxiety rose with each incident. People on both sides were on the move but, unfortunately, the professor didn't know the stakes because the Bone Man refused to confide in him. As dicey as this made things, David had committed to coming–there was no backing out now. The trick would be to get Karen and slip away before being trapped in something neither could handle–if it wasn't already too late.

The shaman disappeared, leaving David in the care of two short, scraggly haired women who understood not a word of Spanish. He considered following Balaam to insist on being included in whatever the shaman did, but knew that he would be rebuffed. The women led him to one of the larger huts where an adolescent girl knelt on the ground with a hand stone, grinding corn on a *metate* to make tortillas. In different circumstances the professor would have found the bucolic setting and its inhabitants interesting, but now he sat outside in the hut's shade and stewed in his own misgivings. The women giggled and, he assumed, gossiped about the new men in town. He could use a stiff drink of brandy.

Thirty minutes later the aroma of beans and tortillas tickled his nose. Damn, he was hungry! Up and down the muddy, littered road women feverishly made preparation for tonight's festival. A few of the more prosperous homes had mud brick ovens in their yards, but most cooking was done on barrel lids that hung suspended over open pit fires. The aroma of cooking food made his mouth water, and he thought to venture near in hopes of being offered a few freshly cooked tortillas, but then the Bone Man reappeared. He still carried his bag slung over a shoulder and two men the professor hadn't seen before walked at either side. Balaam extracted several small satchels and handed them to the women. After discussing what was to be done with the contents, the women laughed, one pretended to swat him, and the shaman dodged, feigning hurt. The men stayed behind and Balaam joined the professor near the road.

"Nice village," said Balaam.

David searched the old man's face to see if he was serious. The town of Dolores had absolutely no redeeming features as far as he could tell.

"Yes..." the professor agreed, reluctantly, trying to think of something nice to say.

"Tonight fiesta, *ahua*. Much *ponche*, chicken soup, and beans...festival, eh!"

David couldn't remember seeing the old man so excited.

"Then *gallos* fight!" His chest swelled at the thought. "Come, *ahua*," he motioned, "I me show best bird Chiapas."

"Balaam...what about tomorrow? Have you heard anything about the American woman?"

"My bird legs like goose, claws like eagle."

"Balaam...are we really being followed by the army?"

The shaman stopped, placed his hands on hips and faced the professor. The wrinkles on his face turned down into a frown. "*Ahua*...*manana* talk *gringa*. Tonight fiesta."

"But Balaam..."

The Bone Man held up his hand. "Manana...*ahua*. I promise. *Gringa* is come. Balaam know. I'll hear them me tonight and tell you...eh? Tonight fiesta...tomorrow maybe fight." He turned to go, uncaring whether or not David followed.

"*Padre* my *gallo* father win thirty-four fight in town *Realidad*. He retired. Have *gallinas* make busy."

The professor sighed and frowned, but decided that the Bone Man was serious about letting him in on things, so he went along for now. "What do you mean?" He tried to appear interested. "How many fights has your bird won?"

"My *gallo*? None, *ahua*...no yet, but is strong mean bird. He them cut them in pieces. He black...have red on chest...sign of a fighter," he boasted. "He have white stockings...oh...he macho, this bird."

And so went the talk, the normally loquacious shaman speaking effusively of his wonderful, but untried rooster. Balaam led them to a large hut on town's edge. A surly-looking youth whom David believed he recognized stood waiting for them. The shaman called out and a reticent, middle-aged woman exited the hut. David recalled seeing her when he first arrived. To his surprise, his diminutive guide took her hand and spoke in a low tone, showing genuine affection. She seemed happy to see Balaam, yet embarrassed to be in the presence of the professor. David nodded and greeted her, but her head remained bowed and her eyes downcast. She looked away.

"Look...a*hua*...me machos." Balaam pointed and circled the hut to the backside where six cages of birds sat.

The boy, whom David now remembered as the youth Balaam had chastised at the church in Palenque, was extracting a rooster from its pen. The Bone Man tucked the nervous bird under his arm and stroked and talked to it. It's name, David discovered, was Zapata. Very fitting, he thought. He knew little about chickens, and even less about cock fights. He decided that the rooster did indeed seem to be a good specimen, but would look even better on a plate garnished with boiled potatoes and black beans. David, however, didn't tell this to his guide. Remembering the shaman's earlier comments about the bird, he repeated them back as his own observations, so as not to appear ignorant.

"Si ... good eye, *ahua*. These..." he sneered and pointed at the cages, "fight like *gallinas*. Shit in ring and run. I maybe eat, but is cost much. Is hard find macho fight to death. Luck change with Zapata. Hold you peso, *ahua* bet this *gallo*." He petted the rooster and muttered endearments before handing it over to the boy with instructions for its care and preparation for tonight's fights.

Leaving the youth to tend to the birds, they returned to the front of the hut. Balaam's wife approached holding two plastic glasses and a corked bottle of what David assumed was liquor. Two centimeters of peanuts and sugar lay at the bottle's bottom.

"*Ponche, ahua*?" The diminutive Indian proffered the bottle.

"Er...maybe just a small one. You know...on an empty stomach and everything."

The shaman filled the glasses to the brim and handed one to the professor. "Zapata!" toasted the Bone Man, raising his glass.

"To Zapata," agreed David, halfheartedly, worried that he might never swallow again after drinking the moonshine. He tried not to imagine what ingredients might be added to the sugar cane for flavor. He really hoped it was wood alcohol, which would make him really sick. Sure enough, one swallow caused him to gag and cough. Alcohol fumes seared his nasal passages. "Jeeezus!" he wheezed.

"*Que bueno*, eh?" said the shaman, who took another drink. "My wife...she make best *ponche*." He threw her a smile. "Is beautiful...eh, *ahua*?"

"Whaaat? Oh...yeah...of course. Good looker, Balaam. You're a lucky guy," agreed the professor. He attempted another sip of the paint thinner.

"You stay house with women...okay? They sisters. They give food you. There be hammock sleep you." The shaman raised his glass, then paused and caught David's eye. "The sisters..." he gestured with his glass, "one husband kill by the federal soldiers, the other...he is gone. Maybe dead. Lonely sisters." He winked.

David choked and spewed his drink on the ground. The rocket fuel scorched his windpipe and he couldn't breathe. "Balaam...listen..." he tried to catch his breath. "I'll stay outside or something. I'm...er...married. You know that."

"It's rain tonight, *ahua*. Sun leave, mosquito come. You wife no want *ahua* David. Stay close fire and women...eh? I bring you tomorrow meet." He turned and watched his wife enter the hut, then turned to the professor. "My wife want talk. Time of go, *ahua*. *Mas tarde*." He turned and followed his spouse inside, leaving David alone with a nearly full glass.

No manners at all, thought David, tossing the contents of the glass onto the ground and setting it on a table framed from tree limbs. A quick glance revealed a darkening sky. The sun fled behind forested hills and the air felt even more humid than when he arrived. The jungle loomed menacing and sinister and he could barely see the outline of individual trees or limbs. It would soon be impenetrable without a light. He had no desire to sleep in the rain, especially in the jungle, yet was loathe to return to the sisters' hut. What a dilemma. Balaam Reyes was such an asshole.

His stomach growled and burned from the two swallows of *ponche*. He glanced at the shaman's grass hut, frowned, then turned and slowly retraced his steps. His legs were bone-tired and he reeked of body odor and dried sweat. He itched all

255

over from mosquito bites. His stomach rumbled and he realized that he was ravenous. He was supposed to eat with the sisters, but what would he say to them? They didn't even speak Spanish–just giggled. His thoughts returned to the comfortable ranch at San Cristobal and his wife and friends. Less than a week ago he'd been enjoying a vacation, great food, friendship and the company of loved ones. Less than a week ago he'd slept in a comfortable bed with his beautiful wife. Oh how he missed Alexandra! Now he was in the Lacandon jungle with an eccentric, rude, Zapatista shaman. The federal army was hot on their trail, or so said Balaam, and tomorrow they would supposedly rendezvous with other Zapatista troops. What was happening? How had things gone so wrong? Bile, burning and tasting of cane liquor, rose in his throat. He belched painfully and thought again of the sisters. It certainly wasn't their fault. The reason for his predicament was simple, really. Bad decisions, one after another, he decided. He was hanging out with bad company. Maybe he should've listened to Luis.

CHAPTER TWENTY FIVE

The evening thunderstorm blew east, leaving a beautiful red-orange corona with wispy magenta wings hovering above the forested mountain range. It glazed the sky with a ceramic sheen, but faded as it slid behind the sierras into the Mayan underworld. Luis stood on the consul's verandah looking west into the terraced foothills. His stillness and lack of facial expression belied his inner turmoil. He stared unseeing, his mind focused on his friend's disappearance into the jungle in search of the missing archaeologist. Despite the professor's protests, the federale believed that David's primary motivation lay in his hope of finding that cave and those infernal Indian books.

The two of them had shared much over the years, and an unlikely but enduring relationship had developed–Luis, the uneducated but streetwise policeman/federale and David, the university professor. But events of the last few days, especially yesterday, had sorely tested their bond. His friend's obstinacy and apparent lack of common sense remained baffling and out of character. Irritated and more than a little angry, Luis was tempted to return to Chihuahua with his wife rather than pursue the issue. However, upon relating events to Alexandra and seeing her expressions of disbelief and concern, he knew that he would stay and see this thing through.

Thus far, he felt stymied. Where to begin? Who to involve? Where would they find allies? What were the right questions? In order to know the seriousness of David's situation, Luis must know the players and their motivations. Alexandra, always practical, had put aside their marital spat, her jealousy of the beautiful *gringa* archaeologist, and dropped all pretense of supporting Joaquin over her husband. She joined with Luis in urging her brother to use his connections to investigate Colonel Herrera's story and insisted that he call Interpol for information on the two Americans, Dr. Depp and his henchman. She also wanted him to follow up with a call to the embassy people in Mexico City. Despite Joaquin's claims of inadequacy and no authority, Luis and Alexandra extracted a promise of help. But five hours passed with no news, and Luis was drawn tighter than a piano string. He believed that the consul deliberately dragged his feet, which in itself was a mystery. Considering the stakes, Joaquin's reluctance seemed almost callus. With the passing of each hour a sense of hopelessness gnawed at Luis. Was the situation growing worse and uncontrollable, maybe beyond resolution? How could they proceed if Joaquin didn't provide them with information? Rescuing a man from the jungle who didn't want to be saved in the middle of a war was daunting, maybe even stupid, and now that Luis thought about it, probably pointless.

Luis now realized that the temptation had been too great when the shaman showed David the location of Council

Valley on the map. And what of the female archaeologist missing since last week? Luis didn't believe for a second Joaquin's insinuations that David was crazy for her. That was bullshit and very unkind of the Consul to say in the presence of his sister. No, even though David felt responsible for Karen's plight, it was the books that drove him mad. Anyway, that devil Indian–that Bone Man character–claimed that she was okay. The possibility of finding her, the caves, and maybe even the books had overwhelmed the professor's good sense. It allowed him to assuage his conscience while enticing him with the possibility of a big discovery. Now instead of one, two innocent people had fallen into a Zapatista maelstrom and an out-of-control Mexican army. What hope did Karen and David have of surviving the greed and violence, the politics and ancient feuds of Mexico? Even more perplexing, what would they do if Joaquin's efforts produced nothing? A plan was built on knowledge, not happenstance and guess work. If they began badly, it would waste time and accomplish nothing, which was exactly what he was doing right now–nothing.

At that moment, the slap of Alexandra's sandaled footsteps drew his attention. The screen door opened and she stepped outside. Luis, roused from his introspection, turned and searched her face for a sign as she approached.

Her hair, cut short and fashionable, still shone a lustrous black at fifty. Her facial bones recalled Spanish ancestry and she wore a flowered print dress with a thin white belt. The knuckles of her right hand shone translucent as she firmly gripped a handkerchief, betraying her inner dread. Her eyes were red and worry lines creased her forehead.

"Luis...Joaquin has some news. I....I think it's worse than we thought. He says..."

"Where...where is he?" huffed Joaquin. The screen flew

open and the Honorary Consul stepped onto the verandah. "Ah...here we are." He walked to the cedar plank table and motioned for all to take a chair.

Luis dropped his big frame onto the lattice mesh of a seat and leaned forward expectantly, his eyes on Joaquin. "So..." he began, anxious to know. "How bad is it?"

The consul, every hair in place, still wearing dress clothes, including tie and jacket, picked at table crumbs and frowned, reluctant to begin. He bent and made a big production of straightening his pant leg, then reseated himself.

"It's the drugs...tell him Joaquin," blurted Alexandra. "He's being chased by criminals in the army...bad people who kill and..."

"Drugs? Who's involved with drugs?" asked Luis. He looked first at Ali, then at Joaquin.

"Ali...maybe it isn't as bad as all that." The consul glowered disapproval and placed a consoling hand on her arm.

She jerked away. "Tell him!" she demanded.

"Come on, you two," admonished Luis. To the consul, he said, "Shoot...give me both barrels. I can take it."

Joaquin, one eye on his sister, sighed and began. "Er...the situation could possibly be described as quite grim, Inspector Alvarado. Your friend," he said, putting as much distance as possible between himself and his brother-in-law, "involved himself with traitors and perditious interests. By aligning himself with anti-government rabble, he..."

"*Calma...calma, hombre.*" Luis held up his hands. "This is me, Joaquin." Luis pointed to himself. "I'm not a PRI flunky. Cut the crap and talk to me here. What about this Herrera? Is he the one dealing drugs, or is it that damned Indian?"

Alexandra and Luis captured Joaquin's gaze, daring him to lie. He shifted uncomfortably, scowled and shot Luis a sour look.

260

"Yes...well...according to my sources in Guadalajara, there is...er...talk that Herrera might be involved with one of the southern cartels..."

"The Medellin," interrupted Alexandra.

Wham! The consul slammed his hand to the table. "We don't know that!" he roared.

"Save it for the conference room, Joaquin," replied Luis, unfazed by the theatrics. "So...Herrera runs dope. Should I bother to ask why he hasn't been arrested or relieved of his position?"

Joaquin raised a hand and inspected his cuticles. "Since it is so rare and inexplicable for a person of such high standing in the military to engage in such an egregious offense, there is speculation as to whether or not others might not be...er...involved also."

Luis, used to plain words and straight talk, seemed perplexed, but then his face lit up. "Oh...you mean that his military buddies are suspected of running dope, too." The federale shrugged, unsurprised. "Hell...anyone with a lick of sense knows that the army runs drugs and that government officials take bribes to turn their heads the other way. But what about this Captain Chavez and the story that his army was routed two days ago on the Guatemala border? Any truth to that and the story about the American girl?"

"Officially? That is another zapatista lie," snapped Joaquin.

"But in fact, they got their asses kicked?" insisted Luis.

The consul sighed again and nodded, resigned to conversing with a barbarian. "It would appear so. Actually, we have little information on the matter. Chavez is missing, presumed dead, and his soldiers are straggling in. His men report seeing the woman in the village. Actually, the matter is quite...er...sensitive." Joaquin fiddled with his pant leg again and inspected the shine of his shoes.

261

"Yeah...I bet," added Luis, knowing that it would be kept secret from the public, and if it couldn't, PRI spin wizards would tout it as an example of zapatista treachery. He leaned back, never taking his eyes from Joaquin. The consul refused to meet his stare.

"What about that Bone Man character?" continued Luis. "He up to his neck in shit like I thought?"

Joaquin winced and Alexandra frowned.

"Sorry," Luis apologized for his lapse. "Is he dirty or what?"

Joaquin didn't hesitate this time. "Balaam Reyes is a well-known zapatista sympathizer, a Quiche Indian from Guatemala who left that country many years ago. Yes, he's involved...we just don't know how."

"What about these *gringos*...the ones that landed on your strip...Depp and Bill. Interpol have anything?"

"Depp is an archaeologist and an administrator at a museum in Washington D.C. He's...er...kind of a mystery man. Seems as though he did some field work in Chiapas and Guatemala."

"Tell him the rest, Joaquin." Resignation tinged Ali's voice.

"Tell me what?" Luis looked first at Alexandra, then to the consul.

"CIA...or used to be." Joaquin spoke as if he had a bad taste in his mouth. "Mainstreamed in the mid 70's. Retired spook...semi-respectable guy. Been at the museum ten years, but he's missing from his job. He took a week's leave of absence, but never returned."

"Bill?"

"The same. CIA scum. Real name is Guillermo Santiago. Salvadoran mother. His father's dead, but was attached to numerous embassies in Latin America. Probably CIA, also. Guillermo was assigned as an anti-guerilla operative in Guatemala in the late 60's. Murderous bastard...nasty reputation...big gaps in his record, though. Next appearance was 1982, burning highland coca farms in Colombia for the U.S. Drug Enforcement Agency. He's an international outlaw wanted by a half-dozen countries, but has the protection of the United States as long as he stays inside their borders."

"And now he's loose in Mexico." Luis' big shoulders shifted and his eyes sought out the expensive interlocking patio bricks beneath his boots. A malignant silence engulfed the trio as each assessed the news within their own context. A sense of helplessness, of near sadness, reigned.

Suddenly Luis' head shot up and he snapped his fingers. An epiphany had presented itself. "Joaquin...I read somewhere about a joint American-Mexican drug thing...a task force or something. You know...they supply helicopters, guns and cowboys and we supply intelligence, maps, guides, that sort of thing."

"I read about it too," added Alexandra, "but how can that help us?"

"No!" said the Honorary Consul, slapping his hand on the table. "Don't even think about it." He stood, seemingly agitated. "That group...er...that agreement is highly political...very sensitive...a problem, you know. It's not very popular among..."

"The drug dealers in the army, Joaquin?" interrupted Alexandra. "The Sonoran Drug Cartel?" She shrugged her shoulders. "What else is there to do? You have to listen...have to help Joaquin!" Her mouth was a tight line and she squeezed the handkerchief even tighter. Her voice conveyed naked desperation.

Luis decided to let them argue it out. Even though he was involved as a friend, this was a family squabble. If she started to falter he would join ranks and help advocate.

"Alexandra...dear...you just don't understand," soothed the

consul.

"Don't patronize me, Joaquin!" She stood like a she-lion and glared at her brother. "What will it take? Calling in a few favors? Asking a favor? Worried about your career, brother? Afraid? What is it? Tell us! Why are you so reluctant to help?"

"Alexandra, we have guests! Calm down. You have no idea what's required...no knowledge of government...no..."

"Oh..." Alexandra's eyes grew wide and her mouth took the shape of an 'O'. Joaquin...you're not involved, are you? The drugs...I mean...you're not part of..."

"Outrageous!" shouted the consul, coming out of his chair. He stomped his foot. "Have you taken leave of your senses?" A black cholera had seized him. "Of course I'm not involved! Be careful, sister," he warned, waggling a finger.

Luis looked at Alexandra with new respect. *Caramba*! That had provoked a reaction. But was it guilt or genuine outrage?

"Prove it, Joaquin." Luis stood also, towering above the suited dandy. "I showed you about where that Council Valley Place is supposed to be. Help us...help save your brother-in-law and the American archaeologist. You could be a hero, you know? The word's out. I called the American Embassy and Federal *Policia*, remember? Somebody somewhere is starting to make inquiries."

"You're lying," challenged Joaquin.

"David and I called from Palenque two days ago while you and the ladies were in Tuxtla Gutiérrez. The investigation's already starting," he bluffed, not knowing if it had. He held the consul's stare. "It's better to be a pitcher than a catcher, Joaquin, and something's goin' down. Too many players...too much money...egos. There's a damn war going on! You can't cover it up anymore. It's more than just a kidnapping at your hotel. You want to direct and control this thing, or get caught in a shit storm with someone else calling the shots? What would being a suspect rather than the investigator do to your career?"

Luis watched while his words took effect. The consul's anger cooled and he appeared hesitant and unnerved, calculating his position and vulnerability. He pursed his mouth as if to whistle, started to speak, then stopped and bit his bottom lip.

"I...I just don't know. I could...maybe get some information...contact Guadalajara and see if they have any knowledge of these events."

"And if they don't—inform them yourself, right? That way it would look good," encouraged Luis.

The consul reluctantly nodded his head, still not sure how far he wished to go.

"And...maybe you could call someone you know in Tuxtla Gutierrez who would leak the story to the Americans," suggested Alexandra.

"Yeah..." agreed Luis, "and you could tell them that we know where it's all going to happen. I've seen David's maps." In truth, Luis wished he'd spent more time looking at them, but he did believe he could point out the general area that the professor had studied. Besides, if Herrera and his men were kept under surveillance, they would unwittingly lead the way to David and the American woman. With a little luck it would work, he told himself—but not without Joaquin.

"Well," said the Honorary Consul of Chiapas, "I don't suppose it would hurt to test the waters...make a few calls."

Alexandra shot her brother a wan smile and look of affection. Luis, however, wasn't finished.

"Joaquin...this cooperative drug enforcement thing...it's got to happen. We need help from someone outside the army...someone with access to guns and helicopters and such—an agency that doesn't answer to the military and isn't full of informers, someone who will involve the Americans."

"Yes...yes, I suppose we do." Joaquin's face drew into a scowl. He looked at his sister, and then to Luis. "Yes...I suppose we do," he repeated, "but it just isn't that easy." He opened the screen door and stepped back into the house.

CHAPTER TWENTY SIX

The sun, a lazy blushing orb, perched above a wall of pine sentinels carpeting the sierras. Shadows congealed into black monoliths, urging daylight to succumb to the inevitable, filling the rocky canyon with urgency and foreboding. A white water creek, much of it bordered with trees and fern, coursed vigorously through the rocky valley. Swollen from the recent storm, it flowed strong, and rapid along its concourse. Thunderheads still blew east toward the Petén and the Yucatan peninsula. Caves, some shallow, some high and unapproachable, hid in the shadows of canyon walls. Beyond tired and past caring, Karen sat with her back to a boulder in the shade of the western wall, watching a trio of scouts depart from the main group which now quickly pitched camp. The patrol headed south along the stream where they would rendezvous with Marcos' father, the Bone Man, and Professor Wolf in a village called Dolores. According to Marcos, all would meet at noon tomorrow and trek together into Council

Valley.

Chonala, the dead youth, was buried with little ceremony within two hours of his death. Pulling a travois while fleeing their pursuers slowed them more than expected. Rafael had ordered a group of scouts to back track in hopes of discovering their foe, but they returned empty-handed. Marcos, wanting to lend dignity to the boy's death, wanted to bury the body with full observances and ritual in Dolores tomorrow. Rafael, however, complained openly, calling it foolishness and insisted that such a plan placed them all in danger and made them vulnerable to attack. Finally Marcos agreed to a quick, inauspicious burial.

Aware that they were being followed, guards were placed to secure the area while others dug a shallow grave in the sodden earth. The body was interred beneath a massive-trunked, lofty ceiba near the swampy lowlands, a jungle watershed where several streams and rivers merged to shed water from the highlands. The stifling heat and humidity made the task nearly unbearable. While Karen sweltered in the shade and watched them dig, she could see and hear dark clouds of mosquitos swarming around her. Even with Chonala buried, the blood-hungry insects had tracked them mercilessly for another two hours before the Zapatistas walked west out of the swamps and up into the forested foothills and canyons that lay on the periphery of the Lacandon. Marcos had moved up and down the line, encouraging and exhorting everyone to keep pace. Karen gave her best but, inevitably, the jungle and heat stole her strength. A numb exhaustion nearly felled her, making every step a conscious effort. She forced herself to ignore the rank body odor of her guerilla companions, the biting insects, and birds and spider webs. Forgotten was the jaguar that frightened her earlier, and she was oblivious to the screaming parrots and monkeys. Deep breaths became shallow gasps in a parched throat, but she had struggled onward, her mind focused on the rhythm of placing one foot in front of the other. She felt as if she was on a death march, hurrying to an inglorious fate, madly intent to arrive at an unknown destination.

Fortunately they experienced no more attacks and the grueling trek ended. As she sat and rested, she remembered Chonala and the swamp in which he lay rotting. How long before scavengers dug him up? Sweet Jesus! The mosquitos, slithering snakes and the ever-present mud. When had she ever endured so much?

Karen took a deep breath and closed her eyes, feeling as if she might fall asleep immediately. Guards paced above on the canyon ridge while others pitched camp beneath the overhang of a cave. A search revealed no jaguar spoor or other evidence of habitation, and Marcos and Rafael agreed that it was a good location. Besides, it would likely rain later and the cave would provide shelter if needed. It seemed that she had just closed her eyes when Marcos plopped down beside her.

"You okay?"

"Yeah...sure. Now I know what the Bataan Death March was like."

"The...er...what?"

"Nothing. Just a bad joke." She sat upright, adjusted her skirt and slowly stretched her legs. "God I'm tired. Everything in my body aches." She reached to rub her lower back.

"Are you too tired to bathe?"

Her head swung around. "A bath? Oh...course not! But where..." she looked askance at the soldiers building their camp. "No...I'd rather not. The stream looks great, but I don't see anything resembling privacy. I've gotten used to a lot in the last week, but I'm *not* undressing in front of a bunch of soldiers."

269

He chuckled. "We won't ask you to entertain us, *querida*…as much as the men would enjoy it." He leaned closer. "Remember my idea? The waterfall?"

"It's near here?"

"Yes…a half kilometer more up the canyon. *Muy bonita*."

"It's secluded?"

"What? Oh…yes…no one can see us there."

"Us?"

"But of course. You will need a guide and a champion to accompany you." He smiled, but stared brazenly. "There are wild animals and…"

"The only wild animals I'm concerned about are sweet talking zapatistas." Her eyes slid from his. "I don't know…" she bit her lip and reached for a lock of greasy, stringy hair, feeling a sudden flush of warmth in her face.

"I promise to be a gentleman," he coaxed.

"What about them?" she nodded toward the soldiers.

"Rafael will tend to the men and the camp. He doesn't need me around all the time…says I talk too much and get in his way. Come on…let's go…eh?" he urged. "Last time I was here, I found a pool beneath the *cascada* big enough to swim."

"Are there snakes?"

"Si…anacondas as big as a Humvee…" He stretched his arms wide.

"Oh, quit it!" She gave him a coy swat. "Anacondas are only found in the Amazon."

"You'll go, then?"

"Er…yes…it sounds nice." She adjusted the ill-fitting skirt that did little to cover her legs, then looked upstream to see how far it might be. "How do we…er…you know."

"How do we go?"

"Yes?"

"Like this." He stood and helped her to her feet. "Bring your

270

rifle."

"What? Oh…yes…of course." She retrieved the gun that she had lugged so far under such trying conditions. "It seems heavier."

"You're arms are tired."

"Everything's tired…not just my arms."

"Need me to carry you?"

"Down boy." She pretended to step away. "Don't push your luck."

He turned and trekked upstream and Karen joined him.

She thought it seemed terribly obvious what they were doing, and imagined the soldiers' eyes boring into her backside as she went. "What if we're followed?"

"No one will follow. Rafael will see to it."

He reached for her hand and she hesitated, but then relented. "I hope it isn't far," she said, "I'm really too tired to walk much farther."

"You'll find the water to be *muy fresca*."

"Refreshing?"

"*Si*…and it will…" he hesitated, reaching for the right word. "Calmarse," he offered.

"Ah! Soothing. Refreshing and soothing." She gave him a coy smile. "I feel better already."

She resisted the temptation to look over her shoulder until a bend in the river hid them from prying eyes. He loosely wrapped an arm around her waist and she lay her head on his shoulder, allowing the hardships and fears of the day to dissipate, to be replaced with cautious trust. They negotiated the rubble-strewn banks and huge bushy ferns and walked in companionable silence until they disappeared into the dim obscurity of the western shadows. When the stream dog-legged west, they followed its meander another fifty meters until it curled into a copse of fir trees and eroded hills that studded canyon's end. Once inside its protective cover they paused to embrace. She felt his urgency grow and broke away, grasped his hand and led him upstream. The muffled sound of cascading water grew stronger and a sense of anticipation, a wanton thrill, coursed through her, invigorating her. Her fatigue forgotten, she urged him to keep up, pulling him through the prayer plants and palms, the fern and scrub trees, until a cool, light mist coated her face and the exquisite splash of the falls caressed her ears.

She stopped at bank's edge to watch the swirling water, then turned and looked upward, nearly thirty meters to the crest of the falls. The water flowed like a diaphanous veil, a sparkling curtain of glass that crashed into the bowl at her feet. Enchanting, she thought, succumbing to its allure and magic.

Marcos pulled her close and she yielded completely this time. Long kisses fueled their passion and his hands stroked and explored her body. When he attempted to raise her dress, she balked and pulled back.

"Close your eyes," she ordered.

"Please, Karen…"

"Close them!" She cast him a mischievous look.

"*Solo un momento.*"

When he complied, she began stripping her filthy garments. She was peeling her panties down when he peeked and stared boldly, feasting on her body. Her face felt warm and she let loose an uncharacteristic giggle, then dived into the pool. When her head broke water, she saw Marcos feverishly tearing at his own clothes.

"Can you swim?" she teased, doing the breast stroke. She glided around the pool, swimming in and around the falls while he struggled on the bank. The waterfall lay hidden in the late afternoon shadows at the base of a cliff. Broad-leafed ferns, bush, and trees dripping with moss and vines rimmed the bank. When she completed her second lap and glanced toward the bank, she saw him standing on a boulder near water's edge. He stood naked and erect, unashamed of his tumescence. Magnificent. A thrill of lust mixed with fear jolted her and a primal ache grew in her loins and uterus. She fought to look only at his face.

"You said you would be a gentleman," she said, hoarsely.

"You excite me very much."

"Yes...I see that I do." Emboldened, she stared. "You're so...so...male." She floundered for the right word. "So..."

"Karen..."

"Yes?"

"I'm coming in." He creased the water with a shallow dive and surfaced in front of her.

"Do you want to swim first?" she asked with trembling voice.

"I want to make love, Karen. I want to do it now."

"Like a gentleman?"

"Like a man who loves a woman." He reached for her and coaxed her toward the shallows. While he explored her body, her passion exploded and reticence disappeared. He lifted and placed her legs over his hips. Small swells radiating from the sides of the pool buoyed her breasts.

She saw the hunger in his eyes and looked away, and then he entered her. She moaned and fell into his embrace. He moved slowly within her, stopping to kiss her lips and lick and suckle her breasts; and so went the primal ritual. She felt his ardor grow and he stiffened, trying to forestall his release, but she was nearly there herself, and urged him on, following his climax with her own.

She lay her head on his shoulder, her legs still twined about him, reluctant for the moment to end. He was nuzzling her neck and tracing the path of her spine with his fingertips when a **Crack**! echoed through the canyon. **Crack**! Another gunshot broke the silence and the water exploded behind Marcos' head! She screamed and he shoved her beneath the water, and motioned for her to follow him behind the waterfall. Terrified, she swam and kicked with a fury, surfacing between the cliff face and cascading water.

"Stay here," he gasped. He took a deep breath and slid beneath the shadow-blackened water. She hid behind a slimy, moss-covered boulder and tried to peer through the falls. She listened for footsteps or voices, but heard only the thundering crash of water. Suddenly shots popped in the distance, but they sounded different. Rifle fire! Had the guards on the canyon ridge been alerted and returned fire? *Sweet Mary, save us,* she pleaded silently. Lord, she wished Marcos would return. Naked and alone, she recalled the terror of her internment at Piedra Blanca with the drunken, out-of-control federal soldiers. When would the insanity end? Would she live to see tomorrow? The mossy rock felt icky, but she skirted to its back side and lowered herself even further until only her nose was exposed for breathing. The mountain water was cold and her skin pimpled with goosebumps. She bit her lip and resisted the impulse to run, even though her heart pounded and her breath came in gulps. She sought comfort in a familiar litany and silently prayed: *Our Father, Who art in heaven, hallowed be Thy name...*

****

Marcos, swimming beneath the surface, burst from the shallows and sprinted into a cover of ferns and broad-leafed alocasia. His clothes lay nearby, but in a fairly exposed area. What to do? The shots came from the south, near the wooded foothills. He tried to see through the leaves and brambles, but to no avail. Whoever fired the shots might be waiting for him to recover his clothes. He must dive to retrieve them, or hide naked in the bush like a hunted animal—not a satisfactory solution. At that moment a shot rang out, a rifle this time, from higher up. Good, he thought, believing it was his men. He bolted for the cover of the boulder and his clothes, hoping that his men's rifles had distracted the attacker. Squatting low and crawling, he recovered his rifle, then his pants and shoes. Still no movement in the underbrush from where the shots had come. Thank God for the thick vegetation or they would both be floating dead in the pool. He struggled into his clothes. Now he heard distant voices—his own men. More shots rang out. What and where were they shooting? Heartened, he called out to Karen.

"Hold on...the men are coming."

"What?" she answered. "I can't hear for the noise," she yelled.

He repeated his instruction.

"I'm coming out."

"No. It isn't safe."

Her head popped from the water. She gasped. "Not with twenty soldiers coming and me here naked it isn't!"

"Karen...don't..."

She scrambled from the pool and ran to where he hid.

"Crazy mujer!" he accused, but her breasts had captured his eyes and he could only stare.

"Help me get my clothes—and quit gawking," she commanded.

"*Chingada*," he mumbled, but helped retrieve her clothes.

"Marcos!" called a voice. "*Gringa! Donde estas?*"

"*Aqui*, Rafael...*cerca de la cascada*," shouted Marcos.

Karen fought to put a wet foot into a sock. "I am so sick of this...this crap!" She stomped her foot, and then snatched the other sock. "This is the craziest country I've ever been in.

Someone always trying to kill or rape you!" She tightened the velcro strap on her boot. "I want out, Marcos. Now!" she demanded.

Several guerillas, including Rafael, snaked through the bush. Marcos looked south and saw the brush and tall grass move where others searched the pines. He tuned out Karen's diatribe and cursed silently. *Chingada*! How stupid of him. He was thinking with the little head instead of the one with the grey matter. The joke was on him, and this little foray into the bush would do little to engender respect among his men. Still ignoring Karen's complaints, he mustered what dignity he could in order to meet his troops. Catching El Commandante with his pants down made a good story. Even Balaam Reyes would likely learn of it within minutes of their arrival tomorrow. What an ass chewing that'll be, he thought. With rifle in hand, he glanced down to make sure his fly wasn't open, then waded through the ferns to greet his saviors.

****

Hungover from drinking *ponche*, tired, reeking of sweat and fatigued to an extent that he couldn't recall since his youth, Captain Chavez cowered in the darkness of a shallow cave southwest of the waterfall. Mosquitos and gnats swarmed about his head. He no longer gasped for air, but his breath came shallow and rapid. Outside, zapatista soldiers searched the valley and hillsides, scouring the forest for the assailant that had tracked them deep into Lacandon. Chavez risked a peek toward daylight and the small entrance into the cave. A stand of brush hid the opening from all but the most observant eye. They would leave soon, he hoped. The sun had set behind the foothills and twilight would become darkness in minutes. The filthy Indians, rabble that they were, would most likely withdraw to their camp and post sentries.

So far the black shadows of the forest had been his friend,

but in this case they had resulted in his missing the kill. *Chingada!* His pistol shots were wide of the mark. He forgot how much the pistol bucked when fired. He should have been more patient and used a tighter grip on the .45 automatic. A rifle would be best, but the vegetation surrounding the waterhole limited the distance one could effectively sight a target. Thus he had decided to stalk the rebel leader and his American whore with the pistol. The situation seemed ideal– naked prey cavorting in the water, oblivious to all but the surging heat in their groins. *Chingada!*

So far things had not gone as planned. The Indians were wily and practiced at woodcraft. Not since he had killed the young one guarding the American *puta* had he found the opportunity to take another of the rebels out. They were wary and better organized than he supposed. He put a stinking, soiled sleeve to his forehead and wiped away muddy sweat. The emptiness in his stomach went from rumbles of discontent to a persistent ache–distracting him even more. Water did nothing to satisfy his longing, and his legs and hands had developed slight tremors. Where were the *cabrones* going? Surely they planned to meet someone soon. Why were they heading south and west into the jungle? They were in the foothills now and mountains loomed to the west. What was to be gained by taking the cocaine and the *gringa* farther into the wilderness? Didn't they plan to cash in? Surely the female wanted to return to San Cristobal or, more likely, the U.S.A. Although the traitorous scum made his task doubly difficult, he had no choice but to follow his original plan. Without recapturing the cocaine there would be no returning to his wife and children, or to society as a whole. He was a dead man when he showed his face. Better to suffer an ignominious death in the jungle than have his family witness his killing or learn of his humiliation and murder.

Meanwhile he needed to eat–soon. He would only grow weaker in the enervating heat of the jungle. He could make it through the night, maybe even another day–he wouldn't starve to death–but he couldn't maintain the scorching pace of the guerillas much longer. Even if he found an animal to shoot, he couldn't discharge his firearm so soon after this debacle–not with the rebels alerted to his presence. Later tonight maybe, when everyone was sleeping. If an opportunity didn't present itself soon, he'd have to create one by forcing the issue. Maybe he could steal some food, or perhaps he could capture something. But now he must bide his time. Patience, he had discovered, was more than a virtue. At war in the jungle, it was a requirement if you wished to stay alive.

****

Lasting but five minutes, a torrential thunderstorm rudely buffeted the village. The bonfire survived the rain, but had driven the pungent smoke low to the ground. Logs popped and snapped, blowing sparks and small red coals over the edge of the fire pit. Black, moist smoke heavy with debris, hovered like a cloud above the village. The acrid fumes stung David's nose and his eyes burned and watered. Above the hazy carbon cloud, the moon and stars took refuge behind a steady stream of thunderheads. Shadows, dancing like wicked wraiths, issued from the light of licking flames.

The professor sat on a wet stump near the fighting ring, his back warmed by the fire, his stomach full, nursing his second helping of *ponche*. The first cup had stung his brain like a red wasp, but now he sat complacently, albeit numbly, sipping cane liquor and listening to Balaam argue, accuse and make excuses, anything but pay his bet. Zapata, the Bone Man's prize macho, had quickly suffered an inglorious defeat and was hustled away by the two giggling sisters to be plucked for the soup pot. Zapata's razor-sharp spurs had been no match for the red and black bird of his rival. The winner, a bird named *Garras de Piedra* (Stone Claws), had made quick work of Zapata. David mused that, based on the bird's names alone, he could have predicted the outcome. The only difference was that, unlike Emilio Zapata, hero of the Mexican Revolution, Zapata the bird would not likely be remembered beyond tomorrow's meal.

The professor felt content. Prior to the cockfight Balaam had unexpectedly invited David to attend a war council at the shaman's hut. This had both surprised and pleased the professor, who had grown resentful being out of the loop and treated like a second-class citizen. The shaman had even gone over the maps with him. The council itself was an eye opener. From where had come all the zapatistas? He didn't remember seeing them enter Dolores, and hadn't noticed their presence upon arriving with Balaam. The meeting was conducted in at least three languages, one of them Spanish, and the professor now had a good idea of what would transpire tomorrow. A zapatista known as Marcos sent three soldiers to Dolores. His guerillas pitched camp in a nearby valley and would rendezvous with them tomorrow around noon. Balaam, in turn, sent a scouting party ahead with machetes to clear a trail for tomorrow's journey. Upon joining forces, everyone would follow the scout's path until arrival en masse, late in the afternoon at a place called Council Valley.

Karen was indeed alive, according to Marcos' scouts, and this did much to assuage David's guilt in accompanying the Bone Man. Moreover, he would finally piece together the mystery of her disappearance and, if time permitted, explore the cave complex to which Balaam had promised to guide him. The last, he realized, remained a big 'if.' With zapatista guerillas converging on Council Valley, and in light of the fact that they were being followed, a violent altercation seemed a distinct possibility. Whatever the Bone Man planned, he had yet to reveal itself. If David assumed the worst, which, he decided, was perfectly reasonable when dealing with the shaman, tomorrow would cast them all into a crucible from which individual lives, careers, and politics would emerge permanently changed.

But for now he enjoyed the comedy. It wasn't every day that he witnessed Balaam Reyes defensive and humiliated. What goes around comes around, he thought, remembering his own debacle in Medina's Bull Pasture. The only thing that would be better, he realized, was if he had bet on the other bird. Aw...well, he reminded himself. Don't be greedy. Can't have everything.

CHAPTER TWENTY SEVEN

Karen groaned, mired in restless slumber, her dreams replete with knife-wielding pursuers. Exhaustion ensured that she sleep the night, waking only when a fast-moving thunderstorm blustered through the area. Now someone shook her, exhorting her to get up.

"Go away," she whispered, unable to rouse herself. Sleep, that mindless state of satisfying torpor, held her inert in the netherworld, insulated from the tyranny of consciousness and the demands of reality.

"Karen…Karen," someone shook her, urgently. "Time to go, *querida*. You must get up." Again the nudge, this time more gentle, and she felt a rough hand brush matted hair from her eyes.

"What the…" she moaned, then jerked awake. A cold dread enveloped her. Her mind wasn't connecting. Where was she? What had happened? She could remember Bill and his knife, recalled herself running naked through the jungle. A dream, she realized. Then she recognized the shadow at her side. Marcos. She was inside the mosquito netting, still in the Lacandon jungle, and a sullen darkness blanketed the sky. Why must she rise so soon? She tried to focus, but a thick fog engulfed the valley. On the periphery of her vision she saw the dim flicker of a campfire and the quiet silhouettes of soldiers roasting corn tortillas on a small barrel lid. The excited chatter of birds and the rhythmic tick of insects heralded the impending dawn. She turned to meet his eyes.

"*Buenas dias*, lover boy." She muttered, giving him a weak smile.

"*Si...si...buenas dias,*" he mumbled impatiently. Or was he embarrassed? "We must go to meet Balaam Reyes and your professor amigo in Dolores."

"It's night, for Christ's sake. I just went to sleep," but she set up and stretched. Every joint, every muscle ached–especially her back. God...what had she slept on, a granite boulder?

"It's the *madrugada,* the early hours before dawn. The scouts are back and...here...eat this." He handed her to two warm, stuffed tortillas. "We leave in fifteen minutes."

"What's this stuff?" she sniffed, but then bit into them greedily.

"Frijoles," he replied. "Eat... you need your strength today."

"Yeah," she agreed, her mouth full. "You can never tell when you might run out of gas."

"*Que*? Run out of gas? What do you mean?"

"Never mind." She waved him off. "Here...help me up." She extended a hand and he pulled her to her feet. "Aw...Jeez." She stretched again. "Okay...I'll get ready. Where's the latrine? I need to do my face."

"Eh...do your face?"

"I have to pee, Marcos."

"*Si...si.*" His teeth shone white. "In the bush behind the big rock," he pointed. "Watch your step," he added.

"Yeah...I bet," she replied ruefully, searching for the outline of the boulder. "Can't see anything for the fog."

"It's there...trust me. You'll smell it!"

"I trust you, Marcos. It's the jaguars and the creeps chasing us I don't like." She turned to go, but then stopped abruptly. "How far to this Dolores place?"

"Two...three hours if we leave on time."

"Don't wait for me. I'm ready." She swept the netting aside, traced the gradual incline of the valley through shifting curtains of fog, then picked her way through the rubble up into the bush. The mosquitos waited, and she slapped at them without enthusiasm, still filled with lethargy. She could use another ten hours of sleep, she told herself, or maybe a week. The too-rapidly eaten tortillas sat like a rock in her gut. As she climbed the hill she remembered that she would see David Wolf today, and this perked her up. Finally she could tell him of her research, her discovery. And this Council Valley she'd never heard of–hadn't Marcos said it was riddled with caves? She passed a huge limestone boulder, detected the tell-tale odor of feces, and slipped into the bush to do her business. As she squatted and bared her bottom to the mosquitos, she remembered a class she had taken in graduate school called Field Methods. Time and again the professor had preached how field work could be rough and primitive with unexpected crises. But had any of her teachers ever endured anything like this? Not likely, she decided, nor would she again if she ever escaped this tropical hell.

****

Absolutely beautiful, thought David, watching the crimson orb break the eastern tree line and layer a honey-like golden evanescence across the hillside into the village. Not even the muddy squalor of Dolores with its many campfires, mangy

283

dogs, and trash strewn paths could sully the bucolic ambience of the morning. Wispy remnants of the morning fog remained, and he imagined that he could see the mist evaporating, trailing up into the sky.

The cockfights and drinking ended after midnight when the second of two gusty thunderstorms crested the mountains and scattered everyone with lightning bolts. Tired from his trek through the jungle, soaked and just a little drunk, David had wandered through the dark until he came to the sisters' hut. With no hassle, and apparently no expectations, they led him inside to a hammock where he had quickly fallen asleep. The cries and laughter of children and the smell of cooking fires had awakened him in time to enjoy the tropical sunrise.

The younger of the two sisters, her hand covering her mouth to hide a giggle, approached with a plastic plate laden with two thick burritos, sliced avocado and four cherry tomatoes. His nostrils spread to capture the aroma and his stomach rumbled with recognition. When he thanked her, she cackled and ran to join her sister by the hearth. He had grown fond of the diminutive Indian widows. Unlike yesterday when they dressed as Lacandon Indians, today they wore their colors–the multi-colored, beautifully embroidered *huipil*, the bodice and shoulders smocked from breasts to shoulders. Tiny tassels dangled from each sleeve.

A bit of chicken had fallen from a corn tortilla, and so he retrieved it and called out to them, pointing at the burritos. "Zapata?" he asked. They nodded yes and tittered. He smiled his appreciation, took a hearty bite, and grunted his appreciation. Balaam's fighting cock would never pay its losses, but David could savor what the bird was destined to do best.

The breakfast was delicious. He finished by popping a tomato into his mouth and chasing it with clear stream water.

The sister made motions to ask if he wanted more. He almost said yes, but remembered that he planned to explore the outlying expanse of the village. Even though the area was studded with hills, he sighted numerous earthen bulges with exposed mortared stone. It was well known that many Indian villages were located within or near old Mayan towns, and he was not surprised to find that this true of Dolores. Ruins were hallowed ground, and the Maya were spiritually connected to the land and the underworld of Xibalba–the Mayan underworld, the domain of the Nine Lords of Darkness. Cenotes, deep sink holes eroded over thousands of years through layers of soft limestone, were found throughout Yucatan and Chiapas states. Oftentimes they were found in conjunction with caves, some of them inter-connected by passages worn smooth by flowing water. The Maya world view was that of a large reptile floating on a subterranean ocean. Cenotes, like caves, were viewed as an entry into Xibalba and were used to sacrifice cross-eyed virgins, war captives, and an occasional "volunteer" to one of the many gods in their well-stocked pantheon.

Yesterday, just north of the village, Balaam had led him past a small but deep cenote, probably no more than thirty meters in diameter, as they wound their way along the creek path before arriving at the village. The cenote sat at the foot of a crumbling rock wall laced with thick, sinewy vines. Its crumbling edge clogged with fern and bindweed and appeared nearly inaccessible in the late evening shadows. The professor's curiosity was piqued and he wanted to search the rocky hillsides for caves, but Balaam had ignored David's entreaties to stop and investigate, and had maintained a blistering pace through the underbrush until their arrival.

David had studied his maps earlier and now believed he had pinpointed their location, including the approximate location of *The Place Where the Gods Sing*, in *La Cueva de Vidrio*. The jungle was rife with unexplored or unknown ruins and he remained eager to search the area further before moving on. Much of the Lacandon was a highland tropical jungle. Though densely forested with mahogany, towering ceiba, and an incredible array of plants, the forest floor was nutritionally poor. Its topsoil was thin and rocky and its sustenance heavily dependent on the moisture of the rainy season and the rapid decomposition of leaves and forest detritus.

David estimated that they had traveled close to thirty kilometers yesterday. If Balaam was correct, they would struggle through at least another twenty today before arriving at Council Valley. He judged the time to be about 9:30 a.m. The zapatista platoon from eastern Chiapas might not arrive for a couple of hours. Meanwhile he had nothing to do. The time was ripe for exploring. He returned his plate to the sisters, grabbed his maps and strode away from Dolores, downhill on the path in which he had entered yesterday evening.

The trail was well worn and more or less parallel to a rill of water that tumbled from the forested highlands to the west. The village disappeared from sight and the path veered north toward the lush, wide canyon that served as an entry into Dolores. The monotonous sounds of the village receded and were replaced by the busy, raucous jungle. Birds protested his coming and insects chirped in alarm. He was alone now and imagined that he saw animals moving through the brush, slithering through the grass, and stalking him through the tree tops. A rush of pleasure, a feeling of being unencumbered, quickened his step. Downhill, threading the damp gravel path, then up a rise and around a copse of mahogany until he arrived at the place in which he had spotted the cenote. There it lay, a bowl half shaded in the morning sun near a protruding rocky bluff on the eastern wall. He gripped his maps and exited the trail, stepping carefully, working his way toward the cenote. Plants and bush blocked his vision and impeded his progress. Grasping bindweed and tall grass caused him to stumble. He wished that he had borrowed a machete. Another twenty meters and he stood at its edge. The jungle, he saw, had extended its dominion into the cenote. A multitude of lichen and moss, ferns, orchids and vines clung tenuously to the irregular limestone walls all the way to the bottom, where a brackish pool lay calm. It was perfect. He had seen larger and deeper, but never one like this–undisturbed, in pristine condition, far from the despoiling feet of man.

He decided to skirt the edge and walk east toward the bluff to see what, if anything, lay in the darkness beneath the overhang. Again the going was difficult, and then the mosquitos found him. Suddenly he was slapping himself and cursing. He walked beyond the cenote and struggled to free his boots from the bindweed when he kicked too hard and lost his footing. The ground disappeared and he tumbled head first over a ledge, his maps flying in the air, a fall of ten meters, to land splayed on his back. He lay dazed and hurting, gasping for air.

"*No mueves, cabron!*" Three well-armed men in camouflage fatigues stood with rifles aimed at him. A fourth, a clean-shaven hatchet-faced man wearing green khakis and a thin long-sleeved T-shirt, pointed a nickel-plated, white-handled .45 automatic at him while stooping to pick up the professor's maps. A radio hung from a clip at his belt.

"*Cuidado,*" he cautioned the other three.

David, surprise mixed with anguish, tried to sit. His breath returned, but his neck and shoulder ached as though severely sprained. When he gained his feet, he couldn't straighten completely and his head wouldn't swivel. Riveting pain accompanied any attempt to move it to the left. He massaged it gingerly. Satisfied that nothing was broken, he turned his attention to the gunmen. A quick glance convinced him that they were not friendly. They were not Indian, nor did they wear the black scarf of the zapatista. He doubted that they were lost. Were these the pursuers that Balaam expected?

"Who are you?" he gasped, holding his neck. "What do you want?"

No one answered. The hatchet-faced one had a map in hand and studied the lines and notations David had made. This one was in charge, he decided.

"I asked who you are."

The leader nodded and a booted foot plowed into David's solar plexus. His knees buckled and he fell to the earth, again unable to breathe.

"I ask the questions, senor," smiled the leader. While David retched and fought to regain his breath, the maps were spread on the ground for perusal. The soldiers talked among themselves and seemed pleased with their good fortune.

"You are the archaeologist David Lobo, yes?" asked the leader.

David nodded.

"I've heard of you, *senor*. I'm told that you are a loco...eh...and that you have joined the traitor rebels."

"Absolute nonsense. I'm trying to locate some caves...and...uh...I'm looking for a woman who was kidnapped...an American archaeologist. Actually, she's supposed to meet me in Dolores over there in a couple hours or so." David pointed in the direction of the village.

This statement inspired meaningful looks among the four, and the leader positively radiated happiness. What had David said to provoke such a response?

"Yes...we have heard of this woman...and we want very

288

much to meet her in person. We appreciate your help." His smile resembled the toothy grimace of a cat. "Like you, I'm told she has joined the zapatista scum. You are a gringo, too, I believe. Correct?"

"I'm an expatriate...yes...but I'm a tenured professor at the National University. But you're wrong about Karen, she..."

"No, *senor*." He waved the pistol beneath David's nose. "You're a meddling foreigner, like the *gringa*. When we find her she'll be like you...dead." He barked an order and David was gagged and his arms bound with rope.

"My name is Ramon. Don't forget it, okay? It is very nice of you to supply us with this map and information on the *gringa*, Lobo. I've never heard of this Council Valley, this *Place Where the Gods Sing*, but I'm a resourceful man. With my brains and your maps I think we can make a surprise for the traitors, don't you agree?"

David struggled with his bonds.

"Save your energy for the march, senor. We leave in fifteen minutes...and we move fast." Ramon gave orders to prepare to leave, then unclasped the radio from his belt and spoke into it as he walked toward the wall—no doubt alerting his superiors, whoever they were, of David's capture and the maps.

Despair battled pain as the professor recognized his folly—venturing alone into the Lacandon with the maps when Balaam had told him several times that they were being followed. And why had he even mentioned Karen? Stupid, that's why, he berated himself. He allowed curiosity to overcome common sense, committing the same offenses of which he warned Karen. *Oh, God*, he thought. Would he ever see Ali again?

CHAPTER TWENTY EIGHT

Sweet Jesus! thought Karen. What next? Mexico was one big illusion. Nothing was ever as it appeared to be. Professor Wolf was missing–vanished into the jungle according to those Indian sisters. And that cranky old Indian that had chewed Marcos like a Rottweiler with a butcher's bone–was she to believe that old dwarf was the leader of this mess? That old fart was supposed to get them all out alive? If so, God help them! He smelled like maggot poop and dressed like a cartoon caricature. And rude? Mercy! Had that been a snarl he'd given her when she tried to ask a question? Contempt. That was what she'd seen in his eyes. To hell with him, she thought–and Marcos, too. She hadn't understood a word when Balaam Reyes yelled at her lover, but from his hang-dog expression and quick glances in her direction, she got the impression that he did nothing to defend her honor. Idiocy, disrespect, and an altered reality–surely this is what Alice felt when she fell into the rabbit's hole–except this wasn't Wonderland, it was an undiscovered level of Dante's *Inferno*, a hell-hole masquerading as a tropical paradise.

She had envisioned a wonderful reunion with Professor Wolf, followed by a scholarly discussion of the Gould Stelae and a brief sojourn spelunking the caves of Council Valley. She hadn't been told otherwise, although Marcos was infuriatingly non-committal when answering her questions. David Wolf's unexpected disappearance changed things. How, she didn't know, but she'd bet a hundred dollars that the curmudgeon Marcos referred to as father was not giving him the answers she wanted. In fact, she could tell the old Indian viewed her as a pain in the ass. Period.

In view of the fact that they were in the midst of a war, David's disappearance concerned her greatly. What was happening and why the secrecy? She didn't like it. The last week was a descent into a personal hell, but her luck had held so far—meaning she remained alive. But if she didn't get some answers, or if things didn't look better by late afternoon when they reached Council Valley, she would insist that they return her to San Cristobal.

Her relationship with Marcos had become a problem. In retrospect she knew that their torrid, three-day affair, though exciting, was doomed to failure. He was supposed to have died fifteen years ago, but was now leading a band of Indian traitors, trying to overthrow his government. This was *not* the profile of a man with a future. Dynamic and attractive, he had saved her from God knows what, finding her desperate and vulnerable, ripe for the plucking. She had no regrets—not regarding him anyway—but knew that they must talk soon and that she must not linger overly long. His world was too different, too crazy. Bingo with Aunt Rose on Saturday nights had never looked more attractive.

The mosquitos weren't as bad today, but the heat remained

constant. Again they moved rapidly through abundant shade, but the terrain had changed–still tropical, still forested, but the vegetation less dense. The hills became small mountains and the trail rockier and covered with lichen and moss. The guerillas moved fast, covering twice as much ground as yesterday, hiking a winding wooded trail along the face of a mountain. The serpentine stream that they had followed into Dolores was sometimes visible. It had a wide trough and flowed full of water.

Their entourage had grown to more than thirty. Scouts came and went in all directions, bringing information to which she was not privy. After all, she was a woman and a *gringa*, she thought bitterly. The scruffy Indians appeared grim and focused and alert, as if expecting something to happen. The more she considered it, the more alarmed she became. She gripped her own rifle and peered ahead into the brush, then over her shoulder at the human chain snaking along behind her. Was there safety in numbers? Why were they hurrying to this place, anyway? It wasn't for her benefit, of that she was sure. Why didn't they stop for a rest? She wanted to talk to Marcos. She felt lonely and vulnerable, the only female in a male army–and worse, a big foreign gringa ignorant of all they considered important. She imagined that they watched her every move and talked about her, making jokes about her ridiculous appearance. *Aw...Sweet Mary*, she thought. *How did I ever get into this mess?*

****

Death would be a welcome respite from this, thought David. His back felt better, but his neck hurt terribly. Every step aggravated the injury, and he sometimes clenched his teeth to stifle a moan. Fortunately they were marching in the shade of a mountain. Long thick vines clung to the sheer prominence of the wall. A few plants, seemingly without soil, basked in the sun above, and except for an occasional tree growing at an odd angle, the cliff face remained forbidding and unassailable.

His captors–there were now eight of them–removed all the ropes except those on his hands. These men were not the average Mexican soldier, he realized. They were extremely well armed. All of them carried automatic weapons with tubular folding stocks, grenades, Glock knives, expensive watches, and packs containing who-know's-what. They were a Special Forces unit, but representing whom he had no idea. Only a few had the speech or mannerisms of Mexican nationals and David suspected that they were mercenaries. Ramon, called Colonel by the others, was always whispering, usually to himself. Sometimes he would stop to ask the professor questions about the maps. David was little help since he had never been to Council Valley and knew only what he had been told or shown by Balaam Reyes.

These commandos were not ignorant Indians, nor were they fools. They spoke good Spanish, and David overheard talk that the zapatistas tracked them. In fact, they were engaged in the same intrigue. Four new commandos, one of them an enormous black man with a Caribbean accent, had returned after spending the night watching zapatista soldiers machete a path for others to follow. This news created a big stir, especially when the Colonel compared David's maps with the topographic descriptions given him. It didn't take a genius to figure out the two were related. The question tugging at the professor's mind was "why?" Why were these specialized killers here? Was it the missing drugs to which Balaam had alluded? Were they searching for Karen, or had someone finally decided to hang a bell on Balaam Reyes? David was no military strategist, but he hadn't seen enough commandos to take on the guerrillas here on their home court, the jungle, regardless of how well armed they might be. What were the surprises to which the Colonel had referred, he wondered? Something in one of the backpacks they guarded and handled so gingerly? Aw, Christ...what did it matter? he despaired. If these professional killers didn't shoot him first, he'd die from the pain in his neck.

Just when he'd reached the end of his endurance, Ramon called a halt. David dropped to his knees, then onto his side. An anguished groan burst from his mouth. He reached with both hands to support his head in order to control the pain.

The Colonel's lip curled and he eyed David like a leper. "Keep up, gringo, or someone might slit your belly and leave you to the ants."

"Go ahead," urged the huge Negro, appearing suddenly from the rear. His massive arms and shoulders glistened with sweat and his teeth shone like pearls. He pulled a jagged bladed Glock from its sheath. "He'll get us all killed. Better now than later. We may have to move fast later."

"No," said Ramon, stepping between them. "Maybe we'll need him. He could be useful."

The black behemoth sneered, looked at David, then into the Colonel's eyes. His grip relaxed on the handle and he reluctantly sheathed the knife. He cast the professor a look of disgust, a lion not yet hungry enough to kill the prey, and turned his attention to the Colonel.

"How about now? This place look okay?" he asked.

"Definitely," agreed Ramon. "Get Diego and *Flaco* (Skinny) to help. We're running out of time."

****

Chingada, cursed Captain Chavez, silently. His reeking body odor wafted upward, causing his nose to wrinkle. He smelled like a Juarez whorehouse latrine. Scratched, fatigued, filthy and demoralized, he slumped against a tree to support

294

his aching back. Below, two more of the filthy guerillas, boys of no more than fourteen, he judged, were returning to Dolores with freshly killed game–three rabbits and a coati. His stomach waffled with hunger pangs and his mouth watered as he envisioned skewered animals roasting over an open fire. From his hidden perch in an ancient mahogany tree, he could view virtually every movement in the village–and what a shit hole it was.

He thought to try out the sniper skills he acquired at the academy, but decided that two days of training eight years ago in a North Carolina forest might not have provided him with everything he needed to know. Not that he didn't feel like killing something. It's just that he preferred something edible at the moment, and that wasn't going to happen for a while. He knew that he could go a long time without food, but he was obsessing on it. Food appeared to be in abundance, or at least the zapatista vermin seemed to have an endless supply. The trite analogy of a man starving at a banquet took on meaning as never before. He felt tempted to find one of the rebels and kill the scumbag for his food, but their numbers had increased to thirty or forty! Shooting a gun would only alert them to his whereabouts, and his strength had diminished to where he couldn't chance a knife attack. Besides the countryside was increasingly more open. Trees and bushes still dotted the landscape, but open spaces were more abundant. Very tall rocky hills replaced the verdant, rounded mounds covered with ancient rain forest. Staying invisible in the jungle was no longer feasible. He must remain farther away from them and keep his eyes and ears open.

Actually, now that he thought about it, his plan hadn't worked at all. He believed that the rebels would simply meet with a few more of their kind and the cocaine would change hands–hopefully into lesser or fewer ones, and that this would make it easier to recover. *Chingada*! Such was not the case. In fact, he hadn't seen the familiar packs since the rebels arrived at the village. What had they done with them? What was their plan? *Chingada! Que mal suerte!* The only thing worse than repressed hope was hunger, he decided. With his luck, he'd fall out of a tree or be strangled by a boa. He'd become a meal for someone else. *Cabrones*! he cursed again. With shaking hand he reached to peel a ribbon of bark from the tree. He eyed the moist white underside, then removed the rough outer skin. Grimacing, he took a deep breath and tossed it into his mouth. He chewed tentatively and found that his mouth watered. He sighed and slowly worked his teeth into the fibrous pulp. Satisfied that it wasn't poison, he tore another scrap and chewed it also. A poor meal for a poor man, he thought. He had nothing, he decided, nothing at all–not even his life if he didn't recover the drugs. He spat the bark from his mouth and looked longingly at the tree leaves as a sense of hopelessness came to roost on his shoulders. Then the cramps gripped him and he began to retch, but only a thin putrid liquid escaped his lips.

****

"I'm coming along," insisted Luis, following Joaquin into the room that served as sanctuary and office-his first time being inside. A quick look around revealed a man's room: leather and smoke, mahogany furniture, big desk, walls covered with daguerreotypes from the revolution and pictures of Joaquin mixing with various PRI power brokers.

"Absolutely not...too sensitive...it's..."

"It's my friend and your brother-in-law out there." Luis placed his hands on the desk and towered over the sitting consul. "I'm going. Get used to it. Someone besides you and your government buddies has to go and see this thing stays on the up-and-up."

296

Joaquin's back stiffened. "What are you implying? Do you have any idea how dangerous this could be? This operation is political dynamite. You'll have no authorization from the *Federal Policia*. The Joint Narcotics Task Force is under the auspices of a few people handpicked by *El Presidente*. No one wants you along."

"Fix it then. I know you can do it." Luis glared a challenge. "The staging point is here, isn't it? It's a natural; private, secluded airstrip, no prying eyes and within easy reach of the target by helicopter."

The consul's face flushed and his jaw clenched. His eyes slid from Luis and he peered out his window toward the distant airstrip. Nervous, he tapped a pencil on his desktop while summoning a retort. The pencil, Luis realized, was striking a map of Chiapas State. Lines and words were scrawled upon it. Although the map was upside, Luis recognized many of the names and could even read some of the hand-written notations. Council Valley and *The Place Where the Gods Sing* had been scribbled and circled on the map. The area, surprisingly, appeared no more than two hundred kilometers south–halfway to Guatemala–where the Lacandon forest rose into the highlands. It was remote, with no roads in or out. The nearest town, a small Indian village, lay fifty kilometers west in the mountains. Something about the map bothered him. He wanted a better look, but was hesitant to mess with anything on the consul's desk.

"All right," said Joaquin, unexpectedly. "It's your neck. I'll see if it's okay." He glanced at his wristwatch.

Luis tried to catch Joaquin's eyes. He'd given in too quickly. "How long?" he asked.

"*Perdon*?"

"When are they coming? When do we leave?"

"Er…that's still in the works. Two…maybe three hours."

That translated to four or five at least. Nothing ever went as planned in Mexico, but with the Americans involved, who knew? Luis was anxious to meet them. He heard that they were all cowboys–swaggering no nonsense John Waynes, quick to use their guns. So be it, he thought. Come to think of it, he'd better clean his own .45 auto and make sure he had plenty of ammo clips and, let's see, wasn't there something else? Wasn't he going to ask Joaquin something? He couldn't remember. Distracted, he said, "Joaquin...don't say anything to my wife about this, okay?"

"I would think that by now she'd be used to your adventures." The consul gave him an insincere smile. "Alexandra's the one you need to speak with. My poor sister isn't thinking too well right now." Joaquin stood, but didn't extend his hand, sending a clear message that Luis' visit was over. "It hasn't been pleasant, has it, Captain Alvarado? If you and David don't get yourselves killed, maybe you and I can start again and do better next time, eh?"

Luis didn't think so. In fact, he had decided that he shared his friend's antipathy for Joaquin. The man was a stuffed suit– clothing with nothing of substance inside. "I think we'll be leaving tomorrow, regardless," replied Luis. "We've taken advantage of your hospitality long enough." He turned abruptly and walked from the office, still troubled by something he'd seen or heard, but unable to identify it. Must be lack of sleep, he thought. He was losing his edge. He wasn't sure, but as he exited the office he imagined that he heard, "Yes, perhaps you have."

CHAPTER TWENTY NINE

Protesting and stumbling, the professor was half dragged, half shoved along the trail liberated from the brush by the zapatistas. Fatigue threatened to overwhelm him as he struggled to stay abreast of his kidnapers. Although the forced march was galling, it had proven beneficial. Whatever had jarred loose in his neck slipped back into place and he felt only soreness where before excruciating pain had jolted him with each step.

They followed the stream to a waterfall that seemed to have burst through and split a mountain wall. David and the commandos climbed high above the rushing water until they were able to pass through the mountain on a narrow trail that hugged the wall far above the stream. After negotiating the corridor, they arrived on a substantial ledge overlooking an immense jungle-filled canyon. The sound of cascading water had subsided to a whisper. The valley, oval shaped with sheer cliffs, extended nearly three kilometers before narrowing at the south end. Caves, most with small openings, pocked the walls of the valley. The ridge on which they stood and the remnants of a path skirted below them, ringing the valley. Pictographic glyphs, all of them Mayan, had been carved into the walls along the trail. David gaped in wonder and felt a surge of energy as his captors led him along the path.

After traversing the trail the length of the valley, it began a precipitous descent, and they slipped and slid downward until reaching the canyon floor. When David collected himself from the near free-fall down the narrow path, his eyes beheld the most amazing cavern opening he'd ever seen. Huge and gaping, it could easily be the birth place of the Maya, the maw of Xibalba, the entrance into Mayan hell and the abode of the Nine Lords of Darkness who had tried to destroy Hanaphu and Xabalanque, the ancestor Hero Twins of the Maya. He forced himself to take deep breaths to calm himself. He looked more closely. Tendrils of vines and roots hung like gossamer curtains, and fern, lichen, moss and scrub trees obscured the mammoth opening. Below it, guarding the entrance, was a small cenote nearly forty meters in diameter. It, too, was overgrown with vegetation. To the side sat a man-made structure—a ruined altar of mortared stone covered with glyphs! This, he knew, must be *La Cueva de Vidrio*, The Glass Cave, and inside was *The Place Where the Gods Sing*.

A joyful tingle spread from David's spine. He turned to continue his inspection. High earthen mounds overgrown with tall grass, fern, and bindweed were too conspicuously situated around the perimeter to be natural. In fact, upon eyeing the area more closely, he realized that he was standing in an old ball field, now reclaimed by the jungle. For a moment he forgot the peril of his situation; forgot Ramon, Balaam, and even Karen. This was an incredible discovery, almost certainly pre-classic, maybe proto-Mayan. His imagination began to run amok at what he might find here and inside the cave.

While the professor regained his breath and studied the area, Ramon checked his wristwatch and talked on the radio. Still conversing on the radio, the colonel imprisoned a lizard with his foot and took out his knife. It seemed that Ramon was always on the radio, and the professor was more than a little curious to know with whom he spoke. If the Colonel was nervous it wasn't apparent–unless one considered his slowly torturing the green lizard to death as nervousness. Unable to watch, but afraid to protest, David turned and tried to concentrate on the cave entrance while Ramon casually peeled and fileted the reptile. The Colonel's actions, David feared, were a harbinger of what the day might bring. An involuntary shiver wracked him and he looked up the mountainside to see if anyone had followed them on the trail.

****

"So…why's Balaam acting like a jerk?" demanded Karen. She leaned into the shade of the wall and fumbled with her canteen. She uncapped it and took a long satisfying draught, then wiped her sweaty forehead and felt the gritty dust kicked from the trail by the soldiers' feet.

"Well…uh…on the best of days he doesn't talk much. He's worried that Lobo was killed by the drug militia…and that he told them our plan."

"Oh, Jeez…the guys that followed them from Palenque?" She fanned herself with a hand.

"*Si. Padre* knew they were close, he wanted to lure them here, but we lost them last night."

"Yeah…probably during that chicken fight thing you told me about. That was sure dumb. They could be anywhere now. Might be looking down a rifle sight at us." She squatted to rest, but then succumbed to fatigue and plopped onto her bottom. Her skirt was filthy, and scratches and welts from two days of wading through jungle brush stung her legs.

After leaving the village and backtracking for nearly two hours they had turned west, sliding through a narrow passage that would be impossible to find without prior knowledge, then marched steadily uphill along the base of a mountain. To her surprise, the entry into the canyon lay above the waterfall where they had made love last night–and where they had nearly been killed.

"Any idea who's shooting at us?" She pushed a greasy strand of hair from her face and stood on the mountain path's edge, surveying the forested valley below.

Marcos grimaced. "Not really. Probably the same people that got Lobo. Word is out that we have the cocaine and someone followed us."

"What are you...no let me rephrase that...what will your father do with the dope?"

"Use it for bait."

"Bait? For who...the guys following us?"

"Yes...but there are others. People who control them...the federal *policia*, the army, the drug cartels, the highest levels of government. All are involved."

"Together? You mean the people in charge of fighting drugs are actually running drugs...the people in charge of kidnap prevention are running kidnapping rings...that sort of thing?"

"Exactly."

"God...I hate this place." She took another swig from the canteen. "So...who in particular is the old bird hoping to lure into his trap?"

"The federal *policia* help the governor transport drugs in and out of Chiapas. They give lots of money to corrupt politicians and landowners that stole our land. Zapatistas hate the drug people. There was this village called Acteal with lots of zapatista sympathizers. When the *policia* tried to move drugs through the area, the villagers drove them off. Several months ago the *policia* instigated a massacre in Acteal. They hired killers do their dirty work. My sister and her husband lived there."

"Consuelo?"

"Yes."

"He's trying to lure the people who did the massacre into a trap?"

"Yes."

Sweet Jesus, she thought, add a blood feud to the list of reasons for the rebellion. She definitely had to get out of this place.

****

Captain Chavez crouched in the mouth of a shallow cave, one of several curious and nearly identical structures found along the cliff footpath. Keeping his distance from the Zapatistas had probably saved his life. Now he watched while unknown, but well-equipped soldiers planted land mines on the mountain path above the canyon. Who were these guys? When he secretly stumbled upon them, they remained totally focused on their task and his presence had gone unnoticed. They must have climbed the mountainside to booby trap the passage and prevent the zapatista scum from leaving. The fact that he had not accidentally stepped on a mine only supported his feeling of invincibility. He followed the mine-layers up the trail, stepping around the explosives, all the while trying to factor in this new piece of the puzzle. Hererra, or more likely, someone above the Colonel sent them. In a sense they were on his side. They were after the cocaine, he was sure, but it would be stupid to view them as allies—not yet, anyway. They moved like tough no-nonsense people, outfitted and armed, trained killers with a plan. He must proceed with caution and improvise as necessary. Being alone had its advantages. It gave him options, which is what he needed, since he didn't have a plan anymore. Maybe they would leave some food out. Maybe they could help each other. If not–well, he'd just wait and see.

While a soldier covered the mine with dirt, his four companions–one of them an enormous negro–quietly and carefully returned via the trail's edge. They moved with stealth, confident in their abilities. Chavez could have sworn that he knew the black fellow. Hadn't he seen him in San Cristobal about a year ago? He'd had an accent, a wad of American dollars, and a pretty white girl on his arm. Bahamas! That was it. Maurice the Bahamian, Herrera had called him. Claimed he could lift a horse off the ground and stick a dagger through a bull's skull. The captain surveyed the mercenary's bulging ebony shoulders, trunk-like arms and long stout legs. It would take more than a bullet to stop that one, he decided.

The Negro spoke into a hand-held radio while the others worked. They extracted rope and climbing tackle from backpacks. In less than two minutes all four were rappelling down the cliff face. The ropes followed, and Chavez was left on the path pondering his next move. This, he discovered, wasn't much of a decision. He could do like the mercenaries and chance walking the outside edge of the trail, or he could turn around and go back. *Chingada!* he cursed, silently. *Cabrones!* He didn't need this shit! His wrath boiled over. He gripped his rifle until his hands hurt. Finally, calmer, he took a deep breath and tried to reason his way out. *Chingada*, he whispered. There was no choice but to go on.

****

Karen took another drink from her canteen, then shook it to gauge how much remained. The more she thought about it,

304

the more urgent it seemed that she leave. Had she known that that arrogant shit Balaam was planning a war, she would never have come along–caves or David Wolf notwithstanding.

She turned to Marcos to make her point, but before she could speak, he frowned and said, "I need to check on something." He stood to go.

"Marcos?" She took his arm and gave him a beseeching look. "I've been meaning to tell you...but there hasn't been time. I...want to go home. I mean...I want..."

"Tomorrow, Karen. Father has ordered it. It's too dangerous here. He didn't think things would work out like this." Marcos bit his bottom lip and shifted his weight to the other foot. He pulled his arm away, and looked down at her, as if to say more.

"And?" she led him. "What else?"

"He...er...there won't be time for you to investigate the caves. Besides...he promised Lobo, not you...and...uh...they're sacred to the Indians and he doesn't want you to disturb any...."

She shrieked and jumped to her feet. Betrayed! A black cholera seized her, her fists doubled and a scream caught in her throat. But an explosion drowned out her cry of frustration. The mountain wall sagged and flying grit stung her face and arms. The force of the blast toppled them both.

Automatic rifle fire erupted from the woods below. Cries of alarm and pain mixed with shouted instructions. Marcos rolled to shield her with his body.

"Get away from me!" She struggled to rise.

"*Calla te!*" he commanded, and bodily shoved her along the path. "That was a grenade. Here...behind this boulder," he pointed. "I'll be back." Rifle in hand, he bent low and ran toward the source of the explosion.

Bewildered but unhurt, Karen gripped her rifle and slid

behind a pile of slumping limestone to wait. What happened? Who attacked? Confused, the guerillas ran back and forth, up and down the rocky path seeking the enemy. Rifle fire followed another explosion. She waited with heart pounding, taking quick shallow breaths, feeling strangely light-headed and fighting an impulse to run. The gunfire subsided and two injured men were hustled by–up the incline, then down–out of sight toward the valley floor. Then Marcos appeared and gunfire erupted from below.

"Let's go." He took her arm and urged her forward.

This time she didn't argue. Shock had replaced her anger. They were exposed and vulnerable–like targets in a carnival shooting gallery. She threw a quick glance over her shoulder and fell in behind the scurrying zapatistas. As she crested the rise and headed down, she remembered Marcos' statement that his father "didn't think things would work out like this." She shuddered as a cold chill rippled down her back. She gripped her rifle and picked up her pace, the specter of fear lending wings to her feet. More gunfire and shouts rang out. *Aw…Sweet Mary…*she thought. She'd never sit at a bingo table with Aunt Rose again.

****

Chavez waited a few more minutes to ensure that no one heard or saw him before exiting his hiding place and creeping forward. He looked below, nearly forty meters to the valley floor, but saw no one. The drug cartel commandos had rappelled down and disappeared without a sound into the forest. Again he took a deep breath, switched his rifle to the other hand and stepped toward the trail's edge. Three minutes later an explosion rocked the canyon, startling and causing him to totter and nearly fall! Struggling to keep his balance, he dropped his gun over the edge into the forest, then dropped to the path stricken with fear. The explosion was followed by gunfire and distant shouts.

"*Chingada*!" he swore, this time loudly. "*Cabrones*!" he cried out, shaking a fist. Trembling with fright, he crawled away from the edge and back toward his shallow hole in the wall. Without a gun he was half a man. He must get another from someone—one of the traitors up the hill, maybe. He would wait a few moments to hear how the fight went, then try again. He moved into the shade of the cave, looking for a place to hide, then realized that he had wet himself. "*Chingada*," he cursed again, this time without passion. He sat and buried his head in his hands.

****

While David watched the trail above the tree line, two commandos jogged from the woods. As they approached, an explosion roared from the north end of the canyon near the stream leading to the waterfall. A plume of dust rose, and then began to settle on the forest floor. The cave was forgotten. Stupefied, he eavesdropped while the Negro detailed their success in laying land mines. Mines! What else did they have in those bags? His head buzzed with uncertainties. Where were Balaam and the zapatistas? The mercenaries talked as if the professor was not present, and what they said unnerved him. They would force the zapatistas to follow the mountain trail down into the valley. The path behind them had been mined to prevent a retreat. Four of the six killers were left to launch grenades up onto the footpath and fire round after round of bullets into the group. This, Ramon hoped, would drive the remaining guerillas down into the south end of the box canyon. Once the zapatistas fled down the path, the commandos would return and help the Colonel, the Caribbean giant and two men called *Flaco* and *Mota* Boy trap and kill them, recovering the cocaine in the process.

To David's horror, while Ramon talked with his black assistant, *Mota* Boy and *Flaco* (pot head and skinny) scooted into the bush to place mines across the south end of the trail on a line leading west, blocking any passage to the cave or cenote. Any attempt by the zapatistas to charge the commandos would be lethal.

"Hey…"protested David. "You can't do that! This is an archaeological site. It'll destroy…"

"Let me kill him, Ramon." The black giant pulled his Glock again. "He's a liability…he'll get us killed."

David stood rooted, his objections forgotten.

"I've got orders to keep him alive at all costs." The colonel pulled his pistol and stepped between them. "I get paid to follow orders and so do you...understand?" Ramon positioned his gun at the tip of the giant's nose. "We don't have time for this. There's work to do. Move…now…while we can."

The giant looked confused. His knife blade pushed Ramon's pistol barrel aside. "They don't pay us to take captives. Prisoners are bad business…you know that." He sheathed the knife.

The colonel lowered his pistol, then used it to point. "Up there," he said, indicating the opposite, west wall of the canyon. "I'll take the traitor and tie him up. If things go bad we'll make our stand beneath that cliff overhang so that they can only come at us from one direction. For now we'll wait and hit them from here." He indicated a fence-like structure of mortared stone near the cenote. "Leave your gun and pack. Go help those two with the mines...and don't forget to leave us a path through the bush. If there's a shit storm, we'll need an escape route." He pointed his pistol at David. "I'll put the gringo away for safekeeping and be right back."

The black giant scowled and cast the professor a withering look. He handed the colonel his AK-47, then glanced toward a line of trees where his brethren busily placed munitions. He spat, took one last look at Ramon, then he headed to join *Mota Boy* and *Flaco*, moving with enviable grace for such a large man.

Automatic gunfire erupted from the south forest floor, followed by two concussions. Grenades? David wondered. A shiver caused him to jerk. He wanted to bolt and run.

"Go!" Ramon poked the gun in his back. "Move it!"

David walked west toward the canyon wall into heavy brush, his arms held high. His legs trembled as much from fright as fatigue and he imagined that he would be struck by a bullet at any moment.

"What's this all about, Ramon? Who told you to keep me alive?"

"Shut up and hurry, *cabron*. I'm not supposed to kill you, but I'll kick the shit out of you. Move it." The Colonel's head swiveled to see the eastern wall where he expected the rebels to emerge.

"Why are you laying mines?" asked David. "This is a valuable archaeological site. It's priceless."

"So is the cocaine these pigs stole. They're all traitors…not that I give a shit personally," he added, "but the people who pay me care a great deal."

"Well," demurred the professor, "if you're not going to kill me, tell me what's going to happen so that I can stay out of the way. I don't have anything against being alive, and I'm allergic to shrapnel."

Ramon chuckled. "Yeah…I imagine you are." He fell in behind David, poked him again and said, "Faster, *cabron*. Lead will fly any minute." Then, as if he didn't have a care in the world, the Colonel began to talk like he was conversing with a friend, relating to the professor what he planned to do with his windfall once the operation was over. He and the black

309

giant had reservations somewhere on Abaco island in the Bahamas. Maurice knew some Bahama Mama's with huge *chi chi's* and legs like deer.

The professor assumed that 'bipolar' was only one of many personality dysfunctions from which Ramon suffered. David personally didn't care if the Colonel buried his loot in a coffee can, or gave it to a stable of Caribbean prostitutes. But he listened anyway while deciding what to do. These commandos were impressive–he had underrated them. Maybe they could get him out alive. But then what? He would be aiding and abetting the drug cartels. These men were *sicarios's*–professional drug soldiers. But then he already had, he realized. His maps had been used to locate this place and lay mines in an archaeological site of incalculable importance. This thought soured him even more.

Balaam and his men had a righteous motive for their actions. They also had Karen. David thought of the cenote and huge cave and the wonders it promised. He couldn't just go along placidly. Now was the time to do something, but the explosion and rifle fire meant that it was too late to warn the zapatistas–except for the mines being placed. He could warn them about those. Or should he? If the Colonel could be believed, David was to be kept alive. For what? To be prosecuted? Kept as a hostage? He was a marked man because he'd thrown in with Balaam and accompanied him to Dolores to meet the rebel army. Although his motivation remained Karen's rescue and The Cave Where the Gods Sing, his involvement with the zapatistas looked bad and might be impossible to explain away. In retrospect, he knew that Balaam had used him to get the federal army's attention. This was too bad because, in truth, he preferred the Indian's cause to the government's–but that wouldn't win him any points. Once the word treason was associated with your name in

Mexico, you had big problems. A pine box and an unmarked grave was your only future.

He made his decision. As he climbed the hillside, his feet slipped in the loose shale so often that it was necessary to lean forward and climb on all fours. The colonel, though physically fit, experienced the same problem. Scaling the gravel mound with a swaying back pack while carrying a pistol in one hand and the Caribbean's rifle in the other proved too difficult. After a couple of false starts, he holstered the pistol and began again, following the professor's lead.

Two minutes later, his hands bruised and nicked from the hardscrabble climb, David paused to get his breath. His hand he gripped a heavy, palm-sized rock. Ramon, concentrating on the climb, seemed unaware that David had stopped to rest. When the Colonel came in range and lifted his head to look up, the professor turned and struck him on the back of his skull–the impact literally bouncing the commando's face off the hillside.

"Umph..." grunted the colonel, but he tried to push himself to his knees. David smashed him again, but slipped and lost his footing. He lunged against the slumping Ramon, pushing him aside, then kicked him in the jaw as hard as he could. The Colonel moaned and collapsed against the hill.

Seized with fear, his breath coming in painful gasps, David glanced quickly to ensure that the mercenaries didn't watch. He relieved Ramon of his backpack and stole his automatic pistol. With adrenaline-induced clarity and energy, he slid down the rubble pile and bolted for the cave entrance as fast as his weary legs would go, all the time expecting a bullet in the back. He was half way past the cenote, moving toward the decayed steps leading to the cave when he sighted the Bahamian's face in the tall grass. The black man looked surprised, then angry.

"*Para te, cabron!*" cried the giant, and he burst from the bush to give chase.

A quick glance over his shoulder assured the professor that his nightmare was indeed chasing him with a Glock knife. David pushed himself even harder until he arrived at the steps. The stairs were eroded and covered with rubble and brush. He tripped and fell, but clambered on hands and knees toward the cave entrance. Certain that the giant was nearly upon him, he swung around and pointed the pistol at his nemesis. The Caribbean, no more than twenty meters away, hesitated. David saw indecision in his black eyes, but then the Bahamian grinned and charged. David's finger curled around the trigger when, unexpectedly, gunfire pinged the stone and raised dust at his feet. The black man stopped abruptly and turned. Ramon, blood streaming from his nose, stood at the base of the rubble hill, his legs spread wide, his AK-47 aimed at them.

"He's mine, Maurice. Get your ass over here with the rest of us." Upon hearing the gunfire, *Flaco* and *Mota* Boy had hurried to join the colonel. Their guns held at waist level, they walked toward Maurice and David.

The professor, beaten, knowing that he had lost everything, lowered his pistol. He would pay dearly for the escape attempt. His shoulders slumped and a piteous moan slipped from his lips.

Crack! Crack! Crack! David traced the sound to the east canyon wall. Five guerillas, with more descending the trail, arrived and fired at the mercenaries. Maurice bolted and ran south for the cover of the cenote. Ramon staggered momentarily, then stooped forward and jogged awkwardly to join the black man. David, exhilarated at his resurrection, gained his feet and climbed until he made the cave entrance. Thank God! he thought, experiencing what could only be the euphoria of a miracle. He swore that if he survived this nightmare he'd go to church again and give thanks for his deliverance. *If* he survived, that is....

****

His gut cramping, his mouth dry and dust-filled, Marcos pulled Karen along behind him. Damn women! He jerked at her arm, urging her to run faster. The Zapatista's return path was cut off. Two Indians were blown up by land mines when they tried to retreat. The Indians had been set up and walked blindly into a trap. Up ahead, guerrillas practically flew down the mountainside and disappeared into the trees of the valley. Down they went. The tree tops were now above them as the forest floor approached. The grade was steep, making it difficult to maintain footing. Brush, scrub trees and tall grass lent poor visibility, and he realized that he hadn't seen Balaam since the attack. What had hit them—a grenade? Who could throw a hand grenade up a mountainside? Marcos was alarmed that his soldiers fell into disarray so quickly. And what awaited them in the Valley? Were they hurrying to their deaths? Was Rafael with the front group? He couldn't remember.

Although he had never been to the forbidden canyon, Marcos heard his father speak of it with reverence. In fact, as he grew older, he wasn't sure that it truly existed. He had no concept of its strategic layout—where to hide if there was cover, or where they should stand and fight. Then he heard gunfire below and realized that it was a moot point. The fight had found his group, too.

The trail swung west toward the canyon. There! He could see them—thirty meters ahead. He drew up short and shoved Karen into the safety of the shadows.

"Stay here," he ordered. "Don't come down until I send for you...got it?"

"Got it," she gasped, and collapsed on the ground.

He sprinted the last few meters before arriving at the valley floor where his men engaged the enemy. They were pinned down, but Rafael had managed to spread the guerillas across a forty-meter area of the woods bordering the bush. Three men had back tracked up the trail to protect the rear. The enemy appeared to be four or five Special Forces soldiers taking cover behind a row of stone near the north end of a cenote. They were well-armed and showed no inclination to reduce the level of their fire. Worse, they began to loft grenades into the bush.

Itching to return fire, Marcos stationed himself behind a ceiba tree trunk and sighted his rifle, waiting for someone to expose themselves. He selected a target and waited for the head to expose itself again when he first heard the voice. What could that possibly be? Who was doing the yelling? He followed the sound until he saw a shirt waving like a flag behind a boulder near the cave entrance. This drew the mercenary's fire, and the shirt dropped from sight. But, as he watched, it rose again and the voice called out above the din. What was it saying? Irritated, he thought to fire a few rounds in the shirt's direction himself, when suddenly he understood. Mines! The man was trying to warn them! Or was this another trap?

While digesting this information and debating his next move, Balaam Reyes trotted from the forest. Marcos saw that he was finally carrying a rifle. Though stooped and wrinkled, he moved with the ease of a younger man.

"Father!"

"*Oye, hijo*. (Listen, son) *Ahua* Lobo...a good man. He try warn me us something. Do you..."

"Mines, father. He's saying that they've laid mines in front of us."

314

"Land mines?"

"*Si*, father. We're trapped. They mined the trail behind us too, so we can't retreat. Charging their position would be suicide, even though we have more men."

"Unh," grunted the shaman. He squatted on his haunches and rubbed his nose. Finally, he said, "Balaam have a plan, *hijo*; must run escape federal scum."

"Let's hear it."

"We have rocket gun?"

"The mortars? Why?"

"We shoot mountain."

"So?"

"Big bang blow rock ground. Hit mines."

"No, father." Marcos shook his head, believing the old man was wasting his time. "They won't land far enough out." He motioned toward the mercenaries. "Those guys are nearly forty meters west. The rock will fall close to the cliff face."

"Si!" exclaimed Balaam. "Are mines…explode, right?"

"Unhh…yeah…theoretically, or some of them anyway. Can't be sure. But what good will that do? We can't get to…"

"Is safe path to cave."

"The cave? Father…we've got to take care of these guys first. We're pinned down. Why don't you go back up the trail and stay until I send…"

"*Oye hijo*! Fire rocket wall. Rock rain ground. Pop, pop mines. Then fire rocket enemy." He pointed to the mercenaries. "We run cave…big cave. *Muy grande*…many rooms. If enemy us follow us, we kill."

A counterattack? Not likely. It would leave them too open, too vulnerable. But inside the cave? Inspired idiocy, thought Marcos, visualizing the damp earth and darkness. He didn't have a better solution, though, and they were running out of time. Some of their packs still carried lanterns, flares, and rope taken from the woman killer, Chavez, in Piedra Blanca. Maybe it would work. Anything was better than being pinched between two groups of mercenaries. Father had really screwed up, but just might have discovered of a way out of this mess.

Two grenades exploded behind them almost simultaneously and they ducked. "Jesus! Okay...it's worth a try. Rafael will set up. Wait here...I'll have the men move down here before we blast the wall. Those mines can spray shrapnel a long way."

He rose to leave, but then remembered why they were being pursued. "Where's the cocaine?"

"Drugs?" The shaman shrugged. "Why matter?"

"If this doesn't work, maybe we can negotiate."

"Zapatistas no use drugs argue federales." Balaam's mouth set in a firm line. "*Olvidalo, hijo*! (Forget it, son!). Better bullet in head than make talk federale. *Hijo* think federale want talk?"

"Uh...no...just thought..."

"Forget it. Get rocket gun! Andale (hurry), *hijo*!"

Because of the unrelenting gunfire, the guerrilla army remained pinned down along forest's edge. With one last look toward his enemies, Marcos turned and ran into the tree cover where he last saw Rafael. How many mortar shells had they brought? he wondered. Would there be enough to blast the wall into rubble and still lob shells at the mercenaries? If not, they would take heavy casualties while crossing to the cave. He shuddered, thinking of how easily they might be massacred if the plan went awry. Upon reaching the south end of the tree line, he searched for Rafael–to no avail. His soldiers were hunkered down and not returning fire. Expressions of despair hung like funeral shrouds on their faces. For some, this was their first battle of the war, the first time they were tested.

He grabbed a young guerilla by the arm. "Where's Rafael?"

The soldier pointed to a cadre of six zapatistas above on the trail, two of whom had been injured. "There Commandante…dead. Shot in the head."

No! Marcos cried, silently. He sprinted uphill to the group. Rafael lay in the dirt, the side of his head missing, bloody gray goo leaking onto the forest floor. Marcos' gorge rose and sorrow buffeted him like an ocean wave. Nausea gripped him. The personal loss was enormous, but the old man's value to the guerilla band was incalculable. Someone would pay dearly for this, he swore. He fought against vomiting, gritted his teeth and slowed his breathing.

"You two," he ordered, "up front… thirty meters up the canyon until you find Balaam Reyes. You…find Victor and have him bring the mortar immediately." He turned to the wounded. "Can either of you walk?"

"Si, Commandante," answered a boy. A bloody bandage covered his upper arm and his face was dirty and pocked with bloody pits from the explosion.

"*Bueno*…escort the *mujer* down…keep your eyes open for the three I sent to check our rear. Listen carefully. Everyone except Victor must move south down the tree line. They've laid mines between here and the cave, so we're going to blow the wall to detonate them. Move out." The two healthy ones motioned for their comrades to follow and, bending low, jogged south into the trees as ordered. The wounded zapatista crept up the trail to find Karen. The other soldier lay unconscious behind the relative safety of a boulder, and so Marcos decided to leave him. He looked toward the cave, but didn't see the waving shirt or hear Lobo calling out. Despite their jeopardy, he felt more alive than he ever remember. His body tingled with the knowledge that death waited, imminent if they made a mistake. Hurry, Victor, hurry! he urged, silently. We must avenge the death of our uncle.

CHAPTER THIRTY

A firefight raged below and Captain Chavez was content to be missing it. He had found his nerve and left the safety of the wall's opening to venture near the trail's edge. He would do it, he decided. He would walk the outer fringe like the commandos and hope that it supported his weight. Besides, if he went now, he might still be able to spot the mines by distinguishing fresh earth from the undisturbed soil of the path. He glanced at the forest floor and it seemed to loom suddenly closer, giving him vertigo. He forced himself to look away and focus on the trail. It was then that he noticed the boot prints. The commandos were all wearing the same type of boot, and the print was very distinguishable. Yeow! he rejoiced. He would keep his eyes open for their tracks to know where they had walked. He stepped cautiously. Ten steps and two minutes later he was gaining confidence. They had been in a hurry and had laid their munitions haphazardly, making no effort to completely block the path. He took longer strides.

Then the boot prints disappeared, and he judged that this was where the commandos rappelled down to the forest floor. He continued slowly, carefully examining the ground before taking a step. Five minutes later he knew that he was in the clear. He breathed a sigh of relief and quickly stepped from the rim onto the main path. Maybe he'd made it? His luck was holding.

He was very close to where the rebels were attacked. He must take care. Luck was a gift, stupidity a theft of reason. He drew near the cliff face, stooped cautiously and creeped up the hill. Forty meters later the path dog-legged sharply left. It was here that he found the fallen guerillas–eight of them he counted. It looked to be a grenade attack. All were dead. They lay in every fashion–crumpled against the wall, face down, some with eyes open, but unseeing. The smell of war–feces and blood–stung his nose. He recovered an AK-47 from the arms of a young boy, and a Beretta pistol from the belt of another.

Que bueno! he exulted. *Que suerte*! (What luck!) He was better armed than before. Five of the zapatistas still had packs strapped to their backs, so he removed them to check for food and ammunition. Moments later, gulping stale tortillas like a concentration camp survivor, he heard footsteps. He grabbed the AK-47 and ran back the way he'd come, hiding just behind the turn in the trail. Now he could hear them well. One, two…maybe three voices. They were upset and angry at the death of their comrades. Captain Chavez thought he heard them discussing the back packs, and then someone called the others over to point out a backpack that had been opened. How had that happened, they speculated? The blast wouldn't have done it. It looked like someone had opened it and…look! There were broken tortillas on the ground. An animal? No…not an animal, insisted the other. Maybe they should look around?

Chingada! thought Chavez. It was now or never. Even the stupid traitors would figure it out before long. He took a deep breath, held his rifle at waist level and quickly turned the corner, firing as he did so. Fortunately they were all standing together. It was a massacre. Only one got a shot off—harmlessly above the captain's head. Jubilant at his good fortune, he danced a few steps in celebration. Unbelievable! he rejoiced. He was The Man! The invincible warrior! He walked to his victims and kicked them a couple of times to ensure they were dead. Filthy Indians, anyway. Served them right. He'd kill them all if he got the chance.

First things first, though, he told himself, remembering the tortillas. He was ravenous and began stuffing his mouth again. These gone, he took a swig of water and moved on to another pack. Who knows, maybe he'd find some dried meat or, with luck, a can of food. He stripped another pack from the dead and struggled with the knot. Why had they tied this thing so damn tight? Frustrated, he unsheathed his knife and sliced the leather thongs and threw the flap aside. What was this? It looked like...it was something wrapped in plastic...it was...cocaine! He dropped it, unbelieving and suddenly dizzy, falling to his knees. This wasn't one of his packs! He had them in his hut for two days at Piedra Blanca. The Guatemalans delivered the dope in brown and gray camos. The guerillas must have switched them. Oh, ho! he thought. Too tricky for their own good. Elated at his good fortune, he quickly inspected the remaining packs. On the last try, he found the other cocaine stash.

The closest thing to euphoria that he ever recalled sent his spirit soaring. He was back from the dead! He could show his face without fear of reprisal. He had recovered his manhood. Colonel Hererra would no longer have Chavez's dick in his pocket. That pompous fuck must admit that the captain had done everything within his power to salvage the mission that he had performed well under the worst possible circumstances. *Ahh...cabron*, he thought. Soon you'll be eating the harsh words you spoke to describe me. He would have to praise Chavez's resourcefulness. Who knows? If Hererra wasn't too angry about losing Piedra Blanca and the platoon, maybe he'd even reward the Captain. Life is good, he thought.

Now the task was to return to Palenque and Colonel Herrera. That he might actually recover the drugs had been such a remote possibility after yesterday that Chavez had spent little time entertaining a new plan. He hefted the bag. Damn. They were heavier than he remembered. Was he supposed to traipse fifty kilometers through the jungle carrying sixty kilos of cocaine? Not likely, he decided, and the way he felt, not probable either. He'd been lucky to survive this long. Returning via foot was tempting fate in the extreme. But how, he wondered, could he do it otherwise? As he sat and pondered his dilemma, the rat-a-tat-tat of gunfire and the concussion of grenades ceased. What was that all about? Had the commandos overtaken the zapatistas? Then he heard the noise of a heavy weapon. It sounded like a mortar exploding, and the vibrations from its impact tickled his feet.

Chingada. The fight was escalating. If used properly, the mortars could put their users in the driver's seat. The captain hoped that Hererra's men were the ones with the heavy weapons, because the zapatistas would cut Chavez's throat in a minute. All things considered, he might be forced to approach the Special Forces guys and use his booty to cut a deal to get out of the jungle. They had a radio and were in contact with the big boys somewhere. He would just return along the same path. Meanwhile, he must get organized–he would need ammunition clips, food, and water. He decided to tie the packs together and piggy-back them. It would take a huge effort to transport them all the way back along the trail and through the narrow corridor to exit the canyon—but then, so what? There were no other options. The captain began to hum a song as he worked. He felt invigorated and happy. He felt proud of himself. He was a stud—a macho without equal, he told himself. Who else could have pulled this off? No one, he assured himself. Absolutely no one.

****

While the commandos rained lead into the woods with automatic weapons and grenades, David peeked from behind the boulder and saw that the zapatistas had fallen into a muddle and were changing positions. Had they heeded his warning? As he watched, all but two of the guerrillas slipped farther north into the forest. These two placed a short, thick-barreled device at the base of a dead tree and pointed it half-way up the cliff face. What in the world? At that moment an amazing thing happened. A tall Indian woman, accompanied by a wounded soldier, descended the trail. What was a woman doing here? Eeow! It was Karen, he realized! She was alive! Thank you, Balaam Reyes, he said silently. If they got out of this alive, he'd hold the grouchy old fart down and plant a big wet one on him.

The zapatistas stopped briefly for instructions, then moved into the safety of the woods. The larger of the two unloaded shells from a heavy pack. Mortars! thought David, elated. They had artillery of their own. But why weren't they pointing it at the commandos? His question was answered when the first shell hit the wall. Large pieces of rock, some the size of soccer balls, exploded from the limestone face and fell to the floor. These, in turn, detonated two land mines. The Special Forces guns became quiet as Ramon studied this bizarre strategy. The next mortar slammed precisely into the shale

323

layer beneath the limestone, causing an enormous spray of gravel and creating a web of cracks in the limestone mass above it. A deafening silence reigned. Then the wall emitted a groan, followed by a crunching sound as a large section fractured and fell to earth where it shattered and cast stone in every direction, detonating the remaining mines. The noise was thunderous. A cloud of dust rose between the cave and the forest, and cheers of jubilation echoed through the valley. Seeing that the guerillas had broken their stranglehold and possibly even gained the upper hand, the commandos returned fire with a fury.

After two shells, the guerillas found the range and began to drop mortars on the mercenaries. They returned fire bravely, and still hurled an occasional grenade, but to no benefit. David saw Ramon stretched out motionless on the ground. Cries of pain revealed that others were hit. Now the zapatistas were the aggressors, but instead of remaining in the trees, they scurried for the cave while the mortar and gunfire of their brothers covered them. David backed farther into the cave where he would be safe from stray bullets.

For the first time, he noticed that the cave walls contained glyphs and markings, some of them quite old. The floor was muddy, the air moist and cool, and he saw that the big opening became several passages leading in different directions. If only he had time to explore…but loud voices and the sounds of arriving zapatistas drew his attention back to the firefight.

Upon arriving, the first contingent, including the inimitable Balaam Reyes, dropped their supplies to the floor and returned fire from their perch inside the cave. Karen came with the second group, also toting a backpack. Gasping, her face white with dread, she scrambled up the ruined stairs and into the back of the cave.

"Miss Dumas!" he called. "Here...over here."

"Professor Wolf?"

"Thank God you're alive!" He opened his arms and she fell into them. "Are you okay...I mean...really okay?"

"I'm in one piece, if that's what you mean, but...aw jeez...I'm scared to death, Dr. Wolf."

"Call me David...and so am I...here...get away from the bullets." He helped remove her back pack. "What's in here anyway?"

"God if I know...it belonged to a dead guy called Rafael."

"Let's see what's in it, okay?"

"Help yourself, I'm bushed." She turned, crouched and stepped gingerly toward the entrance.

"Hey...where you going? It's dangerous up there."

"Marcos...I need to check on Marcos."

He shook his head in disgust. Reckless woman. How had she stayed alive so long? Didn't look like she took direction well, either. He thought to follow and deter her but, curious, began sorting through her pack. Bingo! No wonder it was heavy. He lifted two battery-powered lanterns, a length of rope, four boxes of shells, a large hunting knife. Then, unable to distinguish anything more in the dim light, he dumped the entire contents onto the floor.

"Oh, God...oh, Geez!" called Karen from the cave entrance.

His head shot up in time to see the third and final cadre of guerrillas clambering into the cave.

"Get to the back!" ordered a tall, broad man, much larger than the other Indians. "They've got reinforcements!"

Karen embraced him quickly, but then complied and shuffled back to where David stood.

"They're charging the cave!" came an incredulous shout. "There's four more of them."

"Shoot...shoot them," ordered Marcos. "Set up the mortar!"

325

he shouted to the man at his side. "Hurry!" Desperation choked his voice.

"They're in the tall grass on both sides of the cenote! Watch out...grenades!" cried a voice.

Grenades! In the cave? A searing fear pierced David's gut and his bowels felt watery. Not here! He looked beyond Karen toward the light. The heavy, muscled Indian screamed.

"Get down! Everyone...down!" and bolted toward the back of the cave where David and Karen stood.

David launched himself at Karen, knocking her back into the darkness. A tumult of sounds and confusion followed.

"There's two!" came an anguished cry.

The force of the concussion sent bodies hurtling every direction. The world turned upside down and began to spin. The wall and ceiling collapsed, sealing the entrance. Dust billowed and grit rocketed in every direction. Strong cordite odor permeated the room. David felt the soft body of someone beneath him and tried to move, but the force of the explosion had taken his breath. He struggled to his elbows, then gained his knees. He couldn't think for some reason, couldn't get his bearings. Could he hear? What was that ringing? What had happened? Then he remembered the grenades and smelled the cloying odor of blood. Something warm dripped from his forehead.

"Unhh...oh God," said Karen in a barely audible voice. "What happened? It's dark. David! Are you still here, David?"

"Here...hold on. I'll get one of the lanterns." David searched until he found the backpack on the floor. He found a lantern and flicked its switch. The room filled with soft incandescent light. He held it high and walked to Karen. He extended a hand. "Are you hurt? Anything broken?" He helped her to her feet. "The grenades must have collapsed the cave. We're lucky to be alive."

"I can't hear well...the gunfire...anything. We're trapped aren't we? Oh, God. What about the others? Will they try to help us?"

"Only if they're still alive and the fight is over, which is doubtful." He attempted to gaze down the dark passage, then turned to appraise the cave-in. "Looks like we're completely sealed off. Can you believe it? And neither of us badly hurt."

"Marcos...he...he tried to..." she gasped, and her hand covered her mouth.

"What? What do you..." he followed her eyes and saw for himself. Marcos lay prostrate on the floor, unconscious or dead, partially covered with stone. Blood dripped from a facial cut, which, David hoped, was a sign that he was still alive. His legs were partially covered with rock. David and Karen knelt at his side. She placed a hand on his neck to check for a pulse.

"He's still alive! Oh, God...is it okay to..."

"Here...help with this rock. Try not to move him." The professor set the lantern on the floor and cautiously began removing stones, aware that carelessness might cause another slide. Moments later, Marcos groaned.

"Hold on, we're trying to free you!" said Karen, but the cave-in shifted and rocks tumbled to the floor, threatening to bury him even more. He cried out and tried to push himself up, but his face skewed in anguish.

"Leave it," ordered David. "This isn't working. We're going to kill him."

"He'll die if we don't get him out!" she reached to retrieve the lantern so that they could see. Low-throated, barely stifled cries leaked from his mouth.

"Here...down here." David motioned for her to look. "Sheesh...left leg is crooked, broken bad. The other one's completely covered. Look at the size of those boulders. Shit!"

327

"Karen?" Marcos whispered her name.

She knelt and ran her fingers through his hair. "I'm here with Dr. Wolf. We're trying to figure out something. Your leg's broken...are you hurt anywhere else?"

"I...I have...a cramp in my trigger finger."

"Oh sure...make jokes, Mr. Macho. We're trapped in a cave and this wall of rock is going to fall on you."

"What about Balaam...the others?" He grimaced and looked around the dimly lit cave. "I don't hear shots. They charged the cave...threw grenades."

"Don't know, Marcos. Can't hear a thing. Our immediate concern is getting out of here so that we can get you to a doctor. Is there any other way out?"

"Yes...don't know. Father's the one who knows the tunnels. He says that all the water holes are connected."

"The cenote outside is connected to another one? Where?"

"Inside somewhere, I guess. Oh...Dios..." he moaned as a jolt of agony wracked his body.

David thought a moment, then said, "Karen, turn on the other lantern and stay with him. I'm going to look up ahead...see what's there."

"Not without me you don't." Her voice sounded strained.

"Don't worry...I'll be right back. We've got to get some exploring done...make a plan before the batteries run out." He stood and pointed the light down the narrow passage.

"What's that?" he pointed to marks on the wall.

She walked to where he pointed and joined him.

"Could be vandals," she offered.

"I don't think so...it looks like it means something."

"You know...it could be a map. Look how this line goes...then it goes there, then to there," she pointed. "Those could be rooms, you know?"

David's legs trembled as he stooped to get a closer look.

"Hey...you could be right! As a matter of fact..." he held up his light to peer down the corridor... "Let's check it out." To Marcos he said, "Listen...Karen's going to leave you the extra lantern while we look around a bit...er...we're not leaving you, we just need to...

"Okay...s'all right," he mumbled. "Don't worry...I'll be here when you get back."

Karen turned off the lantern and lay it by his side. "God...I can't believe this." Her voice broke.

David knew that Marcos might not make it. Trying to move the rocks, though, might certainly kill him. Time to get to work. He pushed the image from his mind and looked again at the glyphs and striations on the wall. His interest piqued, he abandoned all caution and began to tread the muddy floor of the corridor, his eyes on the walls for more writing.

He turned. "Be careful," he warned, motioning for her to accompany him. "The floor might drop off or something." He took the lead, heart pounding duly, his breath coming in shallow, anxious puffs. They needed a solution fast. Maybe the Zapatistas would dig them out, or had they been killed in the grenade attack? Damn it all! What they really needed, he mused, was luck—lots of it.

****

Now Chavez knew why drug couriers were called mules. Every footfall was an onerous task requiring a conscious effort. The weight of the packs caused the straps to dig into his shoulders, already blistered and chaffed. His thighs burned and quivered and his breath came in gasps. The gunfire was silent now, and this concerned him. Was the fighting over? What if someone was backtracking the trail at this moment? What if it was the traitorous Indians? He must hide soon, but couldn't until he had negotiated this damnable path.

The escape corridor was narrow, rocky, and filled with

gnarled, woody trees that clung to every crack in which a root could find purchase. Being relatively unencumbered, he had slid through with little effort the first time. But now he thought he might collapse–have a stroke or a heart attack. Fatigue tightened on him like a sinuous boa, slowly squeezing until will and strength dissipated into nothingness. He had never been so tired.

Up ahead he could see white water breaking at the crest of the falls and hear the crash of water against rock. It sounded so inviting, so refreshing. He longed to be done with his struggle and kick back, but not yet–not until he was safely hidden. To do otherwise would invite death. If he must encounter someone, he wanted to pick the time and place. His mind began to phase out and focus solely on taking the next step, then another, and more, until he finally arrived at the waterfall's edge, looking down the thirty-meter drop into the pine forest surrounding the cascading water. He had made it– almost. Now he had to climb down. *Chingada*! What a life, he complained silently. How terrible that he had to endure such injustice to stay alive and feed his poor family. Herrera was a swine, an unthinking brute who asked the impossible of his men. Captain Chavez swore he would transfer to the Gulf Coast if he got out of this jungle alive. *If*–he thought ruefully, looking at the rocky wall beneath him. *Chingada*–might as well get started. His breathing under control, his courage up, the captain put his mind to the task and began descending the cliff face.

CHAPTER THIRTY ONE

After following the passage about thirty meters, it dog-legged right. Twenty meters farther and they stood at the periphery of a cavernous room. It's like being on the moon, thought David. A mirror of creamy calcite coated the floor, reflecting lantern light throughout the room. Thousands of pearly cones, stalactites of unimaginable beauty, dripped from the ceiling. Three small craters, underground cenotes, sat in the center of the room.

"It's like being in the mouth of a wolf," whispered Karen, staring slack jawed. "Incredible…it's so…so…"

"Incredible," repeated, David, inanely. The calcite formations did indeed look like wolf canines–thousands of them.

"Look," she pointed. "Glyphs."

Sure enough, just to the side of them, a broad column of calcite held a message. It began with a period-ending date, but neither Karen nor the professor could make out the message.

The light of the lantern revealed glyphs and stunning pictures painted on the walls and stalactites throughout the room–a veritable treasure trove of Maya art.

"This place is a miracle. Can't believe it even exists." Karen followed David as they toured the room. "Look," she pointed, "more entrances and exits. I bet there are more rooms like this one."

"Could be," he muttered, noncommittal. Then he stopped dead, causing Karen to bump him from behind.

"What the...?"

"Look....look!" he pointed at a manmade structure near the wall. A narrow path between two cenotes led to a shelf-like structure of milky calcite laid down over hundreds and thousands of years. Carrying the lantern aloft, they carefully treaded the course between the cenotes. The floor was moist and slippery and the footing treacherous. The lane widened, and they approached the rack for inspection.

"What is it? It looks..." she gasped. Her hand flew to her mouth. "No...it can't be."

"Can't be what, bitch?"

Stunned!

They both whirled around to see who spoke.

"Who are..." began David, then Karen screamed and dropped to her knees.

Bill stood with a knife in one hand, a long heavy flashlight in the other. His scarred face and milky eye lent the appearance of a ghoul in a B movie. A smirk hung on his face. His eye shifted from Karen's breasts to her face and back to her bosom.

"Glad you made it, slut. Didn't recognize you in the Indian Guccis...but the titties brought it all back." He turned to David and stepped closer. "So...this is the joker you met in Washington. Professor Wolf, I believe? I would never have imagined you so adventurous." He swung and struck David across the face with his flashlight, causing the professor to stumble and almost fall. "On your knees, puss. Try anything and I'll cut out your eyes."

Bewildered and dazed, David dropped to his knees. His heart beat painfully and his jaw was agony. Blood oozed from inside his mouth. He swallowed, then glanced at Karen, "Is this Bill?"

She nodded, biting her knuckles, speechless.

"You deaf as well as stupid?" Bill held the knife point to David's   face.
"Please don't," cried Karen.

"What happened back there?" demanded Bill, pointing toward the cave entrance.

"Grenades collapsed the entrance. Big rock slide," mumbled the professor.

"That so. Anyone alive back there but you and big tits?"

"No," he lied. "Just the two of us."

"The guerillas get away?"

David shrugged. "Who knows? It didn't look good."

"Where did you come from...how did you know where to go?" interjected Karen.

"I didn't, bitch. I followed Chavez. Bastard tried to kill me back in Piedra Blanca. I decided to tag along until the pickins' were good. Last night I ran into that commando group and followed them and the guerilla scum into this valley...decided to stay behind when I saw this place. I knew you or Chavez would show up soon." He placed the knife point inches from her throat. "This is the place....isn't it? The cave with the...whatchamacallit's Depp was always talking about...that Nine Lords of Darkness, shit. There's a treasure here somewhere. That's what the inscription's about, isn't it?"

They all turned to the structure that was the focus of their attention—an altar built by the ancients. Nine shiny skulls, all of them encased in creamy calcite, sat upon the top rack. The heads seemed surreal, alive yet dead, laughing silently at the prey that had crossed the forbidden portal into their realm— Xibalba, the Mayan Hell.

"This is the place," asserted Bill, "and you know the rest. You translated the stone, didn't you? That Red Snail character brought them here, didn't he?"

David listened as the drama unfolded. Karen had never actually repeated her translation to him, there wasn't time. Although he had done his own translation, he had never conversed with her about it. "Just because the Nine Lords of Darkness are mentioned doesn't mean that this is the right cave. Any cave could suffice…any cave could…"

"Shut up. If I want something from you, I'll step on you," he threatened. To Karen he said, "I'm out of patience. I'm tired…I'm hungry and I've been waiting a long time for this chance. I figure there's a ton of gold in here somewhere. The Death Man wouldn't have gone to all this trouble for a bunch of shiny bones." He flicked the knife to her eyes. "What did it say, bitch! Where?"

She swallowed hard and raised her chin, feigning defiance, but her eyes were wide with tears and fear. *"In the lair of balaam beneath the nine deaths of Xibalba lies the World Tree."*

Bill's one good eye twitched. Puzzled, he looked first to David, then to Karen. "You're speakin' riddles, slut. So, what does it mean? Balaam is Maya for jaguar, right?"

She nodded. "Yes…and Xibalba is the equivalent of the underworld or hell."

David, despite Bill's earlier threat, added, "The nine deaths could be the Nine Lords of Darkness, the mythical inhabitants of the underworld who tested Hanaphu and Xabalanque, the ancestors of the Maya." Although they never discussed her translation, he now understood her extreme reaction when she had sighted the skull rack.

The knife swung toward the professor. "Keep talking."

"Well...er...point is...the Maya viewed all caves as entrances into hell. I mean...theoretically almost any cave–and there are hundreds–could fit that description." David maintained a poker face, fully aware that a creamy pink stalactite with the thickness of a supporting column extended from the cavern ceiling to the floor in front of the altar of skulls. An ancient artist had painted the Maya World Tree on its crystalline exterior. The tree symbolically represented the Maya universe with its roots in the underworld, *Xibalba*, and its branches and leaves in the heavens.

"Yeah...but you think it's here...don't you?" The cretin's flashlight flickered weakly, and he shook it, but it continued to flicker. "Battery's dead in this one." He dropped it to the floor. "Hand me yours, fuck-face, before I give you a prostate exam with it."

"No! Don't," protested, Karen. "We'll never find our way back."

"It's okay...here," David made as if to hand it over, but when Bill's hand drew near, the professor switched off the light and rolled aside, scooping up Bill's long-handled flashlight as he did. Karen's scream echoed through the dark cavern.

"You fuck!" cried Bill. He lunged for the professor, but his foot skated on the damp floor and he slipped to one knee.

In the confusion, David gained his feet and circled behind his assailant. The skull rack to his rear, he gripped the heavy flashlight and charged blindly toward Bill, hoping to drive him back onto the path and into one of the cenotes. But in the darkness he misjudged, and his shoulder struck a glancing blow. When he whirled around to strike with the flashlight, a

335

searing pain pierced his abdomen as Bill's knife sank home. David grunted in pain, fell forward and collapsed into Bill, his weight propelling them both toward the cenote.

"No...off you bastard! Turn loose! Noooo!" screamed Bill, tumbling backward over the precipice into the cenote. The professor latched on to a stalactite and collapsed. He counted five seconds before he heard the splash of water. The hole was deep and black. Bill would not be returning. Then, holding his side and falling to the floor in a fetal curl, he passed out.

****

Captain Chavez rejoiced in his good fortune. Completely spent from his trek, he sat at water's edge on a boulder surrounded by leafy ferns and broad-leaf dieffenbachia, basking in his accomplishment. But he could rest only a few moments. When his breath returned, he would take his cargo and hide. The gunfire had not resumed, thus it was a certainty that someone would be hurrying to escape the valley at any moment. It was then that the captain would have to make a decision. He could only hope that the cartel soldiers appeared first. If not, depending on the number of zapatistas remaining, he might have to kill a couple of men and recruit the rest to carry his bags. This plan lay uneasy on his mind–too many contingencies. Maybe he should bury the drugs and lead Herrera's men back to them? No–that wouldn't work. Herrera might torture and kill him if he showed up without the cocaine. *Chingada*! What should he do?

He rose from his place of respite, looked longingly at the pool of water, jumped down and trekked back into the bush. After fifteen minutes of searching he found the ideal location. Although it was closer to the falls than he liked, the three boulders–two on bottom and one on top–formed a triangular cover from which he could clearly observe anyone coming. He dropped his load and gathered palm leaves to disguise the

336

slender opening. His work completed, his chest swelling with deep breaths, he plopped down behind the barrier to rest. He closed his eyes for a moment, the AK-47 resting comfortably in the bow of his arms. As he considered the problem of finding help to transport the drugs, he grew drowsy from the easy woosh and splatter of the falling water and nearly fell asleep. Dozing, his mind began to focus on a distant but rhythmic sound. What could that be? he wondered. Then he heard the sound of boots on gravel and his eyes flew open. There–he heard it again. He grasped his rifle and came to a crouch behind his small fortification, waiting for his quarry to appear. Now the far-away noise grew stronger, a whump– whump–whump. It sounded like–a helicopter! He searched the sky. Was it coming toward him? Then he heard sounds of somebody from above. Whoever was coming was in a hurry and making a lot of noise. Maybe they didn't want to be seen by the helicopter?

Someone in fatigues and T-shirt appeared at the cliff edge beside the waterfall. It was the giant black man, Maurice the Bahamian! Chavez's heart skipped a beat. *Que bueno*! But where were the others, he wondered? Was the giant the only survivor of his group? Were the Zapatista's close behind? *Chingada*! Only questions–never resolution.

Maurice paused only briefly. Removing his backpack, he tossed it to the cliff bottom only twenty meters from the captain. Then to Chavez's amazement, with gun in hand, Maurice the Bahamian jumped! *Caramba*! exulted the captain, silently, enjoying the spectacle of the giant's arms and legs churning the air to maintain balance. Water mushroomed from the pond as he hit, but Maurice quickly surfaced and exited the pool. He checked his gun, then, with a fast glance in the direction of the incoming helicopter, he jogged to the cliff wall to retrieve his backpack. He turned to run into the safety

337

of the fern and pine forest.

Dazed at the swiftness of events, and fearful that a potential ally would disappear, Chavez stood and called out.

"*Alto* (stop), Maurice! *Esperame...soy un amigo*." (Wait! I'm a friend.)

The immense Negro spun and hit the ground, pointing his automatic rifle in the direction of the voice. His eyes narrowed dangerously and his gangrenous scowl jolted Chavez's composure. Meanwhile, the helicopter moved slowly by, pausing to hover above the canyon as if looking for a place to land. The captain knelt also, but waved again. So happy was he to talk to someone besides himself, he lost all caution and gushed his plan.

"*Cuidado*, Maurice. *Soy un amigo*." Chavez professed friendship. "We both need help to escape. I have the cocaine you were sent to recover, but I need an amigo to carry it. Join with me and I'll see that..."

Maurice fired a burst into Chavez's abdomen and chest, killing him instantly. When the chopper disappeared behind the cliff wall, the Bahamian jumped to his feet and inspected his kill. Satisfied that Chavez was dead, he opened his bags for inspection. Initially puzzled, he chuckled and shook his head. A joyous smile fixed his face. Shaking his head in disbelief, he dropped the bags and retrieved his own. After extracting two clips of bullets and pocketing them, he threw his pack into the brush. He strapped his rifle over his shoulder and chest, easily placed a pack of cocaine under each arm and disappeared into the jungle.

CHAPTER THIRTY TWO

The helicopter was brand new, which was good, Luis reassured himself. It's just that he hated the damn things. How they stayed aloft was a mystery, and when it lurched, hovered, dropped, or yawed to the side, his eyes and inner ear disagreed on what was happening. This, of course, resulted in becoming a little green around the gills. The equipment, the chopper and half the personnel on board were courtesy of the *gringos* on the other side of the border. They had strange, fierce-looking guns, too. He'd never seen such hardware in his life. Their money and commitment were impressive–and they were polite and professional, something that pleased Luis greatly.

While Joaquin had stood by nervously, the gringos perused his maps and marked their own accordingly. Then twelve men, including himself, rode the iron bird swiftly over the Lacandon. They had skimmed the emerald forest and muddy rivers until they found the forested, bushy foothills of the sierras and flown to this location. No one in the entourage had first-hand knowledge of their destination, but according to the map this was the most likely location of Council Valley. In fact, Joaquin insisted on it, and Luis found his confidence to be peculiar in the extreme for a man who had never had a dirty fingernail or read a geography book in his life. Why was he so sure? Where did he get his information? Luis was only been able to provide approximations from memory.

Nonetheless they arrived, and the bird hovered, looking for a place to land. Except for a narrow stream, the valley was heavily wooded with pine, hardwoods and towering ceiba. As it turned out, their choices were restricted to a small pond at the north end of this rugged, bushy area near a cenote and cave at the south end of the valley.

"There's been a fight…look!" Richard, the American copilot, pointed toward the east wall. "Three…four dead, at least. There's four more by the…hey this place looks like a…a ruin or something. Look at that thing by the water hole there." He pointed to what appeared to be a stone wall near the cenote.

"Bodies, too," said the pilot, grimly. "Bodies all over the friggin' place. Look at the dust hanging over this place. That ain't natural. Could be dangerous to land."

"No…we're going in," asserted Richard the *gringo*. His face was darkly tanned and crow's feet wrinkles splayed from his eyes. Black face paint was streaked below each eye and he wore tan khakis and a black beret. An automatic rifle lay between his legs and a pistol, knife, and grenades decorated his belt and chest. He turned to Armando, a short broad-chested man with a cheerful face and massive arms. "Ain't that right, amigo? We're going in."

"*Si…loco*. But not to kill everything that moves. We have our orders."

"We're looking for drugs."

340

"*Si*...but our priority is recovering two American nationals–your own people. Remember?"

"Yeah...this is a rescue mission," added Luis. "Joaquin made it perfectly clear–first we recover the hostages, then we chase bad guys."

"Hostages my ass," grumbled Richard. "What are we supposed to do if they start firing when we land?"

"Shoot back," replied Armando, "but we're here to get the gringos out alive."

"Over there...look!" The pilot pointed toward the east wall. "Trail up there...on the wall...looks like more bodies."

Richard craned his neck. "I'll be damned...yeah...more over there, too. Christ...put this thing down before the shooting starts again."

Luis asked. "What's the plan?"

Richard turned to Armando. "What do you think? Send two up the trail...check out the bodies by that hole and ..."

"Cave," interrupted Armando. "The consul and the inspector here say that the Americans were looking for a cave. Do the trail...send three or four. Post guards around that big hole. Leave two with the bird...the rest up to the cave."

"Done," agreed Richard. "Lock and load."

Everyone inspected their equipment for readiness.

"You...federale...stay with the copter," ordered Richard.

"No way...I'm with you two. I've got special status and I'll go where I please." Luis caught and held the American's eye. A staring contest ensued.

Finally, Richard's eyes dropped, and he said. "Yeah...well...it's your ass then. If you're not part of the team, you're on your own. Get ready to move...we're almost down."

When the door slid open, the soldiers jumped to the ground and moved immediately to their assignments. Luis sniffed the air. Cordite. Lots of it. He glanced at Armando. "Been a big blowout here."

"Smells like it. Come on…maybe you can help identify your friends' bodies."

His words jolted Luis back to the task at hand. He'd witnessed gruesome scenes in his twenty years of police work, but never anything like this–the aftermath of a war with bodies strewn where they died, grisly expressions locked onto their last thoughts and emotions. With his own .45 automatic in hand, he followed the task force, scaling the broken, gravel-strewn steps leading to the cave.

While soldiers stood guard, Luis, the American, and Armando searched the cave entrance. The mouth yawned like shark jaws, toothy stalactites threatening all who ventured near. Hundreds of leafy vines roped the cliff face and hung like tattered curtains. Inside, limestone boulders were piled to the ceiling on the east side of the cave. A narrow tunnel extended back into the mountainside. Further examination revealed footprints, brass shell casings, and bullet pocked walls.

"Think they're inside the cave?" asked Armando.

"Possible…footprints everywhere. Someone made their last stand here…and that there…" he pointed, "looks like a fresh cave-in. Might be a tunnel leading the other way."

Luis, storm lantern in one hand and pistol in the other, stooped and stepped warily into the corridor. Richard joined him, his automatic rifle held waist high. Pictures and glyphs covered the walls. Fresh footprints from a variety of shoes disappeared into the darkness–heading into the cave, not out.

Luis turned to Richard. "What do you think? Could be dangerous."

"Of course it is. Here…hand me the lantern. Tell Armando to bring three men and follow us. We'll search a little farther."

Luis, his flesh crawling at the prospect of a cave shoot-out, offered no argument this time. He turned and moved with alacrity toward the cave entrance, one hand on the wall, until he saw light. Armando had four soldiers removing stone from the cave-in while two others stood guard. The three he'd sent up the trail had yet to return.

"Richard needs more men. Looks like someone ran inside the tunnel to hide."

"*Cabron!*" growled Armando. "*Pinche* cowboy! Always taking chances. Tell him...*chinga tu madre*...eh. We're not going anywhere until my men return from up there." He pointed to the eastern wall where soldiers were dispatched to investigate the bodies on the path.

Crack! Crack! Crack! Automatic gunfire echoed from the corridor. Richard had found his action.

"*Chingada!*" cursed Armando. He gave orders for the two outside to stay put and motioned for the others to accompany him. Luis, heart pounding and palms sweating, brought up the rear.

"What is it?" demanded Armando when they arrived.

"Thought I saw someone...but look at this." His lantern illuminated the face and sparkled in the eyes of a soldier sitting with his back to the wall. His clothing was filthy and his hands bloody and mud covered. His right leg was wrapped with a tourniquet to prevent bleeding from a wound. He appeared to have crawled some distance before stopping. He showed no fear, but pain was clearly etched on his face.

"This is Lucas Buenoaño. Says the zapatistas escaped down this corridor into another room. He and some guy called Maurice chased them. When he caught a bullet, his buddy deserted. He's been trying to pull himself out of the cave."

"Who hired you?" asked Armando. "That uniform doesn't belong to any army. Mercenaries? Cartel? Who are you with?"

343

The wounded man looked away. Impatient, Armando kicked his leg.

"Ahhg…*cabron!*" The soldier grabbed his leg and moaned.

"I have no sympathy for mercenaries, asshole. No time, either. Get that tongue working or you'll wish the guerrillas had caught you."

The prisoner released his wounded leg and leaned against the wall. "Don't know. I work for Ramon. He's dead…got it outside. Never told us shit, but the money was good. I'll fight for anyone if the money's right." His expression turned hard and defiant.

"Tell me about the gringos–the professor and the female with the guerrillas," demanded Armando. "Where are they?"

Wrinkles creased mercenaries' forehead and a look of perplexity held his face. "The old man with the maps? The tall one?" He hesitated. "In the cave…the other side. We blew the shit out of them." He smiled at the memory.

"There's another passage?" asked Luis, agitated.

"Yeah…behind the cave-in…two grenades." He smiled with satisfaction. "Hell of an explosion."

Richard appeared to take issue with the commando's attitude and kicked the wounded leg himself, sending the mercenary into convulsions of pain.

When Lucas quit writhing, the American asked, "Where're the drugs…the cocaine?"

The mercenary grimaced and held up a protesting hand. He pleaded. "I don't know…really. That was Ramon and the Bahamian's business. We were told to kill the woman…big bonus for killing her."

"Who's the Bahamian?"

"Maurice…cutthroat…big, mean, black from the islands."

"Drag him out," ordered Richard. "We'll interrogate him later." The task force soldiers lifted the protesting Lucas

344

beneath his arms and carried him away, protesting and groaning.

"Let's go," said Richard, "they're in there for sure and not going anywhere. We'll come back for them."

"No," protested Luis. He directed his appeal to Armando. "We're here to find David and the woman…remember? The drugs are secondary. We have orders, remember?"

"I hate you political fucks," spat Richard. In the pale light of the lantern his harsh expression seemed threatening, horrific in appearance. "This task force is supposed to be above that, Armando. Our purpose is…"

"Enough!" Armando pointed his rifle at the American's stomach. "This is Mexico, *cabron*. Why do I keep reminding you? Everything here is political. You take your money and your expensive toys and get the fuck out of our country for all we care. Inspector Alvarado is right. We're here to rescue hostages." He turned toward the cave entrance and retraced his steps in the darkness. Luis followed, leaving the American to stew in his anger.

****

The fight in the dark had occurred so quickly that Karen did nothing but stand still. So great was her fear of Bill that his sudden appearance shocked her into paralysis. When the lantern light died, she heard Bill's fearful protests, David's yelp and groan and the deep, distant splash of a body dropping into the cenote. But who fell? The room was pitch black and she was afraid to call out, afraid to breathe. Was Bill waiting for her to make a sound so that he could grab her? How long should she wait? She stood motionless and listened. The barely audible sound of singing floated on the air. Singing? Surely not. Was she losing her mind? Maybe it was running water, or was it breathing? Imagination fed her fear and she fought to hold still. The suspense was unbearable. She could hear footsteps now—and voices! Oh, God! she cried silently. Oh, God! Quit it! Quit it! Then a voice moaned at her feet, and someone seemed to be struggling on the ground.

"Karen...Ms. Dumas...help me. The light...Karen are you there?"

"David!" she gushed. Her legs almost buckled with relief. "Thank God! Oh, David...where are you? I can't see...I can't..."

"The floor. The lantern's on the floor. Feel with your hands."

"Are you okay?"

"No...got stabbed...hurry before I bleed..."

"Wait...what's that noise? Are those voices?" She listened again. Yes, and they were nearer.

"Someone's coming?"

"Yes...what should we do?"

"Find the lantern...fast."

She dropped to her knees and groped around. Seconds later she found it. "Got it," she whispered.

"Turn it on... help me up...need to hide."

"David," she whispered, urgently. "I think it's too late. I can hear them really well. I think they're here...in the room with us."

"*Gringa*?" A voice from the other side of the room posed a question. "*Gringa...donde estas*?"

"Balaam," grunted David. "I'll kill that raisin-faced charlatan," he threatened, benignly.

A lantern flickered on from the west side of the room. Four zapatistas knelt in front of Balaam Reyes. Their guns were pointed at her. She felt herself swoon.

"Balaam," called David, weakly, "Balaam."

"*Echalos*," ordered the shaman, and the guerillas lowered their rifles. He hoisted the lantern higher and walked toward Karen.

"*Ahua*...you hurt?" he asked.

Karen switched on her lantern and knelt beside David. "Bill? Is he...did he fall?"

"In the cenote. He won't be back this time."

Balaam and his men arrived. Karen saw that two were wounded, though not seriously. They still carried rifles and one carried a backpack.

"You find Place Where the Gods Sing, *ahua*. You hear?"

"Yeah...sounds like a funeral dirge." David struggled to sit up. "Got a knife in the gut, Balaam. Don't suppose you have anything in your bag, do you?"

"Si, *ahua*, but Balaam leave bag at stairway cave. Here...have a look." He motioned for two men to roll the professor to his back.

"Ouch...Jesus, Balaam! Ahhg..." David's face distorted in pain.

"You be fixed," pronounced the shaman after much poking and prodding, "but Balaam no can fix. You have need white man medicine, *ahua*."

"How much blood?" David grimaced.

"It missed big blood, but I smell shit in you white tube. You very sick *muy pronto*."

"Don't feel so great now."

No one spoke, then Balaam looked at Karen. "My son...Marcos...run you. Did he..." the shaman hesitated. "He no make it no?"

"Yes...but he's hurt. Ceiling and wall collapsed on him. He's alive, but his leg's trapped. We were afraid more rock would fall, so we left him a lantern and gun and went looking for another way out. But...then...Bill...I guess you don't know him...this man tried to kill us, but David knocked him into the cenote."

Balaam wheeled around and pointed toward the corridor

that led to Marcos. He barked orders and his men took the lantern and raced for the tunnel. The shaman turned toward the passageway his men used to enter the chamber. He listened intently then, satisfied, turned his attention to David.

"Balaam...is there another way out?" David sat up holding his side.

"Three tunnels before the explosion, *ahua*. Now is one, but is controlled by drug man...*sicario*. We go come here."

"Did they follow? Are they inside?" Worry lined his face.

"Many follow, but zapatista shoot shoot. No know how many. We set trap. We wait. No think they fight in cave. Balaam know cave, *sicarios* no. Drug soldier no want Balaam, want drugs...is outside. All want is drug is outside, he repeated"

A silence ensued, each delving into their own thoughts. Karen knew that two days was too long. The old Indian's showing up was a Godsend, might even be their ticket out of this hell hole. For her anyway...it didn't look good for David.

"I'm not going to make it, am I Balaam?" mumbled the professor, echoing Karen's thoughts. "I mean...even if I could get out in the next couple of hours, there's no way to get help."

The shaman hesitated and looked around the cavern, but didn't answer.

"Why you *gringa* want to see cave, *ahua*? Is book...old book?"

"Yes," interrupted Karen. "Here, or somewhere else. They're hidden in a cave...I'm sure of it. I found a stelae...an inscription that tells of..."

The shaman waved her off. "They here, *ahua*...you book...but water kill. The Nine Lords of Darkness hide book in rock. Water kill clean book, bury book hide from ladino eye. Save from bleach skin Spaniard.

"What do you mean, they're here? Where? Quit talking in

riddles, old man." The shaman had taken to never addressing her directly. Now he refused to look at her.

"In the rock?" croaked, David.

"Si, *ahua*. Are one with cave soul. No see book?"

Karen, baffled, glanced at the floor, then the stalagmites hanging from the ceiling.

"There," pointed Balaam, "by head bone."

Carrying the lantern, she walked toward the skull rack, but saw nothing unusual–just layers of cold lava-like calcite. It was breathtakingly beautiful–everything shining and covered with glass. What was the grizzled old poop talking about? Her eyes fell to the floor. Streaks of color had bled into the calcite– blues, blacks, red–lots of red. Where had that come from? She knelt for a closer look, then spotted a fold in the floor, then another–shiny, colorful calcite ripples, anomalies in an otherwise smooth floor.

"What is it?" called David.

Then she understood, and the enormity of the discovery caused her heart to skip a beat. She couldn't breathe, and grasped her chest.

"Karen…what…are you okay?" David extended a hand to Balaam. "Help me Balaam," he demanded. "I've got to see this."

"Sit, *ahua*. You bleed, you die." But seeing David's determination, he helped him to his feet and led him staggering to the skull rack.

"He's right, David. They're part of the floor. The dripping calcite completely covered them over the years. Look…you can see edges. There's more…over there and there." she pointed. "Look at the streaks where the calcite bleached the colors and rotted the pages. See those lines? They look like beautiful feathers buried in the rock."

"My, God!" said David, falling to his knees. "They're here!

They're really here." His face twisted in pain and he grabbed his side. He took a deep breath and turned to the shaman. "Why, Balaam? Why did you offer to show me this place?"

As Karen watched, the old man hesitated, then fondly placed a hand on the professor's shoulder. "You shit white man, *ahua*...no bad...no like others–ladinos, PRI scum, those kill Indians...steal land. Loggers, Pemex *petroleros* come soon. Three, five years they here. Mexican army build road. Make fort in jungle. Cave be hurt, be kill like all thing white man touch. I think you help, *ahua*...but..."

A cry came from behind and all heads turned. Speaking dialect and gesturing as they approached, two guerrillas jogged from the tunnel. Although Karen couldn't understand a word, she saw the look of concern on Balaam's face. Three men staggered through the door–one of them groaning and protesting.

"Marcos!" she cried, elated, yet sickened at the expression of agony on his face. His leg hung crooked and bloody, and a jagged bone pierced his shin. Her stomach buckled and she felt her gorge rise. She quickly handed the lantern to the shaman and bent over the cenote and vomited. Her stomach empty, she plopped onto her behind beside the listless David and concentrated on looking away from Marcos.

Balaam, meanwhile, listened and asked questions. He argued in dialect with the four guerrillas, then stood pensive and silent.

What had happened? she wondered. Why were they so excited?

The shaman turned to face them. He placed his hands on his hips and stared intently, considering his next move.

"*Ahua*..." he began.

"Please stop!" she demanded. "Quit ignoring me! If you've got something to say, tell me. I'm the one that's not hurt, the one that's thinking clearly. He's wounded and dying."

The shaman frowned his displeasure, then addressed David again. "They dig dig through big rock. My men hear. They are call you, *ahua*...you and...er...this Karen." He finally looked at her. "These different men...no drug soldier. But is all same me you. They enemies and we fight." He paused, pursed his lips, and said, "Unless want, *ahua* and *gringa*. Balaam think come look *ahua* David and *gringa*."

Karen sat rigid and listened. Someone had come for them? The mercenaries were gone? How could he tell? How would the newcomers know her name? For the first time in days a glimmer of hope shone within. If only...

David reached toward the shaman. "Take us to the wall, Balaam," begged David. "Please...it's my only chance," he croaked.

"You chance? Yes...maybe, *ahua*...but zapatista is problem." He paused, but then said, "Okay, *ahua*. We bring *ahua* David. Zapatistas no want no take hostage. But when men make path, move rock, you me tell stop, understand? They take *ahua* David and *gringa* and go. They come cave we will fight kill all enemy. Is big cave." He nodded and agreed with himself, "Is many room this cave. We set trap...kill soldier."

"Take us...please," groaned the professor.

The Bone Man gave the order and two guerillas lifted David and carried him back toward the cave-in. The other two grabbed Karen's arms.

"I hate you!" she spat at the shaman's feet. "You...in your filthy clothes and your big patriarch act. I hope you...you..."

"You me wife I'd beat with stick, *mujer*." Balaam stood with his arms across his chest. "Then me you go bed...please Balaam." He gestured and the two diminutive Indians shoved her toward the tunnel leading to the cave-in.

"*Ahua...un momento.*" Everyone halted. Balaam trotted to

where the professor stood bent and sagging against his helpers. The shaman glanced at Karen, then stood on his toes to whisper into David's ear, all the while eyeing her.

What the hell? This guy was too much. What's the big secret? He was doing this just to piss her off, she fumed. As she watched, David's back straightened perceptively, and he grunted. Balaam whispered to him again. *Oh, pleeeaze!* she thought. What a jerk!

The shaman gave the professor a friendly whack on the back, shot Karen a sly smile and motioned them onward. As she passed, she caught his eye and mouthed silently, "I hate you."

"Remember, *mujer*," he replied. "Is stick and bed next time."

****

"They're in there…I heard voices."

"You're hearing things," groused Richard, standing to the rear, doing nothing to help.

"No…I'm sure of it." They had created a hole at the top near the ceiling and Luis knew that he heard voices. He scrambled up and bent his back to the task. They had made remarkable progress. With so many men, they were able to tumble heavy boulders to the floor. Sweat soaked his clothes, and his large hands displayed bruise and scrapes, but he labored on, certain that he would find his friend. He could only hope that David was still alive. There it was again. A voice. A woman's voice?

"There…hear that?" he called down.

Two others climbed to join him. Soon they were pulling stones and clearing a path over the top. When he called out this time, he got an answer.

"Who are you?" replied a querulous voice.

"Inspector Luis Alvarado…Federal *Policia*," he gasped. "Are you Karen Dumas?"

"Federal police…oh, thank God!"

352

"David Wolf...is David there with you?" called Luis.

"Yes...but he's hurt...a knife..."

"They're here...it's them!" cried a joyous Luis, and he attempted to stand, then slipped and rolled head over heels to the cave floor.

Armando grunted an order and everyone hastened to free the captives. "Take a break, *senor federale*. We'll have them out in no time."

"Yeah," agreed Richard. He tossed a cigarette butt to the floor and blew smoke through his nose. "We'll be empty handed and back in Guadalajara in no time."

While Luis caught his breath and checked for fractured bones, the American descended the broken steps and walked toward the helicopter.

"Fuckin' cowboy," muttered Armando. "Stupid fuckin' Americans."

"Yeah," agreed Luis. "But I wouldn't be getting my friend back without them."

EPILOGUE

Legions of snowflakes fell steadily for three hours. It was Halloween, and Omaha's mayor was on the news earlier to cancel the traditional trick-or-treating activities and warn everyone to stay home in the Snow Emergency. More white stuff was forecasted and he worried about the snow-removal crews. Besides, children didn't vote and this was an opportunity for him to further consolidate his power and boost his ego by micro-managing the holidays. As of yet he hadn't figured out how to control the weather and bring it to its knees. But just wait—maybe next term.

Aunt Rose heated water for tea in the kitchen while David, his friend Luis Alvarado, and Karen made small talk in the living room and watched the snow fall. Luis, standing in front of the picture window, stared awestruck at the incredible vista. He came along hoping to see snow for the first time and was disappointed. The professor glanced outside to the black sedan and driver that had driven them from Eppley Airfield.

Why hadn't he accompanied them inside? Had he changed his mind?

Five months had passed since Karen's disastrous trip to Mexico. Although she was delighted to see David Wolf, his visit conjured up memories that she would rather not revisit. She thought his insistence on coming to Omaha to be peculiar, but could hardly refuse. Karen wasn't busy–didn't have a job, or even the prospect of employment. She wasn't looking. Money wasn't an issue since the death of her parents. Apathy now reigned supreme in her life. All her fire, her desire to excel, to become a world-renown archaeologist was abandoned in the Lacandon jungle. Her view of the world, of herself, was shattered in that terrible week.

Aunt Rose, ever caring and nurturing, dropped hints of late that perhaps Karen needed to talk to someone. You know, a professional, she suggested. Someone who did that sort of thing for a living. Sure, said Karen, but like everything else, she hadn't followed up. She didn't need a shrink, she needed a life. Since returning to Omaha she'd spent innumerable hours analyzing her adventure in Mexico, her time at the Smithsonian, her failed marriage and her college days at New Mexico State. Karen's introspection revealed much that she didn't like, and suspected that her present state of mind resulted from a careless, shallow approach that she brought to every endeavor. She had never made really good friends and could only assume that she wasn't very likeable. How could she have been so blind? God had given her so much–brains, looks, and money–everything she didn't need to be a real person.

"...so I was really happy that you agreed to meet with me, Karen. I know it was terrible for you. I hope you've recovered and that you're not...er...suffering from any...uh...emotional problems."

"I'm fine," she lied, sweetly. "You're such a miracle. I'm so happy that you're well again. You saved my life in that cave. Bill was going to torture me...kill me...you know that don't you?"

David's head dipped and a look of sadness gripped him. "Karen...I feel so bad about what happened. I've spent a lot of time thinking of how I might make it up to you."

"No need. Don't worry about it, David. Sure it was terrible, but...well...I'm an adult and I've moved on. I'm just..."

"You said you're not working right now."

"True...but I'm considering some things...you know...maybe something different."

"Consider this then, young lady. I can get you a job as the director on an archaeology project that will boggle your mind."

"More lost Mayan books?" she joked. "God, what a disappointment."

"Well...yeah...sort of."

"Huh? What do you...no...no," she held up her hands as if to fend him off. "I've learned my lesson, Professor Wolf. I didn't do that very well. If I'd listened to you...listened to a lot of people, maybe that nightmare would never have occurred. Besides, I'm looking for something solid, something real. I'm ready to slow down and do it like everyone else...quit taking short cuts, build some relationships with others in the field, you know?"

"Wonderful! And this would be the perfect project," he insisted.

"David...can you believe this. It's so white!" gushed Luis.

"Hush up, Luis." The professor edged to the front of the couch. "Listen...I got this on very good information. It's a certainty. I just need someone...a young, knowledgeable archaeologist to take on this project."

356

"I'm not going back to Mexico, David."

"Even for Mayan books?"

She laughed. "Especially for Mayan books."

"Even if it was a certainty?"

This gave her pause. "How could it be a certainty?" She took the cup and saucer offered by her aunt. She sipped and set it aside. "Frankly, David, I'm a little surprised. I thought you were the skeptical one...the person with the common sense," she chastised.

"Can I go outside?" asked Luis.

"Please do," grumped the professor. To Karen he said. "Do you have a snow shovel?"

"By the garage door."

Luis threw his coat on and was out the door like a shot.

Karen stared at the Mexican archaeologist, but his eyes never wavered. "Okay, professor...what do you have? Let's hear it."

"Remember Balaam Reyes?

"Don't get me started."

"Remember when he stopped and whispered something in my ear?"

"How could I forget?"

"The guy in your stelae...Red Snail."

"Yah?"

"He transcribed everything in the books onto the cave walls."

"What!"

"Balaam swore it was true. I went and looked. It's in a room adjacent to the one we were in."

"Everything? Glyphs, dates, stories?"

"Everything. Covers most of three walls."

"But why? Why would anyone do such a thing? Especially if it was already written in the books?"

"Who knows? Maybe he was afraid that someone might find and destroy the books. Maybe it was Red Snail's way of ensuring that his people's legacy–their religion and way of life was left behind for future generations. I don't know...but it's there."

"You've seen it?"

"Yes."

"Why me? I don't deserve this and you know it."

"Wrong. You've earned it, Ms. Dumas. It isn't a gift. You deciphered the stelae."

"Why not yourself? You'd be famous."

"List me as co-author on anything that you publish and it's yours."

"I don't know..." she vacillated, "...sounds good, but...will the authorities cooperate this time?"

"Absolutely. Luis made the Honorary Consul a deal he couldn't   refuse."

"Oh yeah? How's that?"

"It seems my brother-in-law has been aiding drug traffickers."

"Oh?"

"Yes, but he made a mistake and Luis caught it. It wasn't terribly incriminating, but after Luis brought it to Joaquin's attention, his attitude toward Luis improved measurably."

"I'm listening."

"While planning our rescue, Luis was in Joaquin's study at the ranch. At the time he couldn't figure it out, but later he realized that Joaquin's map was marked with information that the consul shouldn't have known unless he was in contact with the mercenaries. Thus, he deduced that Joaquin was the person who had sent the mercenaries and was giving the orders."

"What information?"

"He knew two names, only one of which Luis told him– Council Valley, but Luis never showed him where it was, or at least he didn't remember doing so. The other name, *The Place Where the Gods Sing*, was known only to Balaam Reyes and me. Luis had never heard of it, or been around when Balaam and I went over the maps. Both names were on the maps the mercenaries took from me."

"That's kind of scary isn't it...a corrupt brother-in-law with that much power?"

"Yes and no. It can be very useful in a country like Mexico. After I was released from the hospital, I sent Luis to talk with Joaquin and propose an archaeological expedition fully funded by the government. Luis claims the consul was quite excited about our offer and agreed to come up with all the money himself," deadpanned the professor. "So...knowing how difficult it can be to finance an archaeological expedition...and in view of the fact that Joaquin probably has more money than he needs, naturally I accepted."

"Naturally."

"What do you say, Ms. Dumas? It's the chance of a lifetime."

She hesitated, but not from reluctance. A moment of sheer joy–of anticipation and certainty–swept through her. She felt renewed and challenged, a woman with a purpose. Her skin felt electric.

She gave him a huge smile. "I'll do it, David, provided you take the lead in setting up everything. It's your country, you know the ropes. You hire the help...edit the reports...everything. Agreed?"

"Agreed!" he jumped to his feet. "Let's shake on it!"

She stood to offer her hand, but then the doorbell rang.

"Expecting someone?"

"Actually, no. Not in this weather." She opened the door and there stood Luis with another man at his side. He looked very familiar; a tall man with broad shoulders with a thick black beard and long dark locks reaching to his shoulders. Her eyes grew wide and her hand covered her mouth.

"It was getting cold out and I thought our driver might want a cup of that there tea," pointed Luis. "Anyway..." the federale glanced at David, then to their driver. "It's time to get this over with. You know that..."

"Marcos!" exclaimed Karen.

No one spoke. All waiting to see how she responded.

"Marcos...you were...but how?" she looked to David.

The professor grinned. "Luis knows some people, and Joaquin was willing to jump some hurdles for us. No problem getting him a passport. Marcos looked me up after I got out of the hospital. One thing led to another and, you know..." David looked at the floor, then shifted his weight to the other foot.

"Marcos thought maybe that if he agreed to provide security at the site, that you might come back to Chiapas."

He did, huh?" Karen's eyes locked onto those of the handsome, bearded Marcos. A staring battle ensued.

"What is it Stinky?" Aunt Rose exited the kitchen for the living room. "Why don't you introduce me to your new friend?"

"In a minute, auntie." She looked to David, then back to her former lover. She felt her face begin to color. "This wasn't necessary. I've already agreed to come." All resistance faded and she extended both hands to Marcos. "So...back from the dead again, eh?"

"*Si*, Karen...I was talking with Lobo and thinking that I have much to live for, even that maybe I am willing to give my life to the right woman."

Aunt Rose stood transfixed, her mouth the shape of an 'O'.

"Do you love this woman?" she caught and held his eyes.

"More than my life. This woman, she completes me. She is my...er...my other side, my other spirit."

"Please come in, Marcos." She took his hand and guided him across the room toward her aunt. "Aunt Rose, this is the Marcos I told you about."

"Oh my...oh yes...he is, isn't he?" The old lady stared, but extended her hand. She looked at her niece, then to Marcos. "So you've come to fetch her back to Mexico, have you?"

"That is my plan, *senora*."

"And you're positive you love her?"

"*Absolutamente, senora!*" Marcos' smile broke into mirth.

Aunt Rose appraised him from head to foot, then looked at Karen. She turned to Marcos and asked, "Do you like children, young man?"

"I love children, *senora*."

"Good...because this girl..."

"Aunt Rose!

"...because this girl needs to settle down and..."

"Well...I guess that's all settled," interrupted the professor. "They've much to talk about, eh Luis?" He looked to the federale for support.

Luis, of course, understood none of the conversation in English, and merely smiled affably.

And...Aunt Rose...I believe you agreed to be our guide to this new Oakview Mall place somewhere near here?" coaxed David.

"Oh...I don't know...it's snowing out and..." then she looked at her niece and saw that Karen's eyes were fixed on the hirsute hunk in her living room.

"Chance of a lifetime for us, Aunt Rose. Besides...I think they've lots to talk about."

Rose looked at David, then to Karen. "They do, don't they?" She gave a wry smile. "Let me get my coat." She struggled into

361

it, took another look at her niece, then Marcos, and added. "This should maybe take a while too, huh?" She nodded at David to indicate the two lovers.

"Yes, mam. Maybe just the three of us could have dinner together after we do the mall."

"Well...yes...I suppose so. An old lady with two handsome men. My friends will be jealous."

Aunt Rose buttoned her wool coat. "Well...Stinky..." she said loudly, "I suppose we'll be gone three or four hours. I guess you'll just have to fend for yourself." She motioned for David and Luis to accompany her outside, and both fell in behind her. The old lady let the two men pass, then shot Marcos a smirk before shutting the door behind her.

"Stinky?" Marcos asked, puzzled.

"Don't ask," she sighed with resignation, then reached for a strand of hair. "So...how do we get to know each other again?"

"Like this, *gringa*." He reached, and she fell into his embrace.

"I have many wonderful things to tell you, Karen," he whispered in her ear.

"About Mexico?"

"No...about how much I love you, *querida*. Do you have time to listen?"

"Oh...I've lots of time, you zapatista bandit. How long will it take?"

"Hours."

"Mmmm...I was hoping so." She looked into his eyes. "We have three or four hours."

"We have forever, *gringa*," and he kissed her long and passionately.

"Yes...I guess we do, don't we?" And she melted into his arms.

THE END